I0775663

Each
Wave
That
Breaks

This is a work of fiction. Names, characters, places, and incidents are products of the author's imagination, are used fictitiously and are not to be construed as real. Any resemblance to actual events, locales, organizations, or persons living or dead, is entirely coincidental.

Copyright © 2023 Birdcage Ink

All rights reserved. No part of this book may be reproduced, distributed, or transmitted in any form or by any means, including photocopying, recording, or other electronic or mechanical methods, without the prior written permission of the publisher, except in the case of brief quotations embodied in reviews and certain other non-commercial uses permitted by copyright law.

First Paperback Edition July 2023

ISBN: 979-8-9863386-2-0 (paperback)

Published by Birdcage Ink
www.Birdcageink.com

Each Wave That Breaks

Lori Worley

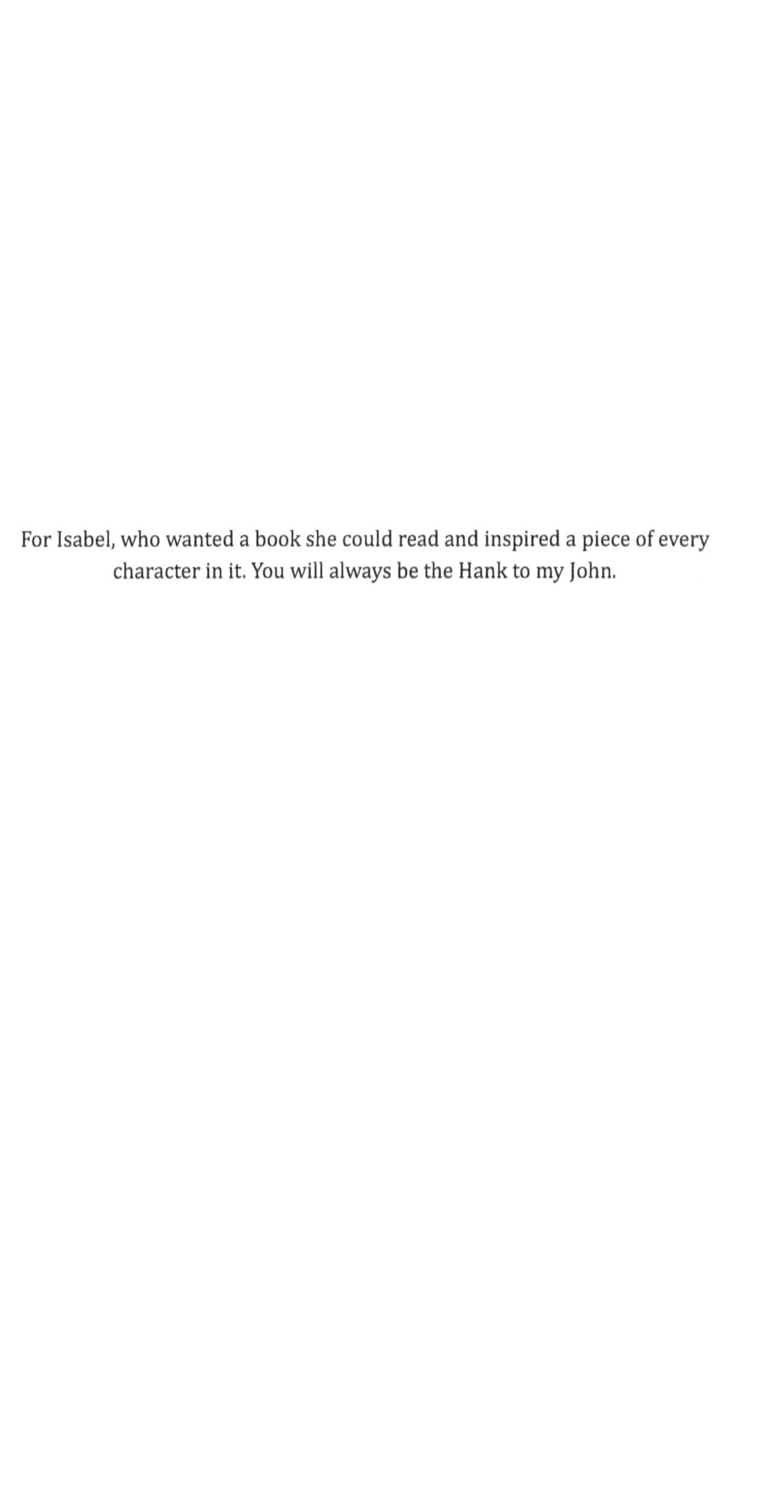

For Isabel, who wanted a book she could read and inspired a piece of every character in it. You will always be the Hank to my John.

Present:

WINTER

When the rains came, so did the days when my feet could barely withstand the cold of the ocean as it lapped my ankles, nor could I withstand the weight of all the memories that came with the change in temperature. The sand was firm beneath my feet, cold and unmoving, unlike the shivers that shook my jaw and ached in my bones. I shouldn't be out here, alone with the ocean. My mother would be frantic with worry when she found my bed empty, save the twisted sheets and the pillow wrinkled on the floor. She would only worry for a few minutes out of habit before she remembered that I was lost, and had been lost to her for a year. She would make my bed and leave my room empty again.

She didn't run out to the sand and shout my name down the small stretch of beach any longer. She had given up on trying to save me in the fall, when the leaves had first clung with desperation and then finally let go with colorful abandon. She had given up on the version of me that had moved through the last three years of high school effortlessly. I had too. I didn't dream anymore, I walked instead of sleeping.

I wandered the stretch of beach below our house until my feet felt raw in my shoes. I dumped my damp, sand-crusted Converse on the wooden deck outside my room each morning. My feet were red with blistering, the skin rubbed pink from the sand caught between my foot and the canvas. This was my life now, as the one who survived; I was the only ghost haunting the living. That was what I had discovered when I awoke from that night—a ghost isn't the dead haunting the living, it's the living who are left behind by the dead. So now you know that everyone dies. You just don't know who, and I just don't understand why…

Past:

TWO YEARS AGO

SPRING

"Are you ever going to finish cleaning your room?" Her voice was full of boredom and impatience on the other side of the door. I laughed out loud. The rule was that spring break only began when my mess of a room was clean. I should have started cleaning it a month ago. I didn't, and I wasn't technically cleaning it now. I was sitting on the other side of the wooden door finishing the last three chapters of my book. It wasn't my fault she had come in with the sun, always expecting that I'd changed my terrible ways from years prior. Nope. Procrastination was my name.

"Come back after lunch and we'll ride our bikes into town!" I smiled at the wood that separated us.

"Are you kidding? Why do you insist on the bikes when your mom always offers to drop us off?" I could hear the annoyance and fought to stifle a laugh. She hated my love of bikes. I could hear her tapping her fingers on the wood floor, her nails already manicured for the boys she knew she would meet and fall in love with over spring break.

"Is that you turning a page? Are you seriously reading and not cleaning right now?" The annoyance was shifting into frustrated disbelief, but still I struggled not to laugh at her words, pitchy and mad in the hall.

"No. Why would I be reading?" I held the book to my chest and smiled into the clutter of my room. It wasn't that I hated cleaning, it was just that it never seemed as important as whatever else came up. I wasn't lazy, I was just distracted.

"Of course you are reading. God, you are such a nerd Laney. A nerd. I am going downstairs to eat the breakfast your mom made for you. You should know that I plan to eat it all." Her words trailed down the hall behind her as she walked away from my room. She was right. I was a nerd. The books called to me more than the sun and the boys she wanted to chase. How had we been best friends since we were five?

I finished the book and set it on the stack that reached up to the nightstand by my bed. I hadn't slept in it since my father had slung a hammock across the room against my mother's wishes. I spent almost every night swinging in the net, a captured mermaid. I fingered through the box of records that once belonged to my uncle. I needed music to do absolutely anything, and cleaning was no exception. I stopped on the beat up cardboard folder containing my favorite of the inherited records, Creedence Clearwater Revival. I set it on the turntable and watched it spin into a black oblivion. I moved around the room plucking jeans and t-shirts from the floor. "Fortunate Son" played while I swayed between piles of clutter. My blonde hair had fallen loose down my back, and the cool air coming in through the windows caused it to match my sway.

There had been more mess than I realized, and by the time I could move across the room in any direction without tripping it was almost noon. The only mess left was the pile of records scattered down the length of my bed, discarded after use. I picked them up carefully and returned them to the box crate next to my dresser.

I stared at the reflection of myself in the mirror beside my dresser just to be reminded that everything was changing. My hair now fell to my waist, the blonde having darkened. My face thinned out after the summer that followed eighth grade graduation, and my body had followed the summer after sophomore year. My eyes were still green, bright and wide with gold rimming the pupils. I traced my mouth; my top lip was still too thin. It was my mother's mouth, though the voice that came out was never hers. I was much noisier than the woman below who had probably saved breakfast for me. I stared harder into the mirror, trying to find myself.

I could hear them in the living room even before I saw them. My mother and my best friend were sprawled on the couches watching some weird reality show.

"I've finished my room!" I shouted down the stairs.

"But not before you finished that book I bet!" Leave it to Edie to say that right in front of my mom. I paused midway down, not ready to show myself. All the time spent staring into the mirror defining my reflection in my mind made it occur to me that everything would always change and that I should embrace it. So I did.

"Laney Wilder, you better not have been reading when I specifically woke you up early, as requested, to clean that hoarder's den." Her normal light tone was gone, and for good reason. She loved spring break as much as kids and teenagers did. She had the whole week off from teaching and I had begged her to give up sleeping in because I was notorious for sleeping through alarms. I heard Edie snort with laughter. I grimaced. If my mother thought she was annoyed now she was in for a shock. I prepared myself, running my hands down the jean shorts that had crept up my thighs a bit higher than I had expected. Growing two inches over fall and winter does that to your clothes, though. I breathed in to steady myself and slowly began descending the stairs.

"Holy shit!" These were the only words to tumble from Edie's lips since she was the only one facing the stairs. My mom slapped a hand at her arm.

"Watch that mouth Edie…" She stopped speaking mid-sentence as she caught sight of me. The remote clattering against the hardwood unmuted the TV. For the first few minutes all I could hear was a Kardashian going on and on about her dress.

"Say something," I whispered at the two faces that were twin looks of shock and speechlessness.

"Something," Edie sighed. I felt my brow furrow in annoyance. I needed her to stop staring and break the silence. My mother just smiled. No words, just a blinking owl and a frog-like smile twisted and staring over the back of the couch.

"Do you hate it? Mom…?" I felt the heat in my cheeks turning them pink and the burn that swept across my lower eyelids like sloppy eyeliner.

"You are beautiful as always, kid, just going to take a while to adjust. Your father is going to have a meltdown, but we will ride it out. No bikes today, girls. I insist on driving you, and yes, Laney, you will be getting that cleaned up and evened out." She turned back around. "We will leave after I see what Bruce has to say about this." I smiled at the back of her head, the light brown waves alive in the sunset. I wanted to hug her with everything I had in me, but these days I felt awkward showing my emotions.

My hand moved of its own accord to the hair that now touched the bottom of my jawbone. I didn't know why I had taken the black-handled scissors with me to sit across from the mirror. I could hear the sounds of The Band behind me. Whenever he sang, "take a load off," I cut another handful of hair. All those blonde strands slipped from my palm but clung to my fingertips. I just wanted to see the changes I felt everywhere. My body had changed, my face was changing, but my blonde hair still hung loose and long like it had since I was seven. Now I could feel the uneven lengths of it around my face, and my whole being felt lighter.

Edie was still watching me, leaving the couch and circling around me to get to the perspiring glass of lemonade she had left on the counter. It was like she was desperately trying to figure me out without having to say anything directly to me. I expected shock and dismay from my mother, but instead here was Edie, estranged from me by a simple haircut. She should have seen me upstairs, cross-legged and webbed in my own hair with "The Weight" playing in the background, the record emitting little hiccups of static. I had done more than organize and declutter my room this morning.

"Stop staring at me like I'm a freaking alien, Edie. I cut my hair, that's all." I grabbed the lemonade glass from her hand and took a long drink. I sputtered. I had forgotten that she always added more sugar to her glass when my mom had her back turned. She came from a long line of sugar abusers. Her mother's coffee was always two parts sugar, one part coffee. She smiled smugly and retrieved her glass.

"It's just so unexpected and weird that you read a book, clean your room, and change your whole identity. I get that it's just hair, but you haven't allowed anyone to touch your hair more than once a year, and that's only for a trim. You would stare too if Rapunzel came out of the tower and was like, 'Oh yeah by the way I chopped off the rope before the prince showed up.' You know?" She smiled, a shy smile from a loud fun girl.

"Why would it matter if Rapunzel cut the rope since you just said she walked out of the tower? It's just hair, Edie. It will grow on you." I smirked at her exasperated face. Leave it to her to have completely botched the emphasis of her point.

"Your dad is going to flip out. You know it and I know it and so does she." She used her thumb to gesture behind at my mother, who was still fully absorbed in the Kardashian drama. I nodded and sighed. She was not missing her point on that one. My father loved my long hair and the idea that if I were still hanging onto my fairytale fantasies, I would never stop being his little girl. Yep, he was going to freak out when he came home next week.

"So let's get this fixed, because I'm not lying when I say it looks like Helen Keller was your stylist. She was that blind chick from history class. I cannot believe you didn't tell me you were going to do that. There isn't a mishap or mischievous plan hatched in the last ten years that wasn't concocted by us. You didn't say a word." She looked sad when she turned to walk back into the living room.

She sat down next to my mom, and they laughed at the eye rolling and annoyed face of Bruce Jenner getting blind-sided again. I didn't know how to tell her that I wanted to have things that were just mine. I wanted to remember sitting alone in the mid-morning light in a pile of my own hair, the sun catching where the snipped pieces went from pale gold to a darker blonde that was almost brown. I wanted to have that moment where a few simple cuts changed my face into a new one. I didn't know how to explain that to her because she was right—we had always shared everything from clothes to boyfriends that we passed back and forth like notes.

My mom dropped us off by the pier with forty dollars and a lingering look at her new daughter, the kind of girl that made changes to herself without asking or apologizing. I could see she was looking for herself in my face and finding it harder to spot now that my hair didn't wave down my back like hers.

"Have fun. Fix your hair with that money, Laney. I want to see even hair when I pick you up." She waved and fell back into the line of cars; tourists flocked here every spring and summer. She was used to their impatience and confusion. I think she enjoyed the driving challenge that the tourist season brought. If she had been searching for our matching personality traits, she would not have left with her sad smile; I was definitely my mother's daughter. If my father didn't return home every few weeks, I could be convinced she made me from thin air.

Edie had already left my side in distracted pursuit of the boys brought by the wave of tourism. I followed behind her, feeling the distance that my decision had put between us. She would get over it because that's what Edie did. She always said if she could recover from having been named after some eccentric cousin to a president's wife, she could bounce back from anything. Her mother tried to show us this old documentary of two women, one of them her daughter's namesake, but turned it off within the first half hour because our mindless laughter was irritating her. I don't know what she expected out of two thirteen-year-olds, one of whom was just told that she was named after some lady who lived with her old mom with their weird accents. We couldn't stop laughing that day if we wanted to. If anyone asked Edie about her name, she just said she had an old name and an old soul. The truth was, if some people were truly old souls then Edie wasn't a day over newborn.

"What about Ruth's?" I shrugged in response to Edie's suggestion. I didn't really care who fixed my hair now that most of it was gone. My friend rolled her painfully bright blue eyes and went into Ruth's.

The inside of the salon smelled of nail polish remover and hairspray mingled with the Chinese takeout that two of the stylists were eating in the corner by the back door. The thing about Ruth was that she cut hair well and everyone loved her, so much so that we all ignored the fact that on any given day her tired face was pulled a little bit tighter by her hair wrapped in a bun with strands hanging limply by her eyes. If she were selling cars, she would be telling you to get a Bentley when she only had a Kia.

"Oh my lord girl, what did you do to that hair?" That was Ruth, straight to the point. I smiled awkwardly. I really hadn't thought it looked bad enough to warrant a "holy shit" and an "oh my lord." I nervously smoothed down the chopped up ends.

"I wanted a change." She smiled in understanding and pointed to the chair in front of a white sink basin. I rolled my eyes at Edie. This was all becoming just a bit dramatic. This wasn't some small two-hundred-people-populated-town where everyone gathered at the diner to discuss gossip. I walked with my chin firm across the room while everyone followed me with their eyes. It took thirty minutes to wash and fix the damage I had caused to my own head. When she held up the cheap plastic mirror warped on the edge, I could see the entirety of my change. I felt it again, the burn along my lower eyelids. What the hell had I done? In one impulse I had wiped away part of who I had always been.

"I like it. You were getting too old to wear your hair down past your waist anyway. Pay Liz at the counter and then go make those peach-fuzz jaws drop." I didn't answer. I was trying to calm myself with the familiar—my thin top lip and the way my newly short hair was the same blonde as my father's. I didn't recognize myself anymore, but this was what I'd wanted hours ago as I sat on the floor. I just couldn't remember why.

"Let's go, Laney. We are supposed to meet up with everyone else on the beach." She was back to tapping, this time on the chair arm. It was like her theme song, mindless tapping in no particular melody. I looked back one more time to see myself, and then blinked back what could have been the beginning of tears. I did not cry in public.

I paid Liz, her face bright with the excitement that anyone here has when spring break comes, only to be outdone by summer. She gave me the change while she hummed. It sounded like Adele.

The sun hadn't warmed everything yet, and I was grateful for the hoodie I'd grabbed at the last moment. There was no fog holding tight to the buildings anymore either. We walked in silence, but the fact that Edie was beside me and not ahead of me meant that she'd already begun forgiving me for excluding her from my momentous change. I smiled even though she wasn't paying attention to me. All Edie would see for the full solid week were the boys. She liked the boys of spring more than summer. Some of them were the same, but the wave of summer tourists is more aggressive, and there is, as it turns out, such a thing as too many boys in one town.

"Can you believe that Hadley decided to make it all official with Nathan the day before our break? Seriously? Nathan is so local it pains me to think that when we come back here after college he will never have left. I mean, he is good stuff, but he is as local as they come. He loves it here. I just think Hadley is setting herself up for heartbreak. She has one more year, one more and then she is probably off to the Midwest for school. Why date anyone long-term when you are that close to being gone?" She shook her head in disbelief. I frowned down at my black ballet flats. I couldn't tell her that I was perhaps as local as they come too, not when she had spent every moment since the whole "this is your future speech" in eighth grade planning our lives together. Hadley had been infatuated with Nathan since he kissed her on the cheek as a dare at her sixth grade birthday party. I was not surprised at all.

"You know she has always liked him, E. You know it, like everyone in school knows it. So what if she wants to be with Nathan even if we all know he isn't going down the same path as her?" Her strides lengthened. My sigh was lost in the breeze as we made our way through one cluster of quaint beach shops after another. Here and there we walked past art galleries squeezed in between clothes shops and souvenir shops. Normally Edie would pause and stare at whatever was on display; she was very much like an infant drawn to bright or shiny things. Today her feet were swallowing up the pavement. The distance we had closed stretched out again. It was another unspoken rule that we went along with whatever ideas the other had, a permanent support network we built. I didn't get it this time though; perhaps in my room I had cut off more than just my hair. I felt like this lighter me had left some of my immaturity in the nest of blonde hair.

When we rounded the corner, we saw the gleaming shells of a hundred cars and trucks. Squat or tall, they shone in a rainbow of metal and plastic. The tourists. The street busking couple with their his and hers dreads were already strumming up easy change and loose bills while their rough-looking dog circled the tree behind them. I could never remember their names, but they showed up right before the crowds, the natives knowing they weren't one of our kind but the foreigners never the wiser. No amount of Jason Mraz played twice an hour on an old acoustic would provide them with enough to stay in this town.

I watched Edie catch her reflection in the last storefront before the sidewalk curved into stairs dusted with sand and met the mouth of the pier on the other side of the handrail. She knew she was pretty the same way someone knew they were short or that their left side seemed a bit higher than the right. She was correct, though—she *was* pretty. Sometime during freshman year she had grown into her light brown hair and her body had curved just enough to make her feel feminine. She had never been an ugly duckling; she had just matured into what was already there. I watched her push her bangs out of her eyes. They swept over her forehead like a gender-bending Justin Bieber. She pulled her always-present lip balm from her shorts pocket and pinched her cheeks. She had been pinching her cheeks in mirrors since my mother had shown us the movie *Mermaids*. It was a habit I had grown out of; Edie clung to it like she was at the front of the line for adulthood, yet a small piece of her held back.

"Stop staring at me. I just need to get used to the new you, the Laney of the future." She had the same voice as the narrator of old black-and-white science fiction movies that played late at night. I laughed, and she returned it. The distance closed in a little.

"You look fine. Your hair looks fine and your lips aren't chapped, not that you have ever let them get chapped since you were old enough to know what lip balm is. Let's go find Hadley. When we find her, don't make that face. They are just dating, for god's sake, not getting married." I scolded her for wearing the look of a grieving friend standing graveside. She was the dramatic half of our twosome. She smirked and kept walking while our steps slowed and began dragging with the dry sand. I hated sand. I loved the water and wanted nothing to do with the land that cradled it.

"Jesus, I wish I had brought my sweater." She shivered in the breeze that came off the water. We had to fight the ocean's roar to be heard, as if anything we could say would ever sound as important as its crashing on the shore.

"No you don't. You wanted to make sure that all that cleavage could be seen from the space station." She grinned but didn't deny that I was right. I glanced at her tank top, black and sprinkled with black glitter around the neckline. Her breasts were obvious, but not in a way that would label her a whore. That was Edie, toeing the same line between her teenage self and the adult self she was nearing.

"Brainy Laney!" I rolled my eyes in Edie's direction, and she was doing the same. The stupid nickname used nearly as frequently as my own was being shouted down the beach at me. I knew who it was without looking, and I didn't want to humor him. I lasted about five seconds before glancing sideways toward Evan. He was a part of the group that met down on the beach every first day of spring break and summer since we had been young enough to still need our mothers, all of them stretched out on nubby towels leftover from past summers. I swallowed hard at the sight of him; I'd had the same reaction since he grew three inches after the seventh grade. He showed up the first day of eighth after half a summer in Nevada with his grandpa, and he had muscle definition and was right at six feet. He was the first of our group to show a glimpse at his adult self.

"Shut up Evan, you ass." Edie's voice was aggressive and protective, but no matter how much she defended me the nickname might as well have been tattooed on my forehead. He smiled at her with a grin that took up his whole face. He looked at Edie the way I had been looking at him for all these years. Edie didn't see anything that was right in front of her face. It should have strained the dynamic of our group, but it never did. That was our way. We weren't raised to be obnoxious and filled with bitterness. We were the children of the sea—that's what our mothers had called us. We were their sun-kissed mermaids, and the boys their sand-covered pirates. We belonged to them as much as we belonged to each other and to the sea itself.

"So, Laney, you look…different." He was studying me now, taking in the lines of my face that had been muted behind all the hair. He could see the shape of me now.

"The hair?" I asked like I didn't know. He didn't say anything. It took a few minutes but he shook it off.

"Nah, it's the shorts. Who knew you had an ass?" I glared at him through my lashes and went back to studying the way the sand glittered against my pale skin.

"You're an ass, Evan!" Edie jumped to my defense, always to my defense. I glanced from her disgruntled look to Evan's face, now sheepish and apologetic.

"Hey guys."

I took my eyes off Evan to find Hadley and Nathan, struggling to walk while remaining wrapped around each other. Evan shook his head and sighed. My god, why was every single person beside me acting like their budding romance was going to bring our seaside town to its ruin? This wasn't a CW show. Edie stared off at the waves climbing up the shore, pretending she didn't hear the greeting. I waved at them as they got closer. There were only two people left to show. They *had* to show. This was our tradition. We were molded by women who longed to have traditions but didn't growing up. The adults that made us created them and followed them with militaristic dedication. That need had passed down to us. We took over and added people to the group as we grew.

"Where is Reese? She called me and said she was leaving an hour ago." Hadley barely got the words out before Nathan was kissing her again, her cheeks pink from embarrassment and the sun. I didn't find their union as unholy as everyone else made it out to be, but I didn't need to see them making future babies on the beach either.

"I haven't talked to Reese in weeks. Have you?" I didn't purposely avoid Reese, but she was post-breakup and my sweater had no room for tears and snot unless it was Edie's. Reese's tears were Hadley's department.

"What happened to your hair, Laney?" Nathan had stopped molesting Hadley's face long enough to get a question out. What a waste of a question.

"I woke up and it had all fallen off in my sleep. This is a wig." Sarcasm was second nature.

"This crazy beezy cut her hair this morning when she was supposed to be cleaning her room. Seriously. She chopped off hair that was, like, almost to her thighs without a second thought while she probably was listening to some weird band from the seventies again." She laughed and looked at me pointedly. This was Edie venting her resentment with a crowd and humor. I let her have it. Besides, she was right about the where and how of it all anyway. She never understood my odd fascination with seventies rock. I didn't understand my fascination with it either. Edie made fun of that love every chance she got. I had inherited it with the record player and box of vinyl. I was the only one of us to even listen to vinyl. They just were not convenient.

"There she is. Who is with her? She knows she can't just drop strangers on us on the first day." Reese, with her wild black hair and the lip ring she acquired a few months back, was in stark contrast with the beach around her. She wore her breakup in the smudged charcoal eye shadow and the looseness of her shirt. If Reese did anything, she did it with passion, whether it was being in love or breaking up. Her brown eyes disappeared into sadness, but still she was walking toward us accompanied by a face none of us recognized. He was average height with a strong jaw, but his attractiveness wouldn't warm us to him. We didn't isolate ourselves often, but this was one of the times we did. She was breaking an unspoken rule.

"What are you all staring at? Did you see a freaking ghost?" She was unaffected by our tension, the rudeness that seeped from our pores unwillingly. I wanted to stop acting like a brat. This was Reese after all, but some traditions felt more important than others and this was one of them. We didn't have many spring breaks left before we scattered.

"Whatever. Don't be weird. This is my cousin Ryland. Ryland, these are my people." She gestured at us with a wave of her hand. It was like her wave rolled over us and smoothed out the tension. Family wasn't against the rule. I smirked inside at his name. I had forgotten that his mother and her sister had both decided as prepubescent girls to only give their children names that began with the letter R. They looked nothing alike. Where she was the color of the moon, he was the color of the sand. Their eyes were identical, though; they could have been siblings in that regard. He was the only one left of the R bunch I hadn't met before.

Ryland smiled and did a half wave that dropped to his side in awkwardness. Could it be that he was a shy R kid? Reese and her two younger sisters were all so loud and excitable. Their mother was the same, her voice the most boisterous among the mothers, her stories the most interesting.

"Whoa Laney, your hair is all gone. However will prince charming find his way up the tower? I mean whoa. How are you guys not just gathered around her right now, feeling and studying this lack of hair?" Her astonishment was vivid on her face. We had been kindred in the way we both had worn our hair for years. Hers had never been as long, but she always looked like a wild girl.

"I just cut it, that's all. Maybe I cut it to get away from all the Rapunzel references…" It might have been true or it might not have. When the last cut was made I had become aware that somewhere between the laundry basket and the records, I had changed who I was. Was it too late to take any of it back?

"Were those cheekbones really hiding under all that hair? Wow." She stopped circling me and moved to stand beside her silent cousin. He didn't talk, but he was studying me as if he could see the changes that were only now starting to rise to the surface even though we hadn't formally been introduced. Evan was staring at Ryland and Edie was putting on more lip balm, absent from the whole staring contest. I think Edie was always a little absent; she already knew that none of these boys would be the one she chased or allowed to catch her, so she didn't bother even thinking of it. I don't know if everyone was as aware of that as I was.

"It looks good, you know, but I don't know what you looked like before." Ryland's mouth moved and words came out, but he was looking off to the side. His shyness truly was remarkable in that it probably wasn't the lasting kind. There was a spark of rebellion in his face.

"Thanks." I tried to push my hair behind my ears but it fell away immediately. It was going to be so hard to break the smallest of habits. Reese was grinning, but it was a tight grin. Her face had gotten used to being sullen in the time that followed her last breakup, yet there was light in her eyes again. No one could stay heartbroken during the break, not in our group anyway.

"Oh my god, get a room already!" Reese shouted over at Hadley and Nathan, their faces hidden behind her hair but mashed together nonetheless. We all laughed when nothing changed. They just kept kissing, and we wrinkled our noses and shook our heads at them.

"Did everyone forget I wasn't here yet?" The deepest of all the voices in the group had me twisting around. Leland was coming up behind where we were gathered with blankets slung over his shoulder and hanging from every arm. We cheered in unison. He always remembered the things we needed but always forgot. The tradition could begin. We all rushed at him to pluck the blankets from his arms. We ran to a few feet above where the shore was wet with seawater and tossed our blankets around in a semicircle. We all scattered out in search of bleached driftwood, rough and littered across the shore. I picked through piles of black-green seaweed swarming with sand fleas. I gathered the wood to my chest and carried it back while Leland and Evan scraped the sand into a presentable pit. Our fathers had taught them the way of the beach bonfire, eager to offer absolutely anything to us. The fathers had a way of getting lost in the contribution of traditions and personalities from the mothers that we held tight. I dumped the wood next to the ring and looked out into the ocean, the waves building and falling, hypnotizing me to wander close. I was startled when the foam slid its cool fingers over my ballet flats and up my ankles. I shivered; the water was too cold for swimming most of the year.

"Hey stupid, what are you trying to do? Catch pneumonia? Take some of this wood. I overestimated how much and how long I could carry it again." I laughed at the voice coming from the stacked wood that obscured Edie's head. I pulled pieces away from her face that was all smiles despite nearly getting a splinter in the mouth.

"I'm not going to get pneumonia, I've the blood of a mermaid." I smiled. Our mothers taught us that we were invincible. Perhaps they were right. Nothing took us down or tore us apart. When she was planning her journey away, I was trying to imagine ever being able to leave. Not just the beach, but my mother and days like these. How could she just walk away from them with no plans to return until we were older, coming home again as women with careers and fiancés in tow? This was where we all wanted to end up; raising our children around bonfires while the stars lay in abandon above us and eating dinner late because every spare moment of freedom was spent on that sand listening to that ocean. I didn't know how I would be able to leave it, even if I knew I was coming back.

"Where are you Laney? La La Land?" Her question pierced through my haze of musing.

"I am the queen of La La Land, as you know. It only makes sense that I return there often to rule my citizens." I shrugged.

"I have the weirdest best friend ever."

"You know I am still walking beside you right?"

"I just assumed there wasn't an echo all the way into your kingdom, your highness," she chirped back with lightning speed. I laughed; it was amazing we didn't have ridiculously cut abs as often as we laughed. We threw the wood and collapsed into each other on one of Leland's blankets. She stretched out so I could rest my head on the space where her knees became her thighs. I pulled my hair up and she sighed. I was sure no one heard it but me, but in my brain she may as well have screamed. Her inability to accept it was baffling. Maybe she could feel that this was just one of many decisions to come where I wouldn't seek out her opinion.

"I can see why some of the guys at school think you guys are lesbians." I rolled toward the sound of Leland's voice and smirked.

"Who says we aren't?" I tried to say it with seriousness, but Edie's laugh triggered my own until we were balled up together with the humor slapping a Band-Aid over the fragile crack in our twosome.

"Edie could never be a lesbian. Have you seen the way she glows like a light bulb the second she sees the first group of non-local men?" There was the thinnest thread of resentment woven through Evan's words. Edie could hear it as well as I could, but instead of hurting her feelings it made her antagonistic.

"It's probably because all you locals are still just boys." She stared Evan down until he glanced at the flames that were slowly building up. It was almost too early for the bonfire, but the thrill of the first one on break couldn't be held to normal hours. It was bright and wavering, but in a few hours it would illuminate our faces half-hidden in our hoodies like skulls on Day of the Dead.

Evan tossed another misshapen piece of wood into the fire and let the tension recede with the tide.

"You know what we need to do this break…" Nathan, who spoke the least, dropped off before stating anything. It was like his boldness tapered when our heads turned in his direction.

"Nathan and I were thinking we should all pitch in for something adventurous. He has the keys to his mom's SUV all summer whenever he needs them. His father gave her a new car last week for her fiftieth." She let the idea circulate while they awaited our returned excitement. I was always trying to wrap my mind around the fact that Nathan's mother was so much older than the rest of ours. My mother had just turned thirty-eight in the fall. I had been her belated graduation gift and arrived in time to celebrate Mother's Day. It was much the same for Edie and Reese. Nathan's mother was a writer; she told us that she was too busy holding onto her feminist rights to bother with babies at that age. She met his father when she moved here; he had been a year ahead of my parents in high school. The age difference never seemed to bother them. It struck all of us as strange to think that his mother was halfway through life already.

"What were you guys thinking of anyway?" The question came from above me, Edie's voice vibrating all the way down through her legs. I could hear her heartbeat as well.

"I don't know. We could drive up to the mountains and go hiking or something," Nathan threw out.

"Are you kidding me? Do you take a farmer away from his crops when it's time to harvest?" Edie didn't hide the disbelief in her voice. They all should have seen it coming, but there was silence before we all laughed so hard our sides ached.

"What if we just put our money together and have a much bigger bonfire with like food and stuff." I sounded like I was five or fifty myself. What was the point about getting excited over Nathan having the SUV if all we did was come right back here? We would be in plain sight of our parents should they come looking, but it was all I could think of.

"Laney, Laney, Laney. What is the point of having The Beast then?" Nathan was of course referring to the nickname bestowed upon the black Dodge Durango that could comfortably seat eight, the one none of us understood his family of three having.

"I vote for a road trip. Let's hit other beaches. It's a win-win if Edie still gets tourists." Hadley spoke up like the voice of reason and wisdom combined. It was perfect.

Agreement murmured around the circle. I sat up, shaking my hair out, and found Ryland and Evan both staring at me like I had grown an extra nose. I scowled at the fire. I wanted to just yell, "Get over it!" but I didn't.

"Will you be here for the whole week, Ryland?" Since I had never seen him I had assumed his visits weren't normal.

"Yeah, I will actually be moved in by the end of the week." His voice was raspy like he already had a pack-a-day smoking habit. He was hard to hear when the burning wood popped and cracked against the slow moan of the ocean. My eyebrows shot up; he was moving in with the R's? I wanted to jump up and plop down next to him, a hundred questions ready, but I didn't move an inch. Laziness and the first pulls of cold kept me exactly where I was.

"So you are bunking down with the unholy trifecta, huh?" I got a mean look from Reese, who was directly across the fire from me. Ryland's laugh was full and overpowered the other sounds around us. The fullness of his laugh was unexpected.

"Yeah, I'm moving into the Bermuda Triangle of women. I will probably lose my masculinity in a minute. Don't look at me like that Reese. You know its true. When your dad comes home he just ducks and smiles with you girls." She punched him in the arm, but her smile was anything but angry. How were they so close when none of us had ever met him in the five years we had known Reese? It didn't matter. Just like that he had become one of us and we all accepted him.

"So should we go Thursday? We could leave in the morning and come back at night." Hadley was looking at all of us like it was Christmas morning. We had never left this beach during break. None of us had ever been able to drive before. Nathan was now clear to have anyone he wanted in the car with him. I was jealous when I thought of the year that separated the rest of us from him. I wanted to drive, but I was still in the studying stages. My mother decided I could wait until summer to take driving school, and I was also expected to start working when the heat rolled in gradually with the unfamiliar faces. It was what she had done and what my father had done. Working at Gilly's Fish Bowl was how my mother had met Edie's. They had been going to school together since junior high but weren't aware of each other until they both smelled like fish and had slaw stains on their aprons.

"I will ask my mom tonight at dinner and text you guys as soon as she decides." I wasn't actually sure she would agree, but the thought of all of us crammed into The Beast with a black ribbon of highway underneath and the scattered beaches ahead of us made me smile. It sounded like freedom. It wasn't as though we were being suffocated, but still—freedom was freedom.

The day slipped into dusk, and all of us were quiet when the sun slid into the ocean. We could never hear it like the adults said you could, but it was our nature to grow silent just in case. Once the darkness spread around us, we fell into smaller, quieter conversations. We all pretended that we didn't notice when Hadley and Nathan disappeared into the shadows of the sea cliffs that rose for miles down the sand. I couldn't put myself in Hadley's place without my stomach twisting with nerves. Kissing was one thing, but I knew Hadley and Nathan had moved past that. They already had years of friendship behind them, so there was no need to grow accustomed to each other. They were finally seeing what was under the wrapping paper like eager kids at a birthday party.

I wasn't naïve. I also wasn't the only virgin. Out of our seven, there were four of us left. We wore it like the odd extra button that's sewn into the side of a sweater or a shirt. We felt safer knowing it was there, although we were more than aware we would eventually lose it. It surprised me to think about who the remaining four were, though, and which three weren't anymore. I wondered if I was the only one keeping score.

"Psst…Laney. Come down to the water with me. You're the only one who isn't afraid of the cold." I looked up into Evan's face hovering over me. The way the flames cast their shadows carved his boyish face into a man's. I could hear the light snore coming from behind me. Edie had been up since dawn and had fallen asleep when the conversation had trailed off. I held out my hand and he lifted me to my feet. I tried to ignore the twisting. We had been friends since the days when he would push me down on the playground. In the beginning it had been Edie, Evan, Nathan, and I. Hadley and Leland came a few years later when we were in junior high and would stand awkwardly around the bleachers during unbearable midday dances. I had liked Evan since the summer our mothers first trusted all of us alone out here. We had been the only ones throwing our bodies with abandon into the waves, soaked and shivering for hours after. It was a tradition within a tradition for us. I didn't admit that once I was picked up and taken home, I would shake in a bath that could have boiled a crab tender in its shell. The ocean here was never really the blue-green bath they showed in movies, but I couldn't say no to him.

We walked where the waves were starting to climb the shore. It would only be a matter of time before it washed away any trace of our having ever been there. He said nothing and I couldn't speak. It was getting more difficult to hide the million emotions that ran through me.

"So why did you really do it?" As he asked me he pulled his shoes off, rolling up his jeans to just below his knees. I stepped out of my ballet flats and set my hoodie on top of them. I had no plans to let the waves entice me in past the knees, but I was depending on that sweater to hold off the chills until my mother pulled into the line of cars trying to leave or looking for a place to park.

"I wanted to look in the mirror and see something or someone different. Everything is changing; I just wanted to be a part of that. I blend in and I thought, 'Why not make people see me?'" Evan looked at me as I spoke the truth. We all told lies and we all had secrets, but rarely ever from each other. It never felt strange to say how you felt.

"Jesus, Laney. When have you ever blended in? You didn't then and you don't now. I see you, we all see you, but no one can touch you. I'm not the only one who knows you would rather spend your time lost in your own thoughts or in a book. You didn't have to cut all your hair off—you just had to look up." He took my hand in his and pulled me into the water. I didn't know if I couldn't breathe because it was so cold or because the cold couldn't break the heat that existed between our hands. I shrieked when the waves crashed into my waist. I didn't anticipate the water to be that high.

"Oh my god, it's so co..col…cold." I barely sputtered out the words when he pulled me tight against him. We stood like that, shivering and swaying in the water, until I pulled away first. He pushed my hair off my cheek. The wind coming off of the water never felt more painful than that moment without all the hair that usually shielded me. We walked haphazardly through the water back to the sand. I didn't know what that moment had been, so I chose not to question it.

I saw Edie sitting up in the light from the fire, rubbing her eyes. It was endlessly amusing how often that girl fell asleep in random places. Hadley and Nathan were wandering back at the same time. I couldn't see her face from where I was, but her giggles stretched down the sand to us. We were both shaking by the time we made it all the way to the ring in the sand. I reached down for heat and to help gather the blankets. We got a few stares, but no one said anything. Evan looked over to catch me staring at him, and then glanced at Edie's sleepy face before he looked into the dwindling fire. I didn't care. He saw me, even if it was only for a minute.

"I am so…" her mouth gaped open in a yawn so hard her jaw should have snapped, "…tired. Thank god your mom said I could sleep at your house tonight."

I shrugged off the annoyance that came when my mother and her made plans without bothering to include me. It lasted about a second when it occurred to me that they were deciding where Edie would sleep while I was upstairs chopping off my hair. I nodded, feeling the exhaustion creep into my bones next to the cold. It was only eight. I knew that we would get home and shower or bathe before my mother fed us and picked out another odd movie from her own youth to share with us. Sometimes her taste was impeccable, and other times it fell somewhere between the amazingness of *Weird Science* and the absolute nightmare of *Fantasia* for the thousandth time. I never once made it all the way through that movie. It was the classical music that killed me. I had no ability to remain a functioning human whenever the strains of Tchaikovsky or Beethoven could be heard. I blamed my mother for that. She listened to it every night when my father was gone and she was grading assignments and lengthy papers.

"See you guys!" We called back to the rest of them. The fire had been cleared and suffocated beneath the wet sand that Leland and Ryland had thrown on top of it. We dropped our blankets on the rail of the stairs for Leland to collect on his way up. I turned around at the top and glanced down at the faces I loved. There was something to be said for tradition.

I barely remembered getting into the bath, but the door swung open and Edie waltzed in with wet hair and my favorite pajama bottoms on. They were a thick flannel in blue and green.

"Your mom said don't make her come up here and carry you down to the table. In other news, she made spaghetti…again. Why do you always do this to yourself? The ocean is too damn cold even if it does get you closer to Evan." She was brushing her teeth with the toothbrush she kept in the drawer. I pulled the drain and watched the blue water swirl away, leaving scraps of seaweed behind.

"God, those bath bombs you buy smell awesome, but gross. Seriously Laney, look at that tub." She pointed to the thin green strips that stuck to the porcelain. It *was* gross, but I refused to give up my bath bombs.

"I can't believe you fell asleep out there." I laughed and reached for the towel hanging beside the tub.

"Really? You can't? I fall asleep everywhere. I don't know why I wake up before dawn, but it's an unbreakable habit even though I quit the track team at the end of last year."

She studied her skin in the oval mirror hanging over the sink. There was something to be said about old bathrooms with freestanding sinks and claw foot tubs. I loved how dated and seaside-town cliché our house was. Whenever I saw houses like mine replicated in movies I felt happier. They were recreating a fantasy of what I already had.

I hadn't really ever put the fact that Edie was used to rising with the sun to run laps together with her unbearable early morning wake-up's. I was not a morning person. In the summer I was seldom seen in public before noon. My mother never minded my sleeping patterns in the summer; she said that was what summer vacation was for.

"You know, we should offer to cook your mom dinner tomorrow night." I smiled at her back as she was investigating her pores. I pulled the towel snug and walked to stand next to her.

"Is that just your way of saying that you don't want one of the five meals my mother cooks again?" I nudged her over so I could brush my teeth.

"You said it, not me. I forgot to tell you that Big Edie is going out of town with the mister until Wednesday, so you are stuck with me for five blissful days." I laughed. I saw her almost every day anyway.

It still made me chuckle that she called her mom Big Edie since the day of the documentary; her mom had been less amused. She called her dad "the mister" since the first time she stumbled on the proof of romance still going strong between her parents. No one knew why.

"Do you realize we just brushed our teeth to go eat dinner?" I paused when I thought about it. I smiled and shrugged on my way out of the bathroom. We were so weird sometimes. I dropped my towel in the basket outside the door.

"Would you please get your butts down here, I'm starving!" We moved quickly down the stairs, with Edie skipping down them while I still clung to the bannister. It only takes falling down them once to leave you skittish, and I had done it at least a dozen times in my life.

My mom was waiting at the table with the usual trio of spaghetti, bread, and the salad that only she and Edie really ate. I tried, but it always felt like the lettuce went from crisp to rotting when I put it in my mouth. It seemed super odd to love eating leaves.

"Mom…" She held up her hand to her mouth, a signal from when I was small to please stop talking when my mouth was full. I rolled my eyes and chewed faster.

"Ahhh…" I stuck out my food-free tongue sarcastically to show her that I was done chewing. She shook her head at me in exasperation.

"Can Edie and I go with the group on Thursday for a day trip down to a few of the neighboring beaches? Nathan has the restrictions lifted from his license now, and he's got permission to use The Beast whenever." She narrowed her eyes in response to my question. She picked up her phone and typed something quickly and sent it. She was texting my father. That was the way it was, every matter discussed and decided upon together. It didn't matter that he was gone all the time; he was present in as many of the details as possible. Her phone buzzed with the clacking keys of a typewriter.

"Sure, but the same rules apply as for the bonfires. You will be in that door by no later than ten." I dropped my fork at her answer.

"Are you on crack because you got bored when we were gone and said, 'Hmmm… maybe I should smoke crack today?' Did you just say ten?" I looked over to Edie and saw her mouth agape too.

"One, don't ask your mother if she smokes crack! Two, I think meth would probably make more sense, or cocaine. Three, don't question something you don't want me to have to rethink." With that, she stood up with her empty plate and set it in the sink. "I'm going upstairs to call your father. Do the dishes and sweep." I barely caught the last part as she climbed the stairs.

"Seriously though, is your mom on drugs?" I laughed at Edie's never-ending face of shock. I had been told my entire life in lengthy lectures and short reminders that I wouldn't be allowed out past nine until I was seventeen. My parents were liberals with a strong belief that the boogeyman comes out after dark. Seventeen was still almost two months away.

"Nope, she is too calm to be high on crack or meth. I'm not entirely sure of the difference." We laughed and pushed the spaghetti around our plates. My blood felt like it was buzzing. This was huge, and if I didn't screw it up it would become the norm. My parents were good about trust and respect as long as it wasn't abused and returned.

"Should I call my mom and ask her just in case?" She was stabbing at the dark green leaves, and my stomach turned at the thought of eating them. She loved salads so much that sometimes I was certain that she could have been my mother's daughter. When we were younger I often found myself having feelings of jealousy. I grew out of it eventually.

"Of course you should. Big Edie will kill you if you do something like that without her permission." I was just pointing out the obvious. "Wait. Isn't Big Edie coming back Wednesday anyway?"

"Yeah, but remind me again how much Big Edie loves last-minute decision making. I believe her favorite phrase of last summer was something along the lines of, 'Don't put me on the spot Edie, if you want something ask me without an audience.' She must have said it a million times." She smiled while she twirled pasta around her fork, sending splatters of sauce around her plate.

"To be fair, you did put her on the spot a lot. I mean like all the time." I remembered her mom's brow furrowing more last summer than the entirety of our shared childhoods. She hadn't been purposely driving her mother insane but she had been testing every boundary she had. She was quicker to push for independence than I was. Our relationships with our mothers were so different. I wasn't aching for the escape she was. Big Edie was an amazing mother, but she didn't understand change and fought against it with everything she had. The only reason Edie had as much freedom as she did was because her mother seemed to be compensating for what all the other mothers allowed.

"I'm going to bed, Laney. I am so tired." I nodded while she picked up her plate to scrape into the trash. "I'll sweep in the morning. Your mother will never know. I get up with the sun and you guys definitely do not." I watched her stretch and yawn. She would be up with the sun the rest of break, but the first day killed her.

"From the stars to the sea." She shouted down at me like an afterthought.

"From the sand to the moon," I yelled back while the rest of my spaghetti slid like intestines into the trash. I smiled in her absence. Would we still text those goodnights when we were separated by miles? The likelihood of me getting into the same university as her was almost impossible. I had good grades, but she had it all. I just couldn't drag myself to the extracurricular activities. I had done cheerleading and it had been unbearable. The skirts and games, smelly buses with boys who tested my gag reflex with the horror of their actual personalities. I stuck it out freshman year, but after that I was done. I still had one silver and teal pom pom on the floor of my closet. I hadn't been fooling anyone, but my parents and Edie were nevertheless at every game, whether it was in town or not. We were all relieved when I quit pretending that I was something I was clearly not.

I got lost in thought as my wrists sunk in the deep sink basins. It was a natural impulse to want to take another bath. The heat climbing up my arms from the dishes warmed the inside of my bones where the ocean water had left its imprint. I sprawled on the couch and looked through all the crap my mom had on DVR until I hit *The Walking Dead*. I was the only one who watched it in the house. It turned my mom's stomach, and unless someone was getting divorced or having an affair, Edie couldn't be bothered.

I could hear the waves breaking outside the sliding glass doors and the sounds of the dead filled the darkness. I buried my head in a pillow twice, but otherwise I couldn't take my eyes off the fake corpses moving in a slow dance down the abandoned backwoods roads.

⌇⌇⌇

"Hey, Laney. Wake up." I squinted into the room trying to find her face. I squeezed my eyes closed against the invasion of the sun through the drapes that hadn't been pulled tight.

"You fell asleep on the couch again watching that crap you call television. Go up to bed." She sounded like my best friend and my mother had unknowingly merged into one person while I slept below them. Edie had no siblings, so when she sounded maternal it threw me off.

"I'm fine. I'm up." I wasn't really, but I felt bad about leaving her alone the few times I was actually aware that she was up before the world.

"You can't even open your eyes, nerd. Go back to sleep. I already swept the kitchen and drained the nasty stuff out of the sink that you forgot." She was whispering; maybe she thought my alertness was controlled by volume.

"Are you going for your run then?" I prayed she would say yes. I was a crap runner, but if she left me alone I could slip back into the weirdness of my dreams, ones where I slayed reanimated corpses and smoked on a broken porch telling younger kids about how the apocalypse started.

"No crazy, I already went." My eyes opened fully for the first time, and I could see she wore the tiny black shorts that made my mom frown and that her shoes were wet and caked in sand.

"Ooooh she is going to kill you!" I leaned over the couch and pointed to her bright pink running shoes marred by her morning run. The trail of sand caught the sunlight and it glittered in a path back to the door. When I looked up her face was pouty with recognition that there was more sweeping for her in the immediate future. Mom had an unbending rule about shoes and sand. She had passed down her hatred of loose sand to me in the womb, and even as an infant I would curl my feet up in protest whenever my skin touched it. I laughed at the way her pretty face drooped like a puppy at the prospect of cleaning up her mess.

"Shut up. Go get dressed if you are staying up. We can put some coffee on for your mom and walk into town for bagels."

"Or we could take our bikes..." She grimaced at my face.

"Fine." I jumped up, knocking the plaid lap blanket to the floor, and ran up the stairs. I took them two at a time—my paranoid precaution about going down them did not apply to going back up. I threw on my thermal and zipped up my jeans. Edie might not mind the early morning chill as she ran down the beach, but I was not into it. I reached for my pile of black hair ties, but my hand stilled halfway to the dresser. I had no hair to pull back anymore. I smiled. Cutting my hair had taken ten minutes off the time it usually took me to get ready. I grabbed my phone off the charger and tucked it into my back pocket. Three cracked screens and I still kept it back there. I grabbed the hoodie I had tossed on the floor and walked carefully down to where Edie was still stretching with her leg up on the couch. She was lucky the lady of the house wasn't up to see her sandy shoes on the furniture.

"Let's go. I am so hungry. I just couldn't eat spaghetti again. When dad is gone it's like two times a week now. Why can't she just do sandwiches and pizza all the time like other bad cooks?" I felt bad as soon as the words left my mouth. It was a fair question, but I knew she tried. She just wasn't cut out for cooking and I wasn't looking to be any better.

We shut the door behind us as quietly as possible. I couldn't remember the last time anyone had a break-in, so I didn't worry that I had forgotten my key. Even with the tourists, it was almost silent outside save for the sounds of wildlife and the fading roar of the ocean as we moved further inland. We were both walking fast today. Edie was never exhausted even after she had been running, but I was surprised at my own speed. Food. It was the best motivation ever. The vacation rental row was now lined up and down the street with cars, and sand had blown over the asphalt. A month ago the whole neighborhood had looked clean but abandoned. We made our way through the side streets and were halfway to The Mad Bageler when I stopped with my face pinched as I glared over at Edie. From her fat smile she knew that I was mad about forgetting the bikes, and since she never spaced on any detail I knew she hadn't reminded me on purpose. She said riding a bike was dated, that we had feet and usually had rides available. She called them my "old lady perks," the bikes and my vinyl obsession. I picked up speed and walked past her. It was my own fault for being so eager to go, but knowing she remembered made me want to shove her.

I groaned when we rounded onto the street and saw the line halfway around the block. I waited a few seconds and heard Edie groan behind me. I kept walking until we filled in the back of the line. It was mostly couples around my parents' age, blowing into their hands and bouncing back and forth on their feet. Edie was on her phone, scrunching her nose as she skimmed through Facebook.

"Seriously, did you see Hadley's status last night? She said, and I quote, 'Nothing like bonfires with your soulmate.' She is killing me, Laney. Ki-ll-ing me!" She was so annoyed she was shaking her leg as she rolled her eyes and kept scrolling.

"So what?" I didn't get why it bothered her, why the whole relationship gave her hardcore ugly face.

"Soulmates? She is sixteen and they aren't getting married. They have been together for approximately how many days again? It is just so ridiculous. Why do girls our age buy into this crap already? Why are they so eager to find a boy and settle down? There is a whole world out there, Laney. I just thought our friends would never be the kind to ignore that. I feel like I'm settling by association." Her voice was lined in her anxiety—this was the Edie almost no one else knew. They saw a carefree determined flirt with a huge sense of humor. I knew this side of her.

"You can't be settled by association. I don't even think that's a thing. You aren't married just because you know married people, E." She looked up, and I saw the exhaustion in her eyes, the tiredness I never thought she felt.

"All of us leaving was the plan, to conquer the world and come back to raise our brats in the sand. Our version of our parents' chosen lives. You don't see it, but I see it. Some of us will stay behind, and when the ones who leave come back we will be different." Her voice fell off when she realized a few people within earshot had paused to listen. Edie had a thousand facets, and I could know her until we died and would still be shocked every time she revealed a new one. This was her vulnerability.

"I don't see why it matters, why you care if some stay and some go." Her concerns made me feel naïve, not smart enough to grasp the bigger picture that caused her to be snarky about two of our best friends falling in love or whatever it was they felt.

"Forget it, Laney. I watch too much TV. Reality shows are warping my brain." She held a finger gun to her head and pulled the trigger. I laughed. God, she was so dramatic. I smiled at her imaginary gunshot to the head, but her words were going in a circle in my brain.

"Holy crap, Laney." She shoved her phone into my hand. I saw a picture of my face with my new hair. I was lying on Edie's legs, my smile wide as I looked off toward the ocean in black and white. It was posted on Evan's Facebook, and above it he had left a vague comment that made my heart drum out of control in my chest. Above my smiling face all it said was: *Sometimes you just have to look up.*

"Right? What does that even mean? By the way, this is stunning. Your hair suits you. I guess I just had to see it from an outside perspective." She clicked her phone off and stuck it in the side of her bra.

"Eww, stop doing that. You're going to end up with like cancer or something." She laughed like I was speaking a foreign language. She poked my back pocket and I sighed. She didn't have to say it.

"If phones really can cause cancer, then I would rather have it in my boob than my ass." She laughed so hard that she turned red, and one of the couples that were much older than us shook their heads in dismay at her language. I laughed with her. We inched through the line at a slow pace, but eventually Edie was carrying two cups of orange juice while I transported a bag of bagels fresh from the oven, making my arm sweat beneath the sleeves of my thermal and hoodie. I gagged a little at the smell of freshly baked bread. I was dying to get home and eat while we stared half awake and half asleep at some show we wouldn't even remember watching ten years from now. I was young, but I believed it when my mom said to enjoy these years. They were the best some of us would ever have.

We kicked off our shoes and snuck in like we were trying to break into the house. Spy status. It didn't work; my mother, usually the queen of sleeping in, was sitting at the table with her coffee and her Kindle. Her hair looked like a dirty blonde nest shot through sporadic silver streaks. She lifted her head and smiled at us like we came in carrying gold.

"You two are saints. Perfect little saints with an armful of my favorite bagels. Mmm…I love that smell. I am not looking forward to the day you two turn into true teen monsters." We giggled—she was always saying that. I couldn't imagine ever turning on her, but who knew what hormones and end-of-high-school craziness could lead to.

I tossed the bag on the table, and she removed the bagels and plastic-lidded bowl of schmear as if they were fragile glass. We plopped down in the chairs across from her as she stopped mid-spread, holding out her hand.

"Card." I pulled her bankcard out of my pocket. "Thank you girls, but Laney, next time clear it with me first." I nodded begrudgingly. A blister was forming from the long walk and she wanted to talk details.

We ate in silence, the drip and percolation of her outdated coffee maker the only sound.

"So what are you guys doing today? The beach again? Cleaning up the deck like I asked you a week ago? Hanging out at Hadley's?" Her conversations were always built on getting the most information in the shortest time. She was good at that. I think it was built into her at this point because she was a teacher in a high school. She only had so long to educate bored teenagers, so she knew how to cram a lot in.

"Slow down, mom. This isn't class." She bit her lip, looking embarrassed.

"Once a teacher, always a teacher, Laney. So which is it? Please say the deck…please say the deck." She smiled from behind the rim of her oversized black coffee mug. The front had an apple on it that appeared to be bleeding down the surface. It was some abstract gift from one of her former students. I rather liked its lack of the usual #1 Teacher logo.

"Yes mom, I will clean up the deck today, as if that was really a request and not a set-in-stone responsibility. I don't know what we're doing later. Maybe going to the pier and just hanging out, or even better, I can crawl back in bed and sleep until it's a normal time. Why are you even up, mom?" I realized she was never up this early. Not on a Sunday. We didn't really go to church anymore, so seeing her up before nine was a mystery.

"Thank you in advance for cleaning the deck. I think you should take a nap, because if I am not mistaken you left a Laney-sized body outline on the couch and deleted all the saved episodes of *The Walking Dead*. Last but not least, I am up because that god-awful dog walking lady took about seven dogs down the street earlier. Is it bad that I keep hoping they will turn and just eat her? Don't answer that. Good morning to you as well, Edie. If you wear those running shoes in my house again, however, you will see two little hot pink dots bobbing up and down in the ocean next time." She narrowed her eyes until Edie looked up, her cheeks pink at having been caught.

"When is dad coming back?" I played with the seeds and dried bits of onion that had fallen off of my bagel. Mom leaned back and looked up at the ceiling while she counted in her head.

"Nine more days, I believe. Just nine, and he will be back home for a week this time." She smiled. We could pretend that Edie and I kept her busy enough, but she got lonely while we were out in the world exploring who we were. I flicked one of the black poppy seeds in irritation.

"So he misses all of spring break then?" She just nodded; she let me have these little fits of unhappiness. I don't know why, but there would be months and months where it wouldn't bother me, and then it would turn into an avalanche of resentment. The thing about avalanches, though, is that they melt eventually. He worked so we could live here, the ocean within view, and a childhood of never having to be the new kid after kindergarten. I was grateful and mom was independent, but I couldn't pretend I didn't notice his absence.

"Can we have a fair moment?" she asked me, her empty coffee cup in hand. I exhaled and nodded; I didn't want to make eye contact. I knew what was coming but I just didn't want to admit it.

"You have almost no time for anyone but your friends during break and we both know it. Your father and I know what it's like when school is in, not always having classes together and then after dismissal, homework. Plus, some of the others have sports or clubs they're involved in. We don't mind that you give your time to your friends while school is out because your priorities are focused when school is in. So is it even fair to be this upset about your father not being home when you have no intention to be here much yourself?" She tilted her head and waited. Edie was silent beside me.

"No." Everything she said made sense, which happened a lot.

"Okay then. That being said, I am sure he would really love for you to call him tonight or set up a Skype date. He just loves talking to you…wait…hair…" She stopped mid-sentence. Even sitting across from her, I think she still imagined me with all my long blonde hair. "On second thought, you might want to hold off on Skyping until he is home."

"You didn't tell him? You tell him everything under the sun, even stuff I don't think he understands." I could hear my tone hitting high and squeaky notes. If she didn't tell him, that meant she was leaving the job to me.

"Bingo, kid. You made that decision all on your own, whether from a thought-out plan or a desperate gesture of growing up. You get to tell him. Go clean the deck and pick up all that mess you made with your nasty bagels." She pointed at the scattering of crumbs and seeds. I watched her rise and rinse her coffee cup before grabbing the car keys.

"Where are you going?" She didn't usually go anywhere on the weekends, instead opting for bad TV and reading.

"The groceries don't just show up in bags containing all your favorite things. I didn't think you would want to go." She was right. I don't think I hated anything more than grocery shopping.

"Okay, I will pick up some more peanut butter, and Edie, I will pick up some more water bottles if you are going out at dawn to race up and down the beach." She left the door ajar so the house could fill up with the morning air, still cold but slowly warming.

We took turns staring at each other and then at the sliding glass doors that opened onto the deck. I loved that deck, furnished with two giant round cabana couches covered in olive green canopies and railings built from enforced driftwood. The deck was my responsibility alone to keep up. I had begged to get a deck from age nine to twelve so I could read outside facing the ocean and sleep in tents on its wooden surface when the sun granted us enough heat to be warm but not miserable. I said I would trade getting any presents until I was an adult if we could just build a deck. So they had, and I gladly skipped a Christmas and a birthday before they started getting me presents again. It was my deck, and I had to keep it swept, cleaned, and weatherproofed before seasonal heavy rains. I didn't regret it once, but that didn't mean I wanted to clean it now. I tried to gauge how much time I could waste before she got back.

"Should we just do it and get it over with?" Edie said without taking her eyes off the doors.

"Nah. Let's just watch some crap, and when we hear her pull into the drive make a mad dash for the brooms." She laughed at my answer. I was being so lazy.

"What a weird caption Evan put on that photo post of you," she mused out loud.

"True." I smiled into my crossed arms; it wasn't that I enjoyed keeping things to myself, but every once in a while it was nice to have something of my own. I understood it and so did he, but no one else would. It felt like the moment was mine and mine alone, so I kept my head down and did not share it with her.

"Are you awake?" I nodded into my warm sleeves at her question but it didn't stop me from closing my eyes. She sighed. My sleepiness was probably driving her insane.

"Well, did you know Evan wants to go to NYU?" Edie was trying so hard to tug at my consciousness while sleep was trying so hard to hold me from her. I shook my head in response but did not look up. It wasn't the overwhelming tiredness that kept my face against my sleeve. I just didn't want her to see my face, because if she saw how devastated I was at the thought of Evan being so far away she might realize I didn't have the same kind of distance from this place in mind as she did.

"He wants to be a photographer, but my guess is you already knew that." I nodded again. Evan had been taking pictures of us since his camera still came wrapped in cardboard and had to be turned into a photo developer. Now he did it for the school yearbook and occasionally for the local paper. He was never without his camera until his parents gave him a smartphone, and now he was never without that. None of us were, but he was the only one capturing all the moments we spent together, filling up his Facebook with people while the rest of us were still taking pictures of our shoes and close ups we regretted when they uploaded to full size. I didn't want him to go, I didn't want to imagine the days on the beach without all of them there, but those days were coming fast. If the future went the way I saw it there would only be Nathan and me left, and our traditions were too intimate if it was to be only the two of us.

"You are being so booooring." Her voice fell flat, but she put her hand on my hooded head and pressed it against my arms. "Do not even nod your head again. Let's go clean the deck and see if anyone else is up." She released my head and I nodded just to be a jerk. My laugh was muffled in my sleeve.

"OKAY." She made a face at my loud volume, but stuck her phone into her shirt and grabbed both brooms while I snagged the garbage bag and cheap plastic dustpan that I swore did not hold anything substantial.

I woke up to the smell of the ocean. It never got old. I looked around and saw Edie sprawled out on the other cabana couch with a magazine, the cords of her headphones coming out of her hood. I remembered sweeping the deck off and picking up all the trash, while Edie had emptied and restocked the small fire pit I had gotten last Christmas. Afterward, we lay down on the couches and texted everyone else, but somewhere in that time I had fallen asleep.

I stretched lazily, feeling the slight chill hit where my shirt had crept up to expose my stomach. Edie pulled her head back and laughed at me. I was sprawled like a cat in the sun.

"So Hadley and Nathan are off somewhere being gross, and Reese and Ryland are doing something with the rest of the R's." She stopped talking and started typing faster than human fingers should allow.

"What about Evan or Leland?" I threw out the question and waited for her to realize I was still there. She said nothing in response. I lay back under the canopy and waited for her to tell me what was going on. I pulled my own phone out from under my side and saw endless notifications and messages. All of the texts came from my mom while she was shopping. I had been asleep for two hours.

"So Leland isn't even in town today. He went on a fishing trip with his uncles. Evan, however, is doing nothing and wants to come over. What do you think?" I glared at her. She knew exactly what I thought. I jumped up and barreled up the stairs.

"Stop running! He's just a boy, not a news crew." My mother leaned back as she was speaking to avoid being knocked over. I groaned, coming to a stop with my lungs in my mouth and my heart in my stomach.

"How do you know this has anything to do with a boy? Did it occur to you that I might just have to go to the bathroom?" I smiled at her, a smug smile at that.

"You're right. I should have just said, 'it's only Evan, not a news crew.' You only run for two reasons: Edie has stolen some of your food or Evan is on his way over. Don't bother to lie. I have your mascara because you lost mine last time we went out of town. Thank god I made you clean your room." She moved down the hallway, throwing a smile over her shoulder. She was right. I would have lied.

I got into the shower so fast that my foot slid and I slammed my head into the wall. Getting it together was clearly not on my agenda today. Everything took less time with my new hair, but when I had finished drying off I caught my reflection. It was marred in the steam but I could still make out my face. I did look different, more defined somehow. I picked up the towel from the floor and wiped the moisture from the glass. I was lost in this moment of rare vanity, but the door shaking from Edie's fist broke my train of thought.

"Your mom is in one bathroom and you are in this one. I smell like armpits, Laney…armpits! Let me take a shower! I don't want to use the sand shower again." I grinned while I crammed all the makeup back in the small striped bag. Last time I made her wait she had stripped down and used the sand shower below the deck. She had a cold for five days because of the wind chill.

"Calm down, pits. I'm coming." When I opened the door the steam rolled out into the hall, but it didn't slow Edie down. She had her shirt over her head and her other hand twisting the old silver knob to hot.

"God, Edie, let me at least get all the way out of the bathroom first. You could have used the claw tub you know." I don't know why I bothered—she was already under the burning spray, trying to erase a long walk into town and a longer run on the beach from her skin. I shut the door behind me. She was always so impatient. I tossed open my closet doors and tried to figure out how to alter my clothes to match my hair. It didn't work; only so much change was possible. I would always be a little less put together than the other girls. I pulled on my skinny jeans and a black tank top. The breeze coming in through the window reminded me that it wasn't as warm today as it had been yesterday. I pulled out a cropped knit sweater the color of blue I only associated with a Van Gogh painting.

Edie tore past me and jerked the zipper open on her huge black canvas duffle bag, sending clothes over her head in every direction. I frowned at her huddled, towel-wrapped form.

"I just cleaned this room E. Seriously, I don't want to do it again." Frustration radiated from my pores.

"Okay, calm down, Hitler. I'm obviously going to clean up my own mess." She matched my irritated tone with her own. I sighed and crawled onto my bed to start the ridiculous process of getting ready.

"Should we walk into town when he gets here? Or even better, ask your mom for a ride?" She twisted around, still only in a towel amid a pile of clothes.

"We can walk. What do you want to do in town?"

"What do you think, hoser?" I rolled my eyes at her question and smiled.

"Stop calling everyone a hoser. Your dad should never have shown you that movie last year." We had watched *Strange Brew* with her dad, who took any opportunity to spend time with Edie. He had shown us some interesting movies over the years in his efforts to bond.

"Hmm…should I go with this dress or the jeans?" She held up a pair of jeans and a blue bohemian-style shift dress. "Or leggings? Or should I go with the olive green shirtdress, you know the one I wore to your father's birthday dinner?" I shook my head at her every suggestion.

"No? No on all of those?" Her distress was apparent.

"Edie, just put something on that body. If Evan comes up and sees you half naked I will never have a shot." She smiled at me, but there was sadness behind it. She stood as she pulled on leggings under one of her dad's old vintage band shirts. I smiled at the faded white face of Jim Morrison trapped against her boobs. She couldn't even sit through an entire record by The Doors, but she looked good in their merch. I smiled at the idea of her teenage father, tall and skinny, listening to music I loved. She was focused on lacing up her black boots.

"I think that Facebook post means he's really seeing you now, Laney. If he doesn't see you, forget him. There's a whole sea of boys out there. What is the deal with everyone wanting to pair off anyway? This isn't *The Breakfast Club* for god's sake." She laughed after she said it. I hated to admit that she was right. If we all just chose one another it would feel a little incestuous. I had ignored every boy last summer, and I would probably ignore the many that invaded during break. Unlike Edie, I didn't like the idea of sharing bits and pieces of myself with lips and faces that wouldn't remember me after the long trips back to wherever they came from. I think I was hungry to be known, to have someone consume who I was, whereas Edie just wanted to keep who she was to herself, only to be consumed if she chose it and not if it chose her.

"What are you doing?" One question asked outside of my own head was all it took to break my thoughts. When Evan said I was untouchable I wanted to say that it would take almost nothing from him to knock it down.

"Nothing." I picked up the brush and covered my awkwardness in attempts at being pretty.

"Where's your mascara? You don't think Evan will mind walking into town with us, do you?" I heard her, but I was trying to remember where my mascara was…my mom had it.

"My mom has my mascara, so I would look in her bathroom. I don't know if Evan will mind. He is a hard read. He isn't exactly an open book." Edie was staring at me while I put the eyeliner to my lid and swept it across evenly. I could see her, but more as a silhouette than a person.

"He is a closed book. Doesn't that worry you at all? What if you open the cover and find out there is nothing more than a Dick and Jane level of material inside?" Her sarcasm ran thick. We both knew Evan. "I think you should leave Evan exactly where he is."

"Where's that? Waiting by your feet?" The resentment I felt only came out in flashes, a strike of lightning and then a blue sky again. "Sorry." I muttered the apology, but said it nonetheless.

She didn't even glance in my direction. She was looking into her compact and pinching her cheeks, praying for color. I softened watching her, seeing a nine-year-old, and then ten, and so on. It felt like forgiving her for a crime that she didn't even know was being committed. That's what it was like when I lashed out, quiet and distant afterward. Edie knew how to be quiet in a fight. Whatever fights raged around her, very few of them actually had to do with her.

"Laney!" My mom was shouting from the kitchen, her voice echoing among the appliances. I ran with my shoes slapping the wood all the way down the hall and into her bedroom. I found my mascara on the edge of the bathroom counter and applied it as hastily as I could without jabbing the wand into my eye. I sped back to my room, tossing the black tube into Edie's lap before pausing at the top of the stairs. Evan didn't give me butterflies; he gave me piranhas, little mouths full of teeth, eating through my stomach and gnawing on my nerve endings. Little bloody mouths starved and feeding on my anxiety.

"Coming!" I walked down the stairs, aware that my lazy lungs were trying to punch out of my chest, leaving a gaping hole and a ruined ribcage. Evan was sitting at the table, my mom having already given him one of the bottled waters she bought for Edie.

"Hey Evan, want to come hang out on the deck while Edie finishes up?" Casual was my middle name, but unfortunately I have two and awkward was the other.

"What is Edie finishing?"

"Her makeup."

"Like she needs it." The boy I love is a juggler. I walked toward the door and he followed me out to the deck. I almost wished I hadn't asked him to come with me. The sun-bleached wood was where I felt safe, not a place to nurse invisible wounds.

"I just meant that none of you girls actually need makeup." He knew. Where he was a closed book, my face was the front page of a newspaper. All the emotions or thoughts I felt were right there for anyone to see.

"Yeah, I figured." Lies for a girl are like Band-Aids—they put a stop to the bleeding. "We were thinking of walking into town, maybe down to the pier to listen to the buskers. There are bound to be a few of them outside the shops." He smiled at me. I had to shade my eyes to see his expression under the shadows. All I could see was the smile.

"That's fine. I was supposed to go with Leland, but I had some other stuff to get done so I couldn't." His attempts at conversation felt stilted. My hurt feelings caused the tension to stretch between us.

"Like what?" I would say anything to make him keep talking.

"Mostly some crap around the house. My mom needed help with chores and such. It was either get them all done today or have something going every day of break." I nodded at his answer, barely listening.

We sat on the couches while Edie was upstairs, completely unaware of how weird things felt below. It was only when I was alone with other people in our group that I realized how much of me relied on Edie to fill up time and space with her endless energy. I didn't want to be part of a duo anymore, but without my crutch all I could feel was the broken limb.

"Hey Evan. Laney, I told your mom we are going down to the pier. She said she would give us a ride home around ten-ish. Evan, she said to put your longboard up on the railing. It rolled away from the door and into the street when you came in." Evan looked up and colored pink at his mistake.

"God, when did it get so cold?" My body shivered in agreement with her question. The air had definitely not warmed with the passing of morning. "I'm going to grab a jacket from your closet, Laney." She disappeared back into my house and left Evan and me standing and staring at the door. I noticed him watching her go up the stairs. My stomach twisted, but I ignored it. I seldom thought Edie was right, but seeing his face ran a tremor of realization up my spine. He saw me now, but just not the way I had wanted.

"Let's go!" Edie shouted from inside the living room, her voice lurching us back to life. I was in a duo whether I liked it or not.

The pier was littered with tourists. You could spot them a mile away. They were the ones who were either completely underdressed for the weather or severely overprotected from the slight winds. The people who were not native to the area couldn't understand the weather unless it was summer. Even then, they all expected the water to be warmer, more like the tropical islands. No one anticipated the cold that the Pacific held close to her heart. We laughed together while I pointed out a guy who looked like the older brother from *The Goonies*, with his sweats under his gym shorts and his basketball bouncing like gunshots against the wood of the pier. Edie was looking, flitting from one male face to another trying to find one that suited her. She was picky like Goldilocks when she was choosing. She didn't want them to feel local, but they couldn't be as absolutely naïve as the guys who shivered embarrassedly in their thin board shorts and nothing else.

"What about him?" I pointed past the guy in sweats to the boy sitting two benches down. He was wearing jeans and Vans, a longboard propped against the side of the pier while he texted, waiting for something or anything to happen.

"No." She kept looking, but I was stuck on the guy on the bench.

"Why not?" I couldn't help it. I was baffled. That guy was perfection.

"Because that boy is for you, Laney Wilder. Please direct your attention to the object sitting to his right." Aha, it was a book, and a thick one from the looks of it. Edie wasn't after an idiot, but she wasn't after an intellectual either.

"You know I have zero interest in tourists, right Edie?" She nodded and kept searching as we walked. Evan was silent beside us.

"So? This isn't just a regular boy, Laney; he brought a book to the pier. You don't even bring a book to the pier. Quit being a total hoser and go talk to him. *Books*, Laney. Most of the boys don't even know what they are anymore, and if they do they are shocked that they come in paper. That's a legit paperback he has with him. Your girly bits should be sighing right now." I blushed under her assessment. The longer I looked at him, the more I was tempted to go sit on the other side of the bench.

I glanced over at Evan, who had remained silent; he wasn't looking at Edie anymore. He was staring down at me like he was waiting for water to boil, like glaring into something can cause a reaction. It didn't with water, but it did with me.

I walked away from them in the direction of the mouth of the pier. I don't know why, but when I looked back I saw what he saw. Even though Edie wasn't looking at him, they fit together, complemented one another. We both saw it, but unfortunately for Evan she never would. Edie was a snob and local fare wasn't what she wanted. This time, though, he wasn't watching her—he was looking at me. I didn't understand what his face was trying to say, but I didn't want to.

The boards breathed as I stepped on them, the whole pier exhaling in time with the ocean as it rushed against it and pulled away. I sat on the bench beside the boy with the book. This was foreign. I didn't know how to speak the language.

"Hey." His voice was lower than I expected, with a rasp to it like Evan's. I never expected the rasp from anyone younger than their thirties.

"Hey. What are you reading?" I asked, feeling my own voice fighting a waver.

"*In Cold Blood*." He was looking right at me. I felt stupid. I shrugged my shoulders to acknowledge that I didn't have the first clue what he was talking about.

"Truman Capote? The Clutter family murders? Nothing?" I shook my head and looked down. I was trying to hide my annoyance. I hated to admit ignorance of something while the other person would prod me with details like they couldn't believe I was so stupid. "Well, do you read at all?" His face was without cruelty, but his arrogance was too much.

"Laney, don't play with the tourists. Come on." I laughed at the face Edie was making a few feet away. The nameless boy next to me colored in irritation at being regarded as a tourist.

"Bye." I paused after I stood to pick up his book. "Looks good. I just finished *The Stranger* by Camus. Pick it up if you haven't yet. It's quite compelling." I dropped the book beside him, enjoying as his face changed from arrogance to understanding. His expression echoed the realization that his dismissal of me was presumptuous, but Edie's assessment that he was just a tourist was evident in everything I had not seen from a distance. It showed in the way he sat on the bench, pulled tight in discomfort. I walked away.

"You looked like you were going to either sink through the boards and drown in the ocean or kill him. I didn't want you to be dead or imprisoned during break." Edie rested her head against my own, and I forgot anything I ever felt toward her but love. This girl was my life.

"I would never drown. I swim like a fish." She laughed.

"You're the only one who can, except maybe Evan." We walked away from the pier, leaving behind any boy who thought he could make me feel small.

Evan was skating in circles around the cluster of palms in their cement pot. My favorite street musician was sitting cross-legged and looking exhausted as he plucked at the strings of his weathered acoustic. He always played me songs, old music, some of which I knew and some I didn't. I never told him that I loved old music, that I would trade my CDs and iTunes cards for stacks of vinyl, that listening to music like that made me feel like time had gone backward to when my uncle was still alive. He just knew.

Today he was wearing his old blue cambric shirt with the sleeves rolled up and his dirty brown hair, dreaded from the roots, hung in a sloppy bun. Evan kept skating while Edie and I slow danced in front of him, lazy sways and dramatic bends. People grinned around us, assuming we were part of the act. His guitar case was open and we kept time to the music as dollars drifted in and change rained down from open palms.

He smiled at us as we left, trailing behind Evan and his longboard. Edie hadn't met any boys and I had met one that didn't matter. Evan had simply skated while we did whatever it was we wanted to pass the time. The lights bloomed simultaneously around the walkway as the shops lit up from within. The sun had fallen back into the ocean. My grandmother had told me long ago that she thought the scientists were crazy, that the sun and the moon were one and the same. When the sun fell into the ocean the cold put it out, it labored all night in the sky to catch fire from the stars again. She never made any sense, but her voice rolled over me as I faded into sleep through a lot of my early years. My grandma hadn't come back to the beach in at least five years. The damp was too hard on her; we went to her for Thanksgiving. She said she never missed it here, but I couldn't find the truth in her eyes, or I didn't want to. I couldn't stand the idea that someone would leave the waves for a sea of dirt, but she had.

"Why do you always drift off Laney?" I shrugged. I didn't know. Memories were for remembering, and that's all I was doing lately—thinking about the hundreds of memories we had created here. After the break, there were only a few months until summer. Each year was dragging me closer to choosing, to growing up.

"Let's get some pizza, yeah?" Her smile was infectious.

"Yeah. Who's going to catch up with Evan and tell him?" She laughed at my question like I wasn't serious.

"He finds us. He always finds us." I followed her. I always followed her.

"This has been the least amazing break yet." I watched Edie pout, leaning against the headboard of my bed with her clothes thrown everywhere again.

"It's only been four days. What were you expecting…a grand love?" She shook her head at my question. "Besides, tomorrow we are all going out of town. Nathan is a decent driver. I am sure we will live to see other beaches." I pulled at the skin under my eyes. I had to stop staying up so late. I'd gotten completely sucked into some strange foreign documentary on ballet. The girls were so thin it pained me, but they were so beautiful when they danced it seemed worth whatever they gave up to look like they did. Edie had fallen asleep the second the subtitles hit the screen. She did not believe in "reading" movies.

"Speaking of that, Big Edie still hasn't given me permission, and the mister has his phone turned off." She said it like it wasn't a big deal, like if she went, she went.

"Really? Call her again Edie, call until she has to decide to break her phone to pieces or answer." I didn't want her to screw it up.

"Shut up hoser, I'm on the phone." She smiled while she held the phone to her ear looking bored. "Nothing." She sounded agitated now.

"Nothing?" Edie shook her head. She now held the phone over her face while distorting her expression into different ugly forms, attempting to give herself as many chins as possible.

"What are you doing?"

"Winning the chin game with Reese! Boom! There are like five chins in this one." I waited for more of an explanation.

"I'm in the middle of a picture message war, the war on attractiveness. I can make the ugliest faces with the most chins, and I just made Reese my…"

"Don't even say it, Edie." We both glanced up at my mom standing in the doorway. She was staring at Edie with her lips pursed.

"Beezy," Edie said with a sheepish grin on her face, all the so-called chins gone.

"That's not any better. You may as well have said the other word." I laughed, and my mother scowled in my direction. My mother didn't allow swearing in the house. Every person had his or her own swear jar. Ironically, hers was the fullest, but she tried. It wasn't because she was opposed to swearing so much as she was trying to force each of us into expanding our vocabulary.

"Jar." She pointed Edie to the jar that she had received at the end of last summer, just like the rest of us. Edie sighed and stood up, searching her pockets but turning up with nothing.

"No quarters?" Edie shook her head no at my mother and genuinely looked sad, but it wasn't because she felt bad. She knew what was coming.

"Hmm…I happen to have a spare quarter right here. What will you trade me for it?" This was my mother's favorite part of the swear jar. If you couldn't put change in, you had to borrow change. The catch was that no one in this household could loan money, only trade it.

"Dishes," Edie said with her face down.

"Catch." My mom tossed a quarter at Edie, who caught it like it was nothing. Athleticism ran through her veins. "I just came upstairs to tell you that your mom left a voicemail on my phone this morning. I guess she and Kyle are hiking today and wanted me to tell you that you can go tomorrow, and to give you half of your spring break allowance." My mom held out her other hand, which held a neat stack of twenty-dollar bills in the palm. "Now go do the dishes and watch what you say." Edie almost took her down in her excitement, the pouty lip over the dishes gone.

I went back to studying the dark circles under my eyes. I put on makeup and pretended I was an excited teenager when all I wanted to do was crawl back in my hammock and sleep. With Edie here, I had been up every morning shortly after she returned from wherever she had run to. I wasn't going to waste all my time on Evan, so I texted Reese to tell her that Edie had gotten busted by my mom. She sent back a photo of her face caught in mid-laugh. Then I texted Hadley to tell her we were all good to go. She texted me back a thumbs up. I tried not to be annoyed with a world that spoke in emoji, but it felt like going backward in time—we were now leaving the English language and returning to pictograms. My one exception was the octopus emoji—that was just stupidly cute. Old lady quirk: 1, Laney: 0.

"Hey." I jumped and almost smacked my face into the mirror at the sound of Evan's voice. I hadn't even spoken to him since two nights before. He hadn't texted to say he was coming over, but he was here, standing behind me in the reflection.

"You look tired Laney." I wanted to say, "thank you, captain obvious," but I continued putting on mascara as I waited for him to speak.

"Why are you so mad at me lately? We have been friends since we had cubbies to put our stuff in at school." He was right. We had been friends since the third grade; his cubby had always been next to mine and he was always next to me at the end of the line. That was the pain of being a Wilder and a Wallace. We came last in everything.

"I get it Evan. You adore Edie and the ground she walks on, but it doesn't make it any easier on me to know that. I was fine with it for the most part, but when you stared at me at the bonfire you didn't feel like my cubby mate, and when you held onto me in the waves, I couldn't remember any of that. You are confusing me, Evan. I hate being confused." I wanted to lie, I really did, but I wasn't good at it. Quick little lies were one thing, but I was awful at being put on the spot.

"Did you ever consider that I'm confusing you because I'm confused?" His face looked lost above mine in our mutual reflections.

"What is so confusing?" I didn't want the answer, but it didn't stop me from asking the question.

"I have fallen asleep with Edie's face in my mind since eighth grade, but she doesn't have a single feeling for me. You…you have been looking at me like I have been looking at Edie since the day I walked you home after Jeremy Uhler broke your heart. It isn't like I don't get it, and it isn't like I don't feel it, but I've never for one minute felt like I was on your level. I don't read a dozen books a month and I have no idea why you like me." He stopped and stared at me. He saw me, yet he hadn't chosen me because he was intimidated by me. I didn't feel it, the pull of his voice on my stomach. Not now. This was bullshit.

"I am no better than Edie. She has the best grades in school, and her two years of track and field will get her into any university she wants. I am not on a higher level than her. If you are not on my level, what makes you think you're on hers?"

"Edie wants good grades and needs the extracurricular to get out of here. She wants out like I want out. You have it and you aren't even trying, Laney. If there is one thing I know about you, it's that you can be lazy as hell." I couldn't help it. I laughed hard until my eyes were full and my chest ached.

"That's where the levels happen, Laney. You are always smart and you don't read just because it will get you out of here. People can grow because of effort, but no one grows based on what you have. It's just a part of you. I love it, I do. I could listen to you talk all day, every day about whatever you've recently read or watched, or what you are thinking. I felt the separation then and I still feel it now. Stop being mad. We don't have to have this all figured out right now. Kiss a stranger, Laney. I'm not going to hold it against you." He lay down on my bed with his head at the wrong end. I felt the blood moving through every part of me. How had I not seen this side of Evan in all the years I'd known him? How could I not have seen him like this before? Scared. After seven years I was seeing past the confidence and ease. I didn't know this Evan at all.

I stretched my arms above my head and stood up, walking over to him. He looked sad, like I could see the outline of his third grade face under the man he was becoming. He made that face when he got picked last or when his arm went numb, the teacher ignoring his raised hand entirely. I leaned down and placed my mouth on his. His hand gripped my neck, and for one minute Edie and all things outside of the kiss stopped meaning anything. I pulled away first, his eyes wide. I could feel my cheeks stain red.

"Why did you kiss me, Laney?" He was completely still below me. He had kissed me back in a single moment of truth.

"You said to kiss a stranger, Evan. I didn't know that part of you. Now let's be friends again, okay?" I smiled and held out my hand to him. If my mom came in as he lay on my bed, his lips smudged with faint pink gloss, she wouldn't be surprised, but I would be in for the *Teen Mom* talk again.

"Okay." He popped his knuckles. I called it his caveman trait. He did it when he was nervous. He had learned it from his cousin the summer we were ten. His cousin had said that men popped their knuckles. I knew so many things about him, and now I knew what his lips felt like too. I hadn't found anything in them that was worth the cost of losing him as a friend, because it was clear that he wasn't ready to be anything more. We were only sixteen, and Edie was right—who bought into this soulmate crap at sixteen anyway?

"Evan? Where did you come from?" Edie paused on the staircase, climbing up as we were climbing down.

"I…Laney's room…just got here." The words came out, messy and disjointed. His face flushed as he looked back at me; it was more of a stare than a glance.

"Huh? You're obviously in Laney's room, idiot. When did you get here?" I watched him, his eyes widening, but he pulled himself together.

"Oh, about twenty minutes ago or so. I knocked, but the door was open and no one was answering so I just came up to see what you guys were up to." There was no stutter this time, but his voice sounded the way a voice sounds when you have lost it and you are trying it out again for the first time in days. Edie shrugged and moved past us.

"By the way, Laney, I have to go, but I will be back in a few hours. I totally spaced on the fact that I was supposed to watch Maddy today. I'll catch up with you guys on the beach in about four hours…we were going to the beach, right?" I nodded, trying with everything I had to communicate silently with her. My eyes begged her to ask me to tag along for help. There was no silent best friend language between Edie and me; she never focused on one person or situation that long.

"Yeah, we were going to swim and surf today since it has finally warmed up. Reese and Ryland are coming after lunch. I just came over early. When are you coming down?" I watched him make plans, having forgotten that I was supposed to walk down to the beach with her after we had eaten. Sleep came and went, and with it my ability to stay organized.

"I should be down there around three or four. Mrs. Caswell gets off at three, I think. I couldn't turn down fifty bucks for a couple of hours. I already told your mom, Laney. She's going to give me a ride since I did such a bang up job on those damn dishes." She smiled and pointed toward the kitchen, which I knew despite her sarcasm was probably sparkling in actuality.

"Anyway, I gotta go. Your mom is in the car. Do you want me to tell her that Evan is here or…you know?" She was asking if I wanted time alone with Evan in the house without my mom knowing. I shrugged and looked away. I really didn't care at this point.

"Just tell her I'm on the deck." He answered for the both of us. She smiled and went into my room, probably for her phone that had been going off all day. I waited in the shadow of the stairs in case I was exposed to my mom if she came back in. I didn't feel like talking about anything. The kiss, although brief and done as an act of closure, had meant more than I thought kisses could. I knew I would grieve what never was. I felt so tired.

"I forgot to put on my bathing suit. I will meet you on the deck." I turned, but stopped when I felt his hand gripping my arm.

"For what it's worth, Laney, I don't want to be confused or feel inferior, but I do. That kiss, that wasn't nothing. God, it was, well, everything, Laney." He let go, and my arm felt warm from where his hand had been. I wanted so badly to appreciate his honesty, I did, but it didn't change my wish for things to be different. I would be his friend; I would always be his friend. I went upstairs as Edie shot past me. I wanted to stop her, to weep for a second or ask her if she had overheard him. I did neither. I went into my room and shut the door.

When I came back downstairs, Evan was stretched out on one of the deck couches with his long legs dangling off.

"Are you thirsty?" I asked, shading my eyes to look out at the ocean. I loved my stretch of beach, but the rocky shoreline wasn't good for surfing or swimming.

"Sorry. I got a water while you were getting dressed." He held up a half-empty bottle in the sun.

"No bigs. Should we just hang out until later, or do you want to walk over there now? If we wait for my mom, she will probably give us a ride." He was staring out into the water, still trying to pop his knuckles.

"Let's take the bikes." I smiled at his answer; he knew we had four or five beach cruisers in the garage. I loved riding them, especially when I was alone and gliding down the sloping asphalt.

"Yeah. The bikes will be good." I stared at him, his efforts to smooth over the weirdness making it impossible to stay hurt. He stretched out the laziness that came with the couches. I walked ahead of him, scribbling a note to my mom on the dry erase board. I pulled my hoodie off the hook and zipped it over my tank top and considered the flip flops I was wearing. I hated riding bikes in flip flops. I dropped down by the shoe basket my mom kept just inside the front door. It was full of sand-dusted shoes that smelled like the sea. I pulled out a pair of beat up, washed out Converse and put them on as fast as I could. Evan was leaning against the wall watching me. His phone was out, but I didn't consider this moment photo worthy. He apparently did, because his phone made a shutter sound that he said reminded him of using the real thing. Most of the time, though, his phone was on silent. He had no interest in posed photos. I was so used to his random photographer moments that I had lost the ability to feel insecure during them.

"Okay. I'm ready." I smiled up at him; he had no idea how simple it was to make me happy…or perhaps he did. I was determined to get past this. I didn't even consider distance, not from Evan and our shared childhood.

The ride was colder than I expected, but I loved the feel of the ocean air trailing across my skin, the exhilaration that comes from riding down a thin strip of road with cars flying past. I smiled into the wind that caused my eyes to water until tears traced across my cheeks and flung loose. It was warmer today, but not in the shelter of the tall pines that lined the street. Evan was pedaling harder and harder, always racing me. When we hit the corner I had to swerve around him, having forgotten to slow down in preparation. I halted just before the line of tourists leading out of Gilly's, my sternum connecting with my handlebars for one crashing moment when all the air escaped me, only to be replaced with pain. I should have slowed down like Evan had.

"Jesus, Laney, are you okay?" He dropped his bike behind me. I was frozen against the handlebars. In my mind I could see the pain spreading like a web across my chest. I wanted to cry, but I was in shock at how hard I had slammed into the metal. I was swimming in the regret of having only removed the basket a few weeks ago. I had to believe that hitting the basket would have sucked less at this moment.

"Seriously, are you alright?" I nodded and pretended I didn't feel the burn of tears that I was blinking back. I *did not* cry in public for any reason. I pushed away from the bars and exhaled shakily. How long had I been holding that breath in…minutes? Hours? Days? It felt like forever, and the bruise that I could feel blooming between my breasts would be horrific. Tears threatened again, but I shoved them back down.

"I'm fine. I just flung too hard into the handlebars." I stammered at the end, my voice feeling like it was in a fight just to be heard. I could feel the ache, pushing up against my skin.

"Are you bleeding or bruised? Let me see!" His inability to understand the embarrassment I was consumed with was frustrating. I ignored his request and walked my bike the rest of the way to the racks beside the pier. He didn't say anything else, but his look of confusion made me want to laugh, if the thought of laughing didn't make my aching chest cringe.

"Come on. I'm fine. Come swimming with me. You know that everyone else won't go in as far as we will. When Leland gets here everyone will be surfing anyway, so come swimming with me now." I smiled at him; I was offering him a truce. I wanted to have the waves slam the awkwardness out of us, to leave us as two kids playing in the waves, wading in farther and farther because our moms couldn't see how deep we were going.

"Are you sure you're okay?" His tone was lined with worry.

"I'm fine. Come on." I walked toward the stairs, the beach already cluttered with obnoxious colored umbrellas and shrieking children. I threw my backpack stuffed with my towel, phone, and sunscreen down on the sand. He did the same.

"Where is your board, by the way?" I hadn't even considered that it was missing until now.

"In the back of Leland's dad's truck. We met up last night and threw all the stuff we would need today back there. You know Jeff likes everything to be organized." I nodded while I slid the Converse next to the towel I had just laid down. Leland's dad never minded driving our stuff down to the beach if we agreed to not do everything last minute. I didn't miss my board. I had been terrible at surfing, so instead of feeling bad at my lack of athleticism I embraced not being a beach cliché.

I tossed my hoodie down on top of my backpack, followed by my tank top and shorts. I bit the bullet and glanced down at the area I could feel bruising. The skin was red with purple starting to edge up to the surface. It looked like I had a jellyfish between my boobs during spring break. Awesome. I turned and watched Evan's eyes become saucers of blue liquid.

"It's really not that bad," I said, poking at the skin and feeling little flares of pain at my touch. Evan let out a long exhale.

"What's the big deal anyway? You cut your leg last summer and bled for a mile. This is nothing." I was trying to get him to say something, anything.

"When did you get that suit?" I looked down at my bathing suit, the blue almost black against my pale skin. Winter had ruined my tan. I shrugged.

"I don't know, like a week after last summer maybe. Why?" He looked away.

"I'm glad you're alright. It was a rough stop. Come on, let's go in." His rasp was heavier, but he held out his hand to me, so I took it. I would always take his hand.

The water had not warmed like the air down on the beach; the sun had clearly not shared its heat with the sea. I shivered violently, willing my skin to acclimate faster than it was. Once the waves lapped into my hips I dove in. The sooner I grew used to it the better. I felt the reverberations of Evan's arms moving through the still water that lasted only seconds before another wave rolled across us. I broke the surface and held my breath as the water swayed around me, the build before the calm familiar to me. Evan was just a head, a shock of blonde hair moving up and down before his face disappeared back under.

I could swim for hours, the ocean tearing me down and throwing me back to the surface. I pushed against the current to reach Evan, to race him until I couldn't go any farther. The water was washing everything away, and the ache from my chest was either easing or being numbed by the cold. I came up for air, searching for his face, but the hand on my leg pulling me down caught me off guard. When he let go, I pushed off his chest to springboard me forward. I swam harder against the tide until my lungs felt like fragmenting, then I let go while the swells pushed me upward. I smiled, my mouth salty and my eyes blinded by the glare of the sun on the water.

I didn't know if swimming in the ocean was love or if Evan was love, but I fell in love with the taste of the waves on my lips and the way his hand felt on my skin. I fell in love with the wildness of being this far out, and with the sunlight that hurt as much as it was beautiful. It was all love, but I could feel the exhaustion tucking into my muscles. I buried it down so it could curl up against my bones. I had to twist around in the blue and green, swim back to the sand. I closed my eyes and sank under the wave right before it climbed higher than my head and let my body drift with it. When I came back up he was beside me, his skin beaded with water and his expression confused.

"What?" I was treading water, but my thighs burned from swimming against the current.

"I didn't see you for a second. It's all good." He smiled, his chest rising and sinking with the water's movement.

"I swallowed enough water to brine my heart. What's that saying about seawater curing everything?" I asked. He laughed.

"Did you just use a pun?" I smiled and shook my head yes, my short hair already drying while the rest of my body was submerged.

"Are your arms killing you too?" I lifted my arm up out of the water and dropped it back in to answer his question. He grinned at my dramatics. "Do you want me to dolphin you back?" He presented his back to me, still annoyingly tan after the winter. He hadn't let me dolphin back since we were still equally flat chested and tan. Once I had gotten boobs, they separated us with their awkward presence. He blushed the only time I had suggested it. Puberty had been rough.

I moved behind him and clasped my hands together on the other side of his neck, holding my breath. He went under the water and I knew that it was all love; even if we were never anything more than friends, it was love. He swam so much faster than I did and my body moved smoothly with him, pulling me along. He came up when I unclasped my hands and shot up for air. I was surprised to see how much closer the shore was than I expected. He laughed and splashed saltwater into my mouth right as I was inhaling. I coughed so hard I was sure my lungs were floating abused and tired beside me in the water. He smacked me on the back, which did not lessen the coughing whatsoever, but left a numb patch between my shoulder blades. The great romance of the ocean was waning with my red face and shaking chest.

"Do you think this is why some of us never leave, never go explore what is out there? Is it because of days like these?" he asked quietly. I looked across the expanse of the water, the sky vivid like a movie scene. This was why. I didn't want to answer too fast, to give myself away. I didn't know how to imagine a life without this day in it over and over.

"I think it's just hard to walk away from, I guess, but not for some—some run as fast as they can." I smiled sadly at his face. There would be two more years of this, and then I would know for sure if I could leave it all behind. Would it be easier if all of them were leaving too?

"I'm not going to run from here. Maybe a quick limp, but not running. I love this place. It's my home, but I don't want where I live to define me. I should see the world, photograph more than just some waves and faces…" He paused and traced my chin while I swayed with the ocean. "Faces like yours, full of life and thrilled with the world you live in." His hand dropped back to the water. The burn in my muscles from treading was almost unbearable…almost.

"What's so wrong with being happy, Evan? Doesn't everyone want to be happy?" It was a legitimate question.

"Yeah, everyone wants to be happy, but if it's all you know then you can't possibly be prepared if it's ripped away. I want to know both—great happiness while understanding the loneliness too. I don't want to be fooled into thinking that can't happen." His voice fell away and he looked up into the too perfect blue sky. I swam closer, pulled him to me. I held onto his neck while hiding my face from him, and his from me. He was scared to become his mother. His father's death hadn't devastated him the way it had his mom. He had only been nine, and time did heal wounds for some. His mother loved him so hard it was crazy, but she was as lonely as she was happy. She had stayed behind after high school, married the local boy, and been deliriously happy. He wanted to be ready if life took back all the good it had given. Knowing that he understood that already made me want to cry. He was still against me, his legs knocking into mine as we kept each other afloat.

"You should see the world Evan, see everything you have ever wanted. Just come back when you have seen enough. That's the plan, hatched in the sand and sworn with spit and blood. We all come back and tell each other about what we have seen and done while all our future kids make a pact of their own." With that, I let go of him and swam to the shore. I could see Reese, her red swimsuit blazing like fire in the sunlight against her skin. I couldn't make out Ryland, but I was sure he had come with her. When I could finally feel the sand, firm but shifting under my feet, I considered collapsing and crawling to my towel.

"Laney! We saw your stuff so we just threw ours down too. Are we hanging here?" I nodded, too tired to talk anymore. The last summer had been carefree, but this break I had grown older somehow, and it pulled at me with different emotions and awareness. She walked over to me, her expression darkening.

"What the hell happened to you?" She leaned forward to hesitantly touch the bruise that was no longer pink and red, but was now completely purple and rimmed in black. "What did you do?" she asked in a whisper.

"I rode down off of Third and took Main Street too hard. This is what stopped me." I gestured to my bruised chest. The numbness from the ocean was fading to remind me of the persistent ache that had been temporarily dulled.

"Wow. Well be careful next time, crazy. That is so bruised." I smiled at her shocked face.

"What was that with Evan?" She raised her eyebrows at me and glanced over my shoulder. "Not that I blame you," she laughed.

"It was nothing. I was tired, we swam too far out." I dropped onto the towel. She looked down at me skeptically, but after a moment the look was gone.

"You guys are crazy. You have always been crazy. That water is freezing. No way am I getting in there unless I am in a wetsuit, not like those crack heads over there." She was looking at the zoo of tourists dipping their toes in the water and screaming in surprise before returning to their chairs and busted-looking sandcastles. Reese wasn't like Edie; she hated the tourists and all the mess that they brought with them. Our group was evenly divided about them. The R's were against, Edie and Evan for, and Leland was like me—we didn't care one way or the other.

"Evan!"

"Reese!"

"Ryland!" We all laughed at Ryland, who had shouted his own name, lying with a towel over his face.

"Where is Edie?" he asked from under the towel. I stopped and wondered. Did Edie's "no locals" rule apply to Ryland now that he was becoming a permanent resident? His mom lived with his other siblings down in L.A., but she almost never returned to her hometown. The relationship had been strained for years.

"She's babysitting. Fifty bucks for a few hours," I responded to his covered face. He pulled the towel off and sat up.

"Nice! Should I start watching kids, Reese? Become a manny?" She laughed and threw the towel back at his face.

"You suck with kids, just ask your cousins." She smiled at him as he shrugged his shoulders with a "what are you going to do?" look.

"I offended the little R's when I told them to pick up their Barbie dolls. They freaked out because *clearly* they were Monster High dolls, and they were obviously too big to still be playing with Barbies. I don't get it, but now I am a pariah." He grinned. I liked his easy going personality. Evan was on his phone with an exasperated expression engulfing his face.

"Leland isn't coming. He has to work with his dad. He got called in, and Leland says he needs the money. He is so sorry. No surfing today. Sorry guys, we should have kept our boards." He was talking to Ryland and Reese, their faces matching his.

"Whatever. We'll surf tomorrow. Nathan said he already put the rack on, and he's getting The Beast gassed up today. He said that someone has to pay for his food since The Beast ate all his money," Reese threw out. I had well over two hundred bucks from a combination of leftover Christmas money, chores, and grades.

"I will cover him," I volunteered.

"You should make Hadley pay, if they even come up for air long enough to eat," Reese pointed out. We all laughed as the afternoon sun grew warmer, drying out my scales from the swim. I lay back on the towel, covering my face with my hoodie. I was pleading with the sun to give me color.

"Sit up for a minute," Evan demanded. I sighed and sat back up. After only two seconds of lying down, I felt all the tiredness of the swim catching up with me. Evan lifted up the top half of my towel, sifting through the sand until he found his sunglasses. He put the flat black wayfarers on his head and smoothed out the towel again, sitting down and stretching his legs out. He pulled on my shoulders until I relaxed against the top of his thighs, his board shorts still damp from the water. He smiled down at me, his eyes as blue as the fake-looking sky, before he dropped my hoodie back down onto my face.

"I don't get it." Reese's voice was somewhere in the distance, my eyes closing against my will.

"Get what?" I heard Evan above me.

"Why you guys don't just date?" I colored under the fabric that I was never more grateful to have shielding my face. "Are you worried Laney's too smart for you? You won't be able to *Legally Blonde* your way into whatever Ivy League kisses her ass enough?" I groaned at Reese's words, loud enough that Evan pinched my neck in response.

"That's it exactly, Reese. That's why," he said. I felt another groan rise up, but he pressed his hand over my mouth. He knew me too well. I bit his finger through the sweater. He laughed, and Reese was laughing too. One thing no one seemed to understand about Evan was that, as sarcastic and witty as we could all be, Evan just said how he felt with nothing attached to it. I closed my eyes again; his fingers were playing with my hair.

I was almost asleep when I heard him whisper, "That's exactly it." I wanted to cry, but instead I fell asleep on the beach with my friends and the boy I wanted to love.

"Wake her up." I could hear Edie's voice.

"No." Evan was still cradling my head on his lap. How long had I been asleep?

"Come on. She's an insomniac. She can't sleep all day." That was Edie, always so impatient and unaware of how much she had absorbed from my mom. I had been hearing that my whole life. Sadly, it was true.

"Shut up, E," I muttered, my face overly warm and my stomach roaring like a sandworm in *Beetlejuice.*

"Hallelujah, she's awake. Now rise, child, so that we might baptize you in the sea." Edie was using her tent revival voice again. She did that when we were deliriously tired and studying for school. I turned over and tried to get comfortable again, forgetting that it was Evan's legs beneath me until he groaned in pain. His legs had to be numb from the waist down.

I pulled the hoodie from my face and looked up for about a second before I became permanently blind. I was now without eyes. They had been burned from my face.

"Here, Sleeping Beauty, your sunglasses await you." He put his wayfarers on my considerably narrower face. They slid down my nose, but I pushed them back up while I rose stiffly into a sitting position. My sight returned, only to find a face I recognized but didn't know why hovering slightly behind Edie's.

I waved Edie closer. "Who is that?" She turned and smiled. "How did you meet someone on the quarter of a mile walk down here, seriously?" My voice was louder than a whisper, but I was trying.

"You don't remember Bryce? Bryce, the guy from last summer. I kind-of-sort-of dated him the last two weeks. Duh, its Bryce." She said it like he was the only non-local she had ever dated last summer. Puberty had helped him in more ways than any of us had benefited from. Even Leland and Evan hadn't become nearly as defined in the almost eight months since she had "dated" Bryce.

"Hi Laney. Remember me?" I nodded, but I was glad that Evan's sunglasses were so dark that the look of vague recognition wasn't too obvious.

"Sorry, I just woke up." I used my hand to muss up my short hair, so tempted to curl back up and sleep against Evan's legs. He was in the process of trying to work the blood flow back through them, never taking his eyes off of Bryce. I wanted to remember Bryce better. His face lit up with energy. He was staring at Edie like a kid at Christmas. Her cheeks were flushed pink and her grin was mischievous. She nodded down to my forgotten phone. I picked it up casually to see that she had texted me twice. I blinked and looked at the time again. There was no way I had been asleep for that long, even if the tightness in my muscles made it seem like it had been a year. The residual exhaustion from trying to swim faster than my heart disappeared with Evan around.

Edie dropped beside me, her eyes widening the closer she got. She looked from my face to Evan's, and for a split second I wondered if this was it. If this was when she saw Evan, saw him like I had for years.

"What happened Laney? Where did that mega-bruise come from?" She panicked like a mother, her lips pressing together. I smiled and looked at the skin that was almost eggplant but didn't pulse with pain like a second heartbeat now.

"It's nothing. I hit my chest on my bike. No big deal, E. Put your phone down!" I saw her trying to be discreet. I knew her like I knew my own face in the mirror; she was trying to sneak a picture. She would then send it to my mother, asking something along the lines of, "Should I be worried?" She dropped her phone guiltily, but not before I saw the picture of me in my new blue bathing suit, the skin between my breasts right above my ribs a purple explosion and Evan's face grinning at me. He wasn't looking at Edie, but me.

"I think we should go home and at least show your mom. What if you damaged, like, your chest bone or something?" She couldn't let go of the maternal flashes that colored her personality.

"NO! I am completely fine. It's not a chest bone, E. It's a sternum." I couldn't keep the laugh out of my voice. She responded with a frown. She thought I was laughing at her, but I wasn't—at least not in the way she was thinking.

"Whatever, but your mom is going to freak out when she sees you." I knew my mom's particular brand of overreacting when someone she loved suffered so much as a paper cut. It was why I planned on keeping my tank top on.

"Wow. I forgot you bought that suit at the end of summer. Jesus, when did your boobs get so amazing?" She looked down while I considered burying her head in the sand. She hadn't thought that I would care, but in a group of people I would pass at such a blatant compliment. I reached over and pulled my tank top on. My stomach ached from the swim and from missing lunch. I grabbed my phone to see what Edie sent me. The first text was from almost an hour ago.

I found Bryce! He was skating a few blocks from Maddy's house! Is this fate or what?

The second text looked more like a letter; I was tempted to not read it. Edie drawing attention to me irritated the hell out of me. I let it go as I read her opus that surprisingly contained no emojis for once.

We made out. I know. I just saw him again and already we have made out. I forgot how much I liked him last summer. I just wanted to tell you that I'm trying to make sure Evan sees you. He does. I know he does. I've seen him look at you. He adores you, but he's afraid of you. We all are. If we

had different lives in a different place we would be the kids you never notice Laney, your nose in the books and your brain working so fast I can't even imagine what it's like to be in your head all the time. I love you, Laney Wilder, and I just made out with a hot boy and regretted not calling him in the fall last year. I REGRETTED a boy for a good reason. I just wanted to tell you, Bryce is doing kickflips and I'm pretending I care about skateboarding. You are probably hanging out with Evan and the group. I will see you as soon as Bryce is done doing tricks for my affections. Lol

I took the sunglasses off and rested them on my leg, rubbing the rest of the sleep from my eyes. I caught Edie's eye and smiled at her. All was forgiven, as we always forgave. You can't stay mad at the other half of your soul. Evan might have a part of my heart whether he wanted it or not, but Edie was the better half of me. She rolled her eyes at Bryce and Ryland comparing skate stories behind her. Her smile wasn't always her best feature, but when she was genuinely happy it was the sun.

"Is anyone else starving?" I asked, pressing my palm to my stomach and grimacing, "Because I am almost dead from hunger, guys, and I need what anyone in this situation would need."

"Pizza." It was answered in unison. No one could argue with good pizza, really cheap good pizza. Gilly's Fish Bowl was only for dates and kids with actual jobs.

"I'll pay," Edie volunteered, her pockets actually full from babysitting.

"No way, I've got it. It's the least I can do for my temporary friends every time my family vacations." Bryce winked at us, helping Edie to her feet.

"By the way, what happened to that tall dude and the girl who lost her top last summer?" We laughed.

"He got taller and he got her. They should be somewhere up there about now." I pointed at the stairs as we picked our stuff up. It felt strange that I had never considered how temporary we must feel to the tourists when I considered them the temporary entertainment.

The wind shifted from warm to cold and from cold to freezing as the night grew darker. I wasn't tired anymore; my mind was everywhere and nowhere all at once. The pizza had been fun, and Nathan and Hadley finally found us. Knowing us well, they quickly found us by looking through the tiny porthole windows of Sailor Pizza without bothering to look anywhere else. We had eaten until we thought we were dying, only stopping to play the pop-infested wall jukebox. Hadley and Edie had serenaded each other across silver pans littered with dismembered pizza slices. The discards of pickiness and Taylor Swift flooded the area of the restaurant we had taken over. The locals ignored us, but the visiting families came in to stare at us like exotic birds in the wild; perhaps we looked ill mannered instead of in our element.

Evan rode me home on the handlebars of my bike while Bryce peddled Edie so fast that she screamed, a sound of joy and terror combined. It felt like being in a Nicholas Sparks movie.

Edie was wrapped in my father's heavy plaid wool blanket, texting and yawning, waiting for me to wind down as we sat on the couches under the stars. How could I? Today had been filled with a million different emotions, but in the midst of them I couldn't remember being happier. I turned my record player on and let the sounds of Janis Joplin struggle to be heard against the ocean. Tomorrow was the day, the moment when we tested our ability to be responsible, as well as the limitlessness that I felt when I thought of driving with the music loud, leaving our homes behind us.

"Did Nathan and Hadley say what beach we were heading to?" I asked. Edie paused, looking thoughtful.

"Yeah, that odd one where the sand looks almost purple. I guess it's not very well known. Should I have invited Bryce? Do you think that anyone would mind?" I tilted my head and considered the idea of someone who wasn't in our group being added in at the last minute. We were so possessive of each other, but I didn't know if it mattered this time.

"I don't know, send a group message." I knew how strange we looked from the outside, how territorial and odd for our age we were. It was hard to explain why we had become like the roots of a tree, breaking out randomly through the ground but always connected. Our parents had built a secondary family with their weekly beach play dates. My phone went off, the typewriter keys barely discernable between nature and "Me and Bobby McGee."

"Not me, Edie. You don't have to include me," I giggled.

"It's a habit." Our giggles mixed, and we jumped at the same time when the sliding glass door opened.

"Hola, Mother," I said without turning.

"Bonjour, Daughter," she said, pushing me over to sit beside me. Her hands wrapped around her coffee mug, her shoulder against my shoulder. The meager flames from the fire pit did nothing to lend its heat to us.

"I trust you Laney, and you too Edie." She said it like it wasn't a spontaneous set of words. It wasn't. Her anxiety to let us go tomorrow was written all over her face, the worry in her furrowed brow.

"We know." Edie spoke for both of us. We watched the fire until it grew smaller and I couldn't bear the cold anymore. When we went in, mom set her cup on the counter and climbed the stairs to her room.

"Goodnight girls," she tossed behind her before shutting her door.

"Are you sleeping in the hammock or on the couch?" Edie asked, the remote in hand. I pointed up. I was feeling the hours of lost sleep catching up with me. She smiled and shut off the TV, tossing the remote onto the couch.

"Girls!" I rolled my face into the net and opened one eye. My mom was in the doorway looking agitated. "How many times do you guys expect me to walk up here and keep waking you up? Nathan is going to be here in an hour, so get up!" I yawned and sputtered, tasting rope.

"Edie Callum! Get up!" With that final yell, my mother slammed the door behind her. I glanced toward my bed and saw a bare foot peeping out, glittered toenails catching the sun. I blinked twice. She never slept in, never. I tried to maneuver my body out of the hammock gracefully, a move I had been practicing for a year that I could never quite achieve. I couldn't believe she was still asleep, and for a moment I thought she might be dead, but an arm and a growl shot out from underneath the blanket.

"I forgot to set my stupid alarm. Now I'm going to be dragging ass." I smiled at an expression her mom used frequently. I was glad that my mom had slammed the door at the end of her tirade, or Edie would be using some of the precious little time we had left to do a chore. Knowing Edie's grumpiness, I wouldn't have been surprised if she threw a twenty in the jar while muttering "ass" all the way down the hall.

"I'm glad I took a shower last night when we came in." She scowled at me. She had wanted to take hers post-running this morning.

"You had to. You had sand in who-knows-where from rolling around with Evan all afternoon," she spit back.

"Shut up. I went swimming, that's all."

"Letting someone sleep on you for god knows how long, hours if I know you, isn't something to scoff at." She made a face and walked out of the room, dragging her half-empty bag behind her like a baby blanket. I went to the mirror and jerked my shirt over my head, seeing my own expression of dismay in the mirror at the same time as I saw my bruise. It had lightened in random places, creating a space nebula in a place I really didn't want to draw attention. No bathing suit for this trip. I skimmed everything on the hangers, from dresses to tank tops, but nothing was working. Edie returned wrapped in a towel, the morning moodiness she usually ran off clinging to her.

"E, can I borrow your boho skirt?" She turned around and tossed a thin black dress at me, bohemian in style but not the skirt I'd asked for.

"Don't say a word Laney, just put it on. There is no time for neurotic teenage clothes confusion today. We have less than forty minutes; I showered so fast I nicked my knee and my armpit. Just get dressed. Wow, that bruise is sticking around for a while. Did your mom see it yet?" She followed the question with a halfhearted attempt at a whistle.

Edie was finally getting to use the black tankini she picked up the day before break. I envied her body, her legs muscular from running and the toned stomach she still hid more than she showed. I should have whistled, but I couldn't find one of my Toms that had been lost in the absolute horror of Edie's clothes. The piles looked like they were mutating and breeding new piles, bigger and less organized than the last ones.

"I'm going to clean it. Don't look at me like that. I will. Besides, I have to go home, and as much as you look great in my clothes they have to go with me. Just forget the Toms and go with your Converse or those insane silver gladiator sandals you bought last summer." She was trying to find them, to pick out the silver shine through the mess.

"I'm pretty sure those are going to be buried even deeper than the Toms. Whatever. Should I go with flip flops?" I looked over at her and she shook her head, her glare burning through me. "Okay, I get it, no cheesy beachwear. I'll just wear the black and white polka dot Keds. I hate trying to shake sand out of the Chucks. I couldn't care less if these ones end up in the sand basket."

"Just get ready," she hissed at me. I growled at her, but I was left ignored with a bunch of sad single shoes around me. I put on my makeup quickly and dug under the heap of her stuff to find my blue cardigan, wrinkled but wearable, at the bottom.

"You know there are other colors outside of black and blue," she said behind me while I pulled the extra tank and shorts into my backpack.

"Can you please go drink some coffee and eat something before I smother you in a pile of your own clothes?" I posed it as a question, but it was more like a threat disguised in politeness. She drove me nuts when she was out of sorts. One slight alteration to her routine and she internally melted down.

"Yeah, okay. Do you want anything?" I shook my head no, going still while I applied my eye shadow. The dark circles had lightened considerably. I smiled, happy enough with my face for now.

I walked downstairs, slowly listening for sounds of life. I could hear Edie, but not my mother. Knowing her, she had probably gone back to sleep to avoid the anxiety she felt from allowing us to go. I wanted to race up the stairs and hug her, the hard kind that you ironically quit giving when your arms are finally long enough to really squeeze the body. When I walked into the kitchen there were two twenties and a banana on the table. I ignored the desire to run up again. While I was in the water with Evan, I had realized that leaving even for a while would feel like ripping organs out. My mother was trained in loneliness in a lot of ways, but I was not. Even if I didn't leave, I needed to learn how to let go slowly.

"Ready?" I looked up at Edie; she had stopped complaining and stressing, staring at her phone.

"ARE YOU READY?" She jumped and narrowed her eyes at my raised tone.

"Why are you yelling at me?" Her face was flustered.

"I have no idea, E. Is Bryce coming?" She looked up, the annoyance gone.

"Yes! I texted everyone, and nobody said they care if I bring him. Matter of fact, Evan said that exactly. Nathan even remembers him, 'cool guy,' he said." Her expression was beaming, proud that everyone seemed to be cool with Bryce. I had never seen her care for more than a week about anyone; it hadn't occurred to me last summer that she had liked him so much, that it had stretched out longer than the others. I couldn't remember her face turning pink with anything other than sunburn.

"You really like this guy. Where is he even from? How old is he? Do you know anything about him besides that his name is Bryce?" She had her back to me now, slinging her messenger back across her chest and grabbing my house keys.

"You know what I know about Bryce? I know that he is new and fun, I know that for some reason he liked me enough to hope to find me when his family came back. I know that Bryce isn't someone that my best friend is hopelessly in love with. Is that good enough for you, Laney?" Her annoyance was escalating toward me, and I was reciprocating it.

"No, not really Edie, not really. I don't need you to do me any favors where Evan is concerned. What I do need is for the person I love most to give a crap if the guy she is hanging out with is worth her time." I stormed past her, wishing I had worn boots so that every stomp would echo through the house in expression of my anger, to make sure she could hear me.

I walked onto the drive and watched for The Beast. The sun was already warmer than it had been; it felt good on the skin exposed by the dress. I wanted it to saturate my skin until I was the same as Evan.

"He's seventeen and a year ahead of us in school. He lives in some crap town I can't even remember the name of in Arizona. His family shares a house here every spring break and summer; every other year they go to Colorado for winter. He's been skating since he could walk and sneak off with his older brother's board. He knows it's a long shot, but he wants to go to school for architecture. If you can believe it, his mother's name is Edith. Just kidding, how gross would that be? I like him okay. I like him and he seems to like me, but today has me feeling all crazy, bouncing back and forth between excitement and being terrified that he won't fit in. He has me freaked out that I actually care if he fits in with us. I like temporary things, Laney. You know that. I can't read series books or watch shows past the first couple of seasons. I have no idea what happened in *Lost* and I couldn't make it to Mordor. I am in love with short-lived stuff, and you need to let me be who I am. Okay?" Her arm was around my shoulder and her point was clear. I had to stop expecting her to change, especially when I didn't even want her to. "There he is." She squeezed my shoulder and walked down the drive. Bryce was in a grey tank top with a diamond on it, his hair almost red in the sunlight. He towered over her with a sloppy smile. They were laughing, and Edie was doing that thing she did when she was nervous, her hands in her pockets, teetering back and forth on her heels.

She screeched when she saw The Beast coming up the hill. I picked up my backpack, the nerves of first freedom skittering around in my stomach. Hadley leaned across the front seat and hung her head out the window.

"It's happening! It's all happening!" She laughed when Nathan pushed her back into her seat. She looked pin-up adorable as usual, her lips as red as Taylor Swift's and her curls in a messy ponytail. Nathan got out and walked to the back, opening the doors to expose a jumbled assortment of chairs, blankets, and an ugly umbrella I knew his mom had shoved in last night. The woman was forever going on about damaging our skin with too much sun. Poor Nathan had a white nose for the first three summers we knew him.

"Hey Laney, just toss your bag back here." He indicated an empty spot. The mess was killing me, each item sorting itself in my mind, but I didn't want to be Brainy Laney today so I threw the backpack into the emptiness and hoped nothing crushed down on it to explode the sunscreen.

"Hey Laney." I hadn't looked beyond the mess, but I saw Evan's face peering over the umbrella, the corner of his mouth upturned.

"Hey Evan. Did you help with the packing?" He laughed. We were the same, always sorting our Legos into shape and color before we would join the other kids in playing. He shook his head. "Come on." He pointed at the empty seat by the window. I walked around and climbed over his legs to drop down next to him. I was trying to figure out how we would all fit, and who would sit by whom.

"Reese is going to ride shotgun, Hadley will either try and sit on Nathan's lap, knowing them, or at least right beside him. Ryland, Bryce, and Edie will sit in the back, and Leland will sit on the other side of us. If no one breathes or moves we should have an easy ride." I sucked in my stomach, my monkey cheeks full of air. He laughed, running a finger across my lower rib until I couldn't hold back the laughter.

"Are we going to that beach with the purple sand?" He glanced at his phone before looking up at me.

"Can I show you something? Oh yeah, we are going to that beach they have been wanting to see." He was skimming through the photos on his phone, his answer distracted.

"Is it another photo of my uggo face?" He frowned at me. I wasn't sure if it was because I called my face uggo or because I used the word uggo in general.

"Shut up. Don't be an idiot, Laney. You don't have an ugly place on your body…well, except for that bruise maybe, or the way your toe turns in…that's weird." I nodded at him because he was right, my third toe did a weird "turn into the other toe" thing. My father's toe did the same. It was an inherited weirdness.

"My bruise is a weird space nebula color combination this morning." He leaned over and pulled my dress forward to glance down at my skin.

"Hey!" The exclamation was unnecessary; he had let go of the dress and sat back, his tan obliterated by the blood filling his cheeks like Christmas bulbs.

"I assumed you would have on a bathing suit. I…I am so sorry. Wow, Laney. I mean, that bruise is something." He was talking to the window and I was staring at the floorboard mat. I tried not to laugh. His embarrassment had eclipsed my own and his red cheeks kept me from being angry, but it didn't stop me from wanting to laugh.

"Wow," he muttered. His knuckles popped like tiny firecrackers. I smiled, keeping my eyes on my shoes.

"So the purple sand, what's that from?" I was trying to bring him back to normal, but instead he handed me the Wikipedia page describing the beach on his phone. It lacked the scientific explanation I wanted. "I know, I tried to find it, but the closest I got was some blog saying it comes down from the rocks above. I knew you would want all the details." I handed him his phone, trying not to smile.

"This is going to be awesome. Can you surf at that beach?" It didn't seem likely with the winds and the jutting rock formations.

"No, we traded a cool three hour drive for surfing. I mean, we surf all year round, and summer is only two months away so no worries. This feels like exploration."

"Where's your camera?" I knew he had it, but I wanted to keep him talking. I heard the doors shut as we pulled away from my house. I glanced up at the closed drapes of my mother's window. I should have at least gone up and said goodbye.

"It's in the back. You know I never forget it. Speaking of cameras, and not your uggo face, I wanted you to see these photos I got of you and some of the others yesterday." He slid his thumb over in the gallery, scrolling through images of my face soft in sleep. There was a black and white one of Edie and I, smiling with our swords of pizza crust. Reese was in another with her hand on her cheek, her expression distant. I dragged to the next screen and my eyes went wide. It was my face looking directly at Evan. I thought he had been playing one of the stupid games with tiny fighters on his phone. I had never seen my own face lit up like this. His talent struck me. I wasn't uggo at all. I was vulnerable and caught with the same expression I wanted to be looked at with. I didn't want to look up, not with the heat shooting up my neck. I stared at the photo and swiped past it. My eyes felt blurry; the world felt blurry. It was unnerving to have someone show you yourself in such a way that even your insecurity has to fall back.

"You should go to NYU or wherever people who can do what you do go." I wanted to jump from the vehicle, curl tight, and bounce into the drive of some stranger's house. I felt like he knew what I looked like naked now, yet he was still a closed book for the most part.

"It's the best I have ever done. You couldn't be uggo if you tried." He took his phone from my hand, my fingertips numb and all the breath trapped in my chest. I had to figure out how to breathe without it shaking out of me, exposing how I felt.

"I thought you would love it."

"I do. I really do Evan, it's so good." I sighed, deflating my lungs slowly and feeling the need to wipe at my eyes. I kept staring at the floor until I was sure my face was the blank kind of happiness it usually was. It was just so hard getting it there.

"Laney, does your chest hurt?" I could see how Edie would assume this. I was hunched over, every inch of me frozen in place.

"No, I'm fine," I said, hoping it was loud enough. I felt a hand rubbing semi circles on my back, and my pulse almost burst from my veins like a busted thermometer. I relaxed; the hand was much too small to be Evan's. After a minute I could hear Edie sit back and whisper to Bryce with the same kind of giddiness that Hadley and Nathan lived in a perpetual state of.

"Music requests. Not from you Laney, and no Taylor Swift requests from the estrogen committee." Nathan slowed down in front of Reese's house; she lived the second farthest out from the rest of us. Her house was down the street from the tiny cemetery with headstones and marble markers sinking into the bright green grass. I wasn't allowed to put them through any more weird classic rock music, unless it was The Rolling Stones. Reese loved Mick Jagger.

"What's up Laney, Edie, new guy, and Evan?" Ryland climbed in and sat down next to Bryce, dropping his hand down for a handshake of sorts. Before any of us could answer, he and Bryce were already talking about some video where some guy ripped his nuts open on a grind. I winced at the idea.

Edie closed her eyes and leaned into Bryce's body. Their familiarity was so strange, like time had stood still between his vacations and resumed seamlessly. Edie was right , it felt paired off somehow. It was as if the group grew smaller with each passing year as we turned into we's and us's instead of me and him or her.

"Last stop, Leland's." I didn't know if it was because he was driving us all around in this monster or what, but it felt like Nathan was an adult, even with his messy hair and pitiful stubble attempt at a beard. He seemed older today. There was more maturity, and we felt gratitude at being independent of our normal routines for one day.

"Thanks again. Nathan. This is so awesome. I mean, this is the best break ever right?" I shouted to the front of the car. The Beast erupted into a series of cheers. If we were in the 1950s, Nathan would be our jolly good fellow. I sat back and smiled into the empty air above me. I could forget everything to always be this happy. Nathan pulled up in front of Leland's two-story house, the wood weathered and the succulents stretching around the whole place like a moat. He waved at us and backwards twerk-walked to the SUV. I laughed; he had been ridiculous ever since we'd known him. He was voted class clown in the yearbook every year. The only time we saw him look or seem responsible was when his father was around.

"Woo. Purple Beach-bound, baby." He elbowed Evan in the ribs and stretched his arm over the back of the seat to ruffle my hair. I leaned forward and scowled in his direction.

"I don't think it's called the Purple Beach, Leland."

"By a show of hands in this car, who knows what it's really called? Well that equals no one. Purple Beach it is." He laughed before twisting around to high five Ryland behind him.

"Now put on music because I need some sleep. I met this girl last night, and she drained my phone battery in just a few hours. I barely slept." He pulled his hood over his eyes and leaned against the seat. The low sounds of some indie music drifted over us. Hadley was using her phone. I slouched and leaned my head into the window, trying to watch the landscape without feeling the nausea from the road as it rose and fell in small hills. This was perfection, and I did not want to vomit all over Evan's lap or my own. I closed my eyes at the feel of his fingers twirling in the hair lying over my face. For the millionth time during the week, I wished he wasn't confused, wished that he didn't feel like less than me. I wouldn't change myself for anyone, but I desperately wanted him to change his mind.

"Are you asleep?" His weight had shifted closer to me, probably because Leland had slid over at the first curve in the road. Nathan was navigating slowly now that the black strip of asphalt had narrowed so dramatically. The ocean a still mirror from this far back and this high up.

"Yes," I laughed, my breath fogging the glass.

"Okay. Never mind." He rested his head briefly on my shoulder before sitting up.

"You know I'm not asleep, right?"

"I just thought you were short spoken while slumbering." His head was back on my shoulder, the heat from his breath sinking through the cardigan.

"Well I am, but in this case I was lost in thought."

"Tell me what to do. I can only give you this much of myself, what you already have now. I still want what I have always wanted, but it's over a year away. I want to know that you're my friend always. Will you really not mind that I didn't see you behind Edie for so long? You have to tell me, though, is that enough for you Laney? You always struck me as a girl that wouldn't settle for less than everything." My shoulder cooled with the absence of his breath; he was sitting up now. I turned to look at him. I was finally allowed to choose what was good for me. I studied his face, the one I had known for as long as I could remember. The little boy in rip-kneed jeans and a striped shirt with sand in his hair was the first image of him that I could recall. I loved that boy best, better than the boy who had suddenly grown into a man beside me. Would I have to give up my messy schoolyard love for this other kind? Was I really a girl who wouldn't settle for less than everything? It seemed that through my pickiness and reluctance to get involved that I was.

"It's enough, Laney, and I never think that anyone, especially a local, is enough for you." Edie leaned up to whisper in my ear, her voice faint next to the two boys in the back who could talk about skating for an eternity. I leaned my head to the side until it was against hers. She was straining her whole body forward to talk to me. Evan was smiling sheepishly next to me, his impassioned speech not having slipped as far under the radar as he hoped. This was how it was supposed to be, the three of us in a world of our own again. Edie sat back and rolled her eyes at Bryce and Ryland.

"You don't have to decide now. I'm not going anywhere, but I *am* telling you that when the sun came up I still saw you, your chin shaking and your hair plastered to your cheeks with the whole ocean around us. You with your chipmunk cheeks full of pizza, trying to sing break-up songs last night. The way everything about you goes soft when you sleep, your body suddenly boneless like a jellyfish. That's all I wanted to tell you, to show you with my photos."

"You are enough. You are everything…well, almost everything, besides, like, school, Edie…" His arms pulled me hard against his chest, stopping my rambling mid sentence.

"I get it. Go back to sleep. I can't decide if you are an insomniac or a narcoleptic."

I leaned forward and kissed the corner of his mouth. "And you said you weren't smart enough for me." He grinned and kissed me back, the ease of it surprising.

Present:

WINTER

I had loved the ocean longer than I had loved any one certain person, but now I wouldn't let it touch more of me than my feet. If it lapped over my feet as I walked beside it then I could ignore it, but the first time I lost myself in remembering and the water hit my knees I screamed. I dropped into the water and screamed until I was faint and my throat was raw. It took four days to get my voice back. I've been more careful since then. I never let it rise up on me anymore.

The walls in my room were painted while I stayed at my aunt's house right after I lost it all. They thought if I came home to different colors, if I didn't have to see the things I knew and be reminded that maybe I would heal faster. That I would go back to school and take my bike that was covered in dust out of the garage. What I did instead was go numb. I had loved a boy in a room that was a Van Gogh sky with cheap plastic green stars that glowed all around me. I came home to walls that were pale and unremarkable, my bedding unrecognizable. The hammock my father had slung from wall to wall was the only piece left. I stopped speaking to them, walked by them as a ghost might walk through walls. There was nothing to be saved the night I almost died, and there was nothing to be saved in what I had become as the one left living.

I stopped crying after my mother showed me the obituaries, their faces and facts in a row. Somewhere in that was a nursery rhyme, but not one anyone wanted written. The school excused me; a therapist came to the house when I would not go to him. All those degrees and he couldn't put Brainy Laney back together again. Who says that crying and healing have to happen to live? I was doing neither, but I still had a pulse.

The winter fell into the ground beside them and spring rose up from the remains of the memories lost that night. I ignored the change in temperature. My jeans hung loosely off of me, but still I rolled up the cuffs and kept the hoodie on—his hoodie and mine. We had both wanted it, so we split up its time with each of us like a divorced parent. I don't know who left it on my bed while I slept curled up on the deck, but seeing it was the closest to crying I have come.

It isn't that I don't want to cry, that I don't want to go over every second and detail of what happened that night. I do. I do so much that it's consumed all the other parts of who I am, but I can't. My mother wants to know all the details, my father stares at me when he thinks I'm not aware. I have dark circles and have lost just enough weight for spring break, but that's not what he's looking at. He's staring at me because he's grateful that he can, and just looking at me rims his eyes in tears. The gratitude is why he can't stop staring and the guilt of feeling grateful for anything to have come of that night is why he looks away when I try to catch his eye. My mom doesn't hide her happiness that she still has her child; she doesn't hide her frustration that I won't let her enjoy it. How could I? That would be a lie; her daughter lies with the rest of them at the bottom of an ocean.

Past:

TWO YEARS AGO

SUMMER

I fell out of the hammock. I saw the time projected on my wall from my space alarm clock and thought I was late. I landed on the blanket I had thrown off during the night, but my body still made a thud. Idiocy—it was becoming a part of who I was. This was summer, the first day of work still three weeks away and the morning sun unusually warm. I dropped my head back down on the blanket and tried to close my eyes in vain. Once I'm up that's it, at least for a few hours. My house smelled of food, actual food that didn't come in black plastic ovals with sweaty clear tops and complimentary chopsticks.

I stretched my arms over my head and crawled out from under the still swaying net. It was my belief that every girl deserved to sleep in a hammock under a *Starry Night* scene made on a whim one lazy Sunday. Most of my favorite things were attached to whims. I believed that my boyfriend was attached more to a whim than the shared childhood between us. I had cut all my hair off on a whim; I had let him see me, the side of me that was slowly changing. I loved him for seeing that side of me. There was more to it than that, but somehow just saying I loved him always felt too cliché. Too many stories began that way; we weren't a Ryan Gosling movie. We were just Evan and Laney.

I pulled myself up and dressed quickly, throwing on shorts and a tank top, the staples of summer. The smell of food was the same as a siren going off, an alert that my father was home. This had been a long stretch, almost the entire month gone. I pulled on my old pullover knowing that if the kitchen were hot from cooking, then my mother would be compensating with fans and the windows thrown open to the colder air coming off the ocean. My hair still wasn't long enough to pull back, so I ran my fingers through it. I missed him, the smell of him cooking and the sound of his deep-chested laugh. I took the stairs down two at a time, throwing paranoia aside for the time being.

"Hey, old man," I called out from the foot of the stairs. I didn't sneak up on him when he was frying bacon. Last time he had spun around in surprise and I ended up with a stripe of pain across my cheek from a greasy spatula he hadn't had time to set down.

"Hi, my little weirdo. I missed you. I'm making something new this morning. I'm frying bacon and then making pancake sticks out of them. What do you think?" He held one out and I took it cautiously. I bit into it and died. Whoever created this genius recipe should receive the Nobel Peace Prize. It was heaven in food, my dad was an angel, and bacon was the currency of the gods.

"That good, huh?" I nodded at his question; sometimes words aren't adequate enough a description. I turned and jumped. My mom was sitting at the table with her feet up on the chair, her chin resting on her knees. She looked tired, or maybe more than tired. The long absences were starting to get to her. They were starting to get to all of us. She only got the weekend off before summer school started. I had signed up for the summer semesters but was denied due to being ahead in credits and space issues.

Working at Gilly's was my only option left. Edie and I had applied, and we had both been hired. She planned on starting after the first semester of English at the community college. She was convinced that she needed the head start on college credits now that her senior year would consist of only the minimum four classes mandatory.

I grabbed the chipped Nikola Tesla mug my mom had found on Etsy for me and filled it to the rim with coffee. I had decided to drink my coffee black, but I was making miserable progress at it. I sat in the old wooden chair across from my mother and studied how time was working itself slowly into her expressions, the faint line on her forehead, and the thinnest silver strands peeking out through the brown. I couldn't imagine her old, not even when the first details were already evident.

"So, your mom tells me you started Gilly's this summer. I can still remember her working, her messy ponytail and laser glares reserved for the tourists that ate well and tipped nothing. She was too feisty for food service, but she made it work. It was that smile that got me, and a little bit how much leg she was showing." He laughed, deep like it sprung out from the root of him. She was giving him her signature glare now, piercing him over her coffee cup.

"Yeah, Edie and I both got hired on. Sander said something about traditions and generations, then held out a stack of paperwork and that was it. The uniforms got an overhaul for the summer so we are now basically wearing our shorts, Converse, a Gilly's t-shirt, and our hair in a bun, but he said it won't be a big deal if I pull my hair into pigtails." I smiled up at him as he set the plate of magical bacon pancake sticks down on the table, followed by the syrup pitcher. I took five or six and waited for my mom to say anything. She was never this quiet.

"So, you have all your stuff prepped for summer school already mom?" She nodded, her eyes fixed on something just outside the window. The silhouette moved slowly in the direction of our house, probably Edie coming over for breakfast. She didn't know my dad was home or she would have come later. My mom sat up, her face aloof like she just realized she was at a table with other people. It was the same switch she flicked while teaching, turning off who she was as a person for who she was expected to be.

"I have everything ready. I've been thinking about next year's curriculum too. I want to shake up my approach, keep the learning experience from getting stagnant. I want to introduce some more current young adult books, and get a dialogue going about the difference between what is seen as controversial now as opposed to the past. You know, school stuff." She looked down in embarrassment. She was never at ease with her tangents of passion. She could have been a professor in some Ivy League university, but she loved her home and had no real desire to leave it. I got that from her.

"Sounds good. Should I bring you some of the books I've been reading then?" I saw Edie walk up behind my mom, her mouth an O when she saw my dad standing by the stove with his back to us. I was about to mouth 'go,' but my father turned and set an additional plate of magic on the table.

"Good morning, Edie," he laughed. Her face was sheepish, but she could smell bacon out like a hunting dog.

"Thanks." Her face lit up with the first bite. "Oh my god, these are so good. What gives, Gordon Ramsey?" Her words were almost indiscernible through her stuffed mouth.

"Not Gordon Ramsey. Pinterest. A lady on the plane showed me this odd little website and now we have these." He swept his hand to indicate the pancakes. I was shocked that my dad was using his time to look up recipes; generally he was up to his eyes in paperwork.

"Mom, do you want to borrow the books?" She hadn't answered and her gaze was distant. Maybe she was coming down with her summer cold again.

"Yes, bring some of your favorites down. Remember, content is everything. Just because I let you read much higher than your grade level does not mean that the other parents will allow it. Try to find a variety, and all published within the last two years. Also, if you have any good indie authors you have found online, there is something going on there. Thanks, Laney. I mean it." She picked up her cup and set it on the counter before going upstairs. Something was completely off. She hadn't even tried the pancake sticks. My father was silent at the sink, the running water and the faint squeak when he would wash a dish too long the only sounds in the room. He was off too. This was probably what my mother referred to as one of the rough patches that couples who started early and lasted longer than expected went through. I wasn't ten anymore, but I really didn't like the tension and awkwardness that was climbing the walls in their wake.

"Thanks for breakfast, dad."

"You're welcome, weirdo. What have you got planned today? Bonfire to kick off summer with the group I'm guessing?" He twisted the faucet off and set the faded hand towel next to the coffee cup. He was right—it was tradition, and we honored tradition with as much passion as he and the other parents had.

"You know it. The first day of summer and the first day of break we gather. It will be good because most of us have summer school or jobs. This moron has both. Edie is taking some early college courses and the SAT testing on the first chance. Nerd over there." I laughed at Edie, who was oblivious to anything coming out of my mouth. She had stopped listening when she had started eating.

"What's your plan for today dad?" He ran his hand through his hair, little pieces standing up all around his head. I didn't notice the light purple rings around his eyes and how thin his face was getting. His exhaustion was severe.

"I'm going to take a nap for a couple of hours before your mother and I go see our therapist. I was thinking of repainting the trim on the house this week. Any color suggestions?" I didn't blink twice that they were returning to couples counseling. It was what they did when it got hard. They probably went for a few months every other year, only letting the help get them upright just enough before casually making excuses about lack of time or need to keep going.

"Black trim?" I always suggested black, and he always looked at me like I had slipped into Portuguese or Latin. He rubbed his hand over his stubble, but he seemed to actually be considering it for the first time.

"So, your suggestion is that our home resemble mint chocolate chip ice cream?" I hadn't thought of that. I was sticking with it no matter what.

"Yep. Right now it's seafoam green with a trim the color of clouds. It's so predictable, so beach town cliché." His eyes narrowed at my dismissive tone regarding the house as it was now. It was too late to take back the tone.

"I thought you loved the beach town cliché. It's why you said you needed a deck with rails made from driftwood. It's why your mother drove four hours up the coast for that clawfoot tub. You may not like what you always used to want, but you can't expect us to change just because you have. No black trim." I could feel the vague disappointment that covered his face, but the irritation at his assumptions made it easier for me to forget.

"Then why bother asking me?" I let my annoyance move me as I went up the stairs and away from his sad expression. I left Edie below. He never seemed to consider that his appearances made it difficult to readjust around him. He didn't want to show change around me, but he was ignorant that I was changing too. It wasn't long before Edie followed me up the stairs.

"God, Laney, why don't you give the guy a break? Your mom looks like a zombie and you are clearly hormonal or something. He made everyone breakfast, and he only got home, what, like last night?"

"This morning."

"Okay. Try easing up on him once in a while. He's not even my dad and I feel bad for the guy." She dropped down next to me. The difference with having Edie as a best friend as opposed to other girls is that she wouldn't stay on your side if she thought you were wrong— she wasn't afraid to call you on your crap. She was calling me on mine now.

"I may be an evil hag, but he should stop pretending that it isn't hard for us all to get used to each other again. I mean, if I hadn't smelled bacon I would have just come down in my bra and those old shorts I sleep in. That's gross."

"You have a point, but at least be a little grateful."

"What are you, my mom now?" I was moody today.

"No, she is hiding from the interruption to her regularly scheduled shows…same as you. Stop making me sound maternal. I feel the need to check if I have grey hairs yet, or if my boobs can still stand up without a bra." She grinned at me, looking down her own shirt. I tripped her, and she teetered and fell over onto my stomach.

"Off," I demanded. She obliged.

"Get ready. I want to go find a new bathing suit before we meet up." She was pacing. How could I have forgotten that she was nervous about possibly running into Bryce? They had not exchanged a single text or call in the two months since break. They were temporary like she had wanted, but it was summer again. I didn't question the oddity of it because it was so perfectly Edie.

"Bryce coming?" She feigned disinterest and shrugged her shoulders. I let it go. I slid on the plain black boat shoes instead of the sandals I bought last week. I was beach sloppy at best.

"Are you seriously wearing just that? I know that you have Evan, but come on Laney, it's the first day of our summer." She wriggled her eyebrows at me. I looked down and sighed again.

"Fine." I tossed the cut-off shorts into the corner basket followed by my faded navy pullover. I opted instead for the dark blue bathing suit I had worn over last break and put on a pair of dark denim shorts that contrasted with the beginning of my summer tan. I found my mom's old mirrored aviators on the dresser. My hair was still wilder than I would have liked, but there was no fixing it without a straightener. "Better?" Edie was startled at the sound of my voice.

"Yes." She nodded after staring at me for a minute. "I wish I had been crazy enough to cut all my hair off. You look older." Her hair was getting long, dropping down in loose waves to her bra line. There were moments when my short hair made me feel naked, but the other moments, the ones where I felt free from the weight of it, made having it shorter worth it.

"Is Evan coming over before the bonfire?" I shook my head no while I dug through the box on the dresser in search of bobby pins. "Why not?" I glared at her persistence.

"We aren't sewn together, you know. He went surfing this morning with Leland and we agreed to meet up at the bonfire. Why do you always make that face, the 'oh no, Laney and Evan are breaking up' face whenever we don't spend every second together?" They all made the face, their idea of love slightly based on the short and disastrous relationship that had been Nathan and Hadley. I understood everyone had assumed that they were going to be the first to marry up, but it had been short-lived. The first month had been sickeningly adorable, the second strained, and the third was just a scattering of public arguments and tears.

"You will not believe how many tourists have swept in just this morning. My mom said summer madness has begun. There were forty people in line for The Mad Bagler at eight a.m. Whether Bryce and I meet up or not, there are a ton of non-local fish in the sea." She took off her shoes, switching into my sandals. The gold-encrusted straps caught all the sunlight in the room and shot it out like we were in Pixie Hollow. Perhaps she didn't think that Bryce was coming, or maybe the odd way in which they orchestrated their relationship meant that there were no expectations.

"I want to get my mom those books before we go." Her phone was buzzing against my nightstand, but she didn't move to answer it. I skimmed the spines in my bookshelf, mostly paperbacks. You couldn't hope a beast in a castle would give you a library someday, so I made my own. I pulled out six decent-length books and stacked them up.

"You need to get a Kindle like a normal person." She laughed behind me, still pretending not to notice her phone vibrating.

"Why are you ignoring your phone, E?" She groaned and flopped backward onto my bed, holding her now silent phone above her head.

"It's Hadley. She's freaking out because Reese isn't answering her phone and she wants to discuss how she should dress and act at the bonfire. I would love it if she would just get over Nathan already. They were friends for years, and now this, stupid petty fights like their friends would really take sides. This is why I only have interest in non-locals. When I come back from school and settle down, it will be with a man who will love my friends, but if we decide to go our separate ways we can do so without the mess of putting friends in an awkward position." She held up my phone that now showed Hadley's huge grin, the smile from our road trip to the purple sand beach. That was the Hadley we knew before she started accusing all of us of preferring Nathan.

"Maybe we should cut her some slack. No one wants to finally give it up to a boy, let alone one she knew half of her life, and then break up three months later." I didn't want to admit the concerns I had of that same thing happening to me, to all of us. Most of the girls I knew had already tossed their virginity out the window like it was nothing. I wasn't about to lose mine like that; when I did give it up, it wouldn't be strewn aside like it had no worth.

"That's not how it's going to go down between you and Evan—there is no way. You aren't ridiculous like they were. You wouldn't run off down the beach with all of us gathered to have sex in the shadows. Evan would never treat you like that, like entertainment."

"Is that what you thought Nathan was doing?" She looked thoughtful, either considering my question carefully or trying to decide how she wanted to word her answer.

"No. That's what I thought Hadley was doing. Nathan didn't use her the way she used him, like she was nabbing the oldest guy in the group to make us worship her. I took sides, Laney. I took Nathan's side."

"I didn't want to choose. Hadley has always been Hadley, overly girl and vain, but she has good in her, Edie. I don't know what happened, but I'm letting them play out the weirdness and trying not to worry that I'll be them in a few months. I'm in love with a boy that was in love with you two days before he changed his mind. I don't linger on it, but I remember what it was like." She frowned at me while I sifted through the contents of her purse for lip balm. She always had one somewhere in here.

"Here." She pulled the little plastic ball from her pocket and tossed it at me.

"Thanks." I spread the balm on as I watched her text. She caught me staring and rolled her eyes with a grin. "His plane lands at four and his father said he could come down after they unpack and eat."

I didn't need to ask. Bryce.

"He didn't love me, you know. He loved the look of me, how we looked next to each other. He's a photographer. Aesthetically we made sense. That was it. I don't know what happened, but it finally clicked inside his head that he could have you, and now here you guys are. Can we please go shopping and find me a bathing suit now? What's going on with your mom and dad, by the way? He just got back."

"I have no idea. I don't know if it's the strain of him being gone for three weeks or the usual fights they have every so often. I can't get caught up in it, but I hope it doesn't last all summer." I stood up and grabbed my backpack; I always had too much crap for a purse.

"Big Edie was freaking out last night. I get today, but after the bonfire I am grounded for a week. I don't know if it was signing up for the additional courses without asking or that my room looks like I got robbed. There's always the chance that the grounding is the extension of my last phone bill being a bit higher than anticipated. Either way, I'm in for a week of hearing how I have to be responsible for more than just my grades."

I laughed. "How much is a bit higher?"

"I think it was about a hundred bucks higher." My eyes went round at her answer. Of course Big Edie grounded her—I would have done the same.

"How did you not notice that your bill raised that much?"

"I went over my data limit. I thought my mom would tell me when I was going over. I don't even know how it all works. I also bought some music. I don't know, I'm irresponsible, Laney. I regret it, though, because now I'm grounded for the first week of summer." Edie was composed of sighs, lip balm, and shoulder shrugs.

"You deserve it; you know that right?"

"I do." We walked out of the room laughing. When we reached the living room, I saw my dad's face buried into the couch cushions. He was so tall, and even in adulthood he never shook off the awkwardness of his long limbs. It was like you could see in his teenage self caught in old Polaroid photos. I didn't involve myself in their marriage problems, but it pulled at me that he was asleep down on the couch like he was banished from the upstairs.

"Crap, let me take those books to my mom. Wait for me in the drive." She turned with a mouthful of the pancake sticks left on the table, the spilled syrup drops forgotten. She gave me a thumbs up, her lips barely able to hold in the food crammed in there. I turned and went up the stairs, stopping in my room to grab the stack of books. I knocked lightly on mom's door and waited. She cracked open the door, her eyes rimmed in exhaustion and her hair pulled into a sloppy ponytail. She smiled and pulled me into her for a hug.

"Is this the divorce hug?" She froze with her arms around me, her head pulling back to meet my eyes.

"A divorce hug? What the hell is a divorce hug?" The sharpness and confusion intertwined in her tone and face. I pulled out of her hug and pushed the books in her direction.

"Thank you, but if you want to step out of this house, Laney, I want to know what you mean by asking me if I just gave you a divorce hug."

"You know, the long hugs and the quiet fights. If you and dad are going to get a divorce, I don't want to hear about it during a hug. Haven't you watched movies? The parents always cheese through it with hugs and sweeping the kids' hair out of their face. I won't be happy if that's what this is, but I will be pissed if you tell it in that tired old way." I could feel the start of tears, but I ignored the impulse to cry. This was their thing, and I wasn't going to be one of those pathetic kids destroyed because their parents couldn't keep it together. She went into her room to set the books down on her desk before swiftly walking back to where I stood. She pulled her sweater around her tighter and leaned into the doorframe.

"At this point your father and I have no intention to divorce. We're fighting and we don't hide that from you because you are a part of this family. What we fight about, however, is our business, and unless it directly involves you, I will spare you the details. If we should decide to divorce, rest assured, little girl, I am not going to tell you with some pathetic hug. We will talk together, cry together…yes even you, and figure out what's next. Don't reduce your father and I to TV show parents and we won't treat you like a child during the big events." Just to be a jerk she leaned forward and swept some of the blonde strands away from my face. I slapped at her hand.

"Can we have a fair moment?" It felt weird for her words to come out of my mouth, but we were close because we never held back with each other.

"Okay." The line in her forehead reappeared for a second before the skin smoothed out.

"He has been gone for twenty-two days. He should be sleeping up here and not curled into the couch cushions." I smiled at her sadly. "I'm heading into town and then off to the bonfire. My phone is charged and I'll be home by ten. I love you. Tell dad I said bye." I walked down the hall and kept on until I found Edie dancing to a song on her phone in the driveway.

"Come on, let's go." She didn't even pause; she just turned and danced into the direction of the street angling away from my house. I was curious what color trim I would come home to. It wouldn't be black.

"No," I stated. Edie glared at me and went back into the dressing room. I smiled at the closed curtain. This was the seventh swimsuit she had modeled and the seventh I had said no too. She was annoyed with my honesty, but later she would hopefully be thrilled that I didn't lie to her. With Edie there was no telling.

"Can you believe we will both be turning seventeen the same week that we start work, only three weeks apart. What should we do?" I asked.

"Hold on, the tag thingie is stabbing me." She stumbled out of the curtains and I smiled reflexively. When something looked good on her, it was crazy how good it could look.

"Yes. That one. Yes." She grinned and looked into the mirror. Finally.

"Oh yeah, seventeen. I know we are supposed to have a huge party, but summer is already a huge party, so what if we go low key this year?"

"I agree. If we go low key, neither of our parents have to put all that money out. Remember that trip out to the purple sands? Let's do that again. I can ask Nathan to drive, and he can decide about Hadley. I think my mom will be cool with it, and I can just have a quiet birthday dinner with her and dad. Oh, and you, duh." We had celebrated every birthday since we were nine together. Our birthdays being only three weeks apart, it only made sense. In the beginning, it had been a merger of whatever cartoon Edie was in love with and my love of mermaids and fish. Some years the mixed themes made sense and other years it looked like our television threw up into the sea. When we turned thirteen we went away for our idea of a spa weekend. Our birthdays made us more sisters than friends.

"I'll talk to Big Edie then. We have to go crazy huge on eighteen though. All the birthdays after that we have to pay for ourselves."

"True."

"Okay, I'm ready. Let's go." She took the swimsuit and the two skirts to the counter to check out. I touched the fabric of the dresses in passing; I constantly dragged my fingertips across things and usually got yelled at for it by my mom. I walked out the door that had one of those annoying bells that rang on repeat even though you were on the other side. I sat on the cement tree planter and waited for Edie to be done.

"Hi Laney." I looked up at the sound of my name, but the sun was blinding me entirely. Ryland's face slowly took shape out of shadows and light.

"What's up Ryland?" He sat next to me, his hairy leg rubbing against my own. His black hair had grown wilder like mine. It was a genetic trait in the R's to have that hair. I envied his skin color; he was striking for a boy.

"Not much. Just enjoying this first day of summer. I have summer school to fix a couple of bad grades from when I was living with my mom." He scratched the light stubble you could only see in the sunlight.

"Are you going home at all this summer? Or is your family coming up here?" I twisted at one of the pieces of hair that had fallen into my eyes.

"Neither. She said I moved here a few months ago and she needs a few more months before she wants to see me again." His nonchalance when speaking of his falling out with his mother saddened me. "She's not so bad, we just don't get along. I wasn't much for listening and she wasn't much for talking. Hard to build something off that, but it doesn't matter. She gets along with my sisters, and I like it here."

"Ry!" Edie had finally emerged from the store. Ryland smiled up at her with the same face Evan used to make, like all the boys made. That was the curse of Edie. She had a ton of admirers but she didn't see them the same way.

"What's up Edie?" He pulled his sunglasses down so he could look up at her. She had changed into her swimsuit and one of the skirts after she bought them. I could see the metallic purple straps peeking out from her shirt as the thin skirt swayed with the breeze. She looked like summer; all she needed was to darken a little.

"Just shopping, getting ready for the bonfire, and summer courses at the college. Don't want to be a hot mess. Why aren't you surfing with Leland and Evan?" He laughed at the idea that she ever was or ever could be a hot mess.

"I wanted to sleep in. I love my sleep. I was shocked that I even woke up before noon, but the little R's set off the fire alarm trying to make waffles. You should have seen the crazy amount of smoke that rolled out of the kitchen. I was tempted to pretend I didn't see it, but then Reese and my aunt came running in. Shrieking girls are deafening. So I came downtown to get some new trucks for my longboard." He shook the black plastic bag full of his goods.

"Well, we're going to get lunch and then to see if the guys have finished surfing." Edie waved and started off toward the tiny hole-in-the-wall taco restaurant where we always attempted to eat our weight in *tacos mexicanos*.

"Later," I called over my shoulder to Ryland.

We groaned mutually at the scattered lines of people, creating crowds outside of all our favorite places to eat. We wandered to the back of the line. I guess the one good thing about Gilly's is that they feed you during your shift. We didn't say much; we spoke in her sighs and my inability to stand still. We shared a lot with our irritated body language. Food was most likely the main reason any of us found ourselves loathing the steady stream of unfamiliar faces. They made the wait times unbearable. If it were a week ago, I would already be on my third taco and my second acknowledgement of needing to work out after I was done. Instead, I was staring at the most ridiculously rough tattoo of stars that formed a swooping line up the neck of the lady in front of me. I was bored with star tattoos.

"You look spaced out, Laney. What are you thinking about?" I studied the uneven lines of the tattoo in front of me.

"I was thinking that I can't imagine getting a tattoo. As if I would really be able to decide on something to be etched into my body that was forever interesting. I don't like anything that much."

"Yes you do. You could get a fat heart that says mom on one ribbon and Evan on the other. I'm kidding! I want to get at least a dozen. I will start with your face." She laughed and pointed to her bicep. I shook my head at her. She was mental.

Finally the line moved up significantly. I watched the table in the window, but it was still overcrowded with a family of five crammed into a table for two. I loved that table; we always ate at that table.

"Do you think Nathan will say yes?" Edie asked, looking at me with a nervous shine to her eyes.

"I'm sure he won't care. I keep telling him that the whole breakup shouldn't be the end of the entire group. I'm sure he and Hadley can work it out. No worries. I will ask him today. Since he's going to be helping Leland and his dad out with work, I think I should ask him as soon as possible. Where should we go?"

"We should definitely go to some of the southern beaches. There's that weird one with, like, the crazy street buskers and juiced-up steroid fiends walking around. I heard it has some pretty intense graffiti. We could just have Evan shoot our senior photos there at the same time. That will definitely sway my mother's decision." Edie's eyes went wide to emphasize her point.

"That's Venice. We should definitely go to Venice. I haven't been there since my mom would cover my eyes up when there was a thong-clad old man, or some lady's boobs were about to fall out of her top. It scared me when I was little." It had more than scared me; I had been terrified of the weirdness, of the possibility that those people were an entire alien race that came up from the seas and out of the alleyways.

"I think the only place that scared me when I was little was when my family took that trip to New York. There was so much noise and that everyone was in a hurry. I thought that they knew something we didn't. You know, like in the movies all the New Yorkers are scurrying about because a huge asteroid is coming or something. The whole trip I was just waiting for the whole city to collapse or blow up. I think sometimes we had a disadvantage growing up, like this whole town is a cove sheltering us. What if we get out of here and the world eats us alive because we aren't expecting it? I don't want to work super hard to leave and end up running back in tears. Do you ever worry about that, Laney?"

How could I tell Edie that it wouldn't feel shameful for me to come back or that I didn't know if I even wanted to leave? I wasn't sure what to say. Edie could read me like a book. She had mystery just like Evan, but I wasn't so lucky.

"Would it be that awful to come back if you didn't like it out there as much as you thought that you would, E?" Her shock was bringing out her flare for the dramatic. I could see every emotion on her face revealed in an instant. She would never understand the choices that tore me in half. She wasn't born with a heart that was nourished by the ocean; she didn't hear its lullaby outside her window every night.

"I'm kidding. Calm down Edie. You almost hit that guy with your hair." I indicated with a small hand gesture behind us. She smiled and glanced over her shoulder.

"I whip my hair back and…" Her singsong whisper fell into laughter as we moved forward with the line. I was still eyeing our table, the family around it almost finished.

"I am going to eat the tourists soon, I am so hungry." Edie laughed at my declaration. She could laugh, but I was considering it. I would chew through a couple meaty spots and then toss their mangled bodies off the pier.

"I thought you didn't mind the tourists. You always take the neutral path." She grinned at me and I laughed. That was true.

"Not when they come between me and my food. I have to eat, and I don't want to go home while my parents walk the tightrope of their marriage. I'll take a pass on that." I said it like it didn't bother me, but that was a lie; it was all I was thinking of, the idea of not having them both in the same house at least once in a while pulled at some part of me I didn't recognize. If the heart had compartments, I didn't like the idea that I would have to put each of them in a separate one from here on out. Edie would be upset, almost as upset as I was feeling. It wasn't farfetched to think that she would have been more surprised by my parents divorcing than her own. For some reason everything felt less permanent with Big Edie, even though her life had followed similar lines as most of the parents. It might have been her ease in and out of arguments, the clear impression that she really didn't care which way it ended up. There was a good chance that Edie's desire for all things to be temporary sprung from that.

"So are they getting divorced?" I looked up at her stricken face—I had been right. I shook my shoulders and fixated my stare back on the window.

"This is serious, Laney. I love them and I love you, but divorce will change all of us. What the hell? Who throws in the towel after eighteen years? I mean, they might as well stick it out, right? They're already old." She was staring at me and I was trying not to laugh. She had some good points.

"We are all going to be fine, Edie. I'll let you know what's happening when I know, okay? No one is changing. I'm not going to become one of those emo kids with bangs hanging over my eye and a general look of despair on my face daily." I looked up and she was glaring at me, her bangs hanging most of the way over one eye. I smirked; it was a good burn, even if it was accidental.

The line lurched forward again and the gust of air conditioning at the door made my eyes water for a second. The smell of tacos revved the slight hum of my stomach, which sounded like a seventies muscle car in full throttle. For a skinny girl, my appetite was endless and street tacos would be my Guinness World Record. The lady ahead of us clucked instead of talked, her words turning her head into a cartoon chicken face in my mind. "No cheese. Bacaw. No onions. Bacaw. What does 'asada' mean? Bacaw." I had to tune her out so I wouldn't flatly inform her that I would drown her in the salsa bar. I squeezed my eyes shut while I dug around in my pocket for the folded up cash, pulling it out and pressing it into Edie's hand. This day was already too long, and I didn't want to spend another second behind a lady whose every word was either the word "no " or another silly question.

"Just get me what I usually get and I will swim the tables." She nodded with worry in her eyes. I hated sharking a table, but I hated the woman ahead of me more and wasn't all that fond of the eyebrows on the man behind. I circled around in the back, watching for the first sign of crumpled wrappers or napkins. It worked; no one was comfortable having his or her table stalked. It didn't matter that I hardly looked predatory. Right now I felt like terrorizing someone. The family of five scooted around the table and out, soda cups tilting and awkwardly bumping into each other in their haste. No one acknowledged me, but still I tried to catch someone's eyes. It seemed easier to take out my issues on strangers, but guilt washed through me as fast as the hostility fled.

I pushed the chip crumbs from the table and sat in the chair that pressed most of my back into the wall, watching the streets frenzy with cars and people. It was like feeding season the first weekend. Between my own horrible mood and the agitation of waiting almost an hour to eat, I was about to jump party lines to stand with Reese in the anti-tourist parade.

"I got you eight tacos, onions, and cilantro." I smiled up at her like wings had ripped through her back to unfold in this taco restaurant. She pulled her hand from behind her back and set a Styrofoam cup full of horchata in front of me. We would always be soul mates, no matter the miles or the boys. This girl knew me like I knew her. She sat down in front of me, angling her chair to obscure the streets.

"Your face gets any uglier, you and Reese will have to buy team jackets." I meant it—she was dragging up her inner uggo.

"I just got a text from Hadley. She isn't coming. I told her she was an idiot and to be there or ruin an entire childhood of tradition just because she let a boy get the best of her." She set her phone down on the table face up.

"What did she say?" I was curious. I couldn't help myself.

"She sent me a picture of her middle finger and asked if she should get a manicure first. I said yes, her nails were looking raggedy." She smiled while rolling my straw wrapper into a tiny ball. I smiled as well, my head shaking on its own at her antics. "What? Look at the picture. She clearly chews her nails. Just saying." She laughed and flicked the straw paper at my face. It hit right below my eye as I picked up the phone. There it was, a photo of Hadley's middle finger with chipped yellow polish and what looked like an irritated hangnail. It was too much. I laughed with my head in my arms, my whole body shaking. Edie was antidepressants and ice cream wrapped up into one magic girl.

"You are the worst, E. The absolute worst, but she does need a manicure. I bet you a thousand dollars she will be there tonight just to see if Nathan will come. These bonfires are as important to him as they are to any of us. I would be there even if I was in a body cast with a halo, like that chick in *Mean Girls*."

"Me too. I told Bryce he can come down and we can hang for an hour, but the night is ours. No outsiders, ever. Except for Ryland but we familied him in when he moved down here during spring break. I know Hadley will be there, she is and always has been too afraid that we will talk about her when she's not." Edie bit into her taco and half of it disappeared. She had manners but still ate like a man. Our lives would officially suck when our metabolisms couldn't keep up with our ability to eat tacos.

"I'm shocked you and Evan have managed to date each other and not be totally gross about it, besides the kissing. The kissing is pretty much going to be gross since I can remember him putting boogers on you. Think about that next time he kisses you and you feel like your body goes limp, think about the boogers." Her eyes were laughing but her mouth was serious. I closed my eyes and felt my stomach twist at the sheer disgustingness of the situation. Later when we saw each other on the beach and he pulled on my hair the way he always did, I would know that he was the boy who made me cry for an hour because I couldn't find the booger he put in my hair.

"I just saved you from teen pregnancy Laney. You don't want to end up on MTV with a towel draped over your lady parts and your mom hyperventilating in the corner. Tell Evan he's welcome for this lunch that determined whether or not he will be working full-time at the gas station so he can afford Pampers and boob pads."

"What? What are boob pads?" My voice and body recoiled simultaneously.

"You know, like gauze for milk leaks. I saw it before. It's weird but necessary when your tatas are basically cow teats for a wailing baby." I pursed my lips while I stared at her. She was disgusting today.

"You're right, there will be no teen pregnancy between boogers and boob pads." I ate my third taco, but she was still two ahead of me. Our orders were identical, but mine was sprinkled with white onions that would help keep me from anything leading up to snot and boob gauze.

"Can I come over when the TV crews arrive at your house then? Promise me if *16 and Pregnant* chooses you that you will wear headscarves and sing Broadway with your huge pregnant belly. I want to be able to say that I remembered when you had promise, while you tell them you will be just fine living in a storage pod and working at Gilly's until the kid is old enough to take over," I said. My question stopped her mid-bite. She was seething. I don't know if it was the Little Edie reference or saying she would work at Gilly's forever, but her face was mutating shades of red.

"You are so funny, Laney. Honestly, I hope you are cursed to this town for all time." She pointed at me like the witches in movies did while casting a spell.

"Not much of a curse. This place is amazing; I have an ocean in my backyard and a boyfriend I have known for as long as I can remember. Life could turn out much worse," I muttered while she glared through me.

"Don't even joke, Laney. For a second there I thought you were serious, but of course you aren't. That is a world that doesn't exist for us after high school. Even if you did stay, you could never keep someone like Evan caged to this beach. Who wants the guy who takes photos for the newspaper that only a few thousand people read? He's going to NYU and we are going somewhere equally amazing, even if it's not together. I don't even think I can get into the same universities as you, but I will try. I'm trying now. August is the start of our last year. I really did think you were trying to tell me something, Laney; I just had a complete meltdown in a matter of seconds. The only way we could ever end up on MTV is if we were on *True Life: I'm Addicted to Tacos.*" Her voice shook with determination. Pretending that a life here was paradise was Edie's vulnerable spot. If you stabbed that spot, she became a passionate and articulate woman who shed her teenage body like a cocoon. It was alarming to know that was hiding in her.

"Calm down. I'm hardly the kind of girl that would think of trapping a boy. You'll get into any university that you apply for and so will I. The plan is carved in stone. Edie and Laney forever." Her visible unease calmed under my words. It was like a chant she put herself to sleep with at night and repeated to get through the day. I thought that kind of desperation to leave was only born into people who needed to get out of bad situations, but she was living proof that some people are just born ready to leave. She had been talking about going away to school since we started junior high and hadn't stopped yet. She had studied for the PSAT harder than people taking the actual SAT. When she looked in the mirror there was a ticking clock staring back at her. None of us understood why she saw it or why she was running from a life that wasn't awful.

"Did you start filling out applications for early admission like the academic advisor suggested?" She was testing me because I had unnerved her. Edie could handle almost anything, but she didn't like to think that her plans could go awry; I was integral to her plans. It was like we shared organs, not to be separated.

"Edie Callum, I am serious when I say that I understand our plan and I don't need you freaking out for no reason. You're acting like a crazy person. Eat your tacos and shut up. I hate when you get so worked up. You have a killer new bathing suit and only one day before your grounding kicks in. I refuse to fight with you like an old married couple, because if this is how it's going to be I want a freaking divorce now, you psycho!" I felt it—when I said the word divorce, I felt it. The ache and tension that had been spreading for hours since the pancake breakfast built up into a gaping wound. I didn't want my parents to get divorced, and whether I liked it or not the burn I felt streaking down both sides of my face indicated that I was crying in public. I wanted to slap the tacos off the table and shove Edie through a wall, but instead I let her hug me, her back shielding me from strangers.

"I'm sorry Laney. I am. Plus, I would never give you a divorce, hoser. Never." We stayed like that for what felt like hours but might only have been minutes, and my tacos sat on the table forgotten.

The wind had picked up by the time we reached the sand. We had just finished walking the entirety of the pier and back so that the stains of my emotional breakdown would be gone when we met up with everyone. The wound had closed, but the ache still pulsed like a heartbeat. I was happy to see Evan's face. Sand was caked on his feet and his wetsuit hung off his hips. He looked like he had risen up from the ocean and not walked out of it. I smiled, my face fighting the sadness..

"Hey, have you been crying? Your eyes look strange. You were either crying or you're high…" I looked away to the water instead of telling him the truth.

"Still down for a swim?" He grinned down into my face. He was always willing to go swimming—it was our thing the way some couples had a song. The cold water and recklessness of how far out we could go connected us more than kissing or long stares. I kicked off my shoes and stripped down to my swimsuit. I once made the mistake of swimming in my clothes when we had gone to the beach that glittered like an amethyst in the sun. I almost drowned.

"Yeah. Let me go up and get some water and change. I missed you." He kissed me, but not frenzied or for too long. He kissed me like he knew I needed it.

"Laney, would it kill you to skip the onions just once?"

"It really, really would." I hugged him to me, absorbing his cold skin and the smell of wet sand. He was the ocean for me.

"Fine, only kisses on the head, or anywhere else you want them…" He wriggled his eyebrows at me.

"Edie was just reminding me over lunch of that fun period in our life when you liked to put your snot on me." His face bloomed red and he looked away from me. Edie was right, there would be no teen pregnancy today.

"Be right back." He kissed the top of my head before running past Edie and knocking her over, leaving her red faced with crooked sunglasses in the sand.

"You're welcome Laney," she shouted up at me. I laughed while Leland helped her up.

"Eww Leland, don't be a perv. My eyes are up here." Leland laughed and jogged after Evan.

"You probably just embarrassed him," I pointed out, ever the captain of the good ship obvious. She gave me the "oh well, all boys are pervs" face. We saw Leland's heap of blankets next to the rather sizable stack of driftwood Evan had helped him gather the week prior. I tossed the blankets out and rubbed sunscreen on my chest and forehead. This was our last summer before we had to actually embrace who we would start becoming. Except for a few, most of us were weighted down with busy schedules and work.

I walked down until the water washed over my feet. I had less than a year to figure out who I was and what I wanted. It was hard to think outside of this place when I was standing in it. If my parents did divorce, I didn't want to see my mom more alone than she already was. The house was too big for one. I could stay and go to the community college; I still didn't know what I wanted to be. I told my parents when I was eight that I wanted to be a marine biologist. So had about twenty other kids. I lost interest in the idea during freshman year. I didn't want to understand the ocean. I liked that it was mysterious. When my mom was in high school, no one expected her to know who she wanted to be. That was for college to sort out. It turned out that she wanted to teach and have me. I had been expected to have some kind of answer since I was thirteen, no pressure.

"I am dying. Do I look weird? Fatter or uglier than three months ago?" I looked over at Edie's face twisted up in anxiety and was tempted to say yes. When she made that face she was as ugly as anybody would be.

"Shut up." Simple answers quieted her rare moments of insecurity. She shrugged and walked back up the beach until she dropped down gracelessly on the blanket. Edie was much tanner than I was. I couldn't compete; the sun didn't hate her in quite the same way. I suffered through the burn to tan even one shade, and for two days I would fight the angry red skin that itched after the heat faded. I watched Evan come down the stairs with Leland in board shorts, their wetsuits gone. Leland could drive now, but not with any of us in the car. Next to Nathan he was the oldest. Edie was the baby by three weeks, but the boys had forgotten that when she had grown breasts and confidence.

I turned back to the water; the quiet wouldn't last when all of us got here. There would inevitably be weirdness between Hadley and Nathan. Bryce would come for an hour, as would Reese's new whatever. She didn't really date long term either, not by choice anyway, but she was always in a breakup. Each one made her moody for weeks, and then she would be Reese again with her wild black hair and eyeliner. She was the closest to shedding her beach cliché persona with music and art. It didn't stop her from living on a surfboard or a longboard most of the time. Other moments found her in black skinny jeans and old metal band tank tops she found in her attic the summer she was fourteen. They had been her father's once upon a time when he had been in a band in Los Angeles. You couldn't see the traces of that in him now; all of it had emptied into Reese.

Her sisters were edgier than most little girls in the beginning, but now they blended into the Monster High dolls and leggings fads. I remember tactless Edie asking her why she was named Reese, making her laugh as she joked that it wasn't a Mexican enough name for her either. Her sarcasm was lost on Edie, that's what bonded them first. I scanned the beach for Ryland and her, but they still hadn't wandered down. Nathan would come after work, and knowing Hadley, she would come right as the sky darkened and the flames licked upward. She had told us on more than one occasion that Nathan thought she was most beautiful in the firelight. All of us had gagged inside, but outside our faces smiled as we let out an "aww."

Hadley would want to see him in the best lighting possible. I didn't get her anymore, yet she was still a part of us.

"You do realize that you spend more time daydreaming than you do awake? Plus there's your frequent napping. Is it possible that you have narcolepsy?" I rolled my eyes in Evan's direction; I hadn't even heard him walk up. I did sleep a ton.

"It's warmer today, so the ocean is bound to be a bit warmer…right?" I knew the answer. It would not be warmer. It never was this early in the summer.

"This is nothing. Wait until you come see me in New York. The Atlantic is going to freeze the marrow in your bones, but tradition is tradition, Laney. Come on." I followed behind him, holding his hand and bracing myself for the first wave that broke higher than my knees. It wasn't warmer.

"Let's swim out. I want to talk to you without Edie or anyone else around. Just us and the water, like always." His head went under at the end of his words, his hand dragging down from my thigh to my ankle. I went under, closing my mouth seconds before it would have filled with kelp. I struggled to pull my foot from his grasp, panic gripping me before he let go to swim up. We broke the surface at the same time; he was smiling and my eyes were murderous. He reached out and rested his hand on the curve of my skull before shoving me under and swimming as fast as he could from my side. I gave chase once the initial cold and fear from going under faded. I was fast, my arms gliding through the water, only pausing while a wave rolled over me. We swam like that until I couldn't ignore the burning in my muscles and lungs.

"Why were you crying?" He moved in closer, treading water while we swayed up and down in the water.

"What?" I didn't know if he would buy my pretense of ignorance.

"Why were you crying, Laney? Your eyes look like you haven't slept, but I know you did. They only look bruised when you cry. I think the last time I can remember you crying was when that boy told you your chest was fat when you first started getting those." He glanced down at my chest with a grin. I scowled in response. I remembered that day. I don't know what had been more traumatic—that some stupid kid had thought I was getting plump or that all my friends found me crying in the hallway next to the office. If I was sad or hurt I chose not to share it. I was surprised he recalled that memory.

"You know I beat the crap out of that kid…umm…Jeremy. I got suspended for a day." He was keeping us afloat, but I was sinking in shock.

"I didn't know that."

"I did it after school by the marina. I couldn't believe that he made you cry. The principal called my mom and me in during first period. He suspended me and didn't make a huge deal out of it. Something about not wanting to glorify fighting for honor or some nonsense like that. He was a confusing man. That was the last time any of us can remember seeing this." He rubbed his thumbs under my eyes.

"I don't really know, but it's looking like my parents might actually divorce this time. I know I'm about to be seventeen and that two people who married young don't statistically make it this far, but I might as well be five. I don't want to deal with the mess of a divorce." I felt it, the crack that happened before I turned into a puddle of pathetic emotions amid a crowd of tourists in a taco bar. I pushed away from him and swam farther out. I kept going until he pulled me up.

"This is what we're supposed to do, Laney. You are supposed to tell me when your heart is breaking, okay? That's the point of all this. Besides, you can't swim any farther out or your arms will fall off. Just be sad out here in the water with me. I won't laugh at you or complain about your perfectly obese chest. Promise." I let myself cry. It wasn't a snotty sob-fest, but rather, the worst kind: quietly. I finished crying in the water, my legs and shoulders aching and Evan's legs against mine. He didn't say a word until I stopped. He just held me up.

"I lied to you, Laney. Your boobs need to go on a master cleanse." He laughed so hard I forgot I had been sad. He was an idiot. I shoved his face down, but he grabbed onto my ribcage before letting me go.

"Dolphin me." I looked at him, my lip pouting and my eyes going wide.

"I just tread water for almost half an hour. You are swimming, kid." He smiled but meant it.

"Stop calling me kid. It's a six-month age difference."

"Six months older." With that he turned for the shore. My body was exhausted, but I pretended to swim hard until I caught a wave and let it float me in spurts closer to the shore. When I hit the sand I sprawled out, the water flowing up against me and pulling away. I couldn't quite comprehend how Evan could surf for hours and still swim out to the calm of the ocean afterward. It was crazy to know I loved him; I hadn't said it or shared it with anyone yet, including him. I couldn't remember a time when I didn't love Evan Wallace. The love didn't begin or change in ways that made sense; it just was. He was Evan, I was Laney, and I loved him. The idea of a love like that wasn't an explainable concept so much as it was a fact. Loving him didn't make me want to marry him or pop out babies, it just made me happier for having seen his face in every stage from adolescence to the present. That was the love I had. Fat-chested Laney loved snot-wielding Evan; it made sense that it never went away. Jealous Laney even loved Edie-infatuated Evan despite how unreciprocated it was at the time. That was who I was and always had been. I wish they asked that on college admission essays. No one wanted to know that, though. Who wanted to hear that a teenage girl knew what love was?

"Get up, nerd, before you drown." I didn't open my eyes, instead reaching around blindly for his hand until he pulled me upright. I leaned into him, drunk on awareness and free from the sadness I had worn all day like a sweater.

"What's gotten into you?" he asked, wiping sand free from my neck and collarbones.

"It's summer, Evan. I love summer." I smiled into his concerned face and kissed him until my lungs hurt for oxygen like they did when we swam, always pushing to pass the other. I pulled back first. His face was a lazy grin. He kissed my nose to the sound of the disgusted groans behind us. They had all seen us, except for Ryland, who was laying on his backpack, mouth slack and asleep.

"Are you done yet?" Edie grabbed my arm, dragging me back. I threw up my hand at Evan with a "What could I do?"

gesture. He dropped down next to Reese, prying her phone loose from her hand and taking a selfie of her mock outrage and his duck lips.

"What? What?" I sputtered as Edie kept pulling me. She finally let go. Her face looked like it hurt with the strain of what she had to say.

"Your mom texted me. She said you weren't answering your phone. She said she needed to get away for a few days and that your dad is insisting on joining her. She's asking if you want to stay with me or just stay home. She's leaving in an hour and not coming home until Monday night. This is awesome right? They might fix it, you know?" Her eagerness was no longer contained. How could I tell her I didn't know? I took her phone and sent a text to my mom. I wanted to stay home. Big Edie would let me stay, but with Edie grounded it would be tense and we would have to sleep in separate rooms. The phone flashed with her response.

"Well, what did you tell her? You're a total idiot if you said you wanted to stay with me. Big Edie will be stomping that big giant foot she set down all over the house. You could have Evan spend the night!" I looked up, my face showing that it hadn't even occurred to me. I wasn't a saint, but I also attempted to respect my parents.

"You never thought about it? You guys planning on waiting forever?" I coughed and choked on a hundred answers that were about to come shrieking out of me. "Oh wow, you *are* going to wait forever, huh? I forgot about that whole 'no sex until college' thing." I glared at her, my throat burning.

"I said that when we first got our periods, dork. I don't know when I'll have sex. Who just walks over and writes it on their calendar?"

"No one. We use the calendars in our phone, hoser." She laughed like it was an obvious conclusion, as if she had not just told me I should have sex with Evan while my parents were trying to figure out if they could still stand each other. This was the side of Edie that was my least favorite—the vapid teenage girl she couldn't rid herself of. This was where her maturity failed her.

"Whatever. It's barely been, like, three months. I'm not about to become Hadley and cry at the end of summer over something I probably shouldn't have done. Are you going to have sex with Bryce?"

"Maybe." I stopped glaring; I could feel my face softening at her answer, her normally loud voice so tiny now.

"Oh my god, Edie. Are you actually considering having sex with a boy you only see on vacations and don't talk to the rest of the year? Please, don't say 'maybe' again like it's not a big deal." I was basically giving the talk you have to listen to when they explain sex for the first time in school. The stern bold letters on the worksheet always said: ABSTINENCE.

"So what if I am? Has it ever occurred to you that no matter if I lose it this summer or in college, it will hardly be with someone I love? I have no interest in love right now. I don't need to understand what love is until I'm done with what I want to do. My mother didn't do anything but talk about what she wished she had done. Not me, Laney. I'm going to do something, and I don't believe losing my virginity before I fall in love will ruin that. I'm not stupid; I would use all the stuff you are supposed to use. Sometimes I could swear we are conjoined twins, but we definitely don't share a brain, otherwise I wouldn't have to try this hard to be smart and you wouldn't have to try so hard to not be perfect." She was mad now; I could see it in the way she was trying not to cry. Whereas I seldom cry, Edie does it every time she's mad. She was crying because she was mad that we were fighting and mad for what she had said. I didn't have any other words to say to her; I had said them all. I was mad too. I wanted to be her friend, but never her mother.

"I'm not apologizing, Edie. I meant it. Why can't you give yourself more self-worth than you do? So, don't wait until you are in love, but at least wait until you are seeing a guy that isn't fine with not hearing from you for months. At least wait for that." I crouched down; this conversation was harder than swimming against the current. I felt like I was drowning, and she was content to let me go because she was already falling under.

"I am who I am Laney. You know that. Make you a deal—you let up on me and I will try and wait until the boy I'm seeing thinks I'm worth texting even after he goes home, even if it's only to see what I am up to. Okay? Okay Laney?" The only thing Edie could deal with less than being mad was feeling bad for making me mad. She was red faced and snotty. What the hell was wrong with us, crying through the first day of summer?

"Okay."

She grabbed onto my hand, swinging it like we'd done when we were little when it was more important to show your possessiveness over your best friend than a boy. I giggled at how different we were and how absolutely nothing had changed. It was so us to have deep conversations, a small argument, and make up in the same time it took most people to do just one of those things.

"If we don't end up in the same place, what will we do without each other?" She held onto me tighter, so tight it almost hurt.

"I don't know. It's been years since we had to do anything alone, years since I didn't ask you about every single piece of clothing I've bought. Isn't this supposed to occur the last few weeks of senior year? Think about it: this is our last summer without great expectations, and we're lost in the future already. We'll be seventeen, but we have to consider that this is it—the last year. I don't want to be sad. It's maddening when you won't tell any one of us what's going on up there. I hate that you do that, Laney." If she hadn't been with me all day I would have mistaken her for drunk, but she was just confused and scared of the future. I was more terrified of it than she was. If my heart stayed the same I might lose them all just being me.

"We should go back. Shouldn't Bryce be coming down soon?" I knew it was still hours until he would wander down to hang out with Edie for an hour, but I wanted to change the topic.

"No, it'll be a while, but we look ridiculous holding hands over here. My makeup probably has tear stains mixed in it. One day you have to tell me what's going on up there. We have so much to figure out. Senior year is going to kill us in all kinds of ways." She was right. The thought of it was killing me now. I wasn't afraid to age or mature, but I wouldn't pass on freezing who we were right now. I would love to have the ability to dwell in this age with these people until I could say I was ready to let some of them go. Never Edie, though, and never Evan. I would hold onto them forever if they would let me. I had known for a long time that I couldn't.

We walked back still holding onto each other's fingers. I counted the bodies moving about, digging the pit, and throwing the blankets around. We were all here except Hadley. I wasn't particularly looking forward to the pointed stares across the fire. Even as a kid, I believed that if all the kids weren't around without good reason that the break in tradition would curse the year. I don't know if it was sad, but I still held that to be true. Would anyone show up after the summer when we all went our separate ways? I couldn't imagine it, except it wouldn't shock me to walk down to the sand and find the outline of a fire pit and only Nathan filling it with wood and Leland looking for more. They felt like me, like their roots weren't just planted here, but had intertwined with the pier and the cypress groves, wrapping through all we knew. They held us here, the roots of our existence.

"You know what E, let's just hang out next week, lay around, and watch bad TV and eat junk until we either fall asleep or slip into a food coma."

"*Real Housewives*? Please say *Real Housewives* of…who cares, of anywhere." She let go of my hands to pray for the women who bartered in Botox and bitchiness. I should have suggested watching a documentary about the food industry; something so gross that we would throw out all the crap foods and beg my mom with desperation for apples and stuff that wasn't unnaturally made. We had become vegetarians for four months after we saw *Food, Inc,.* our young brains traumatized with the sadness in the food industry. We forgot how sick we felt when Thanksgiving came around and our bodies were bloated with food babies as we adjusted to eating meat again. I felt proud that we at least tried. Now I was agreeing to anything they played on E! or Bravo. I compromised by watching plastic nightmares and silly socialites so I could hold tighter to my best friend before she pulled away. If I forced her to let me go it would take a long time before I could reach her again, before she would even let me try.

"Hmm…or we could watch documentaries and eat hummus and pita chips?" I smiled like I wasn't trying to crush her dreams. She crossed her arms and twisted her mouth. No, it was going to be housewives or nothing.

"Fine, we can watch the Real Kardashian Housewives of Project Runway. Deal?" She grinned.

"You really are an old lady, Laney. I love you though. From the stars to the sea."

"From the sand to the moon," I said quietly as we let go. I drifted toward Evan. He had pulled on his black and white poncho, the sun already bleaching his hair blonder.

"Okay, why was she crying? Same reason?" Evan asked, his face losing features to the intense sunlight. I dropped down onto the blanket next to him, my cheek rubbing the rough texture of his poncho.

"I told her she shouldn't have sex with just anyone, that it should mean something. She got mad at me and cried." I said it quietly, my chin on his shoulder so he could hear me.

"That makes sense. I don't even want to know how that subject came up. Now explain why you look like you've seen a ghost." He kissed me where my hair met my forehead and inhaled; he loved the salty ocean smell as much as I did.

"I sometimes feel like I'm looking at ghosts. You guys are still here, but next year we'll come down here knowing it's the last time, knowing it won't be like this again. If we are all here together it will be when we have all changed, our experiences different. Just because our parents held on to this so tight doesn't mean we will. As soon as we were old enough they drifted apart too." He pulled me tighter against him. I didn't understand how he never got tired of my rambling, my worrying. He pulled my face to his and kissed me before he leaned in closer so no one else could possibly hear what he said. His breath moved the hair against my skin.

"Have you told Edie that you don't know if you want to go away to school yet?" I pulled back, feeling my eyebrows furrow. I couldn't recover my expression, nor ignore the look on his face. I didn't answer as I pulled myself tighter against him and tried to find the words. I had never said it aloud, but still he knew. He knew the same way I knew that he would go. In love or not, he needed to go. I wasn't stupid, and I wouldn't ask him to come back for me or wait. I would miss him.

"Don't freak out. I have always known. I don't understand how Edie hasn't figured it out yet. People leave good places because their happiness isn't tied to where they were; it's still out there and they are desperate to find it. Your happiness is here. It's always been here. I've never known anyone so consistently happy as you are. It's not in a sickeningly overdramatized way, but just happy. I'm jealous of how much you feel that, Laney. Edie shouldn't have to find out when she won't have enough time left to process it. Don't let her build a future for the both of you and then burn it down the night before she is set to start it." I felt him talking more than I heard him. Everything ached at how true his words were.

"Why doesn't it bother you?" I could feel him smile against my skin before the heat from his cheek was gone.

"I had to get over it to be with you. I realized that I wanted Edie because she was pretty, but also because she would never tempt me to stay here with her. She would be gone faster than I would. We looked good together and it made sense." I pulled away from his side, but he brought me back. "But I realized that it was always you I wanted. I was just scared of everything about you. You are so damn smart and you don't care. You would and do tempt me to stay here. My heart tries to trick me into believing that I could be happy, or at the least live off of your happiness, but my brain says go. My eyes say go. I will leave at the end of next summer, but I won't be a ghost. I will always, always come back for you, or wait for you to come to me. But if you don't tell Edie soon, she'll be your ghost and it will haunt you like losing your twin. When you really hurt Edie she doesn't forget it. Why lose her?" I didn't answer.

The wind was picking up and it was a waiting game with the sun. I looked up at him, his skin almost as brown as Ryland's had been during break. I still didn't know how to say what I wanted to say. I knew Edie, knew her well enough that either way I would lose her. I didn't know how long I would lose her, so I prolonged the fights, the tears, and her inevitable silent treatment. Once when we were twelve, she didn't talk to her own mother for all of June. The whole month she didn't utter a single word. It had broken Big Edie down, and none of us had been aware of just how deep the stubbornness ran in Edie until afterward. When she spoke again, it was like she had never stopped. She got up one morning and was making eggs when her mom came down and sat with me at the table. Edie turned away from the stove and offered her mother some eggs.

"I will lose her for a while no matter what. I haven't decided if I want to lose her during our last year as Edie and Laney or when she's leaving. I know how selfish I am. I'd like to think that if the roles were reversed she would be making all the same bad decisions too." He shrugged in agreement. He knew I was right.

"Have you ever just considered going? Try out a university and then come home if you don't find anything worth seeing. You could get in almost anywhere. You could come to NYU with me." I smiled up at him; I *could* get in almost anywhere. My grades had never wavered since the third grade, which had been a weird year with a teacher straight out of a *Wayside School* book. I didn't know what I wanted to do.

"What would I do?" He stared at me as if I were suddenly speaking a foreign language.

"You would be a literature major. Or, remember in eighth grade when you wanted to be a marine biologist before you realized that it's the career choice most driven into your head when you live coastal?"

"I wanted to name a species of fish or discover a full-sized giant squid. Books? I could probably read for a living. Are there jobs where you can sit around reading books all day?" He laughed.

"I think there's a job where you can read people's manuscripts all day. I could also drag you along on photography assignments. I would take pictures while you lay around in hotels and read while getting day-drunk from the mini bar." I smiled. It was worth considering. I tilted my head up and kissed his chin.

"I will think about it." I wanted to fall asleep. Swimming was exhausting. Worrying about the state of my parents' marriage and my own future was also exhausting, but the smell of pizza wafting my way made me more alert. I cracked open one eye and saw Reese and Leland carrying a stack of boxes. They had most likely pooled their money, but Edie and I had not pitched in.

"Don't worry, chipmunk cheeks. I covered you and Edie. Go get some pizza." Evan held his arm out so I could push myself upright.

"Not coming?" His face looked a little sad, but it could have been from being tired. He grinned up at me, his eyelashes batting up and down.

"Oh my god, don't do that. I will get you some pizza." Right as I found my balance I saw Hadley descending the stairs, her blue skirt whipping around her calves. The fire was only just flaring up, but even in the faint glow I saw what Nathan meant. Firelight was good for her. She looked elfin and sexy. I glanced over and saw that her timing couldn't have been better—Nathan's entire jaw looked unhinged. The girl knew what she was doing, even if what she was doing wasn't right.

"Pizza!" Edie cried out. There was no joy quite like the joy she felt when she had pizza. She could have been a Ninja

Turtle. "Thanks Evan!" Reese had obviously told her that Evan had covered us. Leland was walking back to his blanket with five slices stacked on top of one another. It was good that he surfed, because if he didn't he would weigh at least a thousand pounds with his appetite. Ryland was following suit, but he only had three pieces. Reese had an edgy exterior but was the daintiest of eaters. Hadley and Nathan moved closer and closer to one another, with neither one acknowledging that it was on purpose.

I picked up the pizza and walked back to Evan. His lips would taste like tomato sauce and pineapple. There were worse things that could happen. I saw Edie eating already next to Ryland, her eyes glancing at the stairs and around to the pier. If I had to guess, Bryce was not coming. As it grew colder, our circle around the fire pit shrunk. Edie fell asleep on Ryland's leg. As much as she made fun of me for my spurts of narcolepsy or bouts of insomnia, she fell asleep just as often.

Bryce hadn't come, and at some point Hadley and Nathan disappeared just as they had during break. The anger between them was forgotten in the midst of their rabid hormones. Evan and Reese were racing each other down the beach. Had Edie been awake, she would have left them with sand in their eyes. There were other fires speckling the beach, tourists drunk on summer laughter among their groups. Women shrieked in protest when their boyfriends or husbands, beer usually still in hand, carried them over one shoulder before dropping them into the frigid ocean water. The shrill scream wasn't just dramatics; the ocean had lost any heat it might have soaked up during the day.

For teenagers we were quiet. We did stupid stuff too, but never here and never on the first night. The summer before, Leland had gone to a party at one of the vacation rentals and had thrown up on and off for two days. He hadn't drunk since. We had recklessness running through us in different ways. Edie's wildness was focused on boys and how much she was willing to push the boundaries with them. It was a line she thought she was ready to jump across. Nathan rebelled in small measures—a fight at school or the time he disappeared for two days. I could still remember the panic we felt, the excitement. We knew he would come back, but not knowing when created a feeling of unrest none of us had really experienced except Evan.

When Evan's father died we were all old enough to know what death was, but nonetheless, it was still our closest experience with it. It was the first time we didn't know what to say or how to act. I wanted to ask him at the funeral if he believed in ghosts, but my mom kept me quiet with long looks that told me she knew that what I was thinking was not a good idea. He didn't rebel against his mother or the school; he rebelled against the idea that he should become sullen and troubled because the world had snatched his father away. He stayed Evan, and after a while we grew used to the absence of his father's deep belly laughs. From what I heard in snatches of small conversations, Ryland was the only true rebel among us. He had rebelled against everyone he knew, and because of that he was one of us, because no one would have him back at home. Reese chose to let her reckless streak show through her breakups. She would become brokenhearted and start smoking under the pier, railing out loud against how stupid it all was with her lip snarled and the ocean beat against the pylons.

Hadley was the least rebellious. She had traded being wild for being manipulative. It was against our standards, but we didn't make her leave. We weren't that kind of group. There were no meetings and no expulsions. The rules didn't exist out loud so much as they grew organically with time. No one had declared that outsiders weren't welcome on the first day, but it was there in the back of all of our minds. We knew it and we respected it.

The moon hung like the eye of Cyclops over the mirror of the water, and in a way the reflection allowed the night to have a set of eyes. It was oddly comforting. We heard another shriek and laugh from down the beach and a drunk man singing by his RV, only reaching us in fragments. I saw Edie sit up, her face disoriented and her hair messed up from lying on Ryland's leg. By her own standard of thought, this must mean that Ryland liked her a lot since he let her sleep on him for an hour. There was no way to really know with Ryland since he was so chill all the time. We were also curious about the side of him that had turned half his family against him. Evan returned to where I was sitting, hunching over with his head between his knees and his breath working to find balance between thick gasps.

"I found my limit. I cannot surf all morning, swim out with you in the afternoon, and race Reese across the beach at night. Is this what old men feel like?" I nodded; I imagined it was how old men must feel just doing normal day-to-day stuff. "I should take it easier on my grandpa next time he visits." I laughed at his joke. His grandfather could still pass for forty and spent most of his vacations kayaking or surfing with Evan. If you didn't know their relationship they looked like any other father and son. I could barely remember Evan's father's face, but it was a lot like his. I imagined that when Evan fully matured into his looks it would hurt his mother at first until she could get used to it. Car accidents were so common that I never considered that every time they announced one over the radio or on the news his stomach clenched. He had told me that while we were lying side by side on his bed at the end of the first month together. We were at the "sharing all our thoughts" stage. His head had been down by my feet and mine by his calves. He said it the way someone would say "It's cold in here;" just words between us.

"What are you thinking about?" His voice was low as his arms pulled me against his chest.

"I was just thinking that you and your grandfather look so similar. It's been months since he and your grandma were here last. He made Edie and I giggle for two hours non stop during lunch. I miss his stories."

"He liked you guys. I told him I was crazy about Edie and that Edie wasn't crazy about anybody. He said I was crazy all right, because I didn't know I was crazy about you. He's funny like that, just says what he thinks. He thought Edie was hilarious, but said she looked sad." I frowned at his grandfather's assessment. Edie wasn't really a sad person. I thought back to the six of us at Gilly's amid greasy fish wrappers and empty tartar sauce bowls. I couldn't remember one moment when Edie could have been sad. I didn't want to be defensive, so I shrugged it off. It bothered me though, the way she had been studied unknowingly.

"I told him he was nuts. Edie is a million things, but I wouldn't use sad to sum it up. He squeezed my shoulder and said, 'Okay Evan.' It was weird." He looked at my face. He made me happy—a crazy, strange happy. I smiled up at him.

"Laney, do you want to take a walk?" Edie called out to me. I rested my head on Evan's collarbone, popping up to walk over to where she was standing, stretching her arms and twisting off her nap. Evan walked over to sit next to Ryland. As Edie and I wandered off down the sand, I wished I had brought my hoodie to the beach with me. I hadn't really planned on walking down by the water, my feet still bare because I preferred cold feet to shoes dense with sand.

"Why didn't he come?" I asked. It had to be the reason we were out here walking next to the water. We dropped our heads down any time someone walked past us. It was mostly couples.

"He said he wanted to, but his family decided to go out to that steakhouse by the side of the highway. The dinner went longer than he thought. I don't know though. I kept checking my messages and the time. I don't like feeling like that needy girl. I *am not* that needy girl. All that was missing was a 'Catch you later babe.' The whole situation is getting ridiculous. What do you think?" She stopped when she stepped on a broken shell.

"Do you like him? Like actually like him, or the idea that you don't have to search out cute new boys every time you want to make out with someone?" She sighed at my question, but she had asked me what I thought and I needed more to go on.

"You know I like him, but it does make my life easier knowing that I can focus on school and my friends during the year and avoid all the drama because I have a hot guy who looks for me every time we're on a break. It was weird tonight though, waiting and feeling disappointed." Her hair shadowed her face; I couldn't see what she was feeling.

"So maybe you should consider that whether you like it or not, you and Bryce are basically in a relationship for a total of three-ish months a year. It sounds like absolute madness, but if it's what you want you'll have to get used to the annoying little things that go with it. Disappointment is a part of that." I smiled at how naïve she seemed, at how oddly her heart worked. Despite her ideas of maturity and the future, she never grasped the concepts of being involved with someone for more than a few weeks.

"How would you know, Laney? Evan doesn't seem capable of disappointing you and it hasn't even been three months yet. Your heart could be in a thousand pieces by this time next year. You don't know."

"Of course I don't Edie, but you keep asking me to tell you what I think. Evan disappointed me for years. I was mindlessly infatuated with him since I was old enough to like boys. You don't think someone taking three years to understand that is disappointing?"

"True. I didn't think of it that way. I should try it—dating—but I don't know how to think about other people."

"Yes you do. You think of me all the time. It's like that. I don't even think about Evan as much as I do you, though. I mean, I'm out here freezing my ass off talking about a boy while my boyfriend cuddles by the fire with Ryland. That's what it's like. Sometimes they are the priority and sometimes they aren't. I'm sure you will be fine. Just try it, and if it sucks be grateful that you don't have to see him for most of the year after summer."

"You make Yoda sense." We laughed at the same time. Yoda sense was superior wisdom harvested from the heart of a Jedi. We had been goners the year my father sat us down and showed us the *Star Wars* trilogy (only the ones he thought counted). He bought enough junk and deli food to last a week, turning a blind eye to our candy consumption from our Christmas stockings. My mother had watched while she graded papers and prepped for the return to school. It was a memory locked in carbonite for both of us. Now that I thought about it, it was the only long-term commitment Edie had made as far as entertainment went.

"Seriously, we are walking way too far. If we keep going, we might even run into Nathan and Hadley," Edie noted. I made a face. I didn't care if they wanted to get back together or not, but I didn't need to see them getting back together in person.

"Please. They will be up there in the dark, being trashy." She wrinkled her nose in disgust. I wasn't about to judge her for judging them. We turned and she linked her arm through mine.

"How weird is it to think that one day, years from now, our kids will be doing this?"

"Pretty weird. I'm guessing we will be up in Gilly's drinking wine and pretending that having teenagers doesn't freak us out." She nodded in agreement.

"You know what the funniest part of the whole thing is, Laney?"

"What?"

"If you and Evan have kids, they will still be stuck in the back of the line in class." Her laughter swelled and crashed down across the sand like a wave. I laughed too.

I saw the outline of Evan walking toward us. I was proud that he hadn't let on that he hated me walking around the beach at night before now. He respected the relationship I would always be in; no one came between Edie and me, and nothing could but my secrets. There was another person walking with him that I didn't recognize.

"Is that Leland? No, too short. Who is that?" Edie asked. I shook my head because I had no idea.

"Edie, I took a vote while you were gone and now I would like my girlfriend back because we are all starving. The pizza wore off hours ago, guys, be fair." I smiled. Evan was such a dork, but he had made Edie's decision for her. Bryce looked the same if you ignored the casted arm, which I could not.

"Jesus, what happened to your arm?" I asked as we closed the distance between us.

"You know, skating." I shook my head like his answer was informative. It wasn't, but I smiled anyway. Evan raised his eyebrows at me and held his hand out.

"Ryland and Leland are putting out the fire. We already carried up the blankets and crap and threw it in the back of Leland's truck. We want food. Judging from Laney's horrendous breath earlier, you guys already ate tacos, so give me some food suggestions."

"What about that little Chinese buffet that has the gold lions guarding its door?" I asked. Edie and Evan both rolled their eyes at me. I sighed; so much for suggesting something.

"Do you guys not like Chinese food, or do you guys not like Laney?" We all looked to Bryce. He was grinning and trying to be casual about moving closer to Edie the longer we stood together.

"We love her, clearly, but on any day for any meal if you ask her what her first choice is, it's always some kind of Asian food." Edie said it like it was common knowledge, despite the fact that Bryce knew very little about any of us, Edie included.

"Well Edie, that's not entirely true. You see, Bryce, there is one thing that Laney loves more than anything else. We are all walking around in a state of permanent shock that she is the width of two fingers, because she can eat her weight in bacon. Not kidding. I saw her eat an entire package of bacon once for a snack." Evan tilted his head in my direction. Bryce laughed and held his hand up for a high five, which I returned because the word bacon should never be said aloud without being followed by some kind of excitement.

"So, why don't we go somewhere where everyone can have what they want? Do you guys have an IHOP or a Denny's or something?" I was starting to like Bryce more and more. I could see plates of bacon already, but unfortunately we didn't have either restaurant. The closest one was twenty minutes away. We did, however, have a diner that kept later hours in the summer.

"We should go to Shirley's," I volunteered. Evan and Edie looked at each other, then over at Bryce, who had no idea what we were talking about.

"Sounds good. Laney and I will go tell the group, and we'll see you there," Evan declared. Bryce was now shoulder to shoulder with Edie, swinging his hand back and forth and waiting for her to grab it. Her face was beaming as Evan and I turned away. I had traded Edie's arm for Evan's.

"How did you get him down here, and why?" I looked up at him, interested in the answer. He steered us toward the pier before looking down at me.

"I was sitting there alone, and I thought how horrible it was that you stole me from Edie, how her constantly stealing you must be the punishment for that crime." I hit him in the arm, trying to fight the laughter. "Anyway, I had all this time on my hands and saw that both you and Edie had forgotten your phones."

"Where is my phone now, Evan?" I felt like I knew where this was going.

"It's safe here in my pocket, so think about that after I tell you the rest, because you took off your LifeProof case a week ago. It wouldn't be smart to push me into the water. Yeah, not smiling now. After I updated your status, actually both of your statuses, I texted Bryce that since the night was almost over he should skate down and see Edie since it had been a while. He was more than happy to oblige." He hugged me against him suspiciously. This was an act of a guilty man asking for forgiveness before confessing the full extent of his crime.

"Evan, what did you put on my Facebook?" He was clever, he had always been clever, but he also never knew when he had gone too far.

"I just said that we were happy, two kids in love." My breath caught between my lungs and my mouth. Was he telling me he loved me in a joke, or just joking about loving me on my Facebook? I would rather it be the latter.

"I said that we were young, happy, and because of that we aren't scared for what the future holds for us…and the baby."

"Are you freaking kidding me, Evan? My grandmother has a Facebook and my mom is out of town and has probably seen that! Oh my god, why did I take off my LifeProof case? I hate you."

"Is now a bad time to tell you that your mom has called your phone about seven times as we've been walking down this beach?" iPhone be damned, I shoved him with everything I had in my tiny frame, but all he did was stumble.

"Good, right? Wait until Edie sees hers." I laughed and groaned in the same breath. It was good—it was horrible and messed up, but it was good.

"What will we name the baby? I don't want to have to decide alone or discuss it in letters from prison."

"Are you going to prison because you murdered me?" he asked while skirting away from my hands.

"Nope. I meant with my father. I'll write to him after he kills you, but I need to know what you wanted to name his grandchild before you die."

"I was thinking Albus or Draco." I pulled him to me this time. "I knew you would forgive me if I talked Potter to you." He inched closer, no longer worried that I would push him into the ocean. I giggled and held out my hand. I didn't want to call my mother back, but I would have too. I unlocked my phone to an influx of notifications.

"Hey, where is Edie's phone?"

"I gave it to Bryce. I can only get beat up by one girl at a time. You're strong for being so small. I think it's from all the swimming, because god knows you suck at team sports." He smiled at me while I scowled. I didn't suck at team sports, I just wasn't as athletically gifted as the rest of them. "Team sports are boring anyway. I mean, who actually likes the rush of the game and having people around you who are as good as family?" I knew his sarcastic voice when I heard it.

"Whatever. I'm calling my mom, so shut up or I'll put you on the phone with her. Don't forget, she likes to use your full name when she's mad, and she can lecture like the world is dependent on her doing it." He backed away from me with his hands in the air. The phone rang and rang without an answer. There was nothing more annoying than having a person call you, but only ten minutes later they don't answer when you call back. I ended the call and tried again. Just then the four-page text came in and I groaned into the sky.

Laney. Cute. Real cute. I found your Facebook post amusing. Do you want to guess what I don't find amusing?

Spending over twenty minutes on the phone with your grandmother who does not understand why you would ever joke about such a thing. I also find no amusement in calling you when I'm three hours away and you don't answer the phone. After seven calls I get no response. NO RESPONSE, LANEY. I am obviously aware that you're not expecting a love child with Evan because my responsible, honest daughter has not requested birth control. Do you need birth control? Never mind, don't answer that, at least not until I get home. Why are you not answering your phone? While I'm rambling, don't worry about your father and me. It's always rough when so much distance is involved, and time. Time is a killer. This sounds like a suicide note. Just send me a text or call when you get this, but if I don't hear the phone I love you and I TRUST you. Tell Evan it's cowardly to update your girlfriend's status and then avoid the consequences. I know it wasn't you because your grammar is impeccable. Love you, mom

I shot off a quick response:

I love you, mom. I was walking with Edie and everything is fine. We should discuss birth control when you get home—not because I'm having sex, but because I don't know when I will. Evan just said we could name our children Albus or Draco, so it could be happening sooner than we thought. Kidding. I'm not going to be a teen mom. Send Grandma my love. I know I just got my Christmas canceled. Lol. Evan sends his love. Where did you go anyway? Btw, we sound like the same person in a text message; I must be rubbing off on you.

I smiled to myself and tucked my phone into my pocket.

"Everything fine?" Evan pulled me back into him by the hips.

"She said you're a coward." His laugh was muffled at the back of my head.

"Coward. That's true enough. She can be scary." I nodded in agreement, the top of my head brushing his chin. His body was like standing next to the bonfire—he emitted heat from his poncho.

"Are we eating?" My stomach was hollowing out and soon I would collapse back into the earth. I would have shared the severity of the situation with him, but he would laugh at my dramatics.

"Yes! I thought I was going to eat Leland earlier. Nathan and Hadley came back and said they would see us later. I'm not surprised that they got back together, but if I were Nathan I would have taken a minute to ask myself if that was what I wanted." I twisted around and buried my head into his heat. I was freezing, and my feet were losing feeling from the cold that had swallowed up the idea of summer. We walked toward the stairs, and I saw the back of Reese moving toward the top, her arms heaped with damp, sandy blankets.

"Laney, wait. Let's wait five more minutes. They will still be up there." His face looked boyish in the moonlight. I paused but he didn't say or do a thing, his arms around my waist and the ocean at my back. I ignored the cold creeping into all the areas that weren't pressed against his chest.

"Okay." He let go and took my hand, pulling me toward the stairs.

"Wait. Where are my shoes?" I laughed and looked around, but I didn't see them anywhere. I saw the gold of my sandals that Edie had borrowed in the light, but no shoes.

"Maybe Reese grabbed them? I don't know." I moved the loose sand around with my foot but saw nothing.

"Yeah, maybe. Text her." He nodded and pulled out his phone. I wandered further down toward the pylons and the water. I tried to remember where I had taken them off and prayed they hadn't been washed away with the tide.

"Reese said she didn't see them, but she is asking the others. Did you take them off way down there? If you did, I think your shoes are gone by now. That sucks." His voice was growing more distant the closer I got to the water. I shivered when the water went over my feet, my toes still searching out anything that didn't feel like sand. I gave up and walked back to Evan.

"Here, take my shoes." He had already kicked off his checkerboard boat shoes that eclipsed my foot size by at least three. I stepped inside them and felt the leftover heat from his feet. I looked ridiculous. I lifted each foot carefully and flopped no matter what I did all the way to the stairs. By the third step I had nearly fallen backward.

"Never mind. Take them off and carry them until we get to the sidewalk, nerd, before you plummet to your death." I twisted around and looked at him.

"You know I'm only three steps up, right? I'm not clumsy."

"That's only true if you don't count your tendency to overshoot and your keen ability to slide or slam into things when you get close to them."

"You have a point." I took off his shoes and carried them up the rest of the way. Ryland and Reese were laying head to head on the palm tree planter. Leland was talking up some girls by the beach cruiser rental shack at the end of the parking lot.

"Must eat." I declared my intentions and stepped back into the shoes, preferring to drag them rather than attempt to take actual steps again.

"Where's Edie?" Reese was sitting up, her fingers caught in the tangles of her hair and impatience all over her face. Our parents always gave us food money on the first day, and then the rest of the summer we were on our own.

"She's coming. Let's go to Shirley's. Bacon! All the bacon." I threw my arms up like the god of bacon was above me.

"Yes! I want waffles!" Ryland was now on his feet, fueled by hunger and excitement. One side of his hair was pressed down while the other side went awry.

"Okay, Donkey. Let's go get waffles," Reese said with a grin. Just the promise of food made them happy.

"Leland! Food!" Evan shouted down the boardwalk. Leland turned and looked back like he was torn. He leaned in to the two girls again before he started walking our way. We assembled like a ragtag bunch of beach bums with a mission. My phone went off in my pocket. It was another text from my mom.

Drove into San Francisco. We'll be back Monday morning, and I will be calling you three times a day until then. This worries me. Did I make a bad decision in leaving my beautiful, brilliant child home alone? Remember, if you hear burglars, all your old toys from your tomboy phase are in the garage. Remember Macaulay Culkin. There was a reason I showed you eighties and nineties movies. *Home Alone* was a survival guide for children with negligent parents who leave their kid at home. Parents like me? I miss you already. Don't say 'gross' in your head. Feelings are fine and all humans have them, including you. Speaking of feelings, your father says 'DON'T HAVE SEX' and thinks our jokes are not in the least bit funny. Honestly, I still believe Dumbledore was too reckless with Harry's life to be up for consideration when naming my future grandchild. What about Luna? I love you. Call me from the house phone so I know you get home alright and what time you got there. This is killing me. I should just come home. Your father said no.

I had to bend over; I was laughing so hard I thought my stomach would rip open. I glanced up to everyone staring at me including Leland, whose brow was furrowed like he had caught me throwing up.

"It's fine. My mom is just so crazy." They nodded. They didn't understand though, not really. My relationship with her was rare.

"What are we waiting for?" Leland asked, looking around like we were the ones who had just walked up. He didn't even ask where we were going. He didn't care because he would eat anything. He wasn't even opposed to things like vegan food or insects. We moved together as a group, weaving against the current of freshly showered, sunburned adults moving in the direction of the bar at the corner. It was a throwback bar that looked like something out of one of my mom's old Patrick Swayze movies.

Shirley's was on a side street off the main thoroughfare. It looked out of place, like someone picked it up from somewhere in the middle of the United States and dropped it into a beach town. The neon sign was pink and mint green and the menus were printed on paper that had cats chasing balls of yarn across the top. It was busy, but not so busy we couldn't get in.

"Hey kids, just wait on the patio. Leland, I better not catch you on that table singing off-tune to the women walking up, do you understand?" Leland looked down, but his shaking shoulders gave away that he was laughing. He was an ass most of the time. Last time we had come here before finals he had sung Bruno Mars at the top of his lungs to a group of bachelorettes who had come up for the weekend. Mostly his antics worked though. Girls loved Leland.

I weaved in between the tables until I was as close to being wrapped around the outdoor heater as I could get. I had my hands up, giving worship to the heat and wishing I could do stable hand stands so my feet would be closer to the wavering flame ring at the top.

"Aren't your feet freezing?" I looked down to Evan's bare feet on the cement. I was colder just from looking, but he appeared to be completely fine.

"Not really. Do you want my poncho too?" He made a move to pull it over his head, but I shook my head at him.

"I don't think that Shirley will be okay with you ignoring another part of the 'no shoes, no shirt, no service' sign."

"That's probably true. What else are you doing tonight?" He moved back from the heat as if to prove his point about not being cold.

"Watching all the *Criminal Minds* I missed during finals. Nothing but murder and mayhem for this girl, at least until the sun comes up. My mom and dad are in San Francisco." He raised his eyebrows. I expected him to wriggle them like he usually did before he said something pervy, but instead his face was concerned.

"They're leaving you alone for two days?" His tone annoyed me, prickled the independent streak in me.

"Yeah, they are. So? I can take care of myself." I could feel my brow furrowing. His question was really irritating me. I loved his protectiveness when it applied to everyone but me. I didn't need protection or an additional parent.

"Come on, don't get mad. What do you expect me to say? I don't love the idea of you alone in your house, okay? I hate it. I don't mind if you think I'm a neanderthal." He moved in closer to me but I backed away.

"Seriously? I'm fine. Fine. I know how to lock doors and dial 9-1-1. How many break ins and murders happened last year? It was, like, two, and it was people who were personal to the crime. Stop being dramatic," I whispered through clenched teeth. His face didn't give me any sign of understanding.

"So have Edie spend the night. Have any of them spend the night." I shook my head no, both out of disbelief and to reject his suggestions.

"Are you kidding me? Why not?" His volume was elevating slightly. It took so much to get Evan upset that I should have been amused.

"Edie is grounded, like deep serious grounded, and Reese helps out with the rest of the R's. Should I ask Ryland or Leland?" His agitated expression shifted into no expression. His face was blank. That was what Evan did when he was angry.

"Maybe you should." He moved away from me, closer to where the little latch on the gate hung open to the sidewalk. For a minute I thought he would walk out of the patio and go home. He didn't, but from the way he fidgeted around I think he was at least considering it. He didn't get angry with me often. I knew how to fix angry Edie, but I didn't know what to do with this Evan. I wouldn't wish that upon anyone. So I chose to ignore him. He didn't even look up from his feet when Edie and Bryce came through the gate. Edie shot me a surprised look and a shoulder shrug that I reciprocated with my own. She leaned into Bryce, whispering into his ear before walking over to me.

"Why are America's sweethearts standing as far apart as possible without actually leaving?" I rolled my eyes at the 'sweethearts' part of her question. There wasn't a sweet feeling in my body, and my anger was growing at his inability to understand that I *could* and *would* be able to take care of myself.

"He's being a total NEANDERTHAL." I raised my voice on the last word to ensure it would carry across the patio to Evan scowling at the cracked cement.

"Okay, calm down Laney. You never get this mad at him. This is usually reserved for me." She grinned. We loved each other like sisters, but we also fought like sisters.

"Can I talk to you?" Evan's voice was next to a whisper. I looked over, shocked. When had he even moved?

"I'm talking to Edie." My dismissiveness was rude. Edie stared into my face in open surprise. She shook her head at me and walked toward Bryce. Traitor, thy name is Edie Callum.

"Stop glaring at her like she just grew a Hitler 'stache. I'm not sorry and you're not sorry. I want to at least walk you home. Let me walk you home after we eat." His angry face was faltering into a smile.

"I get your bacon," I declared.

"I'll even order French toast so you can eat half of it. Truce?" He was still smiling when he lowered his head to kiss me. His lips always tasted faintly of the ocean.

"Evan, party of seven," the waitress shouted from the open door. We went in single file and tried to be quiet. The table was tucked into the back corner and it was a circus act to fit all of us around it. My back was to a shelf of cat sculptures and a painting of a faded red barn in a sea of wheat. Evan was on one side of me and Edie on the other. Reese was merely a pile of messy black hair that had been tangled by the wind, resting on folded arms. Ryland and Bryce picked up their friendship from break as if they had never been apart, the bond of longboards and Xbox strong with those two. I wasn't sure who Bryce was dating—Edie or Ryland? The menus went around the table, and though we fought to keep a respectable noise level, the laughing couldn't be stopped. The waitress eventually came to our table. Her stiff walk and age-wrinkled face lit up with humor. She had known almost all of us since the days when we would order hot chocolate towering with whipped cream in chipped mugs. She was as familiar as childhood and we calmed when she talked. It was like having a grandmother who worked at a diner.

After the orders were given, water arrived for everyone except for Edie and me; we never let go of the hot chocolate. I still ate the whipped cream with my whole face, my nose and chin sticky with it. Edie giggled with her matching mustache and soul patch. It was possible that we would never really grow up, the Lost Girls until the end.

"You look ridiculous." I looked up to see Evan staring at the mess on my face. I wiped the whipped cream from my chin and spread it down his cheek with my index finger.

"So do you," I said, smiling before leaning over to kiss the sticky mess.

"You guys are so cute it's making me sick." We both ignored Edie, but our shaking shoulders probably gave us away.

My phone buzzed obnoxiously against the table. Evan flipped it over and raised an eyebrow at the six texts from Nathan.

"What is that about?" He pointed at the cluttered screen. There was something odd in his tone. He sounded vaguely…jealous. Of Nathan? Gross.

"Edie and I want to go to Venice for our birthdays. We want Nathan to drive like when we went to purple sand."

"Oh. Okay. Why didn't you tell me that? Never mind, ignore that question. I am so off tonight. Are you ever going to tell any of them that we know the name of the beach now?" He smiled and glanced around at the table.

"I'm not telling them. It's always just going to be purple sand." I laughed and sipped at the hot chocolate that burned my tongue. Our plates came and we ate, displaying our horrible teenage manners as we talked about an entire summer of plans with our mouths full.

"Are you ready?" Evan asked in a yawn. I nodded my head against his shoulder in agreement. I was so tired that my eyes periodically closed. I didn't want to think about the long walk home. His arm crossed in front of my face as he nudged Edie.

"E, we're leaving. How are you getting home?" Her answer reminded me of the way you hear someone telling you to wake up—sound without actual word distinction. The sun must have gone to my head. I let my body go through the motions as I got up and lazily waved goodbye with one hand. Evan firmly grasped the other. Where was the whipped cream sugar high I had been expecting? Perhaps it had been smothered to death in grease.

The cold outside the diner shocked me back to life as soon as we hit the sidewalk. It was so early in the summer that the nights still embraced me like winter. I needed it.

"Better?" Evan was pulling me along, laughing at my huge eyes and suddenly alert state.

"Maybe we swam too far out today." My skin felt tight with sunlight even now that it was dark.

"Yeah, maybe," he said. I struggled not to trip him as I leaned in while we walked in silence. If I was more of a girl and this was less like reality, I would make him carry me the half mile we had left.

"I texted your mom while you were eating. Please don't get mad that I went over your head." I pulled away from him the second the words 'don't get mad' left his lips. If he thought he was about to make me mad, then that was exactly what was about to happen. I put a foot between us and kept walking, waiting for him to finish.

"Anyway, I texted her and said that I was not leaving you home alone. I said I would sleep out on the deck in one of the old sleeping bags from your garage that Nathan and I found when we organized and cleaned it out last year. I meant it. Whether you want me to be there or not, I am not leaving that house."

"And she said what back, exactly?"

"She said that chivalry was not dead after all, but if one inch of my flesh touched your bed or any other surface of the house, that was all your father would leave of me." I couldn't stop the laugh. That was probably the exact wording of her reply. It was a confusing feeling to find a situation so funny and so completely agitating at the same time. I didn't want him going over my head. I wasn't looking for a knight in shining armor, horseless and curled up on the deck loungers. I wanted a bath with nothing but hot water. I liked the idea of my big empty house having no one in it but me.

"I don't want you to stay. I don't want you sleeping outside. Are you totally crazy? It's not warm whatsoever." I could hear how flat my tone was, but I didn't want him to spend an entire night huddled under some faded old sleeping bag that I hadn't used since our one and only camping trip a few years back.

"I'm not. She also said I should sleep on the couch and that she trusted us. She mentioned that she was telling your dad what was up so I won't be surprised if I wake up at four a.m. to him spooning me on the couch. They might end up driving back tonight." He reached his hand out for mine, but I chose my pockets over a romantic walk with my neanderthal boyfriend.

"So you're saying that your insistence on staying with me because you don't like the idea of me staying alone might now have ruined my parents' weekend away? The same parents who seemed on the verge of divorce only this morning? My mom doesn't need to trust us. I have zero interest in taking off my clothes and throwing my virginity away on someone who doesn't seem to listen to a word I say. I would have been fine, Evan. I like the idea of you sleeping on the deck more and more." I glared in his direction, the streetlight illuminating my frustration.

"I didn't really think of it that way, Laney. I just didn't want you here by yourself. I'll text your mom back. Okay? Ceasefire? I haven't seen you this mad in so long I forgot what it was like."

"Text her back then." I wasn't bending. I had seen Evan sway people to his side with the white flag approach. He pulled his phone out and texted my mom. The tightness eased in my chest with the typewriter sound of the phone keys. It was done. He would go home, my parents could stay, and I was going to be alone. I liked winning a fight for once, because with Edie there never seemed to be a winner.

I moved back into him under the streetlight, a pale excuse for a sun trapped in milk glass. I smelled the collar of his poncho. Sand. I looked up and kissed the bottom of his chin where he still had the smallest scar from a skateboarding fall in seventh grade. I could feel the tiny indention with my lips and smiled against it with the memory of Evan holding a handful of blood under his chin and watching to see if any of the girls by the pier had seen him. He hadn't been embarrassed; he had been proud.

"Why do you always kiss that stupid scar?"

"No idea. I just like it. I remember you getting it. Those three girls gasping and panicking, you bloody and arrogant. I like to kiss that scar because you're mine." I pulled away and kept walking. We would never make it all the way home acting like this.

"You are what my grandpa calls an odd bird, Laney." He said it with a smile. I always assumed it to be an insult.

"Your grandfather called me an odd bird?"

"No, but he did tell me that it's always best to end up with one. They are usually the most interesting and the hardest to keep. He does that a lot, passes out advice because I am too young for cigars." He pulled me back into his chest.

"Maybe I would rather be a flamingo, or a parrot."

"Gross. Flamingos make me think of trailer parks and parrots are obnoxiously repetitive. You are neither of those."

"Fine. I want to be a bear." He laughed in surprise at my statement and I smiled at him.

"Okay, then you can be a bear." I growled in response and burrowed into his side. We walked like that the rest of the way, tripping and stumbling like a couple of drunks. I hip-checked the recycling can on the way up the drive and he stepped on the succulents.

"I have to come in for a minute. Don't freak out. I need to get my extra board out of the garage," Evan said. I responded with a few nods while I worked at unlocking the door.

He leaned down once we were both inside and kissed my forehead.

"I'm going to go out the garage. Lock up everything after I leave. I mean it Laney. I gave in, so now you have to give me this."

"Okay. Don't be so dramatic." I didn't even look back because exhaustion was pulling me up the stairs and past the bath I thought I would take. I fell into my hammock, pulling the blanket over half of my body and holding still until the sway settled.

I sat up, the hammock almost overturning. My room was awash in light and my curtains were still open from the morning. I looked for the alarm clock but everything was color-blurred and confusing. I climbed clumsily and ungracefully from the hammock and stumbled down the hall. I couldn't comprehend why I was up. I wasn't hungry, thirsty, or scared. I was just following my body down the stairs. I stopped in the living room and looked around. Everything looked the same as it did when I had come home. It was cold though, so cold that I felt it everywhere in my body. I rubbed the sleep from my eyes, walked around the couch, and screamed.

"Why are you on my couch? Why are you in my house, Evan? You scared the hell out of me!" I could feel my heart in every inch of my body; the pounding was even in my fingertips. He looked up at me, sleep pulling the corners of his mouth just enough to be smiling.

"Hey." Clearly my anger wasn't conveying itself strong enough; clearly he didn't understand how scared I had been because he was already back to sleep.

"Wake up, Evan Wallace, and get out of my house!" He startled back awake and sat up looking weary.

"Calm down. I skated halfway home and realized I'd left my phone on the dryer when I was getting my board. I came all the way back and couldn't bring myself to leave you alone a second time. Your spare house key was where it's been since we were in third grade." His hand was rubbing his eyes like he was trying to sink them further back into his head. I didn't know what to say or how to feel. Anger was still in the lead, but there was something else hidden in my thoughts that felt like relief.

"Come here. Stop being mad and just lay down. I am so tired, Laney. Could you throw me out and give me the silent treatment in the morning?" I walked around the couch still holding my hoodie tight. My mom's old blanket was in a pile next to his feet. I didn't want to give in. I had seen couples bend and break to each other, setting patterns that didn't shift until it was into a separation.

"Come on Laney. I'm sorry. I wasn't lying last night—I was sorry then too. Now I'm even more sorry. Lay down. It's freezing in here." His face was soft in the light from the kitchen. I sat next to him, drawing my knees up to my chin while my body slid over toward his.

"You leave in the morning," I whispered.

"I know. I won't even come back for the rest of the weekend." He reached down and pulled the blanket over us.

"No need to go crazy." I smiled up at him and he laughed as he ran his fingers through my hair. He didn't feel cold, he felt like the sun. I unbent my knees and turned into him as he slid down the couch. His sternum wasn't the most amazing pillow, but at least he was warm.

～〜〜

I stirred awake slowly, not eager to follow through on being angry with Evan. I let the light sink into my skin and waited with my eyes closed. When I breathed in my eyes shot open as I realized that the couch was far more accommodating a pillow than Evan's chest. He was gone. I groaned into the cushion. The room had warmed enough for me to have thrown the blanket to the floor sometime in the early morning. I smiled against the fabric; a fire was crackling in the wood stove my father had purchased the first year the house had actually become my parents'. I twisted my body around and stared at the vaulted wood ceiling. When I was little the ceiling reminded me of a church, and all my prayers were said to the place where the beams met. I needed to shower, eat, and call my mom, but all I wanted to do was send thanks to the beams for stubborn boys like Evan.

I jumped at the sound of a knock on the door. I looked down, but boxer shorts and a long sleeve thermal was as good as it was getting for whoever was on the other side. I bounded up and opened it to Edie's tear-stained face.

"Aren't you grounded?" It probably wasn't what I should have led with, but she walked past me anyway and didn't stop until she reached the glass door to the deck.

"Are you coming?" She wiped at her eyes and smiled brokenly. Edie usually never cried from anything but anger.

"Yeah, of course, duh." I grabbed the threadbare horse blanket from the floor and followed her into the early morning mist.

She curled herself like a cat on the cabana couch, her wet cheeks and bloodshot eyes hidden behind the hair that had fallen over her face. I stretched out beside her.

"What's going on?" I relaxed my voice into a whisper even though my brain was shouting inside my head.

"I haven't been home. Don't yell yet. Wait so you can yell at me for everything after I'm done." She looked up at me, waiting for my compliance. I nodded and kept my face blank.

"Bryce. The tears are for the damn tourist. I am crying over freaking Bryce. I called my mom and asked her if I could stay with you last night since your mom was gone and you were being such a stubborn ass about being alone." She paused with her hand up; she wasn't ready for me to talk. I was. She used me in a lie with Big Edie, and right now all I could think about was how hard she would be crying when I shoved her off the deck.

"I just walked around with Bryce until two a.m. He doesn't have a curfew on vacation. I mean, how weird is that? All his rules are suspended when they aren't home. Some kind of stupid 'what happens in Vegas stays in Vegas' clause. I don't even get it." I rolled my eyes at her tear-soaked rambling. "I did it…with Bryce. I had sex with Bryce and it was cold and awkward and I can't ever get that back Laney. I can never get it back. Who does that? We made out on the beach and it just…" Her sobs wrecked her face, the waterproof mascara not capable of covering a regret this big. I wanted to hold her shaking shoulders, but I was numb with shock.

"Oh god, Laney. I can't rewind and I can't take it away. I feel empty. Why doesn't anyone tell you that you will feel like a part of you has been scooped out and tossed aside? How could I do that?" I didn't know how to comfort Edie, but I let her drop her face onto my lap.

"He tried so hard to make me stop crying, but I can't. I don't know how to make it stop Laney." She really thought I could yell at her after this, when she was a sobbing mess? I wiped her face with my sleeve, snot and all.

"It will be alright Edie." It was weak and I knew it. I rocked back and forth as she cried her voice into hoarseness. Her throat and heart were raw without an end in sight.

"You will bounce back from this Edie. You will. You bounce back from everything. Where is Bryce now?" She coughed and shook, letting my question linger between us.

"I told him to go. I screamed at him to leave me in the street and go. It's not his fault, but I couldn't stop crying. I was scaring the shit out of him and all I could think about was how there is a whole summer ahead of me where I will have to see his face around town and think, 'Why? Why did I choose him? Would I still feel this way if it had been someone else?' It's the what ifs and the whys that are ripping my brain to shreds. You don't understand, Laney. You've been in love with Evan since you would write it in pink crayon on white paper doilies during the Valentine's party at school. You won't ever have to feel this empty. I don't know how to make it stop… All the parts of me are screaming, 'Why him?' He did nothing wrong though; he was so confused. The whole situation was good, then awkward, and then this." I watched Edie cry until her body went limp with exhaustion and the tears dried on her cheeks. I didn't know how to help her except for this—letting her sleep on my legs without judgment for her choices. She was the other half of me, and I would lie to cover for her. I would wipe her snot on my sleeves because it was all I knew, all I wanted to know.

She slept for hours and I stayed where I was, my legs dead from not moving. I watched her shake and cry in her sleep until she calmed back down. When she sat up she looked so blank that I thought I would cry.

"You can yell at me now." Her voice was devoid of emotion. I glared at her while I punched at all the places in my legs from the thighs down that I couldn't feel.

"Yell at me, Laney. Tell what an idiot I am. Please."

"No. You've been crying for hours and I'm not that messed up. You made a mistake…or maybe not. Maybe it was just one weird instance and it will get better with time."

"No, I will always regret this. I didn't think it was important. I really thought it was just sex, but its not. What do I do about Bryce? I was awful to him. It wasn't his first time or anything, but I was a pool of tears the second he was done. He was freaking out. How could I do that to him?" I shrugged. I didn't know what words to say or how to say them.

"He'll get over it Edie, and so will you. How could you know it was going to feel like that? You had never even gotten close to it before. God, I want to help you but I sound so stupid." She laughed. If I could keep making her laugh. I could fix her. Even in my mind I knew that it was a naïve idea, but I had to try.

"Did you get sand in weird places?" It was a long shot. She laughed so hard that she started crying again.

"So many places that I won't even horrify you with the details." She smiled and shoved my shoulder. It wasn't better, but it was a start. She had cracks in her now that my awful jokes couldn't fill.

∿∿∿

Edie stared at me from across the room, trying to hold back a laugh. I felt like a moron in my uniform even though it was just shorts and a t-shirt.

"Don't laugh," I chastised her.

"I didn't even make a sound."

"You want to….admit it."

"I can't, because in three more weeks that same outfit will be mine. I will say, though, that you have the absolute worst luck in the shirt slogan you were given." She didn't laugh but her smile was just as insulting. I had unfortunately grabbed the only small shirt out of the stack that happened to say, "Do you smell something fishy?" next to a cartoon fish and chips basket.

"I know. What girl wants to wear a shirt that asks people if they smell something fishy? Zero girls, E. Zero. I don't want to go. I am so nervous, like 'throw up food I didn't even have an appetite to eat' nervous." My stomach twisted in time with my words. I wanted to sit down with my head between my knees before I passed out.

"Is Evan walking you to work?" Her voice came from behind a fat textbook.

"No. I told my mom she could do it. She seems to think she is driving me to a rite of passage. In a way I guess she is. I'm thrilled to be earning money, though. I should get at least one full check before we leave for Venice, and my mom is giving me my birthday present in the form of cash this year for the trip. She said I would want to buy stuff, but not to buy weed or get a tattoo if I can help it." Edie laughed.

"Your mom kills me. I asked for money too, but you know how Big Edie is. I have to wait until our family dinner to find out if that's what I'm actually getting. She doesn't want to ruin the surprise."

"Knowing her and your dad, you will probably get more money than you need. So umm…is Bryce going to come?" The book didn't move and she didn't answer as I stood there feeling like an idiot. I stared at some chemical structure done in teals and yellows on the cover of her book. I shouldn't have asked.

"Well yeah, I mean we're together now." Her voice was strained and she remained hidden. I bit the side of my lip, torn between wanting to push and wanting to leave it alone.

"Just ask," she said. She couldn't see my face, but she knew anyway.

"Did you talk to him about that night?" My voice cracked even though I tried to keep it even. I had never seen her cry like that. It wasn't just the one day, but three days total. He called and he texted so much that I wanted to answer him myself. She stopped talking about anything that had to do with it or with him. I really wasn't sure why they were together now.

"Of course I did. He said it was cool, and that he didn't know it was my first time or it wouldn't have happened like it did. It was never his fault Laney; it was mine. The whole thing was my idea, my mistake, and it was my responsibility to fix it. He asked if it was cool that we only see each other now. I told him that he wasn't obligated to be my boyfriend because he took my V card, but he chose to stick around I guess." There was a sound that was so off in her voice, but I knew that if I pushed any harder she wouldn't say another word. I never had to push her for information but now I did, as if my knowledge of that night divided us somehow. If I could have taken back knowing in exchange for the effortless connection we had before, I would. It was a selfish thought. I wasn't above being selfish.

"So Evan said he would definitely do our senior photos in Venice. He's packing up all the equipment he has. I mean, what goes well with graffiti? A white dress or something?" I prodded the conversation along slowly.

"Don't do that, Laney." Her tone was withdrawn, like her voice was sinking into a place I couldn't see, didn't even want to see.

"Do what?"

"Make pointless conversation because you don't really know how to talk to me now, like you are walking on eggshells. I hate that. I hate that you have been talking to me that way since I told you about that night. You're supposed to be my person, like those two chicks on that hospital show." Her voice had sunk into misdirected resentment. Bullshit resentment. I caught my bottom lip between my teeth and bit down to stop the wave of words from crashing into her book and washing over her face. It was so easy to be horrible with a little barrier between us.

"Okay Edie, whatever. You screwed up, not me. I'm going to work." I didn't so much as glance at her, and I didn't regret it for a moment. I grabbed my duct tape wallet that had been warped in the washer and shoved it in my back pocket before walking over to where my mom was still rinsing off her car.

"You ready?" She asked as she looked up, the sunlight catching in her hair. She smiled; this was a big moment for her.

"I guess. As ready as you can be to deal with crowds of strangers and their unruly children." I smirked, pulling on my sunglasses so I wouldn't be blind on my first day of work.

"You'd be surprised at how fast you'll get used to it. Hell, you may even miss some of those faces come the end of summer. If you do a good job, Sander might just keep you on for the rest of the year." The groan that was happening internally was luckily not audible. The idea of working at Gilly's long term did not appeal to any part of me. Honestly, it was so unappealing that I vowed to consider what Evan had said about going to a university. "Wait, isn't Edie coming?" She glanced toward the house and squinted against the sun.

"No."

"Really?"

"Just no, mom. Okay?" Her brow furrowed in confusion as I walked through the puddles of water and got in the car. I ignored the impulse to slam the door. Was this pre-separation anxiety I was having with Edie? Was this mild emotion compared to what would roll over me if she left for college and I stayed behind? The twist in my stomach deepened at the thought of it. My mom shut off the hose and wound it up before wiping her hands on her pants and glancing one more time at the door. Edie wasn't there. Even I had glanced up one last time to see if she had decided to drive with us at the last minute, but the door was still slightly ajar as I'd left it.

We were silent the entire drive, and guilt curled into the hole my stomach had twisted into. The argument with Edie was ruining this moment for my mother, and for me as well.

"Can you believe that I have to wear this shirt?" She glanced over at the baby blue t-shirt that said 'Gilly's Fish Bowl' on the front.

My mom smiled as she looked at me in the rearview mirror. "Am I picking you up from work at eight?" She switched on her blinker and worked the car into the lane that crawled slowly toward Main.

"I don't think so. Evan is going to buy me fro yo and walk me home afterward. That's cool, right?"

"That's fine. Thanks for letting me drive you, though. I can't believe I'm doing it at all. Seventeen…you will be seventeen in just a few days. God, where did all the time go?" I stared out the window at people who were walking faster than our car could move in traffic. I wanted to know where all the time had gone too.

"Don't look so eager to grow up or anything Laney. It's going to be fine, this day and the next. All the plans for your future, college, and life are waiting for you, but this summer you're still just my kid. Jesus, I sound like a Billy Joel song." Her expression turned to the grimace she made whenever she realized she did actually sound like a mom.

"Who's Billy Joel?" My question was met with a glare and pursed lips. I laughed. Of course I knew who Billy Joel was; she had been listening to him since I was in the womb. I had no choice.

"I'm going to ignore that. Next thing I know you will be asking me who Paul McCartney is. The horrors of growing old, my child." I laughed so hard that I hit my head on the window.

"Duh. I know who The Beatles are, but do you know who Young the Giant is? How about Alabama Shakes? No. That is the horror of growing old mom—losing your interest in music that isn't already familiar."

"Am I really being lectured by the girl who has two crates of albums next to her dresser, not one of them printed after 1989?" I looked at the ceiling. She had a point.

"Whatever. I listen to Taylor Swift *and* The Doors. I'm a well-rounded music lover. You have no excuse to ignore the current music scene. It's not half bad if you find the right stuff."

"Hey, I listen to Kanye and Bruno Mars." I smiled at her defensive frown. She did listen to a lot of Kanye, but I couldn't decide if that was a good thing or not.

"Bruno Mars doesn't count, and you hate Kanye," I said.

"Why doesn't he count? He's good; you know he's really good. I don't hate Kanye, I just hate every single word that comes out of his mouth when he's not performing," she countered.

"He doesn't count because you can't walk into any store and not hear a Bruno Mars song. Oversaturation isn't a good argument when we are talking about exploring new music."

"Oversaturation, huh? I'm going to let you have this one because we're here, but you're welcome for keeping you distracted and worked up. I didn't want you to throw up in my car because you were so nervous." I spun in the seat and hugged her. She was clever and annoying, but it worked.

"Thanks. See you tonight. I'll be home by ten." I undid the seatbelt, my nerves tingling. I didn't know why I was so scared. I had been coming here to eat since I was an obnoxious kid with too much hair and a pile of broken crayons beneath my highchair. I had known Sander since he began working here while he went to the community college. It was pure madness to be letting a summer job get to me. I turned and went through the doors.

"Laney, over here." I glanced around and caught Sander in my peripheral vision, his lanky body not quite filling the swinging door to the kitchen. Everything was the same in the restaurant, but now I was different. I was expected to do well here. I moved through the main room, past the empty tables where I had eaten meals with my family and occasionally my friends. I couldn't remember if we had been neat the last time we ate here, or if Sander would remember. God, I hoped we hadn't been like we were at Sailor Pizza. I pushed open the door and was impressed with the cleanliness of the kitchen. The prep tables mirrored the surrounding room. Sweat prickled along my hairline as I followed behind Sander. His shirt was not as unfortunate as my own. The back contained the original sign from when Gilly's had been established in the seventies by his great grandfather.

He sat behind the plain desk in his office, the walls holding his degree and the faded accomplishments of a high school competitive swimmer. The décor was dated. Old lighthouse prints and the bell and rope pull from the days when my mother had been the one seated on this side of the desk. Sander had only been a kid then, and these same walls had borne his accomplishments in finger paint

"So today is the beginning of your training. I appreciate that your uniform and hair are to code. I will have you shadow Pavel this week and Cass next week. This will be the time for you to take in as much as possible. You have a chance at doing very well here, and if you do then I can't see why we wouldn't keep you on until you leave for school. Bet you never imagined old Sander being so professional, huh?" I smiled but wasn't sure how to respond. I wanted to point out that he was hardly old, and that I liked the Sander that had piled extra cherries into my Shirley Temples. The soda looked more like a lava lamp than something a person would drink. "Okay, well let me call Pavel in here." He picked up the handset and murmured into it, watching me as I looked back at him.

The day felt surreal as I followed Pavel, and slipped back to reality as it came to a close. I wasn't sure if I had learned more about being a bus girl and waitress from Pavel or the finest level of wit I had ever beheld. It was the kind of sarcasm that goes undetected but feels good to pass from one table to another. At the end of the night I watched Pavel's man bun bobbing around while he wiped up tartar sauce and scrubbed the stickiness of spilled soda from the tables. I had been so intently watching him dance that Evan's hand on my arm elicited a shout.

"I said your name three times. You didn't hear me?" I exhaled at his question, my heartbeat drumming in my ears. He looked past my shoulder to Pavel, watching the bob transform into an entirely different form of dancing as the music shifted from pop to Deadmau5. I was mesmerized. I usually found men with long hair gross, but his was almost pure Leto. I looked back to Evan to see his nostrils flare and his eyes narrow. He was jealous. He was sizing up Pavel, who had at least five years on me, and found him to be a threat. I bit my bottom lip to hold back the smile I could feel coming.

"Hey, you ready? I want my fro yo." He glanced past me before nodding. We didn't speak as we clasped our hands together, our thoughts separate.

"Well, he's attractive." Evan's casual observation caught me off guard. He was so calm, but I couldn't take it this time. I laughed so hard I had to stop walking. My sides ached and I forgot that I stunk of fried foods and the chemicals in the cleaning supplies. I forgot that we weren't alone on the street and saw people startle at the sound of my loud laughter.

"Yeah, he is." There was no point in lying to him, not when I could feel my heartbeat in the hand he was holding.

"He kind of looks like that guy you and Edie go all girly over. What's his name? You watch that show he was on together, the one on Netflix. He's in that band…" I watched him try and puzzle it out with the answer on my tongue. I liked to watch him struggle to figure things out. It wasn't that often that something eluded him this long.

"Jared Leto. He is the singer of Thirty Seconds to Mars. My mom used to watch his show, *My So-Called Life*, in college and showed it to us. He does look like that." I smiled mischievously. I was letting myself watch him be miserable for a fraction of the time I had spent mooning over him in unrequited hell while he had liked Edie all those years. His eyes shot down to his feet and his nostrils flared again. That was all I wanted, just a few seconds to feel like we were equals.

"Pavel is old though, and I don't want to hold his hand and laugh at his jealous face. I just want to laugh at you." His hand tightened in mine for a second.

"Nice, Laney. I feel privileged to be the guy you laugh at. You smell, by the way." His pace quickened as he weaved us through the spaces between people that were only really big enough for one. He was walking so quickly now that I didn't even have time to be sarcastic. He was right—I did smell. He finally stopped in front of the long glass windows of the frozen yogurt shop. The inside looked like a tween girl's spaceship with sharp silver angles and bubbled designs in pink and yellow. The fluorescents made my eyes feel as though they had been pulled out and thrust back into my head after hours in a low-lit dining room, the polar opposite of this shop.

"Are you going fatty or thin?" He pointed to indicate the two bowl sizes.

"Thin. I went fatty earlier at work. Free food is the best food." He grinned at my answer and grabbed two of the small bowls, also pink and yellow.

"So, I saw Edie down on the pier today. She was crying. Do you know what's going on with her?" he asked as we waited behind a woman with a thousand kids. I stared into the pink plastic, hoping for answers to surface.

"I don't know. She was crying, like angry crying, or just crying?" He looked at me with his forehead creased, like I suddenly spoke another language.

"Crying like the kind with tears... I don't know. She dried them up when she saw me and said she would catch up with me later. So I doubt it was angry crying; no one can stop Edie from saying what's on her mind when she is angry. Sad, I think. She looked really sad and didn't hear me walk up. That's all I got, sorry." He turned around to stare down the long line of choices. I ate the same thing every time. He was a scientist of frozen yogurt, and I had taste-tested a few of his experiments gone awry. Tonight it looked like he was going down the mad scientist route. I filled my own bowl halfway with tart yogurt and covered it in fruit. I waited impatiently for him to finish so we could go back outside.

"Hey, don't get all crazy. She was probably just having a crap day," I mused. He set down the bowls on the scale and slid a twenty across the countertop while I tried to understand where the Edie I had spent all my time with was, the girl with the loud laughs and flashes of vanity that colored her like permanent summer. I followed behind Evan while the yogurt melted into purple and red stains. He kept walking until he reached the mouth of the pier, the wind caught in the trembling wood. He sat down on the bench and took a hesitant bite of his concoction.

"I have done it again. I have created perfection…taste and be amazed." His face was a moonbeam as he extended his spoon out to me, but I wrinkled my nose at the green mound bloodied in blackberry juice. "Come on. It's just pistachio, vanilla, graham cracker dust, and blackberries. You love some of that." I still shook my head, stirring mine but not eating it.

He stood up, his bowl dangling haphazardly from his hand. "Come on. Let's walk to her house and bang down her door. You won't really be here until you find out what's wrong." I followed him up the street, thanking the universe for him. I mostly drank my fro yo from the bowl and spit the blackberries I no longer had a taste for onto the sidewalk. Evan shook his head at my backward manners.

"How was work? You know, besides being with Pavel." The sound of the people littering the streets waned with the curve out of Main Street.

"Not much to say, I worked with Pavel all day and I will for the rest of the week. I shadow someone else next week. It's cool I guess, just weird to not be a customer anymore. I had to serve that girl who got valedictorian last year as well as her parents. She was chattering away about how she couldn't believe how simple it was to transition to living on a campus and her mom was kind of vacant. She stared off into nothingness until I set her broiled halibut down, then she looked up and blinked a few times before she began eating. No one even seemed to notice that she was just absent from the whole meal. I wanted to hug her or wake her up. I mean, how long have they not noticed that?" He was staring at me, but it felt more like staring through me. "What?" I asked. He had completely stopped walking.

"Just stand here with me for a moment." He pulled me closer until we were pressed together.

"I'm lost. What's going on?" I asked, my voice muffled in his shirt.

"Nothing. Your goodness is intimidating sometimes, that's all. You're an odd bird." His arm pulled tighter before he let me go. He bent to pick up the bowl he had dropped. I didn't know what to say. My cheeks flushed with heat.

"I'm not that good. I can be a brat, and often." He shook his head at my statement.

"Your awfulness never exceeds your goodness. Your sadness is never greater than your happiness. It's unusual in adults and almost unheard of in teenagers. God, Laney. I stop in the middle of my day when I'm skating or just laying in the dark trying to sleep and wish that you were less amazing. This is the last summer of Evan and Laney without distance between us. I know I said I accepted you staying here if that's what you wanted, but I didn't think it would already hurt to consider leaving you behind. It does." I felt the weight of his words on me, the fact that I didn't think anyone was as concerned about next year as much as Edie and I were. I had no idea what to say back to him. I decided not to speak; instead, I hugged his chest with all of me and then punched him before walking away.

"I'm not even going to ask." His words and laughter trailed a few feet behind me. Eventually he caught up and we walked the rest of the way in silence. I knocked on Edie's door. I probably should have cared that it was after nine, but that had never really stopped me before. I just wasn't sure which face would be on the other side. When the door opened it was Edie's. She looked feverish and tired—her flu face.

"You okay, E?" She didn't answer me; instead she shifted her glare to Evan.

"So you told her… whatever." Her lips pinched together and her head tilted to the side. She shut the door behind her, pulling her long cardigan tighter around her. She was uncomfortable and obviously annoyed with Evan.

"I cried, okay? I cried my damn face off at the end of the pier because I thought that no one would notice. There were just some fishermen and they don't care about anything. You could have not said anything Evan. You didn't have to get her all maternal on me." She stopped when she saw my expression slide from concern to irritation. She was always doing that, always getting mad at me for getting "maternal" on her. I hated when she said it.

"Are you okay now? Do you want me to crash here tonight…with you?" I didn't know if I meant it, what I was offering. I hated to see her this way, all the colors in her fading.

"Yeah. Stay. Thanks, Evan. God…I'm sorry. I'm sorry for being like that to you today. I cannot believe the things I said and I'm sorry I shouted." I spun my head in his direction. What was she talking about? His eyes were on her, drilling holes through her.

"I'm going to call my mom and then I'll come up to your room." I pulled the phone from my back pocket. Edie hugged me to her, but I returned the embrace half-heartedly. My mind was not on this hug. The door closed quietly behind her and left Evan and I caught in unspoken tension. He walked away and sat down on the uneven cement curb. I sat beside him and waited for him to tell me the rest.

"I took her by surprise when I saw her. I startled her and she screamed at me to back off. I let it go because I figured she was crying already."

"What else?"

"She asked why she had to be so stupid, that she made terrible decisions and let the ones that made sense pass her by. She said she could have been like you but she was just totally blind. That was it. She turned around and I left. I didn't know what she meant or what to say, so I went back to looking for Ryland. We were meeting up to go to that skate museum. That's why I asked you if anything had been up with her. I didn't think she wanted me going on and on about how she acted kind of psycho out there today." I leaned my head on his shoulder. I wanted to tell him what this was all about but I didn't. He lowered down to kiss me on the forehead.

"What time do you have to be at work tomorrow?"

"So much earlier than today."

"What are you going to do about clothes?"

"I can just wash these tonight and borrow some pajamas from Edie. God, how weird is it that we are talking about my work schedule?" I laughed and looked down the street. Change had happened and I wasn't dying. Perhaps I should be thinking more about going away for school and shoving myself out of my comfort zone.

"Well, I will be there when you get off okay?"

"Okay." I tilted my head up to kiss him.

"What is that?" I asked. His kiss left my lips coated with something.

He laughed and rubbed his thumb across his mouth.

"That is Cherry Pepsi ChapStick. Shut up. It was the only one I could find and my lips were chapping." He took the blue and red ChapStick from his pocket and smeared it sloppily on my lips. When he kissed me again our lips slid clumsily and the kiss was ruined by my hard laughter. He got up and dragged my half-limp body up. I wiped the excess ChapStick from my lips. It did taste like Cherry Pepsi.

"Bye." I kissed the scar on his chin before running up the driveway and going in without looking back. It was nights like tonight that made me want to lie like Edie had and spend the night wandering the beaches with Evan.

"Hello, hon. She's upstairs. Are you hungry? Want me to throw those clothes in the wash?" I stopped mid-step and saw Big Edie coming out of the kitchen.

"I'm not hungry. I pretty much ate all day. Let me run up and borrow something of Edie's and then I will throw these in the washer if you're starting a load." She started to respond but stopped. Her hesitation was unusual. I had never met a woman who knew exactly what she wanted to say more than Big Edie. I waited, unsure if she would say what she had been thinking or not.

"Is she okay? She's not really been herself lately. She suffered through the last of her grounding in silence and didn't try and debate her way out of the house. I don't get it." I shrugged in response. I could feel the lies setting the lines of my face to quizzical. The pretense that I knew nothing was expressed in my nonchalant response.

"Okay, well just bring down your uniform after you get changed. No rush. I have a good book that's twisting my brain into a pretzel, so I'll be up for a while." She tapped her Kindle against her temple.

"What are you reading?" I couldn't help it. Edie needed me, but curiosity won out.

"It's called *Gone Girl,* but I don't think you should read it, and if you do, don't take notes. Most importantly, this must never be treated as the guidebook that it is." She winked and went back to the couch. I didn't have a clue where Edie's dad was, but I went up the stairs two at a time. I could smell the multitudes of fish on me; the odor must have been what prompted Big Edie to want to wash my clothes. Edie's door was closed but I could hear music from this side. I groaned as I opened the door. Her room was dark except for her phone illuminated on the dock and the strings of white twinkle lights she had hung across the ceiling.

"No more Katy Perry, E. No more." I grinned, walking to the dock and stopping "The One That Got Away" from playing one more time.

"Ugh. Laney. That will never be me. I will never have a person that got away because I throw everyone away before they can go. I'm sorry about saying those things to Evan. I feel like my head is all over the place and I don't know how to feel better. I broke up with Bryce and then got back together with him three hours later. I was jealous of you and Evan. I didn't mean it, you know. Saying that I shouldn't have passed him up.

I didn't want that before, I still don't, but I don't want to feel like this either. I am a hot mess. What do I do?" I lay down beside her on the bottom bunk.

I could remember when her mom bought her the bunk beds. Edie was the only kid I knew without any brothers or sisters who had them. She had begged for them because of me, so that I always had my own bed when I spent the night. The funny thing was, I never slept in my own bed. We had always fallen asleep talking on the bottom. It was ten years later and we were almost as long as the mattress and took up twice as much room. I could see the faint outline of where we scratched our initials on the bars of wood that stretched below the top mattress.

I was letting her words settle, figuring out what to say while trying not to find fault in her decisions. I wasn't threatened by her jealousy. She was confused. She didn't want Evan then and she didn't want him now, but for a girl that had always known what she wanted this must have been killing her. She wasn't made of regrets and second thoughts; her blood ran with impulse, not hesitation.

"Why did you and Bryce get back together?" I turned onto my side and studied her face in the glow of the lights. Her eyes were still swollen from crying.

"I feel like I used him to see what the big deal was, and now I don't want him to be that guy that all girls fear losing their virginity too. You know, the guy who takes what he was curious about and runs away after he gets it. That's what I feel like with Bryce. It's just, like, I don't know how many more times I can watch him do a kickflip or brush his hair out of his face. My god, if it's always in the way, just cut your hair." I couldn't keep the laughter from bubbling out. She laughed too, until we were curled into each other and gasping for air. This time tears streaked down both our faces.

"You're not mad at me?" Her smile evaporated, and she stared into my wet eyes with complete seriousness.

"No. If you wanted Evan, you could have had him then, but not now. I think we both know you were trying to grab onto anything that would make you feel normal…well, truth time—listening to Katy Perry on repeat in the dark makes you horribly normal." I wiped my eyes and watched the fear leave her face. She wrinkled her nose at me and twisted so she could use her feet to try and shove me off the bed.

"God, you stink. Go take a shower and I will run your nasty uniform down to the washer. If this is how you smell after work, I am going to quit before I start!" I glared at her before rolling lazily off the bed. I loved that her bathroom was attached to her room. She was saved from having to make the embarrassing walk from the shower to bedroom wrapped in a towel. I got up, grabbed a towel out of the cabinet, and tossed my uniform into the middle of her floor while she cleaned up her face.

The horn blared in an offbeat song of impatience outside of my house. Nathan was killing me. My mom stared at me with a mixture of concern and disbelief. It was the same face she made every time I turned a year older. Every year that took me further away from being her baby.

"Do you need more money?" This was the third time she'd asked.

"No. You guys gave me more than enough for my birthday, and no I won't spend it on medical marijuana or a tattoo from the guy who dad says sang a song about wanting just one Pepsi. Most annoying song ever, by the way. He played it three times hoping I would have a better reaction. "Institutionalized" is the song."

"Hey, don't be mean. The Suicidal Tendencies were a big deal to him. That song was cool once, you know. That guy's tattoo shop is popular too. You will be back no later than midnight, understood?"

"Yep, got it. I also have my outfits for my senior pictures that Evan is going to shoot today."

"Okay. I know you are going to be fine. Just do that, okay?"

"Do what?"

"Come back fine, in one piece, and still a virgin." She laughed, and I stared at her like she had grown a second head.

"Umm okay." I tightened my laces and hugged her briefly on my way out the door.

"Laney!" I sighed and turned around as she yelled my name down the stairs.

"What?" I asked.

"Happy Birthday, muggle." I grinned and shut the door behind me. Nathan, Hadley, Edie, and Evan were waiting in the

SUV in different states of consciousness. Hadley flashed a huge smile and had clearly been the one laying on the horn, judging by the fact that she was slung across Nathan's lap with her head halfway out of the window and her hand on the steering wheel. I crawled into the backseat, collapsing onto Evan's lap. He smiled down at me, and his kiss was like all the things in the morning I didn't know I loved—sunshine and calm while the world is still asleep.

"Happy birthday, Laney. I have a present for you. It's going to make your nerdy heart skip a beat. Do you want it now, or later in Venice?" I didn't hesitate.

"I want it in Venice." I pulled my face up to his, my hands clasped behind his neck and I kissed him while my heart drummed against my ribs.

"Seriously, do you guys do absolutely anything but kiss these days?" Edie's eyes were sleepy. I jumped up and kissed her straight on the forehead, with aggression and excitement.

"We're seventeen, Edie Callum. I'm going to kiss anyone I feel like today." She laughed and pushed me back with one hand. I slumped into the seat next to Evan.

"Did your mom give you crack for your birthday?" She wriggled her eyebrows at me, but I was staring at the thin gold chain with an anatomical gold heart that bounced between her collarbones.

"Where did that come from?" She rubbed the little metal heart between her fingers, the gold going black to define the muscles and arteries.

"Bryce." She said it with a smile; the smile I hadn't seen on her face since the bonfire before she had sex.

"Really?" I was trying to imagine a gift like that coming from him. It didn't seem like his style. She frowned at me. Her eyebrows drew together over her narrowed eyes before she let go of the heart to swing against her skin.

"Don't be judgmental, Laney. He's trying. I only have to watch like five kickflips a day now." She laughed in spite of herself. "He's at Ryland's house. He sent me a picture last night. I cannot wait to see your reaction." She grinned with her secret; she loved knowing things before me. She only got to keep it for a mile. Nathan lay heavy on the horn again. It only took a second before Reese flew out of the house and clambered into the car, her face lit up. Bryce wasn't far behind her; he got in and sat next to Edie, kissing her quickly before grinning out the window. I could see why. Ryland had cut his hair short. His wild black hair that once hung below his chin was gone. His bone structure had risen from the shorn piles of hair. He looked good. I was shocked that he had done it. He seemed to have a lot of fondness for his hair.

"Okay. Stop staring at me. I would like to make an announcement. I have cut my hair, and as of next week I will be going to basic training. I joined the National Guard. I do my training this summer and then after I graduate I will formally enlist into the United States Army." He put his hand up to his hair subconsciously, forgetting that he had cut his hair even as he explained it to us. It had to be intimidating with all of us slack-jawed and staring at him.

"I know I don't seem the type, but I can't just spend all my days skating, surfing, and living on my aunt's couch. I can't go back to L.A., so this is what is left for me. It's going to be good. I've already met some cool guys." He sat back, reaching for his seatbelt as the silence swallowed us up. No one knew what to say.

"Well, it looks good on you." Leave it to Edie to break through the awkwardness. "Who wants to live in L.A. anyway, with all that sun and plastic? Personally, I couldn't survive in the land of perfect hair and glorious cleavage coming at me from every direction." Ryland smiled at her like he had been drowning and she had lent him a hand.

"That's awesome man. Do what you gotta do, right?" Evan threw out, and we nodded in agreement.

"Yeah man, that's exactly it."

I bet your family is proud." Evan was leaning forward while he talked to Ryland, so focused he didn't see the pained expression wash over Reese's face or the way Ryland's fist clenched next to his leg.

Ryland nodded solemnly. "One can hope." Talk of his family dropped off as we continued on to Leland's house. Hadley was already skimming through music with her casual ADD, only giving us partial chunks of songs. When Nathan pulled into Leland's drive, the front bumper was inches from connecting with Leland's shins. We hadn't even seen him walking out from shadows the trees cast across the drive. His smile morphed into panic. He slapped his hand on the hood before walking around to the back. He overshot and his backpack sailed into the backseat. We all laughed except Edie, whose head had stopped it from landing on my lap.

"Hey guys. Let's do this." Leland's face and voice had all the markings he would need to succeed in college…king of the frat. Hadley slid closer to Nathan; there was no lingering tension between them. Summer had plastered the break in their relationship, erasing the fights and tears. Nathan backed up slowly, bumping the blue recycle bin and finally working the oversized SUV back onto the road. We fell into the music that sporadically shifted from one unmatched genre to the next. The freeway stretched out in a slow march of tourists coming in and locals running away from them.

"What do you guys want for your eighteenth birthdays?" Nathan could barely project his voice over the music. I saw Hadley's slender wrist dart out to turn it down.

"I don't know. I just turned seventeen." I did know—I wanted to stop time.

"I want a car, clothes, and a trip to France. All the same things I asked for when I turned sixteen," Edie said from behind me.

"Oh yeah, and how did that turn out for you?" Nathan laughed.

"I have a lot of clothes." Her answer was so matter of fact that we all laughed.

"Why do you ask?" I wondered. Evan was silent beside me, and it was the first time I really noticed how withdrawn he was.

"Because you might be eighteen before we get to Venice Beach." He gestured to the almost still line of cars and trucks in front of us and on either side.

"Well in that case, I want a tattoo when we get there." I smiled at the idea that I would ever get a tattoo in the first place.

"Well I'm going to go ahead and be a gentleman. I volunteer my name for the right side of your butt. Don't ever tell me that chivalry is dead." Evan laughed. I pinched the skin on the inside of his arm.

"Nah, your mom already sent us all a text that if you come home tatted, high, or with a passion to live the life of a street performer she will hang us from your deck." I rolled my eyes at the back of Nathan's head because he wasn't lying. She would text everyone I knew.

"I think street performance is a noble art. You can tell her I said so." I grinned and sat back against the seat. I tried not to feel the tiredness creeping in on me, the reaction to a long drive that was as ingrained into me as my inability to whistle. The car next to ours was almost spilling over with girls with tan shoulders and a rainbow of bikinis. I glanced around at the boys to see if any of them had noticed and saw Leland frozen, his face a sculpture in joy. Nathan was oblivious because of his effort to concentrate, but he was the only one. The air in the SUV shifted as every head turned to the right. There was a sharp intake of breath before I disrupted the silence that had fallen over the car with my laughter. Edie followed suit, and pretty soon we were all laughing except for Leland, whose face was enveloped in a blinding smile and glazed eyes. The girls were far too into each other to glance at us before Nathan switched lanes.

"Sorry. That was crazy rude of me." Evan was sheepish in his apology. I smirked in response. The apology was unnecessary. There was a car of pretty girls, he had eyes, and I was secure. That was all there was to it.

"I mean it, Laney. I only want to see your face." I laughed at him. I couldn't help it. I laughed while he frowned so hard it eventually broke into a smile.

"It's fine, Evan. You have hormones and those hormones are guided by the same honorable code of behavior that your good intentions are." I smiled into his bemused face.

"Oh, Brainy Laney. Why do you make it so easy on me?" I shrugged without an answer. It was easy and that was the point; the complications he always expected were for later, when we were old and the novelty had gone. I didn't want to be a forty-year-old married couple yet. There was no reason for that.

"Stop it!" I could feel Edie behind me twisting the thin hairs on the back of my hair into knots. She was obviously bored. All I heard was the exchange of names, Sheckler and Mullins. Skaters, if I had to guess.

"Want to play the quiet game Edie?" I twisted around to take in the scrunched up expression she always made when I suggested it.

"No. Why do you always want to play that game? Since we were kids you have wanted to play that stupid game on road trips." Her voice was vaguely annoyed.

"Because when you play you fall asleep. When you are asleep then you aren't bored and trying to tie my hair into knots or drawing on me or whatever else you do to occupy yourself." I smiled at the way her mouth dropped.

"Are you serious? I'm going to kill you." Her eyebrow went up to try and menace me.

"You won't. Who else is going to hang out with you when all the boys ditch us on our birthday trip to skate down the Venice boardwalk? Hadley?" My smile was on the verge of being obnoxious.

"What?" Hadley turned her head so it was resting on Nathan's shoulder. She was looking at us quizzically.

"What?" she asked again. Her forehead pressed down at my obvious joke. She turned back around, turned the volume up, and changed the song. Edie was quietly wheezing with laughter in the back seat.

"You guys are like two Regina Georges," Evan said under his breath. We both stopped laughing to stare at him. We obviously got the *Mean Girls* reference, but he was totally off.

"Shut it, Evan. We have never been and will never be Regina George. Clearly I am Janis Ian and Laney is Damian. Nah…we are Reginas sometimes." She said smiling.

"Probably true," I laughed. Evan glanced back and forth between us. It must have felt like he had two girlfriends most of the time. The conversation had caught Bryce's attention and the comparison of skate styles had paused for the moment.

"Oh hey Laney, I got you a birthday present," Bryce said. He extended his hand to drop a small tissue-wrapped rectangle into my hand. Inevitably I missed catching it and it fell between my shoe and Evan's. I picked the tiny package up and unwrapped it; it was a gold square outline dangling from a thin gold chain. It was very interesting for being so plain.

"Thanks Bryce." I leaned over the seat to hug him with the arm I still had feeling in.

"Why did you get her a square, Bryce?" Edie questioned. I watched his face color. I glared at Edie and thought that she could seriously use a class in how to talk to people sometimes.

"Um, well, I know you guys are close so I thought that I would get presents that made sense to you two." He flustered easily. "So I gave Edie the anatomical heart, but there really isn't an anatomical soul, you know? Well I asked the guy at the store, and he said that a circle could probably represent the soul but I thought of how weird you guys are…" His blush deepened, splotching his cheeks. "I mean, like good weird or whatever, so I thought if souls are circles, yours would be a square. Jesus, that sounds ridiculous. Whatever. Happy birthday."

I didn't know how to respond. There were depths showing in him I wasn't even aware he had. Edie was dumbstruck.

"Thanks, I seriously love it. I do." I grinned because I wanted to cry. He clearly got us, Edie and I, twins in weirdness.

"Okay cool." He leaned back into his seat, his face resuming its usual look of calm contentment. My shoulder settled against Evan's as the traffic broke up and stretched out before coming back together in a line. The hours trickled past us while the view changed from wild to urban. Southern California had a lot going for it, but I think Northern California got the better end of the Pacific Coast Highway.

"I don't want to freak anyone out, but there is a serious possibility we are going to make it before school starts back up." I laughed. Once we were off the freeway the buildings and houses rose up, their colors vibrant. Art scattered across the walls lining the street. The hanging letters of Venice strung across the main street down to the boardwalk. The shoppers steadily walked between Gap and the thrift stores and a guy sped past the SUV on rollerblades, his greasy hair straggling from a turban shaped from an old shirt. His skin was leathery and his guitar a pattern of red and white swirls that swung back and forth with his momentum. I wanted to get out, to follow him and absorb his casual eccentricity. He wore weird so well. Music trailed behind him from the radio clutched in his other hand, the wail of Hendrix fading under the call of seagulls circling two kids whose fingers were orange with Cheeto dust. Was this place love?

"What the hell is she wearing?" I turned to follow Hadley's voice and stare. The "she" in question was a study in cultures clashing. Her thick blonde dreads shot light off the coins threaded into her messy bun. Her breasts were free in a peasant blouse and her hips swung with the motion of a loose sarong. It was the old broken-in Dr. Marten's that struck me as strange, a loose expression of hippie values.

"She has a chain stretched from every pierce-able surface." Ryland's voice dropped in awe.

"And?" I asked. His face was practically pressed into the window. "You're from L.A., man. This should be like running into your neighbor, right?" He laughed and pointed, "Wait until she turns. I mean, there are chains spread over that woman like a web!" I draped myself over Leland and let my forehead rest against the glass. I saw it, the light catching on the thread of silver, and sighed. She was walking art. She moved in such a way that she didn't get caught up in her own masterpiece.

"I just want to jump out and photograph everyone on the street right now. It's killing me to stay still." Evan's words and breath twined when they hit my ear.

"So do it. Jump out at the next red light. You know I don't care. Just meet us at the graffiti walls." His smile only lasted a second before it was mashed into mine. He kissed me with passion and happiness.

"Hey Nathan, I'm jumping out at the next light, bro." I watched Nathan nod imperceptibly in his concentration. Evan unbuckled, his lips brushing over my forehead as we switched seats. He repeated the same thing with Leland, minus the kiss.

"Not while I'm still driving man! You're going to get me a ticket," Nathan exclaimed.

"Sorry," Evan conceded.

"It's cool, man." I laughed at Nathan's match flare-like temper; it lit and blew out in seconds. He was even like that as a kid. All he ever needed was an apology and then he was over it, with the exception of fights with Hadley. He switched lanes and pulled into the turn lane. The cars ahead of us were at a dead stop. Nathan waved Evan on with his hand. I watched out my window as Evan kissed his hand against the glass. He jogged until he met up with the woman with her chains and hair full of coins. His camera dangled by his side while his face turned from nervous to animated. She followed beside him as he gestured to a wall mural down the street. I smiled, seeing his concept. He wanted to shoot her against the black and white mural so that all her color would be against a frozen image for contrast.

"E? Wake up!" She sat up, pushing the hair from her eyes.

"Seriously? I'm a foot away. You don't have to yell. I was up at 4:30 a.m. running down the beach with my father. I needed that twenty-minute nap." Her eyes narrowed. She blinked a few times and they widened. "Did I miss something? Where the hell is Evan?" She looked around, not waiting for an answer.

"He got out about a minute ago. He wanted to photograph some of the locals…or not-locals? I really couldn't tell you." I pointed out the window to the silhouette of Evan and his swinging camera growing smaller.

"That's cool. God, I'm starving. What are we going to eat here?" she asked. I laughed. I wasn't thinking of food. I was thinking of bathrooms and bookstores, cheap sunglasses, and the guy on the rollerblades with his red swirl electric guitar. Of course Edie was thinking of food.

"I want something Greek or Indian. We don't have crap for Greek food at home," Edie said. Bryce and Ryland groaned in unison, apparently not fans of either option.

"Babe, I was thinking Ry and I could go skate when you guys do your senior pics. Is that cool?" Bryce said. Edie's nose wrinkled. If there was anything in the world she hated, it was pet names.

"I'm not a little fat pig from a stupid movie that isn't as good as *Charlotte's Web*. No 'babe.' I'm Edie, nothing else. You guys should go skate. Why not?" I could practically feel the irritation seeping out of her pores but I still laughed. She glared at me and then again at Bryce, who hadn't really moved. If anything, he was more still than I had ever seen him.

"Uh, cool. So just text me when you guys are done. Right?" He kept a level tone and avoided eye contact. I thought my stomach muscles would tear from suppressed laughter.

"Yeah, cool. Hey Reese, are you going skating too?" Reese glanced up from her phone like she had just come back down to Earth.

"Oh, yes. Did you see their skate park? I threw my board in the back yesterday." Reese pushed a piece of half-curled black hair out of her face. She seemed happier than I had seen her in a while. Her phone vibrated against the seat. That was why she looked suffused with light—we were witnessing the "Reese has a new boyfriend" face. She turned back around to finish texting as the SUV finally lurched forward. The sidewalks were heavy with people, the lines of cars waiting to get in the parking garages long.

"Hey Nathan, that guy is waving at you." I yelled over the OK Go song that was playing. He was a tiny guy in a red baseball cap and was calling Nathan forward toward the mouth of the alley. A "fifteen dollars to park" sign was in his other hand. Nathan nodded and Hadley rolled down her window as he carefully pulled to the side and edged The Beast into the narrow space.

Nathan swore three times trying to work The Beast into the maze of already parked cars and trucks. I pulled out my phone while he exchanged money with the man in the cap.

My mom had sent me a message and my Facebook was blowing up with birthday wishes. I felt nauseated trying to read my phone while he pulled forward and backed up, the actual level of his driving experience being tested. I closed my eyes until the vehicle was at rest.

"Come on, Laney, let's go find one of those gross beach bathrooms that always smell like saltwater and urine. We have to look freaking amazeballs in these photos. This is the last photo people are going to care that I send them until I either get married or have a brat. After we graduate we're just regular adults who have no reason to send random 5x7s to family we haven't seen in ten years. This will be the photo that all our classmates will look at for the rest of their lives when they show friends or their kids their old yearbooks and say, 'Oh wow…that was Edie Callum and Laney Wilder. God, they were really pretty girls even though that one hacked off all her hair.'" I shoved at Edie's forehead, pushing her chin off the back of my seat.

"You're an idiot, E." She was probably right though. I could tell you exactly what Melissa Mason from my mom's senior class looked like. How many times had she said, "Look at that tramp. She should have attempted to at least pretend she had more going for her than a double D set and drawn on eyebrows"?

"You do have a point though," I said.

"I think I'm going to hang out at Muscle Beach. I want to work out with those guys. You know, get my swell on." Leland looked around at us to see if anyone else was game. I shook my head.

"I want to see that!" Hadley called out from the front without turning around.

"Not surprised at all, Hadley." Leland elbowed me, like we were both in on the joke. Maybe we were. We crawled and climbed out of The Beast, bending and popping the tension from the drive free from our bodies. I grabbed my bloated backpack from the back. Deciding on my clothes had been problematic. Eyeing Edie's backpack and hobo bag, she must have been in the same predicament.

"We're going to go find Evan, guys. Let's all meet back up around three, yeah?" I yawned while Edie rallied the plans together. Bryce, Ryland, and Reese dropped their boards on the asphalt and skated into the masses, their wheels an echo lost under the Mexican music pouring out of the restaurant near the alley. I grabbed Evan's gear out of the back and passed two of the bags to Edie. He had brought a lot of equipment because he was unfamiliar with the natural light, as well as a ton of other stuff I blanked out on as he rattled them off.

"Holy crap, does he think he's shooting the entire town?" Edie asked. I nodded in agreement. I pulled my phone from my pocket and sent him a text.

Meet us under that giant V with all the palm trees around it in like ten minutes. Btw you have too much stuff -_-

I waited, my skin prickling with sweat under the sun.

"This beach is way hotter than ours is this time of year," I noted. Edie was lifting her hair off her neck.

"I was just about to say that. Let's start walking down there." She turned and headed out of the alley, slapping a high five on the extended hand of the over-exuberant parking lot sign guy. My pocket vibrated again when we were halfway to the giant open area between packed storefronts.

I'm going to try and meet you sooner than that. I forgot about carrying down all that stuff. Did you get Nathan's keys so we can put it back when we're done?

I said a few silent curse words before stopping where we were. "I spaced on getting Nathan's keys," I admitted. Edie let out a slow groan. We trudged halfway back to the alley before we saw Nathan jogging toward us and Leland and Hadley waiting behind him.

"Catch…" I saw the sun glint off the keys as they arched through the air. Nathan's brain could obviously not handle the heat, because his brain had stopped working. I slammed into Edie's side as we both scrambled to catch them. They landed with a clang a few feet behind us. Nathan had already turned to jog back. The plastic alarm keychain that hung from the ring was without a back when I picked it up. Edie was still looking around. I said at least another ten curse words before I saw the tiny back a good ten feet from us.

"We suck at being athletes," I said, playing captain to the obvious squad again.

Edie grinned while I tried to get the back to lock into the alarm. "Nah, he just sucks at throwing." I finally got both parts aligned, and they clicked into place. Edie was already walking again so I picked up speed until I was beside her.

"I think you bruised the shit out of my side." She lifted her tank top to reveal a red patch above her hip. I poked it. She slapped at me, the hobo bag sliding down her arm just far enough to jerk her in the other direction.

"You guys look like bag ladies." Evan had found us.

"Shut up," I mumbled, passing his equipment to him.

"Yeah Evan, shut up." Edie dropped his bag at his feet. He layered the straps and bags around him. He had practice at this.

"So there are a few guys working mid-piece down at the wall. I'm going to go test out the lighting and see if they're cool with us basically shooting around them." He headed toward the stretch of cement wall that was saturated in spray paint. We went in the opposite direction to the bathrooms. I had zero interest in getting dressed in the bathroom. The smell was the same at any beach, with only faint traces of the sunscreen smell to combat the other odors.

"Yo Laney, are you doing the white dress?" She sounded a mile away, but the echo reverberated beside me like the wailing ghost in *Harry Potter*. I was still staring into the backpack, looking at the white sundress shoved next to the black-and-white-striped dress with the belled skirt. I sucked at packing and should have carried the two dresses in garment bags. It was too late to do anything about it now.

"No. I'm going with the striped bell dress with the black floral Dr. Martens. I like the contrast of the patterns. I'm going to wear the galaxy Vans, dark boyfriend jeans, and white t-shirt in the casual shots. Should I wear my wayfarers?" I could hear her periodically thudding against the tight confines of the non-handicap stall. Tiny muttered curses were lost to the piercing shriek belonging to the tiny feet that ran past my door.

"Yes on wayfarers in some shots, but if you wear them in all of them your mom will chop you up with an axe." She laughed from two stalls down.

"That wasn't graphic at all, Edie. What about you? What did you decide on?" I groaned as my elbow caught the slide lock. This was not a well thought out plan.

"I'm torn. There's my black romper or the black dress. There are the gladiator sandals or the silver glitter platform heels. You know what there isn't though—a single clear answer to be found—so please throw a suggestion my way. Hurry though; this place is fast losing its appeal." Agitation and claustrophobia stretched through the metal stalls between us.

"Take my white dress and wear it with the silver heels, then use the romper for the casual shoot and pair it with the gladiator sandals. Wear your hair loose in the formal shots and the gold chain around your forehead in the other. Yes? No?" I suggested. I heard her smile; it's a weird thing to hear what you cannot audibly hear, but I did.

"It really sucks that you couldn't care less about fashion because everything you choose works. I want to be buried under all my clothes instead of dirt when I die, but it will still probably be you who has to choose my funeral attire. Bring me the white dress when you're done. Please. I love you Brainy, but fashionable, Laney." She giggled as random body parts continued to slam into the door.

"Laney…" Nothing but my name fell from Evan's lips. He was in shock. Gone were my jean shorts and summer dresses. I stood taller in this dress, the black striped skirt belling out from my waist. The docs were hot, but the sides were folded over and the sunlight caught on the black ribbon laces. Edie had rimmed my eyes in black and foregone eye shadow for a shimmer dust. My hair was wild. I was pretty.

"I was going to say that old line about a stud from *Grease*, but alas I have no cigarette to stub out." I shrugged my shoulders at him. What could I do? He smiled a little but was still silent.

"Oh my god Evan, the wall…" Behind him two guys were surveying their own work. The wall was coated heavily in black about three people wide, and the splatters of gold gave the urban wall class. It was everything.

"You guys took almost an hour to get ready. Mario and Tyler, those guys, well they wanted to help us out. It's not dry, so you *absolutely cannot* lean against it in that dress. This was my vision. A splash of formal in a sea of vibrant art. It's like a spiral staircase in a building with rotting walls." God, I wanted to kiss him, but I could already hear Edie in my ear saying something about smudging my lipstick.

"Edie, you look like summer meets disco. Do not touch the wall. I know you; don't touch the wall!" She wrinkled up her nose at his command. He was right. I gave it twenty seconds before she touched it to feel for herself that it was wet and to find out how wet it was. Mario and Tyler were both watching us; there was clear appreciation on their faces.

"Laney, you're fairer so you will go last. I have to work with the light to a certain degree and Edie's tan is darker…never mind. Edie, just go stand by the wall." I tried to focus on what he was saying, but instead I got caught up in everything around me. I loved it, the looming art on the walls of the building behind me and the ocean in front, the sand covered with scattered people that looked like they had simply come in with the tide and been left behind. My hair lifted away from my ears for one brief moment of relief from the sun. It was soaking through me. I wanted to abandon the dress and boots and throw myself to Poseidon.

"…aney!!!" Edie was shouting at me, but I caught none of her words except for part of my name. I had wandered away from them, drawn to the water. I couldn't even see Evan's head; the silver umbrella light thing obscured him. I came up behind him and dragged my fingers through his hair. It was almost clear at the tips that hit the tops of his ears and curled out. He didn't look up from his camera, but the skin on the back of his neck pimpled.

"You ready?" It was such a quiet request that I paused. Had he even spoken?

"As ready as any non-photogenic person can be," I said.

"Just don't do the frog face because you're nervous. You look so pretty it's ridiculous. Jesus…pretty isn't even the word. I can't see anything but you." He pushed me forward toward the perfect wall. I didn't want to look like an uggo in front of such perfection.

"Lovely. My grandpa said when he married my grandma that she didn't even look like the girl he had fallen in love with. She had been so lovely that he was afraid to take her hand, but if he hadn't she would have tossed him down the aisle. You are…I mean you look…lovely." I grinned, my cheeks flooding with heat. Everyone could hear him. I glanced at Edie and her expression was caught between amusement and jealousy, like when you laugh so hard that you cry.

I twisted, turned, and smiled. I did everything he asked. I also touched the wall. Just one finger pressed into the paint, which I held up for Edie to see between shots. She looked over in Evan's direction, but he was studying the screen intently. She held up one finger, smudged black. We laughed.

"You guys can go change clothes now." His focus was back on his camera. The two guys with the canvas bags of spray paint watched us grinning. They couldn't have been older than twenty, if that. Edie kept glancing back at them, and her smile was her old one, the summer smile.

"I don't want to go back into that bathroom. It's gross, Laney." I wrinkled my nose and nodded in reply. It *was* gross. They all were.

"Screw it, let's just change here. We have dresses on, so we can just pull everything underneath and then over. Old school style." I tossed the bag down on the cement. She grinned over at me.

"Old school style? Is anything we do able to be considered old school?"

"No, probably not, but I meant how we used to change on the bus whenever we knew we didn't have to go straight home. The whole last two months of school we wore our bathing suits instead of underwear just so we didn't have to go home to change. There was, of course, the infamous Edie Callum bra show when we went on that field trip to the aquarium in Monterey," I joked. I watched her face color under the memory of changing shirts and showing the entirety of the back of the bus her bra when her shirt and sweater got stuck together. It was a classic movie moment embarrassment, but she had played it off. She always played it off. If there was one consistent word I associated with Edie, it was "always."

"Well?" I glanced in her direction. She was already assembled and I was still buttoning my boyfriend jeans. She looked like a magazine ad for California. The romper only clung where necessary and the gladiator sandals lent power to her stance. I had been right; her wind blown hair framed her face and was held down by the gold chain headpiece. I never thought about a life in fashion, but this outfit was changing my mind. I had outdone myself. I pulled the rest of the dress over my head, feeling the warm air on all that I was exposing during the brief second that I passed the dress into Edie's hands while using my other hand to tug down the white v-neck that I'd been wearing like a fat necklace.

"Do you think the sand will ever come out of these heels? Seriously, how did I get so much sand in them when I was three inches above the ground?" She was shaking the grains loose from the glittering platforms. I laughed; It was a reasonable question.

"Okay. Is this going to work?" I gestured at myself, using my hands to sweep my body like a girl from one of those game shows.

"Yes, Laney, yes. That is fantastic. You are going to look crazy-good against the graffiti part of the wall. Oh my god.

Where has this Laney been my whole life?" Edie asked. The heat of not being able to deal with compliments rimmed my ears. I pushed the wayfarers back and tried to shove everything that had been packed so neatly before back into the bags haphazardly. She grabbed one bag while I struggled to keep the bell dress contained, the skirt poking out. We walked through the sand, and this time I stepped lightly.

"There's my girl." I laughed at Evan, who was leaning on his tripod with a look on his face that said, "you guys took forever." I probably wasn't lovely anymore, but this was far more what I would normally wear than the bell dress.

"Can you climb up on the wall by the end?" I glanced up at the wall and shrugged. "I will help you, and so will Tyler," he said. He pointed to the taller of the two taggers, who had skinny jeans and a Thrasher hat with the bill up. His hands were splattered in black. I liked the way he was trying to grow facial hair, but the bare patches gave away his youth. His friend Mario was staring at Edie, devouring her without chewing.

"Okay. Yeah." I walked toward the end of the wall and they boosted me up carefully. While it wasn't that high, it was an awkward height for a short, skinny girl to pull herself up on.

"Jesus, girl, you look better than our piece." I turned my body to the side. It was Mario, his mouth twisted into a smile. I half grinned at him, uncomfortable with compliments and strangers. Evan looked from my face to his and I could see the struggle for patience. They had been helpful, and Evan and I were on the same page in trying to remember that. I lowered myself off the wall and dusted my pants without taking my eyes off Mario. I felt Edie absorbing my social awkwardness.

"Let's do this shizz, Evan." She pinched my arm in passing, her eyes bright. Edie was good at pulling people into her orbit. There were days when she absolutely was the sun.

"Okay, E. So I want to play up this look more. Let's skip the wall and just do a palm tree and lifeguard station thing. What do you think?" Evan suggested.

"Obviously I agree with you and that eye, Evan." She spun her body in the direction of the ocean behind her. This was spirited flirty Edie, her spidey senses tingling when boys watched her.

I wandered down the sand toward the water, careful to stay out of frame. When he was done and all the equipment was back inside The Beast, I wanted to celebrate seventeen with him in the warmer water feeling more than just my heartbeat and bones go liquid. I walked further down to the waves, and despite my careful steps I could feel sand shaking loose in my shoes. I stopped where the sand turned dark and the waves left their patterns behind. There was an aquamarine lifeguard station, empty of its occupants, further down in the direction I was wandering. I couldn't remember the last time I had actually seen a lifeguard in one. They rode in little white pickups down the beaches at home, dodging little kids with plastic sandcastle kits.

I could feel the pull of secrets on me the longer I walked. There was something about sharing this celebration with my best friend that felt like betrayal. I rubbed the little gold square outline hanging against my collarbone. Even someone like Bryce, who wasn't a permanent fixture, knew Edie and I went together. It was a weight on my conscience, but even more than that it was the confusion over how to pull us apart, to create two whole people rather than remain a Siamese thought. How would I survive without the other half of me? I didn't entertain the idea that we would be the same. I felt that I should reconsider going away to school, away from everything I knew, to see what I was made of. I turned to walk back to the wall; back to the two loves of my life.

"Are you almost done?" I asked quietly in his ear, his posture bent and his body still while he framed the shot of Edie.

"I am. I want to shoot a few of you guys together. I thought I was going to have to go fish you out of the water, but you found your way back on your own. What were you out there thinking about? You looked lost." I narrowed my eyes at him. How would he know that?

"I have very good lenses, Brainy. I saw you just fine. Probably my favorite of the shots I have done today. Go!" He shooed me toward the wall where Edie was already perched laughing.

"Laney, Tyler wants to spray paint our outlines on the wall. Wouldn't that be awesome?" I glanced over at Tyler; his cheeks were pink and his hair shaggy under the upturned hat.

"Yeah, that's cool. Is that cool Evan?" He didn't look up, but nodded in my general direction.

We stood against the wall while Mario moved my arms into the position he wanted and Tyler did the same with Edie's. Once we were just so, we held still, but our chests shook with giggles each time the paint flecked onto our skin, our clothes, and splattered against our hair. We had on two medical masks that were wrinkled from being wedged between spray cans.

These clothes would be ruined, but we didn't care. We were leaving a mark on something, even if it would be painted over by the next day. The boys laughed at us trying to pose and not laugh at the same time, and I could swear I actually heard Evan laugh through the fog of concentration that surrounded him as he circled around us. I coughed, somehow almost inhaling paint even with the mask, and tried not to laugh through the burn in my nostrils. The steady sound of the spray stopped. We were officially art.

"You look awesome, Laney. Seriously, paint suits you." Edie cracked on the last word, crumpled in laughter. I wiped at one of the wet paint splatters on her temple, streaking white into her hairline. I could barely stand I was laughing so hard. Mario and Tyler had forgotten us for the moment, working around the outlines of our bodies on the wall. They were building a city around us.

"Wow. What have you guys been up to? You look insane, Edie." We both turned, startled by Bryce's voice. His face was shocked as he glanced back and forth between Edie and the wall, back to my face and over to Evan. We all looked nuts except for Evan; he looked thrilled as he twisted off lenses and put things away.

"You missed it Bryce. These two crazies just got painted." He indicated to the way the wall was shaping into a discernible picture. The outline of our bodies was surrounded in the painted buildings of Venice. Watching the picture shape itself into reality stilled me, the laughter gone while I watched.

"Thanks, guys. I can't believe my luck in stumbling on you two. I have your emails, and I will tag you in the photos when I post them on Instagram and my Tumblr." They had stopped for a second to acknowledge Evan with a couple head nods and smiles. The sound of paint hitting the wall resumed.

"Let's go, Laney. The swim might wash some of the paint in your hair loose. I like it though. You have the look of a street wildling." He threw the last bag onto his shoulder and took my hand. His was cool while mine was hot. Edie launched herself at Evan, the bags sliding down in every direction.

"Thank you." She kissed his cheek before turning to catch up with Bryce.

"She seems happy again," he said. I watched her walk away, her slouch dragging her shoulders down slightly. No, Edie wasn't entirely happy; when she was, it was contagious and irrepressible. I thought it was just summer, that once she didn't feel pressured to pretend, the act would fall away and she would be Edie again. I didn't bother to explain this to Evan. He wouldn't understand.

We passed people in all states of dress and undress. The man on the rollerblades passing us was trailing Jimi Hendrix in his wake.

"I want to go there. Will you come find me when you are done?" I asked, pointing to a small shop.

"You're ditching me and all this gear for books?"

"I am." I grinned before leaving him in the opening between buildings to follow the sidewalk down to the small bookstore I had found online. It was love at first sight. There were narrow aisles between the bookshelves with a fat black and white cat curled up. The floor creaked beneath the carpet that sunk a little by the spinning racks of postcards. Nabokov and Kerouac stared up at me from the black and white photos on cardstock. I paced the lengths of the dull blue carpet, running my fingers across the spines until I found the young adult section. I wanted them all.

"Do you need any help?" I looked over and immediately forgot how to use words. The clerk was taller than me with his hair pulled back into a bun that should have looked feminine but didn't on him. He wore a faded Bob Dylan shirt and jeans that hung low enough to show a strip of pale stomach. My mouth was a desert and my heart a drum. I shook it off.

"No. I'm just…umm…looking." I could feel the heat of the sun bloom onto my cheeks and spill down my neck.

"Okay, well just let me know." His smile was small, his eyes laughing, but still there were so few words available to me.

"Thanks." I dropped my eyes back to the book in my hand, the words on the back forgotten.

"Really? Him?" I jumped at Evan's low whisper, the heat of his breath on my neck.

"What do you mean? Stop sneaking up on me!" My heart was still thudding, but now its rhythm was confused.

"I could have run in here on fire with a bullhorn and you wouldn't have heard or seen me coming. He has a bun, Laney…" I scratched at my hair and placed the book in the space I had pulled it out from.

"A *bun*?" he mused. If his eyebrows got any higher they would blend into his hairline. "I don't get it."

"It's nothing. He's just a crazy amount of hot. I would think you were hot with a bun too." I pointed at his hair and his response was comical. Obviously a bun was not happening to Evan any time soon.

"No? No bun?" I smiled up into his face.

"Not a chance, Laney. You are out of your mind, and don't try to convince me that it will be 'amazeballs' or 'fantastical' either." I sighed and pushed my bottom lip out. He pulled on it.

"I'm going to buy this book and then we should go swimming," I said.

"I have a better idea—let's go swimming, and then you can buy the book and have another reason to ogle the cashier." He had a valid point on both things. I sighed as I caught sight of the bookstore clerk again. He was reading Neil Gaiman behind the warped wooden countertop. I felt Evan's hand in mine again, but I sighed nevertheless. Once we were outside I blinked against the assault of the sun.

"You just lost so many girlfriend points." He looked down at me, a smile pulling on his mouth despite his tone.

"You won't even consider a bun. What do you think you just lost?" I laughed at his frown. I paused to let two tiny girls run past me, a blonde with choppy hair and a brunette with her hair whipping into her eyes. It was like a shrunken version of Edie and me.

"That's super weird. Those kids look just like..." he started.

"I know. I was thinking the same thing," I said. Right after the last word, the blonde one tripped soundlessly, toppling into the side of the trashcan. The brunette girl grabbed her friend's hand, peered into her tear-streaked face, and pulled her up. She didn't comfort her, but instead got her standing and proceeded to drag her toward the playground. I laughed again, because even their personalities mirrored Edie's and mine.

"That would almost be creepy if it wasn't so cute," I said. I stopped at the point where the sand had scattered up onto the sidewalk. I pulled my shoes off to avoid filling them even further.

"Hey, I never asked you if you got in trouble for losing your shoes to the ocean that one night," he said. I paused. It had been nearly a month ago. Did I get in trouble?

"I don't even remember. Probably not. I've managed to pretty much avoid trouble this summer. Seeing as how mom had a rough start to it I've been trying to lay low, but the two of them are working their crap out I guess."

"Why do you always just say things are rough for your mom? What about your dad?" His hand reached out, attempting to tame the hair that would always be wild. Why did I do that?

"I guess because I see the struggle with her firsthand, but because he's always gone it seems like he gets to let it go the minute he's away. It's probably not true at all, but I don't know any different either. It's not like I am welcomed into those conversations, but judging on her behavior alone, I would say that's her general take on it too. That's what happens when you have a chatty parent and a quiet parent."

"My dad was the chatty one. I remember him carrying most of the conversations and my mom saying something here and there," he said.

"I like how quiet she is. She doesn't say anything that doesn't feel important. She doesn't need to fill silences." He grinned at me.

"Well, I didn't get that from her. I don't know what to do when you go quiet—give you your space or try to pull you back into the world again."

"Both." I dropped my shoes into the sand, pulling the t-shirt over my head and dropping it onto the pile. He tossed his shirt on mine as I studied him from the side. I left my jeans in the sand as well, having forgotten a towel…again.

"Ready?" I smiled in response. Heat was everywhere, and I couldn't tell if it was from the sun or him. The feverish feeling could have just been from being seventeen and free from all the usual things that pulled me in different directions. I think it was the freedom from what waited for me.

I ran. I moved with the excitement of this day on the beach. The water hit my shins, still cold but different. I waited until it lapped against my waist before diving under. The sound of the water around my head could have been my lullaby, surrounding me. I swam hard against the current, my muscles tightening and propelling me. I could have swum forever if my lungs had allowed it. I would live in the water with my surfer boy and have kelp beds and mermaid babies. I pushed harder until I felt the burn curl around inside my ribs. When I broke the surface I closed my eyes against the reflection of light and let my body go loose.

"If I hadn't seen naked baby photos, I would think you just washed up on the shore one day."

"God, I wish my mom would hide those naked baby photos already. How much embarrassment is enough?" I kept my legs moving, my body rising and falling with the waves.

"So, about your birthday present," he said.

"Not yet. Let it be the last thing of the day, or let this be what you give me." I encircled his neck with my arms out of affection and manipulation; I was using him to hold me up so I would have enough energy left to swim farther out. He kissed me lazily, like we weren't keeping each other afloat in the ocean. I kissed him back like I was in the middle of the ocean and he was my oxygen supply. His whole body went still, and for a second I thought we would go under.

"You are love, Evan." I let go and went under, using the strength I had built up to swim farther out than I would have at home to put distance between my seawater-soaked confession and myself. I lost the war in who would say it first. I could hear him pushing against the roar, but for the first time I was so much faster. My body felt like it was swallowing up the ocean instead of the opposite.

"What was that?" His voice was a wheeze when he caught up to me. I treaded water, up and down, with his eyes boring holes into me.

"What was what?" I feigned stupidity so I didn't have to repeat what I hadn't actually meant to say out loud.

His cheeks were ruddy with exertion, his hair plastered to his temples and too wet to curl at the ears. I had finally worn him out and had to hope he didn't want me to dolphin him back to shore. Once the adrenaline wore off I would have to wash in like driftwood. It was odd, now that I was thinking about it, that this beach didn't have driftwood. The urban seaside was a stark contrast to the wild shoreline of the beaches I loved.

"I am love? I was love and then you were gone, just a streak of skin in the water…" He wasn't smiling. "You finally tell me you love me and boom…gone." He pushed the hair off his forehead.

"How long have you been waiting? I mean really, we have only been together a few months," I asked.

"That's bullshit. We have been together since I wiped my snot behind your left ear and you gave me a mouthful of sand in return. I have loved you since I knew I liked girls and you were still afraid of my non-existent cooties. By the time you realized I wasn't infected by the plague, I was terrified of you; not of your cooties, but all the thoughts in your head I couldn't imagine thinking. We have been together our whole damn lives, Laney. I'm not love, this…" He pulled me to him, his nose and mouth in my hair. "This is love. Us. What we have out here when no one is around, except maybe those guys." I laughed at the two guys paddling out a few yards away. "All of this is love and we aren't even supposed to know what it means. That's what they say, anyway, and maybe we don't. It just feels a whole lot like we do. God, when did I get so wordy?" I smiled into his face. I didn't want to kiss him. I just wanted to stay treading water while he said all the words I knew like they were my own. They were the words I had left unsaid.

"Do you ever feel like you got cheated?" His words were more strained; we couldn't stay out here forever.

"Why would I feel cheated?" I asked.

"You don't get that 'oh my god, I'm in love' moment. This isn't terribly exciting for you, no light bulb realization. It wasn't surprising or shocking. The whole idea of love between us is as natural as swimming or breathing."

I kissed him then to stop him from analyzing and overthinking. I kissed him with a childhood of memories; I kissed him with all the rage of the waves and the roar of the ocean around us. I kissed him because that overwhelming feeling I didn't recognize was the only feeling I ever wanted to feel.

"Let's swim in. I promised Edie I would go shopping with her since we aren't cash poor today."

He laughed. "Cash poor, really?"

"Shut up." I swept my hand into the water and splashed him. He sputtered salt water, glaring at me. I had swum too hard out here to swim that quickly back to shore.

"Dolphin?"

"Fine. Only because you love me." He laughed and twisted around until I had a firm hold on his neck.

"Gross. Gross. Gross." The sand was in between my toes, turning into a muddy mess. I could feel it shifting consistency every time I stepped down. "Oh my god. Gross."

"Laney, jump on my back before I bury you in the gross. I love you, but I will bury you." Evan's face was drawn with the conviction in his statement. I cringed at the very thought of having that much sand stuck to my body. I rolled my eyes and kept walking. I was not getting on his back.

"I am pretty sure I'm super sunburned. It feels like my skin is going to suffocate me." My cheeks and nose felt tight with heat. I caught his expression of disbelief now that he was really looking at me.

"That's definitely going to hurt more tomorrow," Evan said. I squinted at him, that statement did me no good. He grinned back at me.

"Do I look like Mr. Krabs?" I traced the skin around my hairline, my bottom lip jutting out. I did not want to go to work all red.

"Not yet. It's just really pink right now. You look like you are permanently blushing." He rubbed his thumb along my jawline, but it didn't really hurt. "Here comes Edie now." I turned away from his hand. She was on the front of Bryce's longboard, and luckily for her he seemed to know where he was going despite the hair blowing into his face. She was smiling…sort of.

"Whoa. Jesus, Bryce! Stop!" Edie using her shrill voice wasn't the Edie you wanted around. I thought they were going to collide with the poor lady in her motorized wheelchair, her six tiny Chihuahuas trailing behind with their thin gold leashes sparkling in the sun. The woman's face didn't alter in the least. She kept pushing through without a glance at them. I could come to this beach a thousand times, but I wouldn't ever understand its inhabitants. Here I was a tourist, and I didn't know the local language.

"Ugh. Can we please shop now, Laney? I have so much money and so many stores I want to go to. I love these cheap storefronts where everything says 'California.' Did you see the It's Sugar store on the corner?" She pointed down the congested boardwalk.

"Yeah, let's do this, lady." I smiled back at Evan. He was looking at Bryce like he wasn't a hundred percent sure what they were supposed to do. He shook his head at me and grinned. I waved with the hand Edie hadn't grabbed onto, her persistence dragging me down the asphalt. I could see what looked like Reese and Ryland walking toward us. She was in some kind of black tank top that had the bear from the California flag on it, and he was shirtless, rolling lazily beside her.

"Three hundred dollars. I got three hundred dollars," Edie was repeating in a singsong voice, low so it only stayed between us. I laughed at her enthusiasm.

"I don't want to fight, E, I don't, but I have to ask again… What are you doing with Bryce?" Edie looked away before I could stare her down. She dropped my hand and shoved her own into the pockets of the black romper. Her tan arms were still flecked with white and gold paint. She walked faster with her head down. I shouldn't have pushed, but this was getting more strange the longer the summer dragged on. It was like she was peeling off layers of herself because she couldn't just accept that she had done something she wasn't proud of. She refused to move on. Bryce wasn't her summer boyfriend; he was her reminder, a way to punish herself for having been stupid. It seemed unhinged and unfair to drag this idea of a relationship out. It wasn't like she had lay with him in the sand and lost her virginity, it was like she had dug out the core of who she really was and threw it into the ocean.

"Do me a favor Edie, and do yourself one too. Stop pretending that being someone you're not is going to make you feel better. You aren't doing this for Bryce, so why drag him along? Slow down, my calves beg you." I was wheezing, still exhausted after the swim.

"Shut up, Laney. You don't want to fight, huh? I cannot explain this anymore to you. I cannot keep telling you that it's a situation you can't and won't ever be able to understand. Let me deal with this my way. It is my freaking problem, not yours. I just want to shop for new clothes; hell, maybe even for a new me. Teenagers aren't supposed to have a mid-teen crisis, but that's what is happening. Bryce knows none of this is real, come on. I'm the local and he is my boy of summer. I messed up, and now all I want to do is play out the rest of this awful summer movie cliché, get through senior year, and finally get away from everywhere I've already been. I can be the old me again once we get away from here, from all of this!" She swept her arm across the beach and the people wearing almost nothing.

"What if I don't want to get away from this?" I hadn't meant to say those words; this wasn't the right time to drop truth like atom bombs on the small, carefully constructed cities in Edie's mind. Her eyes lit up, glowing with accusation and paranoia. I wanted to turn and walk away, but maybe Evan was right. I would have to tell her eventually…just maybe not today, or tomorrow. Maybe I wouldn't even have anything to say when she was boarding a plane to head wherever she might end up.

"I'm not a blind idiot, Laney, but I'm not discussing this with you today. You're scared to leave what you know. Just wait. I found five or six schools that you need to see for yourself. Don't make insane decisions because I'm weirding you out. I'm weirding myself out too. Don't say crazy things to me on our birthday." Edie was looking at her feet as she talked to me. She didn't want to see that my mind was made up. She didn't want to go alone. As fearless as she believed she was, it was only because it never crossed her mind that she would really be changing her whole life without the one person she hadn't had to live it without since she was little.

"So, It's Sugar? Let's do that last or the clothes we try on won't fit," I suggested. She looked up, and I met her eyes head-on and smiled. My own smiles were becoming lies. Were we bad people if we blurred the lines of who we were to keep the other person from falling apart? I had to believe we weren't.

"Yes. You're a genius. I want a tank top like Reese's. I saw it in neon," she said, chattering mindlessly. As we moved through the people crowding up the boardwalk the man with the rollerblades looped through a third time. His songs were starting to speak to me, the lyrics hitting me. This time it was "Fortunate Son." I paused as the breeze lifted my hair, reminding me that I had cut it to find myself. Maybe the only way that Edie would find herself was to cut her free from me. I did what anyone would do—I grabbed her arm and pulled her into a store heavy with bass and smelling of too much incense.

I didn't know how to let her go yet. I didn't want to let her go at all.

"Oooh, look at that." She was ogling the paintings hung unevenly in the back—an Einstein in splatters and a Marilyn tatted with L.A. pride.

"You need that Einstein, Laney; you *need* it. You know you do." Her voice rose up over the bass that I could feel in the arches of my feet. My blood jarred with its heaviness.

"Nah, it would look crazy odd in my room, but I love it."

"Not for your room, for our dorm room. Or just your dorm if we don't get stuck together."

"Yeah, remember this place so we can come back for it later."

"You've lost it. I'm getting it, Brainy Laney, and there is nothing you can do to stop me. You need this. It will remind you to be curious. It will remind you that you are way too smart to stay in some little beach town, waitressing and hoping that we all come back still believing in the power of tradition." This was how Edie was going to deal with my small admission of truth. She would bury it under her beliefs, dress up the future, and hope I fell in love with it. It was borderline delusional; it was so damn Edie that it was like having her all the way back to herself again. She was flirting with the clerk in the white shirt and blue Dodgers hat. He pulled the print down from the wall, smiling at her.

"Got it! Happy birthday, Laney! We are seven-freaking-teen!" she shouted over the bass. I laughed. The slack expression on the man behind the counter was everything. She had said our age good and loud, knowing what she had been doing. "Joe here just gave us a discount too." Her smile was disarming and he was in defeat. He had been outplayed.

"Thanks, Joe!" I shouted over the bass, grinning. His face didn't shift into amusement, but he nodded with a pinched mouth in my direction. In that small childish victory, Edie's face was like the sun. I enjoyed being in the sun. We moved like a tornado through the stores until we hit the candy store, where we moved through the bright aisles like children in a rainbow-colored trance. This was perfect.

"I'm starving. What do we want to do for dinner?" Her voice was whiny with hunger, and I scrunched my nose at her. I couldn't deal with whiny.

"I don't know. I haven't eaten anything but these Nerds. I know Evan didn't eat either," I said, shaking my half-empty box of Nerds at her.

"Are you guys ever going to do the deed?" she asked. I blanched. She tossed it out like it wasn't personal, like it wasn't important. *Hey, what do you want for lunch? When are you and Evan going to have sex?*"

"Obviously we'll have sex eventually. Next time give me a heads up when you're going to ask me super personal questions like that."

"I read in some magazine that taking someone by surprise is the easiest way to get a truthful answer. I figured you guys would be like rabbits by now." She was smiling but serious.

"Really? Like rabbits? Gross, Edie!" Her wording had definitely been straight from the mouth of Big Edie. She had been telling us for years to achieve all the dreams we could, because once we got settled down and married we would spend the whole first year doing it like rabbits, and naturally babies would follow.

"What? I just thought by now you guys would have done it. Everyone assumes you already are. Evan wouldn't say a word when Nathan asked him, so I guess that's why."

"Are you kidding me? Why would Evan tell Nathan even if we had? This group is getting too close now. Way too close."

"Calm down. I'm messing with you. Look at those rosy cheeks, all pink with embarrassment. You are so easy to tease. You would tell me though…right?" She said the last part like she wasn't sure of what the answer was. Would I? I didn't know how to tell her. If it was an amazing experience wouldn't it be rubbing it in her face?

"Of course I would, stupid. Besides, you would probably already know. You know me so well that I'm sure you'd be able to tell."

"You didn't know with me."

"Be fair. You came to my house hysterical, your whole face drowning in tears. Whose first thought is, 'Oh, Edie must have hooked up with Bryce'?" She paused, looking out past the people who still swarmed the sidewalks toward the water. She had to know I was right.

"Yeah, that's true," she mumbled while looking through the bags hanging from her arm. She had backed herself into an awkward corner.

"Shit." I had just remembered where I had forgotten to return, but it would be more fun to go back with Edie anyway.

"Quarter!" I laughed at Edie's exclamation. My jar wasn't as full as Edie's, but I had the good thought to not swear that often around the Swear Nazi.

"Let's go to Small World Books. It's this little bookshop I was in earlier before Evan and I went swimming. The sales guy is like Leto." She stopped walking and stared at me, her eyes round and hurt.

"You saw a Leto and you didn't call me? You know how much I need Leto sightings," she complained dramatically. She was more obsessed with the singer from 30 Seconds to Mars than I was. Neither of us had a thing on my mom though; that love was long lasting. She followed me, texting away as I maneuvered through the crowds that had doubled since we got here.

We passed a man on the piano, his fat cat curled on the top. The man's dark skin was shining under too much sun, but his smile spread wide and his body shook in time to the song. His wife was sitting still as a Buddha behind her table of knick-knacks, including hand-painted smiling turtles. I missed Evan. He would be wandering through the pop up stalls and street performers, a Cyclops, capturing all the details of what made this beach so infamous. I pulled my t-shirt away from my body; it was gradually growing warmer.

"I love it here, but I miss our weather. I guess like ten degrees makes all the difference." Edie was trying to blow her bangs off of her face, but the hair stuck stubbornly to her cheek. We had walked into a crowd that swelled out around a group of men, their bodies like rubber. My breath caught when one of them ran and launched his entire body over three other men, twisting into a ball and unfolding back onto the dirty asphalt. The applause was thunderous. We finally worked our way out of the cluster of smiling people and to the bookstore.

"Is that our Leto?" Edie had gone still, her back arching to push out her cleavage a little further. I looked past her at the same guy still lazily stretched out behind the cashier and nodded. I chose to stand more casually than Edie. He glanced up for a second and smiled before going back to his book.

We walked through the shelves stacked full with books. I was always overwhelmed in bookstores. There were simply too many choices. The three hardbacks I had pressed to my chest seemed like enough, but still there was more. I was searching for *Looking for Alaska*, my John Green obsession never ending. I had gone backward through his books.

"Do you need any help? I can keep those books at the register if you want." I had no air, no words, and no response. I smiled a silly teenage smile that I could feel forming but couldn't stop.

"That will be cool, thanks." Edie's voice was calm and collected. Her hip was twisted in his direction but she never looked awkward in her clichés. It was one of the many traits I envied her for. She had no books, of course. She read for purpose, not for pleasure. I handed him the books and noticed he couldn't help judging my selection for himself. He raised his eyebrows at me, causing his hairline to rise. I had to suppress a laugh.

"You read Steinbeck? In the summer?" His voice carried more than just a subtle note of disbelief. He looked between the books and me, sizing us both up.

"She reads everything. *Everything*," Edie said before turning her face back down to her phone, the smallest of smiles pulling on her lips. If flirting was an art, she wasn't a mess like me; I was Jackson Pollock and she was Van Gogh. She changed her style to suit the person.

"I read Steinbeck in all seasons. I like the way he writes. Do you read Steinbeck?" I watched the flush of pink that was mostly hidden by his beard.

"Not since high school. I'll take these up to the register." I watched his lanky body move around the tables stacked with display books.

"Nice one. You better stay with Evan because you are awful at flirting," Edie said without looking up. "So, it looks like the vote is split on dinner. Half of us want the little restaurant that's on the other side of where we are standing now, and the other half wants to eat at the Mexican restaurant by where we parked. You are the determining vote. So, I'm guessing Mexican it is?" She glanced up. She knew me too well. "Yeah, that's what I thought."

I left her standing by the last shelf and scanned the YA section until I found what I was looking for. I took the book with black smoke climbing its cover to the register. He rang up the books, his grin widening at the last cover.

"Finally," he said while scanning the barcode on the back of the John Green.

"What do you mean?" I wasn't sure if that was an insult or not.

"Something that was written in the last decade. I wasn't sure if you were an alien or not. We don't get a ton of high school girls that only purchase obscure titles by classic writers. I was beginning to think you were sent down to study our ways and you just hadn't reached this century. You haven't been on your phone once either. See, an alien." I laughed while he put my books in a bag, throwing in rack cards and bookmarks that were stacked all over the wood counter.

"Not an alien, just well read. What about you?" I pushed the twenties still trying to fold themselves back up across the counter.

"Am I an alien?"

"No, are you well read?" I laughed, my confidence climbing.

"Touché."

"*Au revoir.*" He laughed at my reply, a genuine and loud laugh. I saw Edie smiling out of the corner of my eye. Leto smiled at me before resuming his book. Take that for flirting.

Once outside the sun wavered over the water, the hues of it blinding me for a minute.

"Give me sunglasses, please." I kept my eyes closed and held out a hand to Edie.

"Where's your Ray-Bans?" she asked. I groaned. Where were my Ray-Bans? "Now is not the time for questions. The sun is burning my retinas out." I shook the hand I was holding out and felt the cold plastic she placed into my palm.

"Really? The heart ones?" I laughed. She had given me the red heart glasses she had bought earlier. I had called them her *Lolita* glasses, and she had responded with complete ignorance of Nabokov's book, only remembering when I brought up the movie version we had watched on Showtime in the middle of the night when we were freshmen. It had left us feeling weird, but it had also left me loving the writer.

"Shut up, you look adorable."

"Let's go eat. I am so hungry from that swim and your excessive shopping."

"Is it my fault that this place is so cheap and that half the guys hawking their wares were flirting with us?"

"Us?"

"Of course us, Laney. Who did you think the book guy was flirting with? Me? The girl who looked lost and was gawking at the paintings and skimming a magazine? Yeah, no. You got the hottest of the lot." She was using her freer hand to push the stray blonde hair from my eyes. It was just long enough now to cover both eyes. I could feel the wild array it had dried into but there was little I could do about it. That was the only thing that I missed about my old hair—the sheer weight of it held down the wildling in me.

"I see Hadley and Nathan being completely disgusting. Shocking," she said. I followed her eyes and saw them melded into the side of a wall. If they mashed themselves any harder against it they would become part of the mural.

"Well, they are definitely more together than ever," I muttered.

"You think! She says they average three times a week since he has his own truck, and even more if either of their parents are out of the house." I tried not to let my eyes go wide at her admission.

"How do you even know that?" I wasn't hurt; I wasn't Hadley's confidant, but neither was Edie on most days.

"She told me, obviously. Why? Nathan has never told you?" I looked at her with all the shock I felt in me.

"No, why would Nathan tell me that? Seriously, why would she tell you?" I dropped my arm down. I was already sick of holding the Einstein painting no matter how much I loved it.

"Well, you and Nathan are closer than any of the rest of us are with him, minus Leland, so naturally I figured it had come up. She told me because, well, obviously."

"Obviously what?" I asked. She made the one face that made the whole thought of being separated from her bearable. It was dismissive, because on some level she knew something I did not.

"Because of Bryce and I. She didn't want to bring it up with you because she thought you would be judge-y. You would have been, Laney. You always are." I rested the Einstein against my foot and pushed my own hair out of my eyes now that the wind had picked up. I was more than annoyed but also burning with sarcasm.

"I'm not all 'judge-y.' Reese has been hooking up with guys since sophomore year and I couldn't care less. She just doesn't do it in the middle of crowded streets. I didn't judge you for sleeping with some guy you barely know. I covered your ass and let you cry all over me. Yeah, Hadley is right. Maybe I am…what was that not real word you used again? 'Judge-y.'" Her face was frozen, set in disbelief. I walked away from her.

As I passed Nathan and Hadley I made sure to walk really close. "I wouldn't have judged you Hadley, and it's not a secret that you're sleeping with Nathan. All of Venice is aware of it." Their faces broke apart and Nathan looked back and forth between Hadley's and mine.

"Did I miss something? Laney?" I glared at Hadley but didn't say a word. I walked away from them with as much explanation as I had from Edie.

The sound of Edie's shouts were too far and too quiet under the sounds of the boardwalk. I ignored her efforts to pull me back to her, stupid Laney, always quick to forgive. I looked around and it was like being in a movie. The bright spots I saw from the sun and the music made my head spin. The loud neon colors from identical hoodies and all the different people combined into a blur. I should have eaten. My face burned now, and not with sarcasm. The day was catching up to me. I bent over to try and calm the heartbeat I could feel everywhere and in everything. I slowly breathed and watched the confusion fade into black.

"LANEY!" I could feel her hand before I could see her. Her hands were never hot; she always felt like she carried the winter in her veins, even when the rest of her screamed summer. My elbows throbbed, but nowhere near as thickly as the slow drumming in my head. "LANEY!"

"Stop yelling at me. Jesus, E, stop yelling." I didn't know if the words were loud or even outside my head. "Please." I could hear my grandma's voice, always obsessed with manners, over the drumming in my brain.

"Jesus yourself. You scared the hell out of me." I heard sirens and feet shifting but I still couldn't open my eyes all the way. It reminded me of waking up as a kid with my eyelids stuck together in the morning.

I waited for the drumming to die down but there was shouting all around me. A single white light forced my eyes open…or was that fingers?

"Miss, can you understand what I'm saying?" The voice was hard, but webbed with concern. This guy clearly had children.

"Yeah." His hand brushed over my head until his wrist settled again. Definitely, this was a dad. "I can hear you. It's not really like you're whispering." I could feel my lip twitch. He laughed above me.

"Have you considered the merits of staying hydrated and fed, miss?" His arm was under me, lifting me up to a sitting position. He had a nice face. His skin was a deep brown and his eyes were blue, ridiculously bright blue.

"You're kinda hot for an old guy." I must have had a heat stroke that made you pass out and apparently say anything that came to your mind. I could hear Edie's laughter even with the crowd moving closer. I closed my eyes again, not because I felt weak or dizzy, but because I felt center-of-the-sun embarrassed.

"I could be your dad, you know." His face was amused and his voice was low as he timed my pulse. I put my hand on his.

"My mom would have some explaining to do." I smiled. I had caught him off guard again and he smiled openly. It stretched from lips to eyes. He reached behind him to reveal a water bottle.

"This is water, and when girls spend all day in the sun and don't drink it they pass out. I want you to drink it slowly, and I want a clearly quick girl like yourself to not repeat this mistake again. Understood?" Under the lecture his voice had deepened with the seriousness of his job. I nodded while I twisted the cap free and drank deeply.

"That's not slowly." I slowed down, letting the water pour through me. It felt like the cold was tracing the sun's poison down my veins. I stood with his help, the bottle clutched in my hand and my lips tingling for some reason.

"Your friend here is going to walk you to get some light, I stress *light*, food, and then you have to rest. You should be back to your witty self tomorrow. It was a pleasure to meet you and thank you for the flattery. Be smart. I can tell you are." He turned me in the direction of Edie, laden down with our bags from shopping and my painting against her leg. She was pale even with her tan. I was annoyed that my brush with sunstroke had stolen all my hostile energy against her. I didn't think of it long. Her whole face was an apology.

"We couldn't find Evan. His phone is going straight to voicemail. I didn't even think about drinking more water. Who just drinks water like that?" she asked. I grinned lazily. Edie was a runner who still couldn't understand the importance of drinking water outside of a track. She was impossible.

However, I knew that soon I wouldn't have to figure out how to stay mad at her; she would hold the entire grudge we would need when we learned to live apart.

"You look weird. Why do you look weird?" My mom was perched on a chair at the kitchen table. Her salad was half eaten and the stack of papers beside her was teeming with red marks.

"Don't freak out, but I passed out in Venice." I lost my train of thought at her rapid movement. She was a jumble of legs and t-shirt as one hand pulled me to the chair opposite hers and the other hand moved to my forehead.

"No one called me. Why wasn't I called? Laney, why wasn't I called?" Her voice got pitchy when she was upset. I winced at the higher tones. She saw me do it.

"Sorry. We should have called." I turned to the voice behind me to catch the drawn expression on Edie's face and saw that Evan's was a mirror of hers. I groaned, dropping my head on the table. I had told them not to come in. Nothing good could come of them being my support system.

"I told them not to. You would have been in the car flying down the highway before you even heard what happened. I am fine. I was checked over and well-advised by a medic. I'm alright. I'm not high, no tattoos, and I only got four piercings." It worked. Her attention was pulled back to me. If Edie and Evan were intelligent they would run. I wanted to as well, but I could feel the drowsiness that had overcome me in the car pulling at me. I rested my cheek on the table and nodded off while my mom's concern pinged in the background. It was like listening to rain against glass. It lulled me.

I came out of sleep to the same faint tapping I could remember falling asleep too. It was louder and more persistent, not a tap but a knock. I opened my eyes and saw the planets floating on the wall, the neon green numbers blending into all the blue. It was four a.m. I dropped my head back down, my movements swinging the hammock. The knocking didn't fade. I twisted my body, face mashed into the net, trying to see the door to the deck. Evan was shivering under the lantern light. I rolled free from the hammock, and the blanket I had rolled up cushioned my fall. I opened the door and moved to the side to let him in.

"You slept through your present. I know I said it yesterday, but I am sorry, Laney, sorry I wasn't there." I put my cold hand over his mouth. I had heard enough apologies yesterday during the whole drive home. He had been in one of his photography fogs and I was fine with it. I usually was. I held out my hand and waited with my eyes closed. It wasn't a desire to be surprised, but just to have them closed again. It was a snapshot of an inspirational poster I passed everyday in the hall during school, some quote about electricity from Thomas Edison. I sneered at it each time I passed it. I mean every single time. I couldn't help myself; I was so firmly rooted in Team Tesla that even Tesla himself probably minded less. Something was off about it. Tesla's sepia photo was blown up and pasted over Edison's face. There was a quote by Tesla pasted in printed segments over whatever drivel had been there before. The only things that remained intact were Edison's chest, folded arms, and the scrollwork around the edges. I hugged him. I fell in love with him in the way he thought we had been cheated out of. It was magic under a Van Gogh sky. I kissed him like my mother wasn't down the hall and I loved him like it was new.

"There is that nerdy heart beating double," he said. This felt like that moment, the one where everything blurs and glows brighter, where the room fades to black around us; but it wasn't, not with my mother down the hall. It was there though, the readiness everyone was always going on and on about. In its own way it was as all-encompassing as movies and novels made it seem.

"Thank you. Go home, like right now." His eyes widened at my urgency, but he knew my blushes, my awkwardness.

"Ten more minutes. Come out on the deck with me." He pleaded his case with reddened cheeks and earnestness. I laughed at the reminder that we were nothing if not teenagers. I could feel it in the way his hands sweat as he gripped my arms. "That's a no, right? I had to try. God, I had to try." He wasn't even pretending to look me in the eyes.

"I love it though. How did you do it?" He grinned, a Cheshire smile full of secrets.

"Well, it helps to know a teacher who is currently working at the school during the summer session who shares a deep dislike of Edison with her daughter." He laughed at my face. "It's a gift to you from both of us. You should know it's been like that since the first week and we have no plans on fixing it. Happy late birthday, Laney, the girl who slept through the candles and cake." He kissed my forehead, and there was a leftover aggression on his lips from wanting more.

"See you after work tomorrow," I said. He opened the door like he was vetted at sneaking in and out. It seemed that I didn't know all the facets of this boy I loved, and I didn't want to. We knew so much that there had to be something for us later, like peeling back wallpaper and discovering old frescoes. "You should know that even though you guys were arguing, Edie felt like crap all night." I nodded. I knew. There didn't seem to be anything hiding frescoes between her and I. I crawled onto the bed I had not used in almost a year, the sheets stiff and cold, so cold they felt wet against my legs. I felt the drag of exhaustion, the pound of it in my head. The sound of my own heartbeat was caught between pain and thrill, a song to sleep to.

Present:

WINTER

I came out of sleep every afternoon like the way I imagined a coma patient came to: slow and lost. Nothing was familiar but the ache in the muscles was tight and fetal, holding myself together always. I didn't fight being awake, but I didn't understand why I was every time my eyes opened. My room was quiet, but small things changed when I forgot to punish my body, walking and running the same beach until the broken parts of myself stitched back together just long enough to push me back up the stairs, back into that bed, before I lost the miniscule amount of control I had over my emotions.

Today was no different. My record player was open and fingerprints were in the dust as the red light glowed weakly. I must have mistaken the static for waves crashing around me while I slept. The needle undulated with the record that had reached its end. I moved to it quicker than I thought I could but still awkward, my limbs sloppy with too much cold and not enough sleep. No liquid was left in me that I hadn't coughed out onto the sand. Saltwater and tragedy forever a taste in my mouth. I spent a year empty, but my mouth was still wet with it.

I saw the writing, the letters curling in like a girl would write, but the deep black reminding me of an adult. I twisted the dial until the light went out. My mother must be grasping, more than she had with the therapists and the new paint. She had left cups of tea until I shattered my Tesla mug on the floor, stepping over the broken pieces the way I wished she would step over mine. I wanted her to move on and leave me alone with the dead. I recognized the record; I never could have forgotten it. I traced the letters as I said them aloud, my voice like rust flaking into the pipe the first time you turn the water back on. "You found yourself once, you can do it again." I broke the record almost in the same place as the mug, stepping over what had been left to me, what I couldn't consider keeping. The light caught the torn, yellowing record label that had once been white. I would never listen to The Band again. I grabbed the record player by the handle, feeling its fragility in my palm. It broke off and I tossed it over the deck.

It would never stop, these gestures of hope, as if a song could pull me from hell. This wasn't a Greek myth. I felt stronger in my anger, so I used it to propel me, to carry me down to the sand. I let the ocean moan for me, let it be the roar of all I felt but couldn't express. The grief was what filled my veins. If I cut my arm I would bleed, but I wouldn't expect to feel it. Grief was never ending, no tourniquet needed to preserve the body's life. How long could grief alone fill a person? So far it had been a year.

Past:

ONE YEAR AGO

SPRING

There is a reason that they start movies and shows with the sound of a bell ringing; everyone understands it. We were trained as a society to respond to behavioral triggers, and I was no different. When the bell rang in seventh period I was up, gathering and marching, answering its call. It didn't hurt that it was break or that I had a room to clean if I wanted to leave the house. It wasn't so bad. When the ceiling of the room is so pretty you forget the importance of the floor. I weaved through the faces and the bodies that didn't often change. They became the faces I would see every time I worked or went to the store, and some would fade with memory as they took their leave from the crowds.

I smelled Evan before I saw him. He smelled of sand and strawberries. He had gone surfing during lunch, foregoing one of his mom's experimental bento lunches she had picked up from Pinterest.

If I married this sun-soaked boy I would demand that he come directly to the altar with his tux-covered body, damp from the water and trailing sand. I loved his smell. I loved him. It had been a year, but I loved that it hadn't felt like just one; it felt like an entire lifetime. Why don't people talk about the fact that a person doesn't just fall in love with the same person once, but that it happens over and over again as each different piece of who they are slowly comes out of the woodwork? I fell in love with him because of the way he fell in love with me, because of his wit and his ability to be honest about his flaws. I fell in love a hundred times, but for every twenty I fell a little out of love because of something I hadn't seen or known, a part that wasn't loveable. Those pieces didn't outweigh or equal, they just were. It's what made love make sense, to know that it didn't have to be overwhelming or encompassing all of the time. The ocean was the same; it would have intimidated me if I didn't know that it fell apart as often as it came together before it could crash down.

"You ready?" I smiled up at him, at the way his hair was already lightening and how it had grown longer over winter. I pulled a curled-up strand, giving him pause. "I'm cutting it tomorrow," he said. I let go of the piece and turned my face into his chest, inhaling the scent. I leaned up and kissed the scar that would let me find his face should I ever go blind.

"What about you? Are you going to go back to your tower this year?" he asked. He said everything into the crown of my head; he loved the smell of my hair. I shook my head. I didn't ever want to let my hair fall in cascades again. I liked it short.

"Let me give you a ride home," he said. I didn't want to move, but I had to leave for work. "Or we can just stay like this until they close the school around us." I nodded; I liked that choice far better. He laughed and pushed me without any real force away from his chest, using my shoulders to guide me through the halls. I smiled and waved, giving half-hugs here and there. Evan threw his high fives around like confetti, tossing his happiness down the hall at anyone else just as excited as him for spring break. This was the year where everyone went on their last adventures with the friends they knew might not be friends soon enough.

"I don't get off work until ten and my dad is in town so…" I started.

"So, I will come get you tomorrow or we can meet up at the beach."

"Probably the latter." We stopped when we hit the asphalt of the parking lot, avoiding the truck that could have crushed me. I found his Jeep, the parking always off-kilter. "Where's your board?" I glanced around, finding my own answer when I saw Leland's truck, the bed stacked with three boards. "Never mind."

"What?" he asked. I followed the line of his stare and rolled my eyes. It was a bit desperate to strip down to your bikini in the parking lot.

"Really?" I didn't even cover the hint of disbelief in my voice. "Kara? Gross." I walked around to my side even though it was still technically illegal to ride with him for another month. No one stopped us, but we also never left town.

"Laney…her chest is just out there. It doesn't make me want to hook up with her, but come on…I'm going to at least look. You watch Leland wax his board every single time, but I have no worries that you want to hook up with him." He had a point. Leland's body was a study in sculpture and tone. I appreciated art. I was honest about it so that I didn't have to lie, and I was definitely being a hypocrite, but at least Leland was a human with actual thoughts and personality. I couldn't be a hundred percent sure, but as far as I could tell Kara was absent a single thought. She would need that chest because she hadn't relied on anything else since seventh grade. I glared in her general direction, but there was no point continuing a conversation that would eventually paint me into a corner.

"You win. Let's go," I said. That was all he was getting from me. I climbed into the seat and squinted into the sun. It was odd to know that I only had one full day of spring break. The layers of adulthood were starting to show through.

"I'm sorry. I am," he said. He smiled in my direction. If there was one thing he did well, it was apologize. He wouldn't do it if he didn't mean it. It was a trait he got from his mother; she didn't waste words she didn't mean. The Jeep jerked hard, the seat belt cutting into my shoulder. His driving skills had clearly not caught up to his apologizing skills. We said nothing as he moved into town, trying to use side streets as much as he could.

"I got a text from Bryce. You remember him, right? He gave you a soul for your birthday." The volume of his voice was losing its battle with the wind as he gathered speed.

"Of course I remember Bryce. How could I forget him?" A flash of short images came to my mind, like a quick montage at the end of a film. Snapshots slid through the memories, but they were buried under Edie's tears and her brittle confessions on my deck. I hated thinking of him that way, especially with the gold square hanging between my collarbones. The birthday gift haunted me. Edie still wore the heart that he had given her, even if she had never returned the offering. She had done what she always knew she would. She let him go without reason or cruelty. He was her boy of summer and he left with nothing, without any part of her. That was Edie; there was nothing she couldn't seem to say goodbye to.

"Why did Bryce text you anyway?" I asked. I had forgotten what triggered the faded photographs that scattered through my memories.

"He was just seeing what was up. We are basically his only friends up here. I told him we would go drive to the skatepark two towns over, the one that's by the pier. I doubt Edie will even blink twice. She's Edie after all." I turned my face from the sun and glared at him. He wasn't smiling. He was serious.

"Be fair," I said.

"Tell me how it isn't fair?" He glanced from the road to me.

"Fine." I closed my eyes to the sun and wished that the streets didn't turn so quickly into the one that I lived on. I wanted him to drive, to follow the faded black ribbon into the mountains until the road fell away on one side and the ocean stretched out below the other. I was supposed to be reckless, youth making me stupid, but instead I was aware, aware of every day and month that was left until they all went away.

"Do you think it's strange that we haven't had sex yet?" I asked. The Jeep swerved but I kept my eyes closed, the burn of my words tracing through the veins in my neck and swallowing up my cheeks. I couldn't fight the smile.

"Not really. You never seemed like a girl that would be easy to get." I shaded my eyes with my hand and looked at him.

"You got me, or more like I got you. It's been a year," I said.

"Are you checking stuff off a list of things to do before you are left here by yourself? I know you, Laney. It's just going to happen one day. I've always known that." He grinned.

"The entire male teenage race just kicked you out of some unspoken club." I pulled the seatbelt away from my neck, my own conversation making my skin flush.

"I will get back in." He jerked the Jeep to a stop. I saw my mom glance around the garage. The expression directed toward Evan was not thrilled.

"You better start learning to drive that piece of junk better if you're going to have my kid in it," she said. Evan colored under her tone. He hadn't realized she was outside. I had almost forgotten she would already be home now that she didn't have a seventh period anymore. He nodded. It was the tone of a teacher, and he responded like a student used to being chastised. I would have defended him had there been anything to defend.

"Sorry," he apologized. She nodded as we walked past. I saw that she had taken my Converse from the basket and muddied them. I rolled my eyes. Sharing a shoe size had seemed so awesome when all I had wanted was to wear her high heels and old Dr. Martens, but now that the tables had turned I wasn't really loving it.

"Those are mine. The faded ones are yours." I stared down at shoes that used to be blue.

"I forgot that you bought these ones. Oh wait…I did." This was her closing argument. I shook my head at her in passing and dropped my backpack on the couch. Evan already had his head buried in the refrigerator.

"Did you eat all the Hawaiian bread?" My expression sank into a scowl at his question.

"Did we get married and I missed it? Of course I ate it. I was finishing an essay and stress-ate the last of the Hawaiian bread and seven Cuties!" I refused to feel bad about eating my own food.

"One day that habit of stress eating is going to catch up with you. How can you eat all that and not be sick?" I didn't answer him. I wasn't justifying this conversation with an answer. It would probably hit me around my thirties and I would turn into one of those gym rats that watched the news and cried after eating too many tacos. I ducked before a Cutie hit me in the head, slumping down until he was done tossing a few more onto the couch.

"Thanks for the warning." The orange flew out of my hand and over the back of the couch at him, my aim impeccable.

"You know you are going to want that. I'm eating it now." He grinned with a pyramid of mandarin oranges in his hands. I felt around until I found the one that I hadn't tossed back. He acted like he wasn't going to end up peeling the whole pile and only getting half.

"So, there is this thing we have to talk about, Laney." He sat beside me; it was like he had dropped with all the heaviness I could hear in his words. I cringed inwardly with understanding, and it was a struggle to keep the lines of my face neutral.

"I got my letter a month ago, the letter from NYU," he started. I put a hand over his mouth to stop him, not because I wasn't proud, but because confusion wasn't giving pride its moment in my heart.

"A month? You found out you got into NYU a month ago but you haven't said a word? What the hell, Evan?" I had forgotten I was covering his mouth until the heat of his exhale startled me. My hand had tightened. His eyes were wide as he pulled my palm from his mouth, kissing the center of it.

"I deferred a semester, Laney." I didn't move, but let his words hang suspended between us. I felt like I was on a ferris wheel going backward, the emotion polarizing between head and heart. I went with the one that pounded like a second drum in my chest.

"Why would you do that Evan? Why? It's NYU. You can't throw away what you've always wanted. Is it the cost? Jesus, Evan." My words tripped over themselves, out of sync with the slow widening of his eyes.

"I'm not throwing anything away, Laney. It's one semester, and my grandfather is handling the cost. It's already done. I need you to understand what I am trying to tell you. No more interruptions, no hands over my mouth. This time just listen. I'm not giving up what I want, but I am giving you six months after we graduate. God, Laney, I love you so much it feels like if I leave you here I am losing part of myself, but that's all I am giving you…six months to see what life is here without everything you already know. I want you to come with me or go somewhere you want to be. If your heart is here I will love you anyway, but I can't stay for you. That doesn't mean I won't come back or that we are over, but this world, this bubble we live in, might not be what you want when so much of it leaves without you. Think about it and apply to some colleges so you have options if you hate it. Your SAT scores were ridiculous because you barely studied and still killed the rest of us. Please Laney, consider that what you love here isn't going to just disappear, but it's not going to be the same either. Is there even a 'here' without Edie?" I couldn't answer him. It was so much at once. There was a war spreading through me, tearing me to pieces. He didn't let go of my hand. I wasn't going to cry, not now. I didn't even know why I wanted to cry. Was it this boy and his gift of time, or phantom pains of a loss I hadn't even suffered yet?

"Breathe," he said. It was such a simple command, but it was so impossible to do. I could feel the pressure of decisions—decisions that were currently pushing my lungs out. I waited for the crack of my ribs, for the air to rush out of me through a gaping hole in my chest, but it didn't. "Laney, you need to take a breath, dammit. Now!" It wasn't so much a breath that came out of me as it was me trying to pull all of it—him, the room, the ocean that pounded the sand outside of my house—back into my lungs, into me. I couldn't though; I couldn't pull them into me. The time I had left to pretend it was a realistic concept was shrinking, almost gone.

"Don't do it, Evan. Don't stay for me." The words were a whisper, but I was trying to throw every bit of conviction I had into them.

"It's done, Laney. I'll stay for the fall semester and be gone in spring. Either choice you make doesn't change this, what this is between us." He kissed me with his choices, and I hoped his lips couldn't feel my confusion and the weariness of trying to figure out what I wanted. If he could feel it, he loved me despite it.

"Please try and refrain from making babies on my couch," my mother called out as she stopped in the living room, her arms strained with laundry. She never remembered the basket.

"Sorry," Evan said, sitting up and fidgeting with the hair that was touching his ear. I laughed, but not as hard as he blushed.

"It's fine. Congratulations on NYU, Evan. You are going to be an amazing force in photography one day. You'll make us sand moms proud." He blushed even deeper.

"Thank you. I hope I prove you right." She mussed his hair with the hand she had freed up, dropping bras and socks as she moved up the stairs.

"I will be back down in half an hour, Laney. Get ready for work." The sound of her voice was a faded echo down the stairs.

"I love your blood-red face, Evan. I *have* applied to schools though. I never leave myself without options," I said.

"Of course you have, Brainy Laney." He peeled back the skin of a Cutie, the smell of the oranges sweet in the air. I wanted to remember this smell and this moment when the boy I loved gave me time.

"God, finally. I thought you would never get off." Edie was waiting for me outside Gilly's, the streetlight illuminating her face.

"Why didn't you have to work? I thought you were on the same shifts as me this week," I asked.

"I traded with Ainsley. I needed to have Sunday off because Big Edie and the mister are taking me out to celebrate."

"Celebrate what?" I untied the strings of my half apron, the smell of malt vinegar and the beer someone had spilled on me rising up from my body. Edie wrinkled her nose.

"I will never miss those smells, the scent of the hapless waitress," she said. I rolled my eyes at her dramatics and she grinned in response. "They are taking me to that restaurant in Big Sur, Sierra Mar, at the Post Ranch Inn."

"Why? Your mom isn't cheap, but that place takes firstborn children as a payment." We moved up the street, sliding to the side to let people pass.

"I just realized this is the first time since you got your license that I have seen you without a car." Her face colored pink in response. "What did you do?" I asked.

"I lost the keys, I mean they are somewhere in the house, but I couldn't find them," she responded.

"Classic Edie."

"Shut up." She shoved me into the side of a restaurant window, harder than she meant to. I looked over at the startled faces of a family having a late dinner, the kids squirming with tiredness. Clearly tourists. I smiled and mouthed "sorry."

"Wait, rewind. What are you celebrating?" She kept her head down, watching the light catch on the black glitter Toms.

"I got in. I actually got into both, Laney! I can go to either Berkeley or Columbia. I got into both!" I hugged her to me, tight with pride and pain. I poured it into the hug. She could feel it. She hugged me back, but it was possessive, like the hug was strong enough to tie me to her indefinitely. People were staring at these two girls, one soul split into two bodies, not willing to free themselves from each other but unwilling to recognize the distance that was rising up regardless. Could they see it, the pain in the hug, or did they see two weird girls trying to walk without letting go?

"I am so proud of you Edie! It's crazy how proud I am. Where do you want to go?" If she went to Berkeley I could keep her, but if she went to Columbia I would lose both her and Evan to the same greedy state.

"I don't know, but I want to decide by Sunday at dinner. By the way, you are also off work then. Don't ask me how Big Edie swung it, but we can't eat a meal that costs first born babies without you. Your letters will come soon. God, Laney, it's all real." Her smile was infectious and strangers we passed returned it, but I was thinking of the letters that I had put in an unopened box. I didn't want to see what I was possibly throwing away of my own free will. I didn't want anyone to see them. Each envelope contained an outline of my every move and choice for the next four years. Edie shouted up to the gods, or maybe the moon. I smiled then. I couldn't help it. She was one decibel of excitement away from howling.

"Evan got into NYU," I said quietly. She paused and hugged me even harder than before. She was choosing Columbia. I could feel it in the way her arms tightened to the point of hurting. She was comforting me for the loss ahead and she didn't know it. I ignored the flare of annoyance that she assumed her decision to go away for school was also mine. In the stack of letters there were none from Berkeley or Columbia. I hadn't applied for any schools in California. If I was leaving what I loved, I was throwing myself from the cliffs, not swimming to the deep end.

"You can let go now. I'm fine." *He is deferring a semester to let me see if I can live without you in my life. He knows that we don't know how to be apart, and he loves me enough to wait for me, not forever, but for a while.* These were the things I said to Edie, none of them out loud. She released me and twirled into a man in a pullover hoodie and slacks. He smiled at her and she flirted back because she was happy, because she was Edie.

"Are you going to make me eat weird stuff at dinner?" I used the question to lead us out of my inner thoughts and back into actual conversation. It still felt like for every sentence she might say, a silent answer would follow in my head. My thoughts were a cancer that ate away at us. I was a liar and a thief. I was stealing the time she needed to understand why I was doing this. I wasn't being fair because thieves are rarely fair.

"Yes. You will have to try all kinds of crap we probably won't even be able to pronounce. It's going to be amazing. Amazing. All those cooking shows I watched with your mom did this to me, Laney. You only have yourself to blame. Imagine what I would have watched had you not been buried in a book," she joked.

"Do you realize that you going to an East Coast university is going to be like a non-law school version of *Legally Blonde?*"

"I do. Except I am the soon-to-be valedictorian of our graduating class and I know all about the importance of skin care." My smile was genuine this time.

"I'm so hungry. I couldn't even eat tonight. Some kid threw up all down the hallway. I thought I was going to die. Luckily I didn't have to clean it up. It's not so bad though. Sander is pretty much the most chill boss on the planet," I said. She nodded in agreement.

"I am turning in my notice in July so I can use all of August to get ready. Are you doing the same?" she asked. I stared up the street at the blurred streak of light down the freeway.

"Probably." If I left all my answers vague they felt less like lies. "Are you spending the night?" She looked at me like my brain had just leaked out of my ear.

"Obviously, I wouldn't walk two miles down to Gilly's when I'm not working just to walk you home. This isn't reverse chivalry," she said. She had a point.

"You did not walk down here. I call bullshit," I said.

"Okay, the mister dropped me off. Whatever." Her sentence punctuated with a laugh.

"Edie, what if the letters come but they're rejections?" She stopped in front of a house full of light and glass, the ocean a distorted mirror on the other side.

"That wouldn't ever happen, genius. Your SAT scores were mind-blowingly close to perfect. Why would you get rejected?" Her voice was a study in total disbelief.

"I don't know, perhaps it has been my four years of taking zero interest in sports or group activities?" I suggested.

"No, you never should have read that dumb book about the smart girl who didn't party enough or whatever. I can't remember the idiotic title."

"Probably because it was just an okay book, but one of the many you only read half of."

"If that. I was bored to tears and her parents were freaking nuts." She laughed at her own point. What would I do without her?

"You're right. I'm just being ridiculous," I said. I was compounding my guilt with lies. Even if they were just an omission, I was wearing them like lies.

Finally the silhouette of my house rose up. I should have let my dad come get me. He was home by now. I opened the door but immediately slammed it shut again just as quickly. Gross. My mother had been straddling my father's lap in just a bra, and suddenly I was experiencing childhood trauma. GROSS. I wasn't trying to be a child, but there is never a good age to walk in on your half-dressed mother making out with your father on the couch you planned to fall asleep on after catching up on your shows. Edie was standing silent behind me; she had been close enough to see over my shoulder. I could hear my father's laughter through the closed door and my mother filling the swear jar with a long line of expletives. I wasn't laughing. I was horrified. Edie was so silent I knew her face had to be a mirror of my own. We had not walked in on either of our parents since we had been in third grade, when it was Big Edie and the mister doing much more than making out. We still hadn't let go of that. We were the queens of knocking in her house, and now apparently mine.

The door opened to my father's face. The two of us were frozen in yellow light.

"Okay, all clear. Your mom went upstairs to die, and I'm headed that way if you want to send her any last words before her embarrassment kills her," he joked. We didn't laugh or smile, avoiding eye contact until he shut the door behind us.

"It happens, girls. We thought you would go out for pizza or something. Congratulations Edie on your big news. Your mom called earlier. We couldn't be prouder."

"Dad," I said. He laughed again, the humor wheezing in and out like an asthmatic. He left us in the living room, taking the stairs two at a time. Hopefully not leaving to finish what they had started. I wanted to live in the fantasy land of my parents only having sex when I was absent from the house a little while longer. I should have considered that this was his first day home. All I could see in my head was my mom in a bra. The small more mature corner of my mind had to admit that she was holding up well with age.

"That just happened. Your mom's body though, Jesus," Edie said. It didn't matter that I had been thinking the same thing—I glared at her anyway, because I needed to glare at someone. "Your dad isn't looking bad either."

"Shut up." It was all I had to say, coupled with the glare, for her to fall back into silence.

"Pizza?"

"Definitely. You order it and I will pay, or they will. I need a long shower. I smell and I'm grossed out," I said. I dropped my house keys on the counter and set my phone down. I wasn't looking forward to using the shower by their room.

"I think they might need a cold shower more than you." I groaned in response. Gross.

∿∿∿

"Laney." The whisper pulled my eyes back open. "Laney?" I sat up and my body swayed with the hammock.

"What's up, E? I was almost asleep…or maybe I was asleep." My face stretched with a yawn. I glanced up at the time and saw the green light pulsing three a.m.

"I'm freaking out. I have to make decisions that will affect my entire life. All these years and I didn't anticipate how freaking scary this would be. Every second since I can remember this was the plan. It's like the night with Bryce. What if I make the wrong decision and it twists me up again? I don't want to feel that way. Help me, Laney. I'm losing it." Her voice was full. She wasn't crying, but the panic was worse than tears. I eased myself out of the hammock and lay down, curled like a cat at the end of my bed.

"What do I do?" She was still whispering. I don't think it was for my benefit or to not disturb my parents; it was so her own fear wouldn't overwhelm her.

"You have been ready for this before the rest of us could even function in the hallways of high school. You go, E. You do what you have been planning since the womb."

"I want to go to New York, Laney." My heart swallowed back what it already knew. I was losing my heart and my soul. Even if Evan was giving me six months, it didn't mean that I would change my mind. I couldn't follow them just because they might leave me. I had to want it the way that they did.

"Why not Berkeley?" I had thought she was going to choose Columbia, but I almost needed her to choose Berkeley so I wouldn't lose her all the way. So I would only be a few hours away when the day came that she could forgive me. The time for them to leave had to come, but this was the first time I was considering what life would be like if neither she nor Evan did. I had only ever been thinking of her, but Evan deferring reminded me that I really could lose them both.

"I feel like it will be typical of me to talk big, plan an entire life, and end up back here on the weekends doing laundry. Do people really choose Berkeley over Columbia? I don't think they do, and besides, Columbia makes more sense for a psychology degree." My mind reeled at Edie's tenacity. These were plans I couldn't fathom having to decide. I didn't know what I wanted, but I never had. I had the brains but none of the heart; not yet anyway.

"What are you thinking? Tell me." I smiled at how together she always was, but yet she hated making decisions without knowing what I thought.

"I think you should do what you want. Take this opportunity and do what will make you happy. No matter what, you have to do that one thing, Edie—you have to do what makes you happy." She laughed. I had gotten deep and serious and she laughed. Of course she laughed. I sounded like a poster on the guidance counselor's wall.

"I can fix people and you can make them read, Laney. Remember when all you wanted to do with your life was read and make people read the books you loved? You could do that as a professor, like your mom, but without dealing with teenagers that might act like us, all shitty and hormonal. You will get your letters and I will know what we should do and where I should go. It will all make sense. I believe that, Laney. The universe will tell us what to do." I smiled into the darkness; she always trusted the universe and what she imagined it was telling her to do.

"God, go to sleep. I'm so tired. Do you realize for some of us that this will be the last bonfire? Hadley gets on a plane to see family and go to Disneyworld the day after we graduate," I said. Her foot came horribly close to my face and I slapped at it.

"Don't touch my feet, Laney." Her voice carried her yawn into a whine.

"Don't put it in my face, hoser." She flipped over and purposely nudged my shoulder with her toes. I grimaced. "You woke me up, you know!" I exclaimed.

"I know. It was an emergency though. What's your emergency?" I swallowed the truth. My emergency was that this was a lie and it was killing me, that it was changing who I was to her. I didn't tell her. My emergency was that I needed her to understand me well enough to know this was coming and to acknowledge it if she did. My chest ached with the words, but I swallowed them back.

"My emergency is that I am still hungry." I sat up and stretched my arms over my head. She followed me in suit.

"Me too. Grilled cheese? You don't think your parents are down there half naked again, do you?" I hopped up, wincing at how cold my floor felt. There was nothing weird at all about eating your feelings at three a.m., nothing at all.

We tiptoed down the hallway with ballet feet all the way into the kitchen. I climbed up on the counter, she cooked, and I took Snapchats of her cooking. I sucked at cooking. There would be smoke and burned cheese if I made our middle of the night snack.

"When does Ryland leave?" she asked, her back to me. It weighed on me, the time he had left. He had come back from boot camp quieter and more controlled. I missed the wildness that had been in his eyes and his hair. I could still see him in there, but it was like he had grown up while we watched and struggled to understand the transition. He was going this summer, shipping out in June or July. I would write him letters like a 1950s G.I. girlfriend. I didn't want him to go. He was one of us, he fit, and I didn't want to miss him too. It was odd how I couldn't fathom him living a life without all of us already.

"He still doesn't have a definitive date." Her face was drawn, but she wasn't as scared as I was. She was proud of him. My fear overrode my pride.

"You know what we need? Trashy crap TV that will allow us to forget that the future is coming and coming fast for at least a few hours in the middle of the night. I'll laugh at the scripted jokes and you can bemoan the brain cells that are dying while we watch it." She turned away from the stoves, a stack of four sandwiches perfectly browned already done. I loved when she made the food and I just watched. In a dorm room she could probably be Gordon Ramsey with a hotplate.

"You should be a culinary major instead of a shrink, Edie." She laughed small short laughs that she tossed behind her, leaving a trail to the couch. We both sat furthest from the cushion my parents had been on that we could. I tried not to roll my eyes when she turned on one of the ten episodes that she and my mom had recorded of a Kardashian spinoff.

"Aww. I miss your mom. I never watch these without her," she said. I shook my head at her while biting into the insane heaven that comes from bread and melted cheese. It was cheap bliss. We ate and watched, remaining as close as we had ever been. There was a wall between us, but I could never bring myself to call her attention to it. Tonight would have been the perfect time since the fear was fresh for both of us. My fear was greater, I guess, my encompassing selfish feeling of fear. I sat with Edie and my fear until the sky blushed just bright enough for it to be morning. My eyelids were heavy and the sounds of Edie's breathing filled the room in place of the muted TV. As soon as she had fallen asleep I had ended the agony. I didn't need to hear anything else another person on that show said. I didn't move my head off her leg, but I shifted so I could stare into the screen, its colors bright in the darkness until darkness was all I could see.

I felt her wet finger in my ear and the reality that this wasn't a recurring nightmare I had of seven-year-old Edie waking me up after our first sleepover with her spit-covered finger in my ear. This was happening.

"I will break the damn finger from your traitorous hand," I mumbled. Her laughter was louder than an alarm and a pounding of my annoyance in my brain. "That's disgusting!" There were few ways she could annoy me more than this. My eyes blinked open, but she wasn't there. I had yelled at thin air.

"Laney Wilder, jar." It wasn't my mom letting my whole name roll off her tongue like chastisement was a second language she was fluent in, but my father. Having him say it rattled me awake far quicker than if it had it been my mother. "I mean it, tired or not, we don't do that here…anymore." I ignored the hint of humor I heard. I shoved the heavy blanket that had not been there when I fell asleep off of my legs.

"I object to the swear jar and this whole fascist household," I said dramatically. I tossed my arm over my eyes. It was as if they had gone all out on a Cinderella-style wake up. The house was full of fresh air and coffee and the windows were open.

"Not a chance. Mussolini says put change in the jar." His words were more defined laughs than an actual voice.

"Why do you always choose Mussolini?" I sat up, feeling the crumbs of the grilled cheese in my bra. I was a mess.

"It seems in bad taste to pretend to be the other two." I looked over the back of the couch to see his body folded over the table with a pile of contracts and a cup of coffee. He looked over, his eyes blinking like an owl. "What?" he asked.

"Mussolini isn't in good taste either, crazy. No fascist dictator falls under good taste for an impersonation." He nodded solemnly in answer. I wanted to laugh, but I kept my face blank.

"In that case, Kim Jong-un says put a quarter in the jar, foul-mouthed western filth." This time I couldn't help it. I laughed.

"That was not any better, just so you know, and that laugh does not make you pretending to be a fascist any better. There's only one place waiting for you, old man…" I indicated the floor.

"Urgent message for Laney Wilder: Satan says put a quarter in the jar before he charges you interest." This time he smiled and saluted me with his coffee cup.

"Well at least you will be comfortable down with the big guy in red, dad."

"Santa?" he asked. I groaned at his question. Where was Edie?

"Edie left an hour ago with your mom. They hit the beach for a morning run and left us lazy bastards behind," he said.

"Jar!" I giggled as I headed for the stairs.

"Fascist," he muttered from the table. It was nice having him home. This whole last year had been rough. I missed when his witty comments and lingering presence by the coffee pot were as common of a sight as my mom reading at the table. I stopped before I rounded the corner, watching the way the sun caught on his hair that had darkened from white blonde to a brown over the course of my childhood. His face was a little rough from not shaving. He was finally starting to show his age in the small lines leading away from his eyes. We sat in a similar manner and had the same facial lines when we concentrated.

"Dad..." He turned around as I said it, distracted but still trying to give me time. "Never mind. Tell Edie I will be cleaning my room."

"Really?" His face transformed into shock, hugely exaggerated shock. I rolled my eyes in response. I wasn't that bad. When I opened my door I realized something—maybe I *was* that bad. The floor was littered in shoes, the flat surfaces covered in books and notebooks. Even the Einstein painting was hanging off-kilter next to my closet. Clearly I had been robbed and they just didn't take anything with them. Was it silly to cry because you didn't want to clean your room? Yes, it was.

I flipped through the stack of records until I found David Bowie; it had been the very first one I had listened to after my uncle died. I had come home from the funeral after two flights and a drive that never seemed to end to a giant box on our doorstep. It contained his things, the stuff that grandma couldn't keep or even look at without crying. We all had a smaller box within the big box. Mine had been full of his music and an old v-neck argyle sweater with a hole in the elbow. I couldn't wear it then and I wouldn't wear it now. The knit of the sweater held in his smell, the faint remains of clove cigarettes. I had wanted to go to sleep, but instead I had helped my father carry the box to my room, sat with him while he set up the record player, and watched as he wept. That had been the longest weekend I had ever experienced. Once my dad had stood up from the crate full of records, he had wiped his eyes and said he would see me in the morning. That was the first time I had ever heard, really heard, David Bowie, and known my dad as a man who had lost his brother and would never really understand why. No one can prepare you for the first time you see a parent as more than just a parent. It's both alarming and eye opening to know that they exist for reasons other than getting you through life.

I broke out of the memories and cleaned to the variations of Bowie's moods. I was almost done before I considered that this was a sign that I was growing up, fulfilling my responsibilities without my mother hovering nearby or Edie making puppy faces to try and get me to do what was necessary.

"Holy crap. You cleaned your whole room!" Edie filled the doorframe, her arms and legs coated in sweat. Her feet were bare of the running shoes she kept in the basket by the door. Her chest was still rising and falling like she had never left the sand behind, like her body was still mimicking the waves she had run next to. I was reading.

"I did."

"Bowie? Everything okay?" She knew that I loved Bowie best when my head or heart were heavy. Bowie held up either no matter what. Poor Edie. She was the confidant to all my thoughts and feelings, except the important ones apparently.

"Yeah I'm good. I was just thinking about Jared."

"Your uncle?" she asked.

"Yep. All his memories are just this…" I swept my hand toward the record that spun in slow rotation, the red light glowing.

"What brought this up?" I shrugged in answer. I had no idea. That was the mystery of sadness—it came and left at will. I don't think anyone has a say in the methods of melancholy.

"I remember thinking he was so magical and cool, and his sideburns were a little longer than I had really ever seen. I wanted that olive green jacket he wore like it was his skin. I thought I would grow up and marry him. He always smelled like the spices that your mom uses on her ham during Christmas. Isn't that how it goes though, when people are too cool for life?" she asked. I watched her from the corner of my eye, turning in circles with her hair swinging around. I remembered that day too. She had said quietly to me behind the couch that we would officially be family when she married Jared and I smiled because I thought she was right.

"I have to get out of this room," I said. The music had swelled louder in my head than it really was. It was too depressing a way to start spring break.

"Yeah, we definitely should get out of here. Definitely. What we need is tacos, or a sandwich now and tacos tonight," she said with a laugh as she turned David Bowie and my sadness down. "Oh wait. Let me take a shower real quick. I just realized I'm covered in sweat." She pointed to her armpit and wrinkled her nose.

"Why don't you just put deodorant on before you run?" It seemed like a valid question, but her grossed out face said I was an idiot before she could.

"Eww. No. Just no. I would have to wipe it all over my body, weirdo. You would know this stuff if you had an athletic bone in your body," she said.

"I swim, Edie. I'm not your run-of-the-mill Jabba the Hut, you know."

"Duh, you are way too nice to be Jabba, and you couldn't handle Leia. She was kind of a badass, even with the buns." She grinned, feeling proud of herself. I shoved her out of my doorway and continued on down the stairs. My father had finally given up his guard post by the caffeine and had moved out onto the deck. I tried not to gawk at the sight of my father doing absolutely nothing, but that's what I was seeing, no phone and no laptop in sight.

"Did I die?" He turned around at the sound of my voice; I caught the somber expression before he had a chance to pull his lips into a loose smile. "Did someone else die? What's wrong?" I asked.

"I was just out here being sentimental. It happens to the best of us. I couldn't help but hear Jared's David Bowie record, and I was just reeling at the thought that in five years you will be as old as he will ever be. Math is crazy sometimes, kid, and sad. Anyway, what are your plans for today? Never mind. What was I thinking? It's bonfire night." He was smiling at me, but his knuckles were white against the driftwood rail. I moved closer to him, wrapping my arm around his waist and trying to pull some of the sadness I had brought up off of his back and onto mine. It didn't work. He would never shrug off what he was carrying around onto someone else. I liked to believe that I had inherited this trait from him.

"Yeah, last spring break before adulthood," I said. I smiled out at the water that was climbing in slow laps up the shore. I couldn't imagine not living in this house. Not every little girl gets to feel like she has her own ocean.

"It's funny how that works, kid." He loosened his hold on the rail as relaxation replaced the memories.

"How what works?" I asked.

"Just that everything feels like it is the last of something else. The last bonfire of your adolescence, the last year of high school, the last time all of you will be together the way you have been since you were children, and the last time you have no responsibilities. That's where you are right now, at the last of everything. You wake up and you're an adult, and you think it's all going to be different, for better or for worse, but it isn't really like that. It just changes. It becomes the last illegal drink you have before you turn twenty-one, the last job you take because now you have a career. No matter how imminent the future seems, the past is still hanging on. The idea of youth itself is twisted in the fabric of age until you age out of life."

I didn't want to move or to break up the way this moment felt, like he was taking his last chance to impart his wisdom upon me, but I was never good at being serious.

"Yoda, my Yoda. What would I do without your infinite wisdom?" I joked.

"You would turn into the same beautiful smartass that you would have always become, but now you're smarter for having heard me out."

"Touché, old man, touché!" I laughed, leaning into his side. I did wonder how many more times I would have this feeling of such a solid connection between us as we did right now, in this moment. It was a feeling that didn't dull even with his long absences, because whenever he came back I was here waiting. Would we have that when it wasn't as convenient?

"Go enjoy your spring break, girl child." I laughed and moved away from the comfort of him, the humor of my childhood nickname filling in the gaps. I wandered past my sleeping mother, whose whole body was curled into a snail shell in the corner of the couch. She smelled of sweat and sand. My phone went off a dozen times as I drank orange juice and stared out the window, ignoring text after text. It was a subconscious decision to distance myself slowly from everyone, but I followed through when I realized what I was doing. Reese could feel it; her determination to soak up her friends like the sun was apparent. Ryland's decision to part ways with his cousin, who was now more like a twin than ever, left her pulling at the ties she still had. I glanced at the screen, and the guilt rose up like acid in my throat. Evan and Edie were the only ones I was holding onto with both hands.

"What is with you and your winter moods?" I kept my gaze fixed on the window, the sunlight obscuring the reflection of Edie standing behind me. "I mean it, chick. You are like somber as hell lately."

"Jar!" the voice from the couch mumbled sleepily.

"Okay, that's just getting spooky." Edie whispered conspiratorially, her thumb gesturing back at my mom.

"It is. I'm good, and you can relax on your SAT vocabulary practice. When do you use the word somber? Ever?" I set my glass in the sink. I didn't have to turn around to know that she was giving me hardcore uggo faces. I could feel them. "Let's go already. You took like an hour in the shower."

My father was still out on the deck, perhaps using the water like I did to commune with the lost.

"So Hadley and Nathan are splitsville again. I know, you told me so. She dropped him though, and said she didn't see the point when she leaves to her aunt's and then a few family trips before going back East. I think it also matters that Nathan is going to work full-time at that hotel up in Big Sur and part-time with his dad. She said he got into both schools the guidance counselor made him apply to, but he just wants to do what he loves—surf and work. I don't know how Hadley didn't know he was a dyed-in-the-wool local, as my mom calls it. So they are no more," Edie said. I shut the door behind us as quietly as I could and fought every impulse in my body that screamed hypocrite. She couldn't judge Hadley for the same blindness she suffered, but she did.

"Well they lasted a lot longer than I ever thought they would." She shrugged at my response. It was true; none of us saw their renewed relationship lasting longer than the summer. I was pretty sure it was sustained on convenience, but maybe that was the truth in all relationships that sprang up between childhood friends. There was effortlessness to knowing the other person the way you knew yourself, the awkwardness of getting to know them gone.

"Here's the thing, Laney, you have to wonder how it is that the future is also the past. I mean, I think of this almost as often as I think of the other meaningless things in my life. I know I'm a total clothes whore and my attention span is so short it can be measured in minutes rather than hours, but what will fill the emptiness inside me when I don't have to consider this whole adult thing anymore? My entire life has been spent thinking of only the future, our future. My whole past is made up of my entire hypothetical future," she said. I stopped, pausing in the middle of the street. How did my shallow, almost vapid, friend always find depths that I had never considered to explore?

"Perhaps you should consider switching to philosophy, E."

"How about no. I want to make enough money that I can afford to come back here on my own time and on my own terms. Philosophy won't get me that. Also, again, the levels of my attention span will be better served seeing one patient for fifty minutes at a time. I feel like I skipped the majority of my teenage recklessness building myself into a hybrid adult. I just did it in cute clothes and with a brain full of reality show drama."

"You are really reinforcing the whole Elle Woods from *Legally Blonde* stereotype right now." I laughed, but she didn't. We were still standing in the middle of the road.

"Except I don't want Harvard and I would never, never own a chihuahua. I also didn't need some loser to dump me to know where I am going."

"True."

She dropped her musing without questioning why I never really answered her question. She was alone in her abandonment of teenage normalcy. I spent as much time dwelling on my future, but it was *my* future that consumed me, not ours. I followed behind her, watching the light catch in her hair and the way she still swayed more than necessary with each step. I didn't answer, because somewhere below my insecurities was the rooted belief that my decisions couldn't weigh more than the knowledge and the history that we had between us. I would make my choice and wait out her feelings of betrayal before we slipped back into who we had always been, just Laney and Edie.

She kept her thoughts in her head and weaved between the onslaught of spring breakers, her grin already lightening the heaviness of the thoughts that ate at her. I watched her the way you study a painting, wondering how it was so carefully crafted. She wore her flirtation like a talisman that took the place of Bryce's gift from the summer before. I still wore his gift, but I'd forgotten what it was like to bandy about in flirtation because I had never actually been good at it. Guys smiled back at Edie and the girls did backward glances, lips tighter with envy. We all envy confidence and ease. I rolled my eyes directly at one particular man that was all but salivating, his mouth agape and his eyes glazing. He was grossly too old to be looking at my best friend that way. My reaction was justified, and his shame crept into his cheeks as we passed. She never even slowed down, her resolve to absorb their appreciation obvious.

"Slow down!" I hadn't meant to yell, but Edie stiffened.

"Sorry. I was just making lists and, well, checking them out." She waved to indicate the sea of board shorts. I laughed. Of course she was. I didn't have to be inside her head to understand most of what went on in there. "Let's go get something, anything, to eat. I don't want you passing out again. All the boys I'm trying to attract will be swarming to the swooning princess." She blocked the arm that I jabbed at her.

It's a weird feeling to take a step forward and then slide backward. I shrieked.

"Calm down, Laney. It's just me." Ryland set me down but my heart continued pounding in my throat. "I was looking for you guys. I haven't eaten and didn't see any obliterated buildings, so I'm guessing your appetites haven't wreaked any destruction yet. So, food?" he asked. He was all grins and shorn hair; the smile I was used to, but the lack of hair, not so much. I rubbed my hand on his head. The gesture had become so common that he didn't even react. Edie took her turn petting our man-cat after I was done.

"What do you want to eat? I got paid two days ago, so I am open to anything. Suggestions?" I asked. Both Edie and Ryland glanced around, gauging the lines and the options.

"Gilly's? Sailors? I don't know," Ryland groaned, rubbing his stomach to emphasize his hunger.

"Do you think we will have pizza tonight? I don't want pizza twice. I'm not gaining the freshman fifty before I even leave for school. I want a salad," Edie said.

"What? You want a salad? Are you high, Edie? I hate salad," I moaned. There was no keeping the disappointment out of my voice.

"If I was high, Laney, I would want the pizza." Eye rolling was her new look for this break, and it complemented her tan and witty repartee.

"Fine. Let's go get a salad. Ryland, do you want a salad?" I asked.

"No, Laney, I do not want a salad, but I also don't want to keep walking around looking for the rest of our friends that have far better taste than the two of you. I'm sure Leland is somewhere with barbeque sauce smeared all over his face, sipping some sweet tea, but let's go get a salad. After you." His face was as disgruntled as his voice.

Edie laughed and kept walking. There was only one decent place to get a salad in our town, and it was the same kind of place that had creased Trivial Pursuit cards and food smudged on the back of the table. I shuddered but followed behind her despite my reservations about eating here.

I pushed down the impulse to shove over the toddler that was circling my leg. He ran back and forth around Ryland's leg and mine until he tripped on the toe of Ryland's shoe.

"Whoa, guy, you need to slow down. Where's your mom?" The question had barely left Ryland's lips when a hand waved around the child's face distractedly until he grasped it. I saw a flash of red hair and a phone as the toddler was dragged back across the restaurant.

"No kids for me, ever." I pressed myself against the wall and waited, my statement out there for absolutely anyone within hearing distance. A few people a great deal older than me laughed, and one little girl directly to the side claimed she wanted ten under her breath. I fought the urge to stare at her in horror.

"Twenty minutes. Did you guys see that hurricane child a minute ago? Jesus, I'm glad I don't work here. The hostess said 'Here goes round four' while she was writing down my name. I am going to be so happy to not be working in a restaurant filled with tourists and their terrorists," Edie said. I nodded my head in agreement. She was so right. If I was going to stay here, it wasn't because I was completely enamored with my job. I would have to find another. I felt it in my side—a new twinge below my ribs and a pulling in my stomach—as plans appeared in my head. It was a reminder that if Evan was giving me time, something Edie would never be willing to do, then my plans shouldn't sound already decided.

"Table for three for Jane Arry." The hostess's voice was almost lost in the din of noise. I glanced over at Edie, who was shaking with laughter. She had purposely given the mispronounced version of *Jane Eyre* as our name. I tried not to twitch throughout my whole body. Arianna was in my honors English class and was known for her inability to pronounce the names of most people. Despite being corrected over and over, she had butchered *Jane Eyre* for the entire three weeks that it was our reading focus. I still heard Arianna saying it in my sleep. It was basically becoming PTSD. Last semester she had massacred names in *Macbeth* and *The Merchant of Venice* to the point that I hadn't read Shakespeare since. I might never read it again.

I walked behind Ryland, who smelled like skateboarding. I liked it, earthy and manufactured at the same time. If I lost my sight, I was confident that I could find my people in a crowd. They all wore their personalities in their scent.

I glared at Edie as she sprawled across the booth bench.

"Move over, hoser. I don't want to sit by Ryland. What if some girl comes in and thinks we are together? This guy needs an Edie-style relationship before his soul is stamped and filed into the United States Marines. Until summer his body is all his and whomever he chooses." I smiled at Ryland. The skin around his cheeks were stained pink. I wasn't exactly talking with my long-practiced indoor voice. Edie was laughing so hard that she was shaking against the faded vinyl seat. "Seriously though, sit up Edie," I said. She pulled herself upright.

I moved in next to her, giving her ribs a shove. She already had her nose buried in the menu.

"Why do you even need to look at the menu?" It was a valid question that she completely ignored, if you didn't count the raising of her eyebrows. Ryland studied the menu like he would find something incredible.

"Why are you in a mood? Where is my endlessly happy and brainy Laney?" Edie's voice was faint beside me, like she wasn't really asking me but accidentally thinking out loud. I smirked in response. She was right though; I was happy most of the time, happy until a secret bit up my insides and left them infected. I didn't answer and ignored Ryland's now tense but curious face. I waited for her to tell me like she always did.

"Stop worrying about acceptance letters. It probably has something to do with your last name," she said. I felt my eyebrows draw in at her reasoning, that she was as smart as she was and still assumed we would go through all of our grown life in alphabetical order. I had gotten my letters two months before her.

"That's why you two should have signed up, given your life to God and our country." We paused in our own self-obsessed thoughts at the tremor that ran through the last part of Ryland's words. His smile didn't show the shaking going on inside, the fear that his decision had been made for the wrong reason to impress the wrong people. We let it go, let his fear evaporate in the sun that was glaring in through the glass. I glanced at the menu and pointed my finger on a blur of print, choosing my lunch without concern for what it was. If I was lucky it was just a plate of bacon.

"Are you ready to order?" I blinked up into the light coming in at us from every angle. The waitress seemed unamused that I was studying her. The skin of her face showed the first significant lines of age. I remembered her working here when I still got crayons with my meal. Her blonde hair had always been pulled high and swinging, but now it was gathered into a bun with strands falling free. It was sad. I could end up like her.

"Sorry. I will have the BLT." I looked down to where my finger had rested, but there was simply no way I was putting rubber calamari rings in my mouth. I pressed back the impulse to stare at her longer, to look for myself in her slouched posture, the apron already stained with malt vinegar and cocktail sauce.

"I'll have the same," Edie said from behind her menu. I wanted to shove the dull fork in front of me between her ribs. She had made us come here for a salad and hadn't even ordered a salad!

"Just give me the same, I guess," Ryland shrugged with indifference. Once he had realized the food wasn't going to be great either way, it appeared he had resigned himself to whatever. The waitress nodded without eye contact or any life left in her at all. It would appear that there were things that the saltwater and endless sand couldn't cure. It couldn't make you happy if you didn't live the life you wanted. Her face carved the deepest hole in my conviction yet. I didn't want to be her. I didn't want to look at girls like me with disdain, or worse, with absolutely nothing at all. I was Happy Brainy Laney.

"Edie, I don't want to be a douche, but why did we have to eat here? I can smell the sadness," I said.

Water shot out of her mouth in a gross explosion of humor. I couldn't stay mad at her. How many times a day did I think of that and grasp onto the belief that it was reciprocated? We ate and we laughed, but most of the time we grimaced because the bacon was weird and the bread was soggy with overripe tomatoes. This was how it was supposed to be, but these were some of our last days of it.

I shivered, the heat from the flames evading me. I moved closer to the fire, watching flames lick the wood as sand ground into my bare knees. We were out later than we had ever been before. Curfews had been flung aside when our parents mutually agreed through hushed phone calls that we deserved this. The adults were grateful that we didn't journey down to Florida or Mexico with our classmates for the famous liquor-soaked, commercially approved last days of spring break. We were boring—well, most of us were if you didn't count that somehow Leland had found Cancun right here at home. His morning had been thirty Snapchat photos of the wonders that can happen when you combine bikinis and bronzer. He was knee-deep in girls all the time, and tonight would be the only exception. Tonight he was staring through the heat that twisted up in blue and white between us. His hair was turning into Ken-doll plastic in the light. This was carefree, threadbare poncho Leland, the guy who laughed at every joke and still made barely discernible sandcastles wherever he sat. This was the Leland that had just asked me a question that flushed my skin hotter than sitting pressed to a bonfire. I was staring him down, but he wasn't moving.

"Laney, I asked if you and Evan the Great here had swum out into the undertow yet." I could feel my heartbeat in my stomach. I hated how my answer would sound, how I felt about it. Evan was not smiling. He was emotionless and following my lead. I would answer the question myself, and I didn't shy away from honesty. Leland knew this and was the only one with the balls, besides Edie, to ask me. He wasn't talking about swimming and he didn't care about the undertow.

"I swim as far out as I want when I want, Leland," I said. He blushed at my answer. The same boy had lost his virginity the year he realized muscle definition was a key into doors he didn't think would ever unlock. He thought this was my confession. I was vague and he took it for bragging.

"No. No, she doesn't need to answer you, and just no." Evan's voice was like water simmering. It sounded hushed but potent.

"Calm down, Evan. We all figured Laney kept you in the kiddie pool," Leland said. That was it; the flames fell back under the shadows cast by two bodies colliding. I threw myself away from the center, and Edie's eyes caught mine. We were owls blinking side by side in the firelight. It took Ryland and Nathan exactly one minute to rip them apart and toss them to the side. They looked like toddlers sprawled in the sand, faces red and shirts twisted.

"Leland, you have got to stop antagonizing people. Someone is going to beat the crap out of you in college, you know that right?" Evan asked.

"Yeah, I know, Evan. Don't I know it." Leland's grin was sloppy, his body dropping back into the sand. Just the thought of all the sand he would have in his hair caused my face to slide into a frog-like expression.

"The good news is when some frat guy busts my mouth wide open, I will still be close enough to drive home and have your mom kiss it better." Leland barely got the last word out before his face was dusted in sand as Evan landed on him, a pile of sprawled limbs. This time Nathan and Ryland just hung back while this new fight played itself out.

"Ow. Dammit, Evan." They fell apart, the light catching on the dark streak stretching from Leland's bottom lip to his chin. I couldn't believe he had actually split his lip. I wasn't sure if I wanted to laugh or offer help. Evan was half sitting, the light from his phone illuminating his face.

"Mom? Hey, I'm going to put you on speaker okay?" We all went still at the sound of an awkward laugh on the other end. Evan was grinning.

"Okay. What's going on? Have you been drinking? Are you hurt?" His mom's laugh had become panicked.

"No, god, calm down. I was talking with Leland a minute ago and expressing my concern that his personality could get him into some serious fights with people who haven't grown up with him. He said it would be alright though, because he could come home and get a kiss better from you. Turns out his lip is bleeding now, so I thought you might want to head down to the beach. Right, Leland?"

"You are terrible. Tell Leland I will be right there," his mom said. The phone went dead on the punctuation of her laughter. Evan smiled in Leland's direction, "Did you hear that? She will be here soon, bro."

"Wow. That was an asshole move, Evan," Leland said. It was hard to talk while trying to keep a straight face. Evan nodded with his lips pressed together. Leland was laughing so hard that the blood had smeared from his mouth and chin to his shirt and arm. Evan stood and offered him a hand, grimacing at the bloody palm Leland gripped his with.

"Thanks, that's disgusting," Evan said. They walked off down to the water. I glanced at Edie and nodded in Reese's direction. She was engulfed in light, her black hair a tangle around her face. Her phone vibrated on and off against her legs and her smile was vague. She was happy. We didn't know with whom, but this was Reese in a relationship, full of secrets and smiles.

"Reese! Who are you texting? Tell us!" I nodded in agreement with Edie's question. I had a twenty on closing shift on the guy in econ who transferred in two months ago. His demeanor screamed *Reese wants to date and break up with me.*

"Everyone and no one, Edie." If secret collecting was a thing, Reese was becoming a hoarder. I wasn't worried. She would end up somewhere around town with him during spring break. Whatever she was doing with him, it was probably short term. She left for Portland in June. Her application to Portland State came in months ago. Reese didn't know what she wanted to do, but she knew where she wanted to be. I envied that about all of them, the ease in which they shed the skin they had been living in their whole lives. I knew more technically by knowing where I wanted to be, but I didn't know who I would be or what I would do. The pressure of it was like a tumor, pressing my future so hard into my eyes I felt blinded by it.

"So I got into both my schools, guys." Heads swiveled in Edie's direction and Reese leaned over for an out-of-character hug. "I have to choose between Berkeley and Columbia." The only sounds were the pops emitting from the wood, the burning of something that had been lost and drifted in. I looked away from her, this girl that was the other half of me since we were children, to the fire. Little constellations of sparks rose above our circle before burning out in the darkness. I couldn't make eye contact with anyone, couldn't lie even through omission. They glanced at me with pained expressions because they didn't know about the box in my closet of letters that had flooded in that I had shelved without even opening. I was burning hotter than the driftwood, but to tell the truth would be to lose her, for a minute or years. The not knowing stitched my lips together.

"I think I am going to Columbia. Who am I kidding? Of course I'm going to Columbia. I only applied to Berkeley because it was close, but far enough away at the same time. Now we just wait for Laney to decide." The stares deepened in my direction, Edie pulling full attention to me. I pinched the skin on her leg. She mouthed 'sorry' but her eyes were light, her happiness undeniable. The wave of my selfishness fell back and I saw what her face would look like for the next four years or longer, how free she was from herself. The mystery of needing to escape a situation that is good only feels strange when you don't know what better is. She saw better and she wanted it. This was my better, but I would break her heart as well as Evan's by wanting it.

"Let's smother the fire. I want food. Edie made me eat at Bradford's today," I said. I looked around for sympathy and immediately got it. We all hated Bradford's, each of us having suffered family dinners there, and now a lunch for a salad that no one ordered.

"Tacos! No, never mind, it's one a.m. Pancakes!" Edie was up, her university dreams shelved in favor of filling the endless hole of hunger inside her. We were living on ridiculous metabolisms and the high of impending adulthood. This was what being our age consisted of: spring breaks and summers, with all the stuff between them forgotten. It was filler, and we were only interested in what mattered. This was what being born lucky was. Ryland knew the other side, when every day at school counted and winter was more thrilling than spring. He brought equilibrium to our unbalanced way of seeing the world. What if reality was our undoing? What if our sheltered childhoods left us vulnerable beyond it? This was why I didn't want to stray, but instead to stay close and not allow the world to devour me.

Leland and Evan were still down by the water, the waves too strong to mirror the moon. I felt the ache of leaving between my heart and my stomach. The tear was festering with time; I had let it fester for so long that I was afraid the infection of my thoughts would kill me. Edie slung her arm around my neck and rested her head on my shoulder.

"You have to decide, Laney. You're running out of time." Then she was gone, letting me go and gathering our things. I stood still as the fire weakened, my resolve weakening with it.

"I will," I said in a whisper that she didn't hear. She knew, somewhere inside of her she knew, that I had letters in crisp white envelopes stamped with school emblems that could change my life if I let it. She was dropping breadcrumbs and I was following her. The whole time I thought she was naïve, but she was just being patient. There was a rush of blood that flooded through my veins. Why couldn't I be as good to her as she was being to me? It was fear.

I pulled on my shoes and walked down toward Evan and Leland, leaving Edie and her face flushed with happiness behind. My inner turmoil was a result of the distance I would be wedging between Edie and myself, but every chance I got I seemed to be running away from her. I was running away from her now.

Leland and I caught eyes, and I thought that there were reasons why he was so popular, his popularity having eclipsed ours a long time ago. One of the reasons was that water had a way of clinging to him, a merman turned human. It was surreal how attractive he had become in the years between fifteen and eighteen. He was hard not to notice. I noticed him all the time, but it didn't move me the same way Evan's boyish face did. I just appreciate architecture. Leland was genetic art.

"How's your lip?" I asked, pointing toward his face that was glittering with salt water. I would call him a Cullen, but there was no point. He would just roll with the insult. I didn't need to perk up his vanity anymore than it already had been.

"It has seen better days, like against this girl's lips last night. I think her name was Madison or Megan or Megatron. I don't even know…" He trailed off, his words drowned under the call of the ocean. Evan was still ankle deep, his body swaying each time the waves pulled back to the core.

"We are getting some pancakes and then I think we're calling it a night. You guys coming?" I addressed it to both of them, but Evan was somewhere else. "Evan?" I asked. He nodded but remained fixated on whatever it was he was watching.

"I'm going to throw our boards in the back of the truck. I didn't even realize how late it is. Laney, you better hurry up. You and Edie are still legally past curfew and the asshat from the coastal patrol knows it. The one that has been ogling you both since you started filling out bikinis," Leland said. Embarrassment burned around my head like an outline. He was right though. He was talking about Kyle, who was beach trash.

"We're coming, right Evan?" Leland asked. Another slight nod followed, but Evan didn't move. I watched Leland move slowly and reluctantly up the shore to where the fire had faded into blackness. I walked behind Evan, wrapping my arms around his waist while trying to suppress the cold that felt like a tremor driving up through my ribs with my feet submerged, shoes and all.

"Something is off, Laney. With you, with Edie…today all around was off. This isn't supposed to happen until summer, but it is. We are dividing, preparing ourselves for the break. I thought we would be holding on for dear life until we had to let go. I'm letting go of them, Laney. Edie is almost entirely gone, but it's all wrong with her. Something is going on." I held onto him tighter, refusing to let go.

"You're insane. I mean, yeah, they are kind of drifting. Hadley hasn't been here for a while. Nathan is already feeling left behind. What about the rest of us? What about Leland and me? Ryland is holding on harder than ever because he made decisions that would throw him into danger and strange places. He isn't letting go of anything yet. You didn't see Edie. She was smiling so hard I felt like it cut through me. She's happy, Evan, so happy I feel like I'm drowning in it, too selfish to be happy for her. It's us. We're the ones who are off," I said. He twisted around, splashing water higher up my calves.

"We are fine, you and me. Us. We are all the good I know. You will see it one day. This creepy beach prophet is giving you the future, but you have your doubts. I mean it though, something is going on with Edie and the only way you can do anything about it is to talk to her. Tell her the truth. If you don't, soon I will because I love you and I love her. She's my childhood too." It was a threat laced in sentiment and tied up with conviction, but it was still a threat.

"You should take up drinking this break. You are way too serious. Let's get pancakes, more pancakes, and lots and lots of bacon," I said. He grinned down into my face; this wasn't the time for kissing. I was smiling even though my heart was breaking. I didn't need to be kissed. He knew it too.

The door was locked, and I blinked twenty times before the key actually fit. I didn't know how drunk people ever made it in the door. I was drunk on exhaustion and was behaving like Alice, desperate to figure out how to get into Wonderland. We had milked every drop from the curfew suspension. The clock glared at me from across the room and I glared at five a.m. right back. Edie hadn't come home with me. She had gotten a ride from Leland and Ryland. Reese had left after shoveling two pancakes in her mouth, her eyes heavy with sleep and secrets. Her mouth formed a lazy smile as she left at the sound of her phone vibrating against her keys.

"Did you have fun?" I tried to not appear as startled by her voice as I was. There was no cool left in me at five in the morning while my mom stared me down.

"I did…" I didn't finish. I didn't blink. I suddenly had never felt more awake. She was sitting like she usually did, the old mug of coffee in front of the table with one knee pulled up. She was in her pajamas, wrapped up like a monk in a black cardigan. My box of college letters sat in front of her like it was Christmas morning and there were gifts to be opened. I studied her expression and controlled the one I wore.

"These are all postmarked from months ago. Twelve letters unopened. Twelve futures you have decided not to explore, not to share with anyone, not even yourself. Why?" she asked.

"I…" I felt like it was gone again, all the oxygen sucked out with only the particles of dust like gold glitter remaining in the light. "I don't think I want to go somewhere else, move to another city or state. I love this place. This is my home."

"You aren't even going to see what you could have? Laney, I'm lost. What about all those plans? Edie? I haven't got the faintest idea how to talk to you about this. I mean, I knew you were scared, but I didn't realize it wouldn't pass. This isn't what you want, baby. You don't want to stay closed off and without your best friend. What about Evan? He's going to New York, and in all likelihood so is Edie. Have you really considered what you will be missing?" Her eyes were glazed. I didn't need to touch her face or move closer to see that she was crying. The two of us had always been a mirror. She let me see what the future held and I let her remember the past, but right now we were a hundred percent in the present. My father had teased us endlessly. When he did he would say, "Oh god, twinning again?" It had been a joke, but now emotions were sliding down to my chin. This felt more real than any of it had; it felt more real than Evan telling me he deferred but that inevitably he would still leave. I was standing exhausted in the kitchen, bawling my eyes out while my mom was silent and crying at the table. Reality hurt far worse than even I had expected.

"I know we talked about when I would go to college, but you're being unreasonable. Why does sticking around here and going to community college mean I'm scared…?" It meant I was scared because I was scared. I was. I hated to admit it, but I loved this sheltered life. I loved that I had decent parents who were interesting and good. I loved that I went through all of school, kindergarten to graduation, in the same place. This wasn't some tiny town in nowhere America without culture or promise. Why were they all acting like I had to get out? The hurt receded to anger, hot and twisting inside me. It felt like being unwanted no matter how unreasonable the feeling was. I hated them all, but it faded out as quickly as it came.

"I'll open them, all of them, until you feel like I at least tried. I will go if you want me to, but I'm tired right now. So I will open them, and then I want to sleep until I feel like waking up. Fair?" I asked. She wiped the last of her disappointment from her face and softened. I sighed. My mom sat up straighter and pushed the box across the table. When I sat in the chair the night crashed into me harder than ever before. I was tired in ways that only the old understand. Perhaps it was the way my mother felt tired now, having spent all this time with the knowledge that I hadn't trusted her enough to tell her.

"The top one first," she said. I looked down, wishing the box still held shoes instead of futures. Columbia. The tears burned as I picked up the long envelope and tossed it back across the table. She glared at me, but picked it up and opened it anyway. Her face was the moon, bright and pulling everything to her but me. I wasn't capable of being moved, not even by the new film of tears over her eyes. The letter was one for the acceptance stack. I watched her hands press against the paper. I wanted so badly to be moved by her reaction, but no one is moved at the sight of the nail breaking through the wood of the coffin. I lifted the letter from Yale out of the box and slid my fingernail between the glue. The sting of a paper cut felt so much deeper than my finger. This letter went in the rejection stack. It went back and forth as we opened and placed acceptance and rejection in equal measure.

"You got accepted into Princeton, Columbia, NYU, Brown, Bryn Mawr, and Wellesley. You haven't smiled or shed a tear, and you haven't read further down the page than what is necessary. You are so cold, Laney, it's as if you are one of the creepy changelings. Your whole personality is unrecognizable. Ungrateful, probably more ungrateful than anyone could imagine from you. I am so goddamn proud of you, but if I have to stare into that dead expression for even a minute more I will lose my cool." I didn't look up at her, I just pushed the chair back and moved through the living room like the world hadn't just fallen into my lap and like I wasn't throwing away someone else's dream. I climbed into the bed that the woman crying at the kitchen table had tucked me into off and on since I was four. I could hear her voice reading the first story I can recollect in its wholeness. I cried. Ungrateful—I was ungrateful for so many things in my life, but she wasn't one of them and tonight I had broken a small piece of her heart. I wasn't an idiot, I would break her heart a few more times, but this was the first and it felt like I had broken my own.

The sun was glaring so hard into my mirror that its reflection left me blind. I squinted. I was running too late to stop long enough to close the curtains. Mascara was all that was left on my face. Waterproof mascara and courage might be the two things I needed most tonight. There would be tears. It was a natural reaction to cry when your other half celebrated getting into her top pick for schools and allowed her parents to share that joy with her. Big Edie and the mister were being held at bay, the surprise of her choice happening over dinner.

"You look very pretty, my girl." My father's reflection loomed and his back eclipsed the sun. "Stunning, really, how you have grown. Don't be nervous, this is going to be an amazing night for Edie. Give her my love. Don't make that face. Pinching your forehead together makes you look like a demon on *Buffy*." His voice was rough with emotion. He wasn't getting this dinner or a night full of memories and pride. I wasn't giving them anything to celebrate. "Your mother left to run errands. She will be sorry she missed seeing you in this dress. She's disappointed, but it will pass, and afterward we will sit down as a family. Evan too. I don't have a problem giving you until the summer and even the fall if you need it to decide. She will get over this. It's a complicated thing, this parenting. We were taught that in order for us to have succeeded in raising you, you have to desire to make a life better than ours. I think it would have been better if someone along the way had just said that we would succeed if we raised a happy child. Until now we were successful and didn't know it. You have always been happy, Laney. Our expectations were what changed the situation, not your decisions. Expectations…god, how I hate them sometimes, but I have so many of them nonetheless." He started to lean down, to brush his lips on the top of my head as he had done for all the years of my existence. He didn't. It was left unsaid, but it was clear that my mother wasn't completely alone in her sentiments. He was just less petty, or maybe less defeated. He was wrong, she was wrong, and what I was doing felt wrong.

"I'm sorry," I said. It could have gone without saying, but I wouldn't let it.

"I know."

My father walking away from me and my mom hiding from me were revelations. I hadn't considered that this would change if I stayed too. There had been no thought in my mind that there would be repercussions, that disappointment could change what was unconditional before. They would love me regardless, but I would be a reminder to my mom that she had built me to be happy and loved me thoroughly, but ambition didn't fuse my spine in quite the way she imagined. There was a lack of realism in following my heart. I ignored the urge to cry, ignored the urge to scream and sweep everything off the counter, to react to absolutely anything. This mess of confusion and indecision I had woven this last year and a half was destroying the time left I had to be me and the time I had to be happy with the people I was pushing away, because no matter what they were going to have to leave me behind. I wanted to be Happy Laney, the success that my parents didn't realize was the most important. Life was weird, but I hadn't been living it completely for a while.

A horned blared long and loud. Edie must have convinced her parents to let us drive ourselves the hour and a half to the restaurant. She had become a greedy hoarder of our time spent together. Always my needy little Edie. She was just a smile hanging out of a window, her sunglasses hiding her eyes, and the hair that had finally been allowed to grow long hanging in loose waves to the door handle. She was pride personified; it was coming out of her pores and dripping from her fangs. She had hunted this like a predator. She had wanted it so badly, and now she was glorying in the kill. I couldn't even imagine working as hard as she did. It was almost effortless for me in a way that could have alienated her, but didn't.

"You aren't going to kill us right?" I joked. She rolled the window up without bothering to answer. I heard Edward Sharpe and the Magnetic Zeros through the glass, the whistle of "Home" pulling me into the passenger seat like a piper. Her dress caught the sunlight, scattering it like glitter from a parade float. Her dress was the same color of midnight as when we had snuck out when we were thirteen. The sun made her look like a tide coming in and out when she breathed.

"So, are you ready for this? Nine courses of bliss at the cost of one first born and the blood of a virgin. That was the reason we insisted on your company, you know," she joked. She grinned at me, her whole body melding to her door to try and avoid the elbow I slung at her. "Seriously though, nine courses made by a chef that will know food in ways that neither of us ever will. He probably spends all his days moaning in ecstasy over his sauces. So none of these caveman shenanigans where you hit and club me every time I offend you." She hadn't uncurled herself from the door in preparation for any attack I aimed in her direction. "Big Edie was so excited she burned the skin on her temple with a curling iron. It was gross. Watching her is like watching electricity or someone having a seizure. The mister is even wearing real shoes, like not made by either a surf or skate shop. They have an actual shine to them!" I forgot the virgin comment and tried to imagine the mister in clothes without print, his tan feet imprisoned in corporate style shoes. I shook the image out of my head. It was an oddity I couldn't wrap my thoughts around. Kyle Callum was a brilliant beach cliché, down to his flip flops and year-round tan. It was disconcerting to think of him as anything else. I had never in all the years knowing him seen him in anything even remotely formal. He had been the only dad not wearing a tie at our eighth grade graduation, or when Edie had won the presidential whatever award.

"I mean it, E. Turn around and let's just go get some tacos," I said. She snorted with a shake of her head. We sunk into the music and the drive, the black asphalt fading into dark grey with the mountain rising up on one side and the sea waiting below on the other. I felt my stomach twist and untwist. I ignored everything I was feeling and let the genuine joy I had been struggling to feel for Edie flood through me. I smiled. It felt freeing to shake loose the selfishness and suffocation of self-absorption, letting me go back to who I had always been before.

"Once this dinner is over and break is done we are throwing all of our focus back to you, figuring out this school thing. We cannot, I mean *cannot*, be separated at this point in life. You can't split up soulmates. No offense to Evan. I just loved you first, and my love won't break your heart one day or turn you into a teen mom." She was bananas.

"Don't be insane. I can't be a teen mom when I doubt babies are conceived through immaculate conception."

"Oh yeah, there is that." She grinned at me for a split second, one second before she almost sideswiped something sleek and bright. I almost passed out. She wouldn't take her eyes off the road now. The tan she had begun coveting all week was basically gone. Her phone had shuffled "Home" by Edward and the Magnetic Zeros back on, although for the most part the song was lost under our breathing. Our hearts were beating loudly.

"Have you ever considered the sheer epicness of a car crash synchronized to this song? I mean, the metal twisting and the world spinning while they whistle, no harmony at all…" She trailed off. Her eyes were focused on the road, wisps of her hair obscuring her cheek. I wondered if she could feel the disbelief and rage radiating off me? It was absolute insanity that this is what she wanted to talk about. We could have hit that car. We could be free falling into the ocean like a tiny tossed-over Transformer right now. Did death not seem like a final concept to her? I said nothing, because entertaining her weird, wandering thoughts out loud was not an option.

"Okay, I guess you haven't. I'm sorry, you know accident means accident right, and you didn't die, so…" She glanced in my direction. I saw it and looked out my window to the looming mountainside, the stone flush with green. "Okay then." I watched her twist the dial louder, and I didn't hear the last few seconds of the song the way I had heard it the first time. Where was her fear? The drive passed in songs and stretches of asphalt, my nerves going still.

"Wow." It was the first word spoken between us. It was the only word I was thinking, but she said it out loud first. Wow. There were restaurants, and then there was Sierra Mar at the Post Ranch Inn. I glanced over and saw Big Edie, her thick brown hair loose in waves around her bare shoulders. My father always said that women had a glow when pregnant that radiated around them, but this was different. This was the bonfire glow of having done something well that lit Big Edie. She had succeeded at parenting, even if her child was a little reckless. Edie had survived her teens and got accepted into the future she asked to be a part of. It was how it was supposed to be, that glow that I was denying my own parents.

"Laney, good to see you lived through the drive." I grinned, sort of. The anger I felt toward her daughter had revived the color in my skin from our near-miss collision.

"Barely, that's why she looks like she would rather be coming here for my wake than my celebration dinner." Edie's explanation trailed away from me as she walked forward to join her parents, oblivious to the glare she should have felt sliding between her vertebrae. I could hear the beginning of the mister's chastisement from where I still stood by the door. I felt the anger I had been clutching as tightly as I had the handle above the door slide into guilt. This was her moment. I shouldn't have been hanging back while she got nagged to death.

"Stop exaggerating, E. It wasn't that bad," I said. She smiled at me, grateful for interrupting. Seeing the mister chew out Edie in such nice clothes felt like the equivalent of a corporate boss dressing down an underling.

I welcomed Big Edie's embrace. I wanted to keep holding her to me, because she would undoubtedly turn cold for a while after I broke her daughter's heart. Her hair smelled like sleepovers and spring. If her daughter was always summer, Big Edie would always be spring, lilacs, and rain.

"I can't wrap my mind around this. Both my girls are grown and the world seems to have been spinning just a little bit faster in our families, because I could swear that you were graduating kinder just last year. The two of you stained your Class of 2013 shirts with the juice her papa gave you. Just look at the two of you, such beautiful and brilliant souls. God, I am glad you have each other. I would hate to think of my little wrecking ball out in the world alone." Big Edie's lips pressed into my hair and her tears fell on my forehead.

"Jesus, mom, don't cry all over Laney. You huge sap. Let's go eat. I'm ready to eat food I have never tried and sneer at the foods I have." Edie's arm circled my waist as her mother's left my shoulder. The lies burned through me, and for a second I wondered how Edie was holding onto ash, how I had not just been flung to the breeze. She let go and I followed her in.

We were sitting in the dim room, the ocean on the other side of the glass with the reflections of light hanging in contrast, and it was like the floating lanterns in *Tangled*, but contained. It was unforgettable. Edie was light; they all were. They were also impatient, the very skin of them hardly able to contain it. Edie was waiting until dessert to say what university she had chosen. I wanted to let them off the hook, but I let her eat strange seafood while she watched them squirm.

"This is bliss, unpronounceable bliss. Can I have a bathtub of this on my next graduation?" she joked. She smiled, her eyes rolling back in exaggerated ecstasy.

"Only if upon graduating you have secured a position and a signing bonus. If this food is hundreds by the ounce, then filling a bathtub…completely out of my pay grade, no matter how much I love you." We all laughed at the mister. He wasn't in the market for false promises of that measure. He was smart. Edie would have carved it into cement if the promise had left his mouth. That's how we ended up here spending her college tuition on something called roe, whatever that was. I had only agreed to come if they all promised to not answer my panic-stricken questions about what I was putting into my mouth. So far I was holding it against them. Roe was not for me and would never be.

"So Laney, what's on the agenda for you?" The words were barely out of the mister's mouth when he jerked from the elbow aimed directly into his ribs. This sort of abuse was genetic after all. Edie now had a fallback excuse for the times her body had connected with my own rib cage.

"It's just a waiting game, I guess." LIAR. I smiled through my thoughts and re-examined the roe, poking at it as politely as I could. I felt the tension.

"Can't be much longer sweetie, not a girl with your brain." He smiled in my direction and I shrugged in response. Edie and Big Edie could have been molded in wax and set in metal for as still as they were.

"Oh for sure. I'm not worried." I wasn't worried, and it felt good to say it even if it wasn't in the right context.

"Of course you aren't. The universe would not tear apart this terrible twosome." Big Edie's hand touched on my arm briefly. It was an unnecessary reassurance, but I returned her smile. She was going to hate me, hate me in the way adults aren't supposed to hate the young. She was a wolf mother even if it wasn't always obvious, and I was only wearing the fur to be part of their world for a little while longer. What would it be like not spending half my nights in her house, not waking up to the smell of burned coffee every other weekend? It would be hell. It would be almost worth it to fake an entire chunk of life to not lose it.

I leaned back in the muted conversation and watched one plate of food follow another. Everything outside was awash in color. All of these windows and that view and I was stuck in the same self-absorbed bubble I had been for months, maybe over a year. That was how the dinner passed, in plates and easy laughs, smiles, and very skeptical glances at what we were eating until dessert. Dessert was an odd yet beautiful display of sugar magic, and I didn't feel like I was eating experiments.

I was running on pure sugar, the congratulations, and the surprise on not only Edie's parents' faces, but also in the quicksilver sadness at knowing their only baby was leaving them behind and moving all the way across the country. She was too excited to see the way the smiles sank for a second and how the mister rubbed the space between the top of his ear and head, a habit from carrying a cigarette there for two decades. I watched this dance of letting go move from each of the features on their faces. Was I sad that this might never be my mom? I didn't know. I imagine somewhere in the recesses of my feelings I was sad, crazy mind-numbingly sad, the same way I was crazy afraid to lose what already felt like a good thing. This life I had was hard to walk away from.

"Where are you, girly? You look a thousand miles away right now." Big Edie's voice, in its softest moments, was disarming and out of character. Her words took me out of myself and dropped me back at the table, with the potency of dessert still careening down my veins.

"I don't know, everywhere and nowhere, and it's all good." I returned her smile, trying to ignore the pull on me. This other mother of mine was a huge part of my world. Was I using this dinner to let go of them? This whole family knew me like my own, but still not well enough to see me for the liar I was. My heart was breaking.

"To Edie, and her big-ass dreams." I held up my glass in salute, and theirs joined in response. I heard Edie murmur "jar," and my smile felt real this time.

The clock glared at the wall, imprinting two a.m. on the stars. My stomach twisted relentlessly and the hammock hung empty across the room. Nothing was right about tonight, about the way my personality was being lost in my omissions. I climbed off the bed that I only kept for Edie and paced the room, trying to purge myself of the way my skin felt like it was crawling. I couldn't remember ever hiding a truth this big from anyone. My feelings for Evan were a part of who I was, an afterthought or a period at the end of sentence. The secret of them had been dizzying, but this lie was a sickness. I looked for my phone in the pile of blankets and sheets and found it halfway under my pillow. I was sweating from the panic. The anxiety of what I was going to do curled up and hardened inside my stomach.

Hey E, this is ridiculous but I need to talk to you, now. I'll ride to your house or you can drive to mine. I really don't care. I just need to talk tonight.

I waited, paced, and almost cried, but I held it back. The tears were inevitable, but this wasn't the time for them.

Are you freaking serious?

My grip tightened on my phone. Was I serious? I was. I knew it like I knew the beat of my heart, the way I knew I couldn't kill off what made me who I was, so I could be the kind of person who kept lying.

I'm messing with you, Laney. I don't want to wake up the ma so just be outside. We will go somewhere else. Be ninja

quiet though, because we aren't eighteen yet and I want to see the world outside my walls a little more before we leave for school. So like 15 minutes. NINJA OUT.

I laughed. I laughed because I loved her, I laughed because I was going to break her heart, and maybe I laughed because hysterics present themselves in weird ways. I pulled the hoodie I shared with Evan out of the closet. It was my week to wear it. The insides of the sleeves were still intensely soft, but there was some wear on the cuffs, the cost of rubbing the fabric between my thumb and finger. If this hoodie was a child, I loved it but wasn't treating it too well. I yanked on my UGGs from winter, their ugliness completely wiped out with their warmth. I looked like a beach bum. The whole house was silent, so quiet I didn't know how to make it outside without a sound. I gave it my best shot.

I closed the door behind me. The lock clicking sounded like a gunshot in my paranoia. A flinch ran through me like a chill. I moved out of the yellow, milky light until I was more in front of the neighbor's house than my own. It was colder than I anticipated, but I couldn't handle the skill it would take to sneak back in for pants instead of the jean shorts that did absolutely nothing to shield my legs from the sharp breeze coming off the water. It was creepy being alone in the dark. What was I doing? Then I saw Edie's headlights and remembered that I was breaking a heart and hoping it would stitch itself back together. I almost wanted to climb in her car with the cold and pleas of forgiveness on my lips. I didn't. That wasn't the way Edie heard things. There was no point in asking for forgiveness before the crime. She wouldn't understand.

The heater was blowing obnoxiously hot, a furnace blast to the face. It was no wonder though, since she was just in yoga pants, a tank top, and skin.

"Why didn't you bring a sweater?" I asked.

"Why do you think? You texted me at two a.m. because you needed to talk, and imagine my surprise to find you dressed properly and completely calm. What the actual hell, Laney?" I was taken aback. She was seriously mad. She was mad before I could even kick the legs out from our future. I hadn't prepared for her to be mad, I had simply remembered to wear a sweater.

"You know what, don't answer that. I am so tired. I was up talking to the mister until midnight. You know I love my sleep, Laney. You know how much I love it and how much I love you, but would a tear-stained face have hurt? I don't mean to sound dramatic, but its two a.m. and you look like we are about to go shopping…well, except for your hair. Your hair looks like you just broke out of a mental hospital…" She yawned so wide I was tempted to hook her cheek with my finger the way we had done as children. We would laugh and pull on the other's cheek. It was stupid, but I was grasping at anything and everything that I could hold onto between us before I let go of it all, let go of her.

"Where are you even going?" I asked. She didn't answer my question, she just turned up the radio. I reminded myself that it would be ridiculous to be annoyed by her rude behavior right now, but when the chorus of Fun's "Carry On" hit, I just wanted to cry instead. All of me felt like wet eyes. The rim of my nostrils was even getting snotty. This cry was happening, the one she had expected to see. It was the stupid song, it was after two a.m., and it was the fact that she was parking at a hotel we parked at when we needed pier time.

"Okay, come on." She swung her door open and I regretted complaining even silently about the heat. Once I was outside of her car in the freezing wind that was slinging grains of sand into my shins and thighs, I couldn't remember ever feeling hot.

"This is so creepy." She was leaning into the short wall that outlined the parking lot with little breaks to allow people to walk out onto the boardwalk. "I mean, weird horror movie creepy, Laney. What a stupid idea this was. We could get murdered, and the killer can just drag us off into the fog and let the ocean do the rest." I nodded with hands on my cheeks, trying to block the bite of the wind coming up the beach. It was loud, like being caught in thunder. She was right, this was stupid.

"Come on." She was tugging on my sleeve, trying to huddle with me while walking. It was worse than those three-legged sack races they inevitably have on most sitcoms. This wasn't a company picnic and there was no ribbon, but we stuck together, tripping over each other's feet until we reached the mouth of the pier.

"Okay, talk," she demanded. She stopped walking and stepped away from me, the shiver shaking her entire frame.

"Not yet. Let's walk all the way to the end. It's so freaking foggy we won't get busted for being out so late and being underage." She nodded, her top teeth cracking against the bottom row in the cold. She followed me, and somewhere along the way down the wooden boards that groaned and moved, I gave her my sweater.

"Ta..Talk." I felt bad. How I could feel worse than when I was gripping my phone in the dark, about to ask my best friend to meet me because I was nauseated with lies, I did not know. This was infinitely worse.

"I got my letters, all of them. The acceptance letters and the rejection letters, months ago, before you got yours." I stopped talking; I stopped feeling the cold that I thought was going to free my bones from my flesh. Her face was frozen, a look of disbelief turning her brittle.

"I didn't know how to tell you that I didn't want to go away for school…that I can't follow you to Columbia," I said.

"So what? You didn't get into Columbia. Why wouldn't you just tell me? Why did you wait so long?" Her words were clear, the stutter gone and her agitation leaving no room for the cold.

"I did get in. I got into a lot of schools actually. I'm so sorry, Edie…" I couldn't finish the sentence. The coward in me was yanking the words back down my throat, scared to lose my other half, my best friend.

"What? You got into a ton of schools and you didn't say a word? You didn't say, 'Hey, Edie, what if we go to this other school…?' You didn't say a word while we all tried to tell you it was going to be fine. I'm going to ask you again, Laney. What the actual hell?" I flinched. She wasn't a yeller. She was a foot from my face now, her volume just high enough to not get rolled over by the waves. I was drowning above the water. I was lost in what to say and how to tell the truth. I didn't know how to fix this.

"I'm not going anywhere, E. I'm staying here. I want to stay here, go to community college or something. I love it here. We're different, you and I. I'm not looking for something else to make me happy." That wasn't it. I could feel it after I said "happy" that those were not the right words, or maybe they were, but that wasn't the way to say them.

"Jesus. You've known forever… I planned our whole lives, and you helped and didn't say a word. 'It's going to be awesome, Edie. I can't wait until we are on our own, Edie…' You've known this whole time. We were supposed to do this together, like we have done school and summers and work. I can't even look at you." She didn't either. She turned away from me, her body shaking from rage and cold. She didn't cry; this was the death of it all. Edie was usually full of angry tears and shaking shoulders, but right now she was just shaking. I grabbed at her sleeve, but the second I had the sweater in my hand she pulled her arm loose. It was such a sad display of our angst. I didn't know if we were almost adults or back on the playground again, her feelings stinging after I had hurt them.

"I wanted to tell you so many times, but you pushed and pushed. You created an entire future based on my head nods," I said. It was too low, a whisper, but she heard. Her back straightened, and I didn't even realize I was just holding an empty sweater. My nose was running and the rim around my eyes was a fire fueled by exhaustion and crying.

"I did. I wrote out our lives for us all the way down to when we would come back here to this beach and teach our husbands the traditions of our childhood. I thought it was what we wanted. I thought you would have had the intelligence to say it was stupid, but you *nodded* over and over, and I believed we were always caught up in the same dream. That's not true… I think there were a few times when you slipped and I questioned it, but there you were Laney, reassuring me that it was going to happen. When was the last time we spent longer than a month apart? Not since we were in elementary. I have to go. I don't want you in my car and I don't want to see your face. All you had to do was say something and this could have all been different. To hell with you Laney! You were never a liar before, but now that's all you are." She turned and walked away, her thin, tan arms shivering uncontrollably. I didn't follow.

"I did say something," I said aloud. I was talking to no one and I didn't even believe myself when I said it. I had thought things would be strained for months, maybe, but I couldn't get the look on her face out of my head or the way her voice broke on the goodbye. I wiped at the tears. I was crying because her taillights had gotten lost in the fog, and I was crying because I was scared alone out here in the dark. I called Evan.

Present:

WINTER

I woke up violently. Some days I floated out of this nightmare and other days I was thrown from the water. I was tossed back like that night when the world spun backward, or maybe it was just me that went back. I wasn't aware of screaming, but the pounding of feet on hardwood gave me the impression that I had. I was sitting upright before the door was fully open. They didn't come in. I could hear their erratic breathing from where they stood, and I pulled the sheet tighter around my shoulders and waited for them to go. I was waiting for them to return to their lives. I wasn't a part of that anymore. They weren't parents. They were nursemaids. They left food and notes when I had gone without showering for more than two days. Post-its in colors that were too bright and invasive, penmanship that shook with written concern. I balled them and put them in the trashcan below the desk. The top of the desk was coated with dust, but below it was bursting with loud colors. I hated the notes. I hated the food. I broke cup after cup of tea. There wasn't a grateful bone in my body, the same way there is no gratitude when you leave flowers on a headstone. The dead do not feel. I was as good as dead. Going through the motions was all I could give them. It was almost too much.

I pulled on the hoodie that had been left folded on my bed. It dwarfed me now that all I did was walk. I ate the bare minimum. I wanted it to smell like him. I wanted to smell his shampoo and the salty smell that was a part of who he was. I wanted it to feel like I was wearing that scent, but we had shared the jacket and whatever berry-infused conditioner and body wash I had been using overwhelmed the scent of him alone. It hurt to wear it, but I missed him. I opened the door, my eyes burning with the light, and slipped on my old Vans with the checkerboard pattern, permanently damp from the air. I ached everywhere, but I pushed myself down to the sand and away from the room that no longer looked like mine. I walked away from the memories of kissing that boy, from texting all of them with meet-up plans, from closing my eyes as a whole entity and waking up as just a fraction of who I had been. I made it down to where the water lapped the sand, a perimeter of white bubbles and ridges on the shore. I peeled the sweater from my body and dropped it in the water, careful to not let it pull me toward the icy coldness. I waited as the sun lit the surface in metallic brightness. The sweater was too heavy to move with the small breaking waves. I pulled it up, my arms straining with its added weight, and carried it to where I could sink down onto the sand without fear of the waves. I pulled it on. The sleeves were wet and rough as they caught on my arms. I shivered all the way into the center of who I was now and breathed in. It smelled like salt and sun. I didn't cry, but I shook in this sweater we had shared, soaked in what killed him. I ignored the way the smell soaked into me steadily with the cold. It didn't matter that it hurt in places I didn't know I could still feel. I could smell him. I missed him. I missed all of them.

Past:

ONE YEAR AGO

SUMMER

"Are you freaking out?" I could hear my mom asking question after question as I tried to steady both my nerves and my hand. Mascara application was no joke.

"Mom, I am going to end up looking like a clown if you don't stop asking me questions. Seriously, I almost stuck this straight into my eye." I waved the wand around to drive my point home.

"You look stunning. Your hair is almost to your shoulders." I felt her fingers in the loose curls, classic beachy waves.

"I know. I need to cut it again." Her hand paused in my hair. "I'd let someone else cut it though, probably Ruth." Her relieved exhale made me laugh. Cut your hair yourself one time and you'll never live it down.

I stared into the mirror so hard that her reflection blurred behind me. It was a strange feeling. I was done with high school. I was an adult, or would be in July. I was doing it all without Edie. She hadn't spoken a single syllable to me since the end of spring break. The last memory of us was marred by fog and deceit.

"She will forgive you. One day she'll wake up and not be able to bear your absence any longer. This is the longest Edie Callum has ever held a grudge, and it can't possibly last much longer. It can't." The last "can't" she uttered was more of a reassurance to herself that she wasn't lying to my face. Edie was holding the grudge with both hands and all the passion she was composed of.

"No, I really don't think she will. I thought she would be angry and hurt, but this is different. It's like our entire childhood was swallowed up that night. How do you ignore someone you have known your whole life, turn in your work notice early, and manage to still hang with all the same people without ever acknowledging the tension?" I wasn't really asking and she didn't answer. I could hear Evan downstairs; my father's laughter was more of a guffaw than anything else. The ease in which they had grown close, my father and this boy I loved, should have made me happy, but it was just a reminder that I had choices to make and decisions that loomed over me at all times. Logically, if I wanted to be with Evan I would have to decide on a school somewhere in the same vicinity as him. I would have to follow him the way I did not follow Edie. There was wrongness to that choice that I couldn't shake. There was never a doubt who I loved more, who I would throw my entire life down for. Evan was not my answer. I picked up my phone and slid the lock screen off. The wallpaper taunted me with memories; Edie and I in the dresses with the graffiti wall behind us, the whole of summer ahead of us. I missed her the way an amputee misses a limb. She would be making sure my eyelashes were perfectly separated and curled right now. I touched our last text conversation, the plea for her to come. Someone should take a person's phone away after one a.m.

There was never anything good that came out of texts sent after one a.m. Nothing.

Hey. So it's done. We did it. I miss you. I'm just going to text you when I feel like it and one day you should text back. Did I say I'm sorry?

There was nothing. No little gray dots in a bubble. I tossed my phone onto the bed beside me. My body was made of wet sand and sadness, a ridiculous mixture on the day of graduation, but there it was. I pulled the dress from the hanger. The black and white striped dress had been waiting in my closet since we had come home from Venice. The skirt belled out, and I wondered if Edie would wear the black romper in her stand against being basic at graduation. She had said it a million times. I could hear her telling me that every girl wore a dress or a skirt, and she wouldn't do it. I don't think anyone ever told me before I lost my friend that I would still hear her in my head, constantly. Leland had been crestfallen with our separation, really believing that secretly we must be hooking up.

"Laney, the school called and said everyone is waiting." I rolled my eyes at Evan, who was leaning casually in the doorframe. This was the nicest I had ever seen him dressed. Even at prom, his lazy surfer hair had been present.

"I doubt I will be late. We still have like an hour."

"Yeah, we did…like almost an hour ago. Your father and I have gone through all the Buzzfeed videos waiting for you, as well as the Honest Trailers for about four movies. Come on, you look ridiculous hot, and if we can get through this god-awful long ceremony and the even more insane bus ride by tonight we will be making out on Gold Rush. I don't want the ride to be too fast, obviously, and the school was too cheap to do Disneyland, so you are stuck with Gold Rush. Isn't it romantic?" I laughed at his leering eyebrows. He made me laugh. That was what he had been doing for weeks, breaking apart the sadness and emptiness. I was starting to see what he had meant when he told me he would give me a chance to see what life was like when we weren't a group anymore. Hadley had been on a steady drift. She was long gone, her life already a plan in motion. In the absence of Edie, I had grown closer to Reese. With her wild hair growing bolder and black rimmed eyes, she was the physical representation of who I was now, except she was awesome and I didn't want to reduce her to being the dark to my light. They were still all Edie's too, especially Leland. We didn't divorce and divide.

I couldn't focus. The sun was exceptionally bright and I was in a sea of cobalt graduation gowns, the light bouncing off their synthetic splendor. I could see Edie waiting with ribbons of achievement on the stage in front of me. She didn't glance at where I was sitting. I was looking forward in case she did, like some pathetic loser with a crush. If we were talking, I would send her memes about how bored I was and she would send me inappropriate texts at the same time, chastising me for texting her while she was sitting side-by-side with the Dean of Schools and the principal.

I waited for the speech, the speech where she would discuss how broad our future was and how the generation before us and ahead of us was not lost, but struggling to carve new paths. She had been writing her speech since we were juniors, her confidence never wavering. I closed my eyes and pretended it was the sun's invasion and not a tendency to want to cry for months. I didn't cry, and I hadn't since after Evan found me hysterical by the pier. My tears had been a mixture of broken friendship and fear.

I heard her introduction and lost myself in her words, how sure her voice sounded. She touched on everything, the struggle of youth and the unsure landscape of what the future holds. She thanked her mom and the mister, and I laughed. In the silent pool of blue gowns, I laughed at her staying completely Edie even while trying on the adult version of herself in front of an entire crowd. I glanced down my row and caught Evan looking at me, his grin impish. He understood why it was funny. We looked like bookends on a row of matching blue bodies. Everything went into a hum, and my focus to not openly cry in public was drowned out in sound and blurred color. This was drowning. I jumped with the crash of thunderous applause that could not go ignored. I stood, clapping and wishing it was her and I doing our dramatic slow sports movie clap. I did it alone, because she could hate me all the way down to a cellular level, but I was so proud it hurt. She had wanted this since she was old enough to know what this was: greatness.

I went through the motions; all of us went through the motions. I didn't trip and fall on my face and I smiled, sort of. I also paused, staring dead at Edie, who stared back at me. Her eyes didn't register a thought, and her expression didn't move. I kept walking, trying to breathe without a hitch. It didn't work, and I was lightheaded when I got back to my seat to wait. Suddenly, caps were in the sky, a burst of blue movement on a sun-drenched day, and then it was over. I saw Evan's mom, her blonde hair lighter from the sun the same way her son's was. His grandfather trailed behind her, still more fit than an older man normally was and tanner than all of us combined. Pride—they were soaked to the soul with it. She probably hadn't glowed this much since Evan was a resident inside her body.

"Congrats, Brainy, we effing did it!" My body lifted with Ryland's, and I was never happier that I had chosen the untraditional Doc Martens. The idea of my heels flying off in random directions was amusing, but with my luck they would have hit the shins of some person's grandmother. I hugged his body back; it was a different body than the one he met us with. The government was shaping this one.

"Hell yes we are! I see you are toning down the language. I guess it makes sense due to you being a Marine and not a sailor. In another hour, we will be on our way to Magic Mountain!" The sadness that had poured through my veins was shoved to the side with the excitement that ran through us. This was our graduation, and we had all made it.

"I can't believe this is it. By Monday we'll be drifting in different directions. The world is already pulling us apart, but tonight we can be old us, the whole group. You and Edie don't have to talk, but you can't get out of this either. No bonfire, just death-defying drops, churros, and lemonade ice," Ryland said. I smiled into his face, lit with joy, and I hugged him tighter. This strange boy from the city with whom we all fell in love with had foregone his wild hair, but his personality was still thriving.

"Stop molesting Laney under the guise of celebration!" Reese squirmed in between us, her laughter infectious. I looked at Ryland over her shoulder and we both laughed, our gowns suffocating us. Evan was watching us over his grandfather's shoulder, accepting hugs and handshakes. I needed to hug my parents, but they were enmeshed in faculty members. Mr. Danvers had announced his retirement during graduation.

"Is that your mom, Ry?" I pointed at the woman standing next to Reese's mom and the little R's. She was cold looking, harder than her sister. There was a loss of love in that family, and none of the little R's were clamoring for her attention. She was the full-bodied actualization of the look that Ryland's face took on when he talked even briefly about his former home.

"Yeah, that's my mom." That was all he said, neither pleasure nor displeasure at admitting it. I wondered if she would try harder to reach him before he left, but from the way she stood looking out I would guess probably not. He didn't need her. He had all the R's and all of us. Reese smiled at her family, motioning them to come over. That's all it took for a storm of limbs to hit us. The smallest R was climbing up the leg that Ryland extended out, then she calmed with her head against his shoulder. She was staring at her aunt, who had remained exactly where she was with a curious expression. I ruffled her hair, and she scowled before grinning. She hated when I messed up her hair.

"Congratulations, sweetie." I felt all my limbs still, but my head was spinning. I turned right into a hug. "You girls make me proud every day. I don't like how you went about what you did, but I'm not going to fault you for your choices.

That stubborn kid of mine will come around." I tried not to cry as Big Edie squeezed me tighter and let go. The mister gave the back of my neck a squeeze before they walked off together to find Edie. I was stuck between hyperventilating and sobbing. I missed them, the way I would my own parents after months of absence.

"Breathe. It will be good one day, you'll see," I heard from behind me. I leaned back into Evan and forward into my decisions.

"I'm going to die. I am going to die. I am going to die and it's all your fault, but before my body crashes into the ground, I hope yours does first," I said. It was a chant. Evan was laughing at me, but the chant was calming as we climbed higher until I could see clear to the next town. We stopped. My fingers were just white knuckles and nerves while the mock sinister voice of Dr. Doom counted us down…we were falling. He didn't say one. My stomach was in my throat and he didn't say one. I wasn't dead. I wasn't moving or breathing but I wasn't dead.

"Holy shit! Did you love it? Oh my god, that was insane!" My heartbeat almost drowned Evan and Leland out, but I was just glad my body wasn't shattered bones and lost youth. My cheeks stung from where my hair had whipped around my face, my eyes filmed over from the wind.

"You totally did it. You killed it. If you don't count that weird wishing I would die moment and when you said you couldn't do it." Evan's voice was too loud and the ground felt too solid, but I was alive.

"Scariest thing ever!" I shouted in his ear, finally able to process thoughts into words. "But holy crap, I want to do it again." We were moving through the exit, our elbows and feet bumping into people.

"You should have seen your face, Brainy. No color, man. None. I thought you were going to pass out." Leland was walking backward as he talked and generally annoyed every single person he ran into. He didn't care. He was so happy that he had been spinning on energy for the whole day. He was going to UCLA and he was working for the summer, and all of Magic Mountain was going to know it. I laughed at him, at the oddity of how life was already starting to change shape. Evan was laughing too at the way that Leland was now specifically bumping into girls and then profusely apologizing with all the charm and wit he had. We rounded the corner and saw Reese waiting, her eyes wide as she watched the others drop from insane heights. There was not a single chance of Reese riding this ride or X2. Not a single chance. She had sworn at Ryland in Spanish when he tried to drag her. I had forgotten she spoke Spanish, but three or four people in the line had spun around because they knew exactly what she was saying.

"You guys are stupid. Look at your stupid smiles. You could have been dead. Dead." Her eyes were narrowed, her fear real, but we all laughed because she might be the only angry person in the whole theme park.

"Calm down. Where's Ryland?" Evan was looking around.

"He's with Edie. They had to go to the bathroom." She threw a loose hand gesture to the right. I had to go to the bathroom too, but I would wait. Somehow we were making this work, our group minus Nathan moving through the park with Edie and I like the beginning and end of a thought. It didn't make sense and we didn't speak, but we weren't "breaking up the band," so to speak. I don't think it would work in a bathroom, though. I would break down, try and initiate a conversation launched with apologies and finished with tears, and so I waited.

"Didn't you say you had to go to the bathroom?" Evan was staring at me.

"I lied. I didn't want to go. I was scared, so I figured if you thought I was going to literally piss myself you wouldn't make me go." I bit my lip, bit down on the tiny lie. It was the first one I had told out loud since telling Edie the truth. I lied to myself daily.

"That's a disgusting thought, but you are too smart to pee yourself. You would smell, and you hate to smell." He winked at me. I took his hand and we kissed beneath the cheap awning. The kiss was like we did every time lately, like it was the last one, because now that graduation had come and gone they all seemed to count more. I think they always counted, because ever since he braved through his fear, we had known there was a time limit. He had always known me and he had always known how I would choose, but now I had put an expiration date on us. It didn't matter how often he reassured me that him leaving in January wasn't him leaving us. There was this crazy thing called reality, and lately we spent too much time together.

"You're right. I hate to smell. It's gross. So when they come back, what's next?" I yawned. It couldn't be helped. I was so tired I felt drunk. "We have only an hour left." The sun was lightening the sky in waves. My legs were dead from walking and dancing earlier. The music had been all EDM and pop. It was a given that I would get teased because of my hippie music and acid rock, but when Taylor Swift came on I sang "We Are Never Ever Getting Back Together" while practically sharing DNA with Reese, we danced so close together.

"X2. We waited all night for it. Our necklaces are fading and that bus is going to be a crash site. I am out the second we sit down," Evan said. Leland was still bouncing from foot to foot. There was no limit to Leland's manic energy. I wanted to drink from him like a vampire; I yawned again instead. Edie and Ryland wandered up and we turned toward the long walk back across the park to what was obviously the greatest ride of all.

"We are like infinity or something beyond that." Leland's voice shouted into the night that was bleeding into morning. I laughed. He was mixing up *Toy Story* and *The Perks of Being a Wallflower*—the movie version, because Leland didn't read for any reason and the school had never given him one to read that particular book. He only watched the movie because he was trying to hook up with Madison one last time, and he liked the guy from Percy Jackson. I didn't bother to correct him, but I could feel Edie staring at me. I didn't need to look to know that's who it was. I had read her pieces of the book while she skimmed Facebook and Instagram. I had continued reading until she agreed to at least watch the movie with me. She had cried for the last twenty minutes. I smiled because she was forced to acknowledge my existence, but I didn't look back so she wouldn't feel rushed. Every single thing Edie did in life, she did in her own time. Often it was fast, but this was an exception.

When X2 loomed ahead of us, we ran, a broken chain of hands and feet pounding exhaustion into our bones. It was somewhere between the drop and the heat of fire blown toward our faces that I decided I was ready. I was ready to start making decisions, to give Evan the virginity that my grandmother had brow beaten into me was a precious gift, even while I was laughing at her because of the obvious *Lord of the Rings* reference. I was ready for life after high school.

"Hey, wake up. We're home," Evan said. I blinked long and lazily, an owl out of place in a bus. The sun was a Cyclops, a horrible mythical Cyclops that did not regard my need for a longer nap.

"Why do you sound so awake?" Everything felt garbled, words tangled in words in my brain. I was never going to be a morning person, but being a morning person after not falling asleep until six a.m. was just weird.

"Crack. We stopped in some mountain town for gas and I bought some coffee and some crack."

"I think it might have actually been meth, just saying, mountain towns and all." I curled into his side and tried to ignore the sway of the bus as it turned into the parking lot. "I feel like I have this conversation a lot with my mom." I yawned. Maybe if I didn't move or say anything, they would leave me alone, let me sleep until I felt human again.

"You aren't going to fool anyone. You have to move, lazy." I head-butted his shoulder, immediate regret setting in. He had a hard shoulder, but I didn't have a hard head.

"I shouldn't have gone to sleep. They were totally watching *The Sandlot* and I missed it," Evan said. He sounded almost genuine. I needed my bed. Right now I wanted to kill everyone for no reason.

"Jesus, Leland. How can you still be this awake?" Edie's grumpy voice reached all the way from the back of the bus to the front. I smiled. She was struggling even though she was normally a morning person, but Leland was the guy who could stay up until noon and then sleep for a few hours and do it again. His energy when he was happy was boundless. I stifled my laugh. I didn't want the first time she spoke to me again to be this side of Edie. It was more unforgiving than the side I was left with now.

"Come on, I'll take you home." Evan was pulling me down the stairs, navigating the steps for me. I wasn't preparing for my death this time when the flash of wanting him pulsed in time with my heart. I'd wanted to make it past high school without becoming a cliché, and I had.

"Actually you won't." I pointed off to the left where my dad was waiting. He wasn't like a few of the parents wearing excited smiles and exaggeratedly waving, but he was here to make sure I got home safe. Evan squinted in his direction.

"I think he might be asleep. He's using your red wayfarers, but I'm pretty sure he's asleep." He laughed, watching my dad make zero movement in his Wagoneer.

"Yeah, he's asleep. He hasn't looked over once." I laughed. My dad looked bright and obnoxious in my sunglasses. I twisted into Evan's shirt, the smell of him in the fabric mixed with faint hints of sweat and the popcorn he had eaten I leaned up, kissing his scar out of habit and wanting the whole parking lot to drop away, but this wasn't a movie, and I wasn't going to lose my virginity in a crowd of tired graduates and their parents. He kissed the tangles of my hair in return.

"See you sometime tomorrow. I'm going to crash for a few hours and then go out with my grandpa while he's here. He wants to surf and discuss my plans for this winter, flights and dorms and all that NYU stuff." I let go of his body, riddled with dreams and the smell of grad night. I walked toward where my dad was waiting and sleeping.

"Hey Laney, I forgot to tell you that my family wants you to go to dinner with us tomorrow night. I'll text you," Evan added. I nodded, pretending that I didn't want to cry when he talked about his future. I wouldn't do that to him—toss guilt on top of the inevitable. He had given me more time, and to cry about what I wasn't going to have was kind of bullshit.

"I'll be there." *To listen to all the ins and outs of how we end,* I thought. I hated the afterthoughts, the bitterness. I hated that it still felt like it wasn't enough. I couldn't rationalize moving across the country for a future I wasn't sure I wanted, even if it was for the two parts of my soul I knew I did want. I glanced in the direction of Evan's Jeep and saw that Edie and Reese were getting rides from him.

"Hey! Rise and shine, old man." My dad jumped, his body twisting back and forth. The movement knocked his glasses, or rather, my glasses, askew. I laughed.

"Are you going to walk beside me? Get in," he said. He was acclimating and in need of coffee. He wasn't the caffeine junkie my mom was, but he wasn't terribly far from it. I climbed into the car and let my body melt into the seat.

"If you're picking me up, does this mean mom is cooking or we're picking up food?" Starvation coursed through me now that I was forcibly awake.

"Neither. You and I, breakfast at Shirley's and talking about your future now that you are good and vulnerable." I didn't humor him with a response, but the fluttering of panic that had lived in me for over a year was now beating against my ribs, having grown wings. "Sound good? A little scary, but necessary," he said. I still didn't respond to his question. If disappointing my mother at our kitchen table had made me feel like dying, then disappointing my father in an old diner made me feel like crying. For me it was far worse to cry in public.

He waited patiently through Main Street before cutting through the alley,, the driveways overflowing with the vacationers. I hated traffic, but right now I hoped that we grew old waiting in it. I would rather have anything other than the conversation waiting for me, but when he put the car into park I knew it could no longer be avoided. I followed him into the gated garden, the tables full and the wait not as long as it could have been. There were early risers and there was the brunch crowd, and we fell into that hour that was neither.

"Congratulations, Laney. I can't believe you kids, my favorites are all grown and going off to college. I hope I don't die before you all come back," Shirley said, smiling as she walked us to the table in the corner with the wobbly leg.

"Thanks. You know you're our favorite too. It's the bacon." I smiled at her, finding it strange how this crazy place I lived bounced between a small town, a college town, and a tourist trap. There was so much to love in its diversity. I watched my father look over the entire menu as if he had ever ordered anything besides eggs benedict.

"Are you two ready?" Shirley was back with her tight silver curls and notepad.

"I will have the eggs benedict, California-style, please. She will have a roasted pig on a plate." My dad grinned at me. It was basically an accurate assessment.

"I just want two eggs, whites only, eight pieces of bacon, and yogurt with strawberries." I smiled back at her puzzled face. I had been ordering the same thing for as long as I could remember. I hoped the egg whites and yogurt would even out the mass amount of bacon. I doubted it worked like that. I would have to start working out soon.

"I talked with your mother," my dad began. When he said "mother" my stomach twisted; he never referred to her that way. This was going to be the longest meal of my existence. I wanted to text Edie with a 9-1-1. A "please come interrupt the awkwardness the way you did when we got our first sex talk" text. "We discussed this reluctance you have to go forward and I do feel like we have been unfair, but only because it's a difficult process raising a child as easily brilliant as you are and watching them stagnate in one place." He drank his water like it was going to make this less awful, like the weight of his words could be buoyed by fluid. "You know that you can stay at home, work, and go to community college, but why is that what you want to do? That's what we have yet to understand. All of your friends save a few are venturing out. Your best friend hasn't spoken to you in months, kid. The boy that turns your face to light is going, but you still have no desire to do the same. I'm sorry. This is coming out so horribly. I don't know how else to ask you why you are throwing away a stack of opportunities like the ones you have. Do you know what I would have done to have so many universities opening their doors to me? Anything; I would have done anything. You know what, I did do everything. I got the grades and I didn't screw around." He stopped, both of our cheeks going red with his openness. I felt the guilt I thought I had been pushing aside well back up in my throat and my eyes.

"I'm sorry. That's all. I'm sorry, but I'm not you and I'm not mom. I can't be Edie, and I won't chase a boy and his dream if it isn't mine too. You helped create me, you made me happy and loved, and maybe you regret it now, but I don't. I really don't. I love this place. Why would I go looking for what I already am?" It was taking everything in me not to raise my voice, as hoarse as it was from screaming and talking all night.

"That's the thing, kid…you're not. You haven't been in over a year. That secret you were keeping ate you up, and the only time you smile, really smile like the girl I know, is when you are hanging with your friends, when you are neck-deep in first love. We love Evan. He's a good guy. He has made you almost seem like you were before. I don't know why there was so much pressure on you so early, but it ate away at you and scared you off from what should have been exciting. You aren't responsible for Edie's life or Evan's, or even your mother's and mine, but you are responsible for your life." He stopped when she set the plates down, her expression tense. We weren't usually emotional people in public. It wasn't our style, but he was so frustrated right now and my eyes were so full of tears that I was fighting harder than I had in a while. I smiled at her, grateful for the interruption because I was overwhelmed. Truth has a way of doing that to you. She patted my hand with her wrinkled one and walked away.

"I think my chance at those opportunities isn't what you think it is. I wasted time. I lost a lot of those chances while I hid the applications in my closet. I don't know what I want. I know that I love it here, my home and my life. It's killing me that Edie isn't talking to me. It's killing me that I'm not sitting at my own table right now having this conversation with mom because she is so mad at me that she sent you to do it. She did, right?" I hadn't realized that I had anger of my own, but it was dawning on me now. I could feel it. I wasn't prepared for this. These were the reactions of someone else's parents. Mine had spent my lifetime making sure I knew that I was good and that my choices were mine to make. But they had never been just mine; there were always expectations hanging over my head that were never said aloud. I had talked to my mom about what college would be like, about where I would go and what I would study…when I was a kid. Where was my warning that I wasn't allowed to be who I was, that I needed to run on the same ambition as Edie and Evan, that I needed to grow up the second our caps were sent flying into the air? No one pointed out that you couldn't be content when everyone else is hungry, desperate, and gnashing his or her teeth for what comes next. I was so much angrier than I had imagined. I could feel the surprise of it dripping off my chin.

"I wanted to do this, Laney. You're my child too. I know I have been gone a lot, and I'm going to be gone again soon. Your mother wasn't so disappointed she couldn't be bothered to pick you up and talk to you, she's just completely exhausted from wondering where we failed you. It was our job to instill that desire in you, to always be better than those that came before you. That's the way the world is. It's what we know. Your grandmother had nothing, lived in some hell town in the farmlands, and her mother lived worse before her. My father was a mindless drunk. We knew we had to be better. I'm not disappointed in you kid, I'm just disappointed in general. The same way that you are so mad you're crying in a restaurant. Your mother was right. I should have waited and let her do this because I'm no good at it, but you don't get to tell me that it shouldn't be me, that its not supposed to be me." His voice was low and ragged in the din of noise. I was lucky the brunch crowd was trickling in, their arrival so much louder than the emotions being bared in the back corner. He was right. I was terrified of what was next.

"I will get on the waitlist somewhere, but I want the summer to decide. I will keep my job at Gilly's. I am freaked out, dad, completely freaked out. I don't know what I want to be and I don't know who I am entirely. I just know where I want to end up." I said it quietly, pushing my eggs in circles while my bacon went ignored.

"That's every damn kid leaving, Laney. Congratulations. Despite your keen intelligence, you are sadly and honestly normal. I didn't know what I wanted to do until I was halfway through my sophomore year of college. Most nineteen-year-olds aren't psyched for anything with mathematics, let alone accounting or business. I wanted to surf, to come back here and spend all my time in the water with Kyle Callum. We were supposed to be beach bums until we got old. Do we look miserable, kid? I'm not. Your mother knew from the eighth grade what she wanted to be. Some people do, but honestly most don't." He calmed down as he spoke, bites of egg benedict punctuating his sentences. "Just know that both of us are here, and will always be here. You can talk to me about anything. Strike that…I never want to talk about what's going on with your anatomy. I don't know if we are past that yet, but thirteen almost put the nails in my coffin. Sex—I put that on the list. I don't want to know about your sex life." He hid most of his face behind his coffee cup.

"I haven't had sex," I said like I was commenting on the weather, finally starting to eat the bacon. It was amazing, ridiculously delicious bacon, and Shirley had stacked it in groups of four on my plate for me. If I wanted to have sex with anything, it was this bacon.

"I didn't need to know that… But really? You haven't had sex with Evan? I mean, that's good, because I would hate to smack that boy around, but I would," he said. I laughed.

"I haven't. I wasn't going to end up on *16 and Pregnant*. I might give it a go soon though. Sex, not *16 and Pregnant*," I said as an afterthought. My dad spat out his drink of coffee. He was always well mannered; that is, until I brought up sex. He glared at me, his shirt splattered down the front. "He loves me, Daddy." I affected a southern accent and got a soggy napkin in the face for it. He was signaling for our check between glares.

"You must have missed the whole 'you're a woman and it's your body and I DON'T WANT TO KNOW ABOUT IT PART!" He didn't yell, not really. It was more of a growl between his teeth at polite volumes. I was light again, happy. I would have the summer, and I would make decisions without the weight of their disappointment and the anxiety of Edie's huge ambition.

I could feel her shape herself around me. She had done this when I was little and sick or scared of what I could imagine and believe to be real when I was asleep.

"So you're not mad at me anymore?" Half of my words came out in a yawn.

"I wasn't mad," my mom said, her voice in my hair, tickling my ear. I pushed against her forehead with the back of my head.

"Don't lie."

"Fine, I was a little mad. I took you to dance class, Laney. I sat with dance moms and attempted to make friends. I made you try sports and you read through my entire retirement fund. For a nerd you bought cute clothes, and those weren't cheap. Of course I wanted you to go away to school. If you don't, you might just wake up like this everyday, but I will be doing it to comfort myself." She laughed, and the vibrations against my back soothed me. I had an entire childhood wrapped in those vibrations.

"I know it's not fair. I'm not supposed to tell you I am mad or that I was more confused than anything else. I didn't get a handbook for how to do this whole parent thing. When you came out of my womb, I was still wearing flannel shirts I had taken to college like a baby blanket. I just believe that you can achieve greatness, which is what is supposed to come next. I didn't deal with it like an adult. I dealt with it like we were the same age. Your dad, as bad at communicating as he is, was right though. This isn't happiness, my girl, listening to old classic rock records in your room and not being on speaking terms with your friend. You listened to The Band for six straight hours last week. You realize people who are from that time don't even listen to The Band for that long, right?" she asked. Her voice was still a whisper in my ear, but her point was a punch.

"Has it ever occurred to you or dad that I just need time? I think anyone that loses their better half deserves time to get over it," I said. I stretched an arm out from under the blanket so I could push my hair back behind my ear where her whispers had blown it forward.

"Do you really want to get over it? You realize by the time the hurt is starting to fade, Evan will be leaving and it will hit you again, the loss of something you wanted by your side." Her words pulled and dripped down my cheeks. I did realize it.

"I do and I don't. I can't go away to school to make everyone else happy, or what's the point?" It was a valid question.

"Well, it could be like swimming, when I had to drag you into the pool with a face full of tears and snot. You were like a fish after that. It could be like reading. You hated it because it was boring and you only wanted me to read to you, but then I read three chapters of *Harry Potter* and you were suddenly replacing food and humans with books and fictional characters. I have a hundred examples, Laney, of how much you hate change until you are thrown, so to speak, into the deep side and you figure out it was where you were always supposed to be." She squeezed me to her as if she knew that I felt like all of my pieces were flying out of me.

"What if I look through the applications again and see what waitlists I can get on and take some time to do more research? I'll need this summer and fall to figure it all out. What about that? I'll still work." My voice sounded foreign, but this voice sounded reasonable. This voice sounded like she wasn't a terrified liar.

"I see your offer and raise you this—we look over the schools together at your own pace. It doesn't make you less to have someone start a book for you or walk you into the water. I don't need a handbook on parenting to know that." She shifted away, stretching out. I felt like crying again. This could have been decided months ago with them, with Edie, had I not thought it was less to need someone.

"We should have gotten you a bigger bed. This one feels like a coffin," she laughed, the sound of it bouncing off the wall.

"Eww. Thanks for the visual, Morticia Addams." I shook my head at her. She was my mother, but she had always been a little weird.

"Let's go get your haircut and buy some dinner for your father. I think all this epic parenting has robbed me of the energy I need to make dinner." She was a pretty epic parent, but I kept it to myself. There really was only enough room for the two of us if her head didn't swell up.

"Dinner? It's dinner time?" Had I really been asleep that long?

"Oh yeah, it's almost six. If we don't feed him soon, he will be eating yet another can of ghetto tomato soup over the sink," she joked.

"Why do you always call it ghetto? It's fine." My laughter moved me up and out of the bed, every stretch followed by a groan.

"Your father uses water to make his soup, and anyone with a hint of civility knows that you make tomato soup with milk." She walked out of the room with a smile on her face. Victors in a battle always smile post-conquering.

"I like it. I can see all of your face again." Evan's voice was quiet. He was twisting my hair around his finger, shorter than last time. It was only slightly past my chin.

"It's not too short?" I thought it was, but I didn't want to say it. I wanted someone else to say it, because it had been impulsive to go this high.

"Two years ago you were Rapunzel, and now you are just shy of Daisy Buchanan," he said. I smiled at him. A Fitzgerald comparison was always fine. I grinned into his hoodie, or rather my hoodie, our hoodie.

"Do you think they noticed that it's eleven?" He kissed my head and started to sit up, but I pushed him back down.

"I will be eighteen in three weeks, I have a job, I'm a high school graduate, and we are out here doing nothing. They should be fine. When do you have to be home?" I sounded like I had conviction, but the fact that we were still whispering meant that neither of us believed me.

"Well I don't, really. I have jobs lined up all summer, and I turned eighteen in May, so my mom basically sees me as a full-fledged adult; however, my grandfather will still be waiting up. Old habits and all that." I groaned in response. I wanted him to stay.

"So not right now at this very moment, but just to let you know, I'm so ready for all of this business." I used my hand to sweep the length of him in a gesture that was awkward and more awkward. His eyes widened, but not because I had piqued his curiosity so much as he was trying not to laugh. I repeated the words back to myself, and the groan came out before I could curb the sound.

"So you want all of this?" His voice trembled with contained humor. I was trying to find the hilarity of it through the climbing burn in my cheeks.

"You know what I mean. Ass." I crossed my arms even though I knew it wasn't fair. I had made this into the world's most unsexy dialogue between two teenagers considering sex. I sounded like one of the tweens in the sex education and menstruation video that they showed me in fifth grade. "You, me…sex." Even that would have been better. I tried to stealthily bury my head into his shoulder.

"I feel like it's last summer when you said you loved me and swam away. If you could bury yourself in me, you would be hiding beneath my ribcage." He was twisting my hair between his fingers again.

"I love you in ways that are embarrassing to mention. Let's throw caution to the wind, as my grandfather would say, and just do this thing now." His ribs shook again. He was throwing himself like a sacrifice. Quoting family members was his way to make himself appear more awkward than I was.

"Okay," I whispered into the empty space between his collarbone and ear. I don't know if it was the whisper or the agreement, but his hand, his body, his everything went still. Beneath all his humor and teasing, he was still male and hormonal. His patience had exceeded the normal levels of anyone we knew, except a girl named Jade in calculus who was saving herself for marriage. There was another guy who had been doing the same. He had a purity ring a la The Jonas Brothers, but he had literally lost his ring in Madison. I remember thinking it was hilarious yet horrible for her at the same time. I wasn't saving myself for Jesus or to play hard to get. I wasn't saving myself at all, ever. I was waiting for when I felt like I could deal with emotions like that, and the nakedness of it all. The thought of saving and waiting were such clearly different concepts to me. Evan still hadn't moved, hadn't spoken, and was as still as the dead. I would have felt insecure, but I harbored no doubts that it was something he wanted. He didn't have to reassure me.

"I was kidding, Laney." There was so much strain in his voice for just a handful of syllables.

"I don't mean literally at this moment on the deck with my parents inside. I mean come back later and throw beach glass at my window. Use your silver tongue and draw me out." Everything I said was hushed, quiet and insistent against his skin.

"Is that from *Fifty Shades of Grey*?" he asked. I scowled at him. He was laughing so hard that it was an old man's wheeze hitting my ears, not the romance of a poet.

"You know I don't read that, seriously… If I did we would probably never have sex. That is some intense stuff, man. I have read stuff online. Whoa. Look at my face…whoa!" The yellow milk lantern light turned his smile ghoulish.

"My mom has them, all three sitting next to Dumas and Sylvia Plath. It's whatever, she's been alone for a long time. I read a random page in the middle and felt like I should go to church or bleach my eyeballs, but it makes her happy," he said. He glanced over his shoulder into the living room. In reality, if we wanted to walk across the deck we could be in my room and my parents would never be the wiser, not when they were watching *Big Brother*, my dad pretending not to care but never looking away at the same time. Who wants to lose it like that? I didn't. Evan's patience deserved something a little better than a quickie in my childhood bed. Panic and passion aren't always the best mix.

"What are you thinking of? Me? Naked?" he asked. I laughed at him. He was so stupid sometimes. It was like once he felt that sex was finally in his future with me, he was flooded with teenage boy ridiculousness.

"Not thinking of you naked; although, since you wear wetsuits often, not much is left to the imagination in the realm of body definition." I wished I could see his face, really see it, because red would be moving from his neck to his cheeks. He didn't blush often, but if he did it was due to my blunt nature.

"I need to go. Dinner with my family tomorrow. Cracked Crab. Love you." His lips were on my forehead and then I was shifted over, the old black and blue horse blanket letting in the wind. I heard him tossing goodbyes through the house in his hurry to get home and relieve his grandfather of the watch.

"Laney, come in already!" I could tell from my mom's voice that someone she loved had been evicted. I didn't want to know, but she would probably tell me; that's how it was. I would choose not to watch a show with her and then she would explain the whole episode to me. I maybe missed Edie for that as well. My mom filled in that bonding hole and left me with one I could fill more happily with reading. They were both sprawled across the couch and the attached chaise.

"That crazy…"

"Jar," my father and I shouted in unison. She was all narrowed eyes and annoyed mouth.

"I didn't even say it." We both tilted our heads to the side, not buying it. "You both totally suck." I giggled. Anytime she was really flustered, she reverted to phrases from nineties teenage romances that she loved in high school.

"You suck," I echoed back. All the indignation fled from my mom's face. She couldn't stay annoyed after I mimicked *10 Things I Hate About You*; it was basically her Kryptonite. My sick days had been spent watching nineties comedies with my mom, most of them great…some not so much. Anything that included Heath Ledger fell on the side of always good.

"Why did you call me, as much fun as all this cute banter is?" I asked. I wanted to remain where I had been lying for the last hour, to appreciate that there wasn't fog showing up the stars tonight. I wanted to think. I wanted to make decisions. I didn't know what I wanted really. That wasn't totally true. I didn't want the conversation I had with Evan to be all over my face. Mortification wouldn't begin to cover it.

"We're hungry. So hungry," they said in unison. I was staring at two grown adults who were starved after staying up late to catch up on reality TV.

"Umm okay. And?" I asked. No point in pretending not to be confused and amused simultaneously.

"Laney Wilder, is that a tone? Judgment?" Her face didn't break, but my father's lopsided grin behind her wasn't helping her position. I held up my fingers to indicate a smidge.

"We were going to see if you wanted to come with us. You haven't eaten bacon in maybe like a day," my mom said. That was true. I hadn't. Maybe it was all the confusion and excitement, but I was hollowed out yet not hungry.

"I'm good." Gauging by their expressions, I may as well have said I was growing a second head. They didn't respond, just stared for a minute and turned to leave wordlessly before looking back in shock. It was seldom that I turned away from bacon. "I think I'm just going to go read something. Do you have anything new, mom?" I was holding out hope that she had picked some more books up before summer school officially started. She was the only teacher that kept a privately stocked library in her classroom. Her selection was more current than the actual library.

"I have an odd book I found last week and forgot to show you. Something about peculiar children, and another one from Neil Gaiman sitting on my dresser by the door that you can read. Just put them back when you are done. I still have to stamp the insides." With a short wave she followed my father out the door. They would be gone for who knows how long. They were the kind of people who had long talks over breakfast foods.

I found the book where she had left it. My fingers traced the old-fashioned photograph on the cover. Judging on just that, I knew I would love it. She had decidedly great taste in literature, if the stack of bare-chested romance covers in the back corner of her closet didn't count. Her taste in television was a whole different matter. My pocket vibrated, but I ignored it in favor of reading the book. It vibrated again.

I leave tomorrow. I am terrified. Don't send me texts anymore. It's hard and everything in my life changing seems hard enough without having to forgive you.

I set the book down on the dresser, put my phone back in my pocket, and wished that I had never checked it. I don't think there are books that make this any easier. I don't think there is anything that fills the absence of loss, not really. I think there are holes and there are tears—one can be stitched while the other has to heal into a new shape. I would have to heal into a new Laney.

I climbed into the hammock, leaning down to push off the floor and set myself in motion. I swung back and forth under my Van Gogh sky, back and forth through indecision. Would I stay here, waiting for them all to come back as strangers who had seen other states and other cities, experiences, and educations? I didn't know what I wanted to do or who I wanted to be, so leaving seemed like the most illogical decision, but now staying felt like hiding. I *was* hiding. I was safe and happy here. I knew every store and every restaurant for miles around me. I had walked under and on top of every pier. I was all my ages combined here, and if I left I would be a new girl in a new place. Although being without Edie felt like a steady ache, I didn't want to be wandering around behind her anymore. I wasn't a shadow, but she was the sun, and if I followed her I would be. I didn't want Columbia or NYU, or anywhere else that one of them was going. I opened the browser on my phone and stared at the six options I had to consider, all of them daunting and unfamiliar. I pressed the top of my phone and my fears disappeared as the screen went black. My lungs swelled with relief. I let the swinging comfort me, the room dimming with the sway.

Week one. Week two. Week three. Fourth of July, a constellation of fiery sparks over the pier and the bitterness of cold beer snuck from Evan's grandfather. There had been the feel of too many people and too much smoke trailing down from the sky in disappearing ribbons. It was full of flags and the smell of Evan's sunscreen, the sweat of surfing and the sea combined with skin. That was the holiday: an explosion of people more than pyrotechnics.

This had been the progression of summer. Eighteen had crept in. Adulthood. I chose pizza and friends, the ones still clinging to the beaches before summer was gone. I wanted to surround myself with distractions. This was the first birthday in years that I did not share it with Edie. It was the first of many, I was sure. I could feel her absence, and in it the distance of her forgiveness. It was what it was. I would have tonight with Evan and my friends. My family was opting to squeeze into the spaces between plans. My curfew had been abolished with the sunrise, the time left to hear back from the schools I had waitlisted for spring fleeting. I had chosen without fanfare or celebration. I had picked the East Coast, following my love of books to Bryn Mawr. It was strange not having ever considered that I could go to an all girl's college, but the great hall drew me in and the campus kept me online, pouring over images for hours. I could get a degree in the one area of life that was never disturbed or changed: reading. I could have a degree in literature. I lacked the commitment to write novels, but I read them like they were as necessary as air.

I lifted the arm on the record player and dropped it on my early birthday present, the black vinyl of The Band spinning in slow circles. I had worn out my uncle's copy, and the loss of even one of his records had hit me. I closed my eyes and pulled my legs in tighter, allowing "The Weight" to remind me of him. I always thought of him in the weirdest moments, but the one time that didn't strike me as odd was my birthday. Every year that I grew older, he stayed the same age. I was reminded that I was catching up, and one day I would be older.

"Don't do that whole sad face. It's your birthday, just don't do it." Evan was leaning in my door, filling more of it than he had a year ago.

"I love the vinyl. Love it," I said quietly, reverence as I watched the black swirl around and around. He grinned at me, walking over to flop into the hammock.

"I recall you thanking me for it very enthusiastically. Very enthusiastically." I felt the blush coloring me in. I climbed into the hammock beside him, two bodies caught in the same net. We rocked back and forth. It would have been lulling, the music and the swaying, the heat from his body still soaked in sunlight. It wasn't. The heat of him reminded me every second of how the weeks had passed between us, closer, but not the way I had thought until now. In my empty house, wrapped in sound and net. My parents were gone, and my father wasn't coming back until after lunch when he picked up my mother and my cake. She would be trapped in her classroom. I was here. So was he. His body grew continuously more still as the heat was climbing up my neck and settling into my face.

"What about now, under this messy starry night?" I asked. I smiled into his shoulder, filled with a boldness I hadn't known before. He didn't say a word. I waited while his eyes widened and he twisted toward me, careful not to dump us both on the floor. He stared at me, unnerving me completely. I held on to the boldness and kissed him, just us and nothing else. I kissed him until we ended up a tangle of limbs, awkward and ridiculous on the floor. He was kissing me with an entire year of mostly kissing, a year of unspoken waiting. I didn't even know what I'd been waiting for. To figure myself out, maybe, to know myself as well as his lips and hands knew me now. It wasn't magic; it was strange and weird and unexplainable. The whole condom process was odd and I tried not to gawk but it was oddly perfect. My tank top got tangled in my hair, that he was nervous enough to crack his teeth into mine, that it was not the definition of amazing to anyone else but us.

"Laney! Are you coming down here or not?" my mother yelled from downstairs. My whole life felt like conversations I was already a part of that were picking up again, questions shouted from other rooms. I stretched, muscles in strange places strained. I colored at the thought of why my blanket was in a pile at the foot of my bed and why the hammock was twisted up.

"COMING!" I shouted from the doorway, checking my hair again. It felt like everything about me was obviously different, even though my reflection in the mirror showed the same person I had always been. My hair was a little wild, but no different than any other day. I tugged at the black dress and pulled the gold square necklace around to hang between my collarbones. I wasn't disappointed that I didn't look different; I was grateful. Sex hadn't changed me in any spectacular way.

My parents were waiting, kitchen dim and candles lit on my small, perfect cake. It was the only cake I would eat because it was almost all ice cream with seafoam green icing. My mother's face was the same as it had been for the last three or four birthdays, happy yet sad. The guilt of being fine with this small welcome to adulthood didn't last as long as I thought. I felt Edie's absence, but I didn't wallow in it. I allowed myself to acknowledge it, and then I moved on.

"I should probably mention that Evan, Reese, Leland, and Nathan are outside. Ryland volunteered to hold down the beach, so to speak. We love you, but mash that in your face and go. Jesus, you're eighteen, muggle. *Eighteen*," my mom said. I hugged her, tighter than I had in years. I blew out the candles that had melted almost all the way to the cake during all the mush. I waited while she cut it and considered telling everyone to come in. I could hear my friends on the deck laughing, but I wanted this brief little moment with the people who made me.

"So…the mail came in today," my mom said. I looked up, my mouth full of mint chip ice cream and icing.

"And?" My response was garbled.

"You have two letters. One is decidedly strange; the other is possibly life changing. Which do you want first?" My mother was holding up two envelopes.

"I will take odd." She handed it to me, and I stifled the wave of panic and excitement. Bryn Mawr had decided on my deferment. I slid the envelope open and pulled the sheets of paper out, but all I needed was to see the top one, the letter that decided another part of my future.

"I got in. I can start in the spring. They want me." It felt like I was talking in slow motion. Their faces lit up like a dimmer switch in reverse. I pretended that my hands weren't shaking. It was my attempt to not acknowledge that this had been important to me, that I had just figured all this out later than everyone else. "Wait. Why was this odd?" I asked. It was a reasonable question.

"Bryn Mawr is an all girl's school, Laney. Your circle of friends includes boys and has always included boys. I had no idea you were even interested in an all girl's college. If I had known you were game for that, I would have sent you away to an all girl's boarding school instead of celebrating that you've become an adult in every sense of the word today… What, didn't think I knew? I am basically psychic when it comes to you, and even if that wasn't true, your boyfriend is glowing like a pregnant chick and won't meet my eyes. I know all, Laney Wilder. All!" Her smile still held remnants of sadness, but a little bit of arrogance had been allowed to push in. I didn't look at my father and he didn't look at me, both of us not okay with this conversation.

"Okay, so if this letter was the odd one, then let me have the life changing one." I still didn't want to make eye contact. I kept studying my bare feet as I held out my hand.

I looked down and felt my eyebrows rise. My name was scripted across the envelope, the ink black and swirled.

"Did you do this? Did you freaking do this?" I finally looked up at both of them, but they shook their heads no simultaneously. "Oh. Edie." I felt my chest tighten as I unwrapped the thread that held the envelope closed at the back. The paper was heavy and crested; I had been accepted into Hogwarts seven years late. The long bump in the envelope was a wand, a perfect replica of Hermione's. I couldn't ignore the ache, guilt, or absence any longer. I laid the letter beside my plate and cried. Only Edie would have me sent an acceptance letter to Hogwarts, knowing how many times I lamented being a muggle and that this magical place was not real. She sent me a life-changing letter even after I had ruined our plans and lied to her for a year. I had blindsided her with the truth, and she had given me what I had always wanted. I couldn't stop crying. It was messy and ugly. My mom called Evan in, and he smoothed my hair as he held me. There is a certain gratefulness you can't know until the people you love just let you cry. When I finally stopped, I went back to the room and fixed up all that I had cried off, setting my two letters on the dresser and ignoring the emptiness where my missing half should have been.

"I'm going to throw up. Yes, definitely throwing up in the near future. A human body shouldn't consume that much pizza for any reason whatsoever, and birthdays are no exception. Why did you guys have to spell out 'Happy 18th Birthday, Laney, We Love You' across so many pizzas? There was almost an obligation to try all the different combinations. Totally off topic, but it's super weird to be in your house without your mom and without a curfew. I might be freaking out a little. What are we going to do?" I asked. I knew all the caffeine, sugar, and grease were battling for my soul, my words coming out twice as fast and my eyes heavier than usual. Evan looked fat for the first time in his life, heavy with a pizza child. He was, however, wriggling his eyebrows at my question like some middle-aged pervert who had Tinder on his phone. It was just the two of us now.

"No. The experience was awesome, but my body says a very clear 'hell no.' What else you got, perv?" I joked. I laughed at his obvious disappointment.

"I have an extension of a present of sorts. I cleared out my house. I have this weird movie projector thing that my grandpa bought for my mom. You will love it. I have it set up on my deck to project onto the side of my house and a ton of junk food that you will inevitably not eat because you are made out of nothing but pizza at this point. Thoughts?"

"I am terrified about your movie choice, because they tend to be weird. Is that the word I'm looking for?" His response was to flick water at my face. It was ice cold.

"I would say that your movie choices are crap sometimes, and other times completely pretentious. I mean PRETENTIOUS. Who really sits through a two-hour Russian documentary shot in black and white? You. Pretentious, brainy Laney and her endless library of Netflix documentaries and box set collections from that Burns guy. I think you will be apologizing all over the place in a minute," he said.

"Is it the new Wes Anderson one about that hotel? Please tell me it's that one." I did my dramatic plea face.

"Which guy is that?" At his question, I shifted into a pout. There would be no Wes Anderson movies tonight. "Stop asking questions and help me drag my couch out onto the deck, or we will have to use mom's old bean bags. I swear, the red one still smells like that disgusting cotton candy body spray that Hadley wore our whole eighth grade summer. I don't know how, but it really does," he said. I stood and stretched my limbs, trying to balance blood and pizza evenly. I didn't want to drag a couch. I wanted to pass out, but I didn't want to disappoint him.

"Shake off the food coma, Laney, and decide whether you want to push the couch or pull it." Evan was looking at the black couch. I didn't know what it was made out of, but it was heaven in four cushions and a chaise.

"It comes apart right? Like in sections or something? If it doesn't, I think you should know that I'm open to just standing. I have enough food in me that there is no way my body could actually collapse. I will be like a doughy snowman." He pulled me until my chin banged into his collarbone, cloaked in his many scents.

"Stop talking and help me move this couch. I promise you will love it, and I promise that I will drag it back in by myself." He was breathing into my hair, dropping kisses across my hairline.

"Fine." I moved away from him before I was overwhelmed in him; my hormones might want him, but my overly stuffed body did not. We cursed like we only could when no one was home as the couch chipped the paint on the corner of the wall and my toes slid into its base. We wouldn't be operating a moving company anytime soon, unless our selling point was making your house look like you did it yourself instead of hiring out.

"Maybe we should do this for a living, but like, different," I said. I raised my eyebrows at the couch that was wedged between the sliding glass door and the wall.

"Are we looking at the same half-done job? How would we make any money? We would owe more for damages than we were paid to do the work." He pushed his hair back. It was touching his ears now like it had that first summer when just kissing and swimming had been thrilling. It still was.

"Well, husbands and wives, or you know, whoever, can call us, and we will bang up their apartments and load those U-Haul trucks all wonky. Do you see what I mean?" He didn't even pretend to understand where I was going with this. I loved that about him. He didn't pretend. "It will look like they did it. A wife can be like, 'Look, honey, I packed all day and moved three rooms while you visited your brother.' It will look like they cared when really they just chilled in a corner somewhere while we chipped paint and scratched surfaces so they can look like they really listened or cared about what the other person wanted. We can have some cheesy name, Hands and Hearts. It could work," I said. I glared at him. He had completely stopped pulling the couch when it was so close to being on the deck. "What?" I was unnerved by his stare. Unnerved changed into wary as he climbed over the chunk of couch on the deck and walked to where I was standing. "Seri…" I started. I was unable to finish because he was kissing me like he did when we swam so far out that every place in our body ached. He was kissing me with feelings that were hard to comprehend, but I kissed him back with everything I didn't understand and everything I did. It didn't hurt when I toppled over the arm of the couch or when my elbow slammed into the sliding glass door. It probably would later, but right now I only felt him. I felt eighteen and free, and less confused than I had been in years.

"You are a mad genius, Brainy. If you want to start a moving company, I will. If you want to build a rocket ship out of paper plates like when we were nine, then I want to go to space with you. It's crazy, this thing between us. I was an idiot for wasting most of high school adoring Edie and fearing you, making out with a handful of nameless girls while you were just waiting. Why?" he asked. This intensity was rare. I couldn't find an explanation, so I blurted out the first thing that came to mind.

"You smell like home, but feel like places I have yet to travel. You are my past and future, and the only way I can leave here is if I take this place with me. Is that weird? You beat up a boy who hurt my feelings, you once put snot in my hair, and you were the only one who helped build my rocket ship of paper plates. I wasn't waiting so much as I wasn't settling for anyone else." My cheeks were burning.

"Yes, all the words that come out of your mouth are usually weird, but I get it. You smell like Scoops—ice cream and permanent summer. I don't think I could have loved the East Coast if I couldn't have brought California with me. Let's watch this movie. I've been planning this for a while." My chest ached from wanting something, but not knowing what it was. The metal of the doorframe sounded like it was cracking, but the damn couch finally launched the rest of the way onto the deck.

"I'm going inside to get the hoodie. The fact that it's my birthday trumps it being your week with it," I declared. Evan laughed as he tossed blankets out onto the couch. It felt strange to go up the stairs and into his room alone. I couldn't recall ever having been in it without him. I nearly slammed my shoulder into the shelf he had made from a broken surfboard, but eventually my fingers found the hoodie hanging off the end of his bedpost. I hated the creepiness of beach houses in the dark, the way the wood breathed with the cold or the heat. I turned and ran all the way down the stairs, even if it meant falling and breaking my neck.

"Okay, I am here, wrapped up in a hoodie and still cold," I said. The breeze picked up through the trees. Evan's house wasn't as close to the beach as mine, but the dampness moved through the trees regardless. It was beading up on the white wall that his projector aimed at. He almost crushed my hand when he flopped down beside me. As he pressed play, the ache of wanting came back. We were watching *Tangled*. It was my favorite for more than the obvious reason of having been called Rapunzel for years. Everyone naturally assumed I would love Belle because of the books, but I liked Rapunzel because when she escaped to find herself she helped so many others find themselves too.

"I love it." Evan smiled at me. He already knew that.

"You said you hated traditional presents the year we all turned thirteen. You wanted a sandcastle while we all wanted clothes, surfboards, and anything that kept us at the beach. Edie said you were a pain in the ass, but she still paid that sand artist in Pismo a hundred bucks to make you Rapunzel's tower. It was awesome. I mean, I wasn't into sand art, but it was awesome and I know you miss her. So, Laney, on the last few hours of your eighteenth birthday, enjoy feeling like a kid again." So I did.

Present:

WINTER

Evan. Edie. Reese. Nathan. I repeated their names before I fell asleep. I repeated them as a chant and as a lullaby over and over until they were punctuated sounds without meaning. This is how I fell asleep after walking until my legs felt like the bones were splintering. I woke up burning hot and twisted up in the sheets and sunlight. The cup beside my bed was half full with water and ice, the cup sweating into a wet ring on my nightstand. Two Tylenol and the always offered but never accepted pill lay next to it to help me ward off the darkness, to hold off the ocean and the names. The drawer rattled with loose pills as I opened it and added another. The doctor hadn't believed that institutionalization was necessary. I wasn't crazy. I was soul-shatteringly sad. He gave me anxiety medication, sympathy, and time. I rejected all gifts. I did take the Tylenol, my face felt tight with heat.

The hoodie I had dropped as a saturated heap at the foot of my bed was now clean and folded on my desk. Why didn't they understand that every wash took him away from me again, that I had to wrap myself up in it, soaked through with seawater to stop the shaking that wasn't from being cold? They didn't know anything about a grief like mine, so how could they understand how to deal with it?

Evan. Edie. Reese. Nathan. Over and over the names rolled through my mouth and over my tongue, but didn't fall out as I tried to fall back to sleep. I listed them in the order I thought they might have died and in the order of severity of the ache that rooted into my spine and wrapped around like extra ribs. Evan ached harder than Edie, Edie ached more than Reese, and so on and so on. That's what they were now. Names. The memories of them were diminished by the number of people that remembered that they had drowned while I hadn't. I swam until my heart slammed into my ribs, until the bones shredded the muscle, until I was almost dead on the sand. I swam because I was told to. I swam because I believed that he did too, that they all would make it to where I was. It didn't happen like that. I was here, my eyes strained from not crying, and my heart raw from still beating all these months later.

Past:

ONE YEAR AGO

WINTER

It's strange how when you are in school with a routine that is as ingrained into you as your DNA, the only seasons that matter are spring and summer. I didn't think about fall or winter the same way I did when the sun was out and the water was bearable, when my friends were always there. I was feeling what Evan had warned me I would feel, what I thought would hurt less. The town was empty without the hustle of tourists, and my bedroom was empty without Edie's laughter filling the space between the walls. I had Nathan. He swung by every few days to hang out. Evan was my only constant when he wasn't doing odd jobs or freelancing with a local photographer. Reese was all chaos and ambition. She texted me between classes about her love of all things green in Washington, and an occasional sketch she thought I would dig from her figure drawing class. She was busy and she was happy. I could see it in how open her face was, all smiles, and hair tangling over her cheekbones, her head pressed with another girl I did not know. I got a letter once in a while from Ryland, who was stationed in Germany. His tour had come up quicker than expected and was to last longer than anticipated. Leland had a timeline full of frat parties. He was the embodiment of every college movie we had seen. He probably slept on old pizza boxes and takeout containers. I followed Hadley on Twitter, because when it came to Facebook, she "just can't." That was her last post. Now all she did was retweet endless sad dog abuse posts and the contents of her Ipsy. She was still so Hadley it was almost endearing, but unless I was on Twitter I did not think of her. It was basically the same with Leland.

I stared into the mirror, my hair falling to right below my chin. I had considered growing it out, but when I tried to remember why I had it long in the first place I changed my mind. Disappointing choices or not, I was not hiding behind all my crazy hair and in my books as much. I glared at the Gilly's shirt when I noticed the malt vinegar stain that was right above the curve of my hip. I tossed it aside and pulled the spare one from my dresser. This was my day now, work and contemplating why I had ever decided to put my life on hold. I wouldn't be leaving until January. It was still six weeks away. I had already been packed for three. The winters where I was heading called for drastic wardrobe reconstruction. It was puzzling that before, all my memories, both while I was making them and when I was remembering them, seemed expansive, filling so much space and time that each set was like an entire life. Now I was in the early throes of winter, and I had blinked through fall. It was mere photographs compared to film; they both told a story, but one took longer to experience. I wanted the long, drawn out springs and summers.

The car I got a month ago, the one that we would drive to Bryn Mawr, seemed lonely in the driveway. There was no need to use it now when I could walk to work and ride home with Evan. He teased me about my sincere lack of driving experience or interest and said he would get me a motorized wheelchair and sign me up for a bingo club. He loved his Jeep. He would have lived in it from the moment he got it if he could have. We were different like that. I liked walking everywhere. It kept me from getting chubby on pizza and tacos. I had been eating tacos like they would vanish from the earth ever since I'd decided to leave for school. It wasn't that they would disappear, I just didn't trust that anyone on the East Coast would make them the same. I tried in vain to convince my father to drive us to San Diego for a weekend to walk around downtown and only eat burritos. He shook his head and didn't answer. It was like my version of a California bucket list before dying, except I wasn't dying. I was taking a leave of absence.

Gilly's was dead today. I could see how empty it was from the outside. It would fill up in a few hours, but for now I would wander around and dance to Taylor Swift. I always demanded Swifty when Sander was working. He was the only one who could change the music. There was an actual countdown widget on the screen of his computer that told us how long until we had to start playing Christmas music. He was giving us a week longer than the outlet mall did. They started the second families said grace on Thanksgiving. It was less than two weeks until I would be plagued with melodious roasted chestnuts and some guy who wouldn't take no for an answer when it was cold outside. The only song I liked was "Last Christmas," and only because they had sung it on *Glee*.

"Hey Sander, hit me with some Swifty," I shouted into the hallway. Sander claimed to hate her, but he set up a playlist, deciding on the songs he liked more than the others. Sander was all about never getting back together with someone when he compiled it. He was such an odd guy. His hair was always half done, and lately he was rocking a little bit of a lumbersexual look. It was different. If he wasn't old and hadn't picked up my crayons when he was a busboy, I would say he wasn't looking so bad lately.

"Are you sure you can't possibly listen to something else? A little Bublé, perhaps?" His voice echoed in the hall between his office and the kitchen doors.

"NO! No Bublé, Sander! I am trying to hold onto my youth a little longer, and Bublé will be all over the place during Christmas anyway. Only middle-aged women and that one FedEx driver named Petey love him. Hit me with some Swifty, swiftly." I heard his laugh all the way to the dining room. There was a lone FedEx guy who was always playing him in his truck while he looked over his delivery handheld thing in the alley between Gilly's and Bradford's.

"I'm going to miss you, Laney!" Sander shouted with total abandon into the emptiness. I smiled. He had been saying that for about two months. I told him I would work up until the week before I left. He had been a chill boss and deserved that much. I couldn't bear the hours lately. It was like winter was seeping into my person, draining out the light. Evan was worried about me, texting all the stupid memes he could think of to make me laugh. I thought that this must be how people feel when they lose a person they loved. On all fronts, Edie had cut me out of her life. All the preparation for this had left me completely unprepared.

Work passed by in slow motion. A three-year-old threw up on Sander, and the grandfather of a girl I took Government with hit on me. Perhaps this was the universe showing me what a fool I had been.

Edie was coming home in two weeks. Overdramatic or not, I would tell her I was going and beg her to forget that I hadn't come along in the first place. She didn't deserve begging, but at the same time she did. Everything I felt on the subject had become polarized in the time since she left me on the pier. In six weeks, we would only be separated by a two-hour drive, aliens on the wrong coast, but together. I researched Bryn Mawr obsessively; ten tabs always up on my laptop. I found their traditions and buildings soothing, old architecture and history on their side.

The cold was seeping in, first with the tide and later lingering. The fog followed, wrapping around the pylons of the pier and obscuring the town, the neon a dim glow of color in the dark. The tourists wouldn't come back until right before Christmas. It was like I lived in the town that time had forgotten.

There was a nothingness to winter that crawled in with the last of the year. It showed itself in spindly branches and empty beaches, leaching the goodness from my soul. Impatience was eating away at me. The fear of rejection from Edie had drained me of feelings toward anything else. I moved as slowly as the cold, limbs sluggish and senses dull. I needed the sunlight. I missed being up to my chin in cold water with Evan's breath in my ear. I walked through Thanksgiving, giving little thought to the tryptophan comas that would be spreading bodies around our house like the plague. Big Edie had left candied yams for me with my mother while I was out chasing Evan and his camera down the beach. My mother couldn't cook them. Every year but this one she tried, so I almost missed the smell of scorched sugar and marshmallow. We stood and said what we were grateful for, but to keep it realistic my mother insisted we say one grievance first. She thought it added weight to the gratitude. I didn't say my grievance. I sighed and they nodded.

"I am grateful for this home, its lack of normal traditions as we create different ones, and its rough patches. It has been my home all my life. I'm grateful to the house itself. I never really left the womb, you know," I said. There was stillness around the table. I didn't do sentimental well. It was a Thanksgiving miracle.

"We know," my mother said, her voice quieter than usual. She knew me, and she was taking in my rare moment of sentimentality. I sat down, overwhelmed with the smells of each person at the table. The food was like a path leading down between them. I hated to say it, but Thanksgiving was a holiday that I could do without. It was gluttonous and weird, practically a throwback to Roman feasting without that nasty group-puking business. I listened to the gratitude and the grievance, half-listening really. I was already half gone. If I was leaving I couldn't cling tight anymore, so I was letting go before I had to. I could be grateful, but I still had to let go.

"Again," I whispered into the area between his shoulders where the hood bunched up, swimming in the smell of him.

"Really? Again?" His voice was in my hair and in my ear. I smiled against his neck and nodded.

"Okay." He sat up and I curled into his side like a cat. He lifted the record player arm and dropped it onto the vinyl that was just rotation and static. The White Stripes filled the room, our song playing as he dropped down beside me.

"So, in ten years we will dance to this song, if you can call it dancing, at our wedding," he murmured, falling back against me. I groaned, but couldn't help laughing. We would be the only couple in the world dancing awkwardly to "We're Going To Be Friends."

"We have to, Laney. It won't just be us standing up there at the altar saying vows, but those two kids. The boy with sand in his mouth and the pretty girl with snot smeared behind her ear. This was their song, our song," he said. I kissed him. I had to kiss him. These kisses punctuated thoughts and imprinted memories.

"One week until Christmas. Where did the year go? Oh yeah, we grew up and graduated high school, got our shit together," I said. He propped his head up to stare at me.

"Jar." I laughed, covering my mouth. I think it was the fleeting time, when we had nothing bigger than us yet, that made all the jokes funnier and the kisses more important. He was here so often that his jar was now situated between Edie's and mine on the bookshelf. Football season found his jar and my father's in a dead competition, while mine was almost empty. I wasn't much for talking these days. The neurotic waves of growing up hitting me hard, tossing me back onto the shore time and again. I struggled, but I progressed. I had managed to pack three boxes and almost zip one suitcase. It was a monumental accomplishment. Edie had been home for over a week. That was where I had stalled, the cowardice merging with my bones. I kept thinking I would walk over, or be absolutely crazy and use the car my parents helped me buy, a black Jeep newer than Evan's that Evan coveted and I neglected in the driveway. My father had been unmoving when I had pleaded for a small, gas-efficient car. He wanted four-wheel drive. He didn't want me to be caught in a snow-pocalypse. He said that once Edie and I resumed normal communications, when we had sewn ourselves back up like Peter Pan and his shadow, that I would appreciate his bullying. I didn't appreciate the bullying, but I did appreciate how he knew me so well that only a Peter Pan metaphor could reach me.

"She won't forgive me," I muttered into Evan's side, all the volume in my voice swallowed up in cotton.

"She doesn't have to, but you have to give her an actual apology now that the wound isn't bleeding anymore. One apology, and then you have to accept what she gives you. I know she misses you. Anyone that leaves you misses you, even if it's for a weekend. There are nights when I miss you and I've only left you an hour before." I could feel his fingers pulling my hair straight and away from my head, and then letting it go. I blew my breath as hard and as long as I could into his sweater until he squirmed from the heat on his skin. "Yes, Laney, I am being romantic. Don't weird up on me now. Things are going to be different, you know it and I know it. We will get busy. We won't have hours to lie together playing the same song on repeat. Let me love you all the way to tide us over until I can again," he said.

"Okay, you can love me any way and as much as you want." He was right, and I couldn't pretend everything wasn't going to be different. Not when I had boxes packed and a suitcase full of clothes.

"Oh I can, can I?" I looked up and was reminded that he was eighteen, his body more hormones than blood.

"Evan…"

"Laney."

I rolled my eyes at him, dropping my head against his side. I didn't want to move. My bones had become soft with laziness. Time was almost up.

Present:

WINTER

It had been a year…or almost a year. I couldn't quantify time anymore. I would wake up some afternoons, the sun having washed away the cold, and for a second I would believe the summer had returned. I couldn't remember the last time I knew what day it was, but I did know that a year had passed without bringing me a respite from myself, from the emptiness, from this winter. I was never sure if it would be winter today or the winter I couldn't leave behind when I woke up. That winter that swallowed me up and coughed me broken and vacant of feelings onto the shore. That was a lie—it was always that winter, whether time progressed or not. I was caught in it, drowning in it.

The only changes this winter had brought were layers and hallucinations, thermals and the ghost of Edie crying outside the sliding glass doors, her voice faint downstairs along with my mother's. I dreamed her up as I shivered violently in my bed. I heard Edie chastising me for throwing the record player over the deck. It wasn't mine to throw away; it was a memory on loan, and I had obliterated it. I felt her disapproval in the ache of my muscles. I hated these imagined moments with her. I hated her. I didn't know how I could hate her and hallucinate her, or how I could feel such deep sadness mixed with blame. She did this. She left me behind. She left me in an endless winter when she knew I needed the sun, when she knew she *was* the summer. All my thoughts tangled with emotions I hadn't felt this strongly in some time. They pulled at me, pulled me tighter against myself.

Past:

ONE YEAR AGO

WINTER

It was cold, and it was two days before Christmas. Fall was a mere memory. Winters at the beach bit into you, sucking the summer goodness out like a vampire. I had been standing outside of Edie's house for an hour. My toes were a forgotten part of my body that had been numbed into non-existence. I couldn't go closer. I didn't want to see her face the way it had looked when I had last seen it. I didn't want to fall back into the need and codependency of our friendship, but I was halved without it. This was where I was a coward, where my bravery fell away. I was vulnerable and Edie could smell blood. She had never hunted me before, because we existed off of one heart. I didn't trust that she wouldn't now.

I left my need for her forgiveness in a thin gold chain on her door handle, the little square dangling. She would know. She would know that even if my soul was a square, I didn't want to think about it while her heart was tucked into some drawer in her bedroom. I left because I was weak. The entire walk home I shook with the cold. I hated the emptiness of the streets and that I had left my Jeep at home. I had believed I was going to get us out of this rut where we were stuck, together and apart. I cried with no witnesses.

My phone vibrated continuously, but I buried my face deeper into my pillow. I hated Nathan right now. I was so tired, and he was probably flooding me with messages. He had been gone for the weekend, disappearing into Big Sur with Evan and his cameras. Evan had come into my room earlier and fallen asleep before I could make him tell me about any of it. Nathan was home and obviously still high from seeing sunsets and trees that let anyone know their size in the universe. I was still swimming through my own stupidity and lack of conviction. I knew my size without the trees, and I went back and forth between wallowing and anger. I could feel myself giving in.

I had just fallen asleep before the buzzing. Stupid Plants Vs. Zombies. Time and battery life had trickled away, and I hadn't even noticed I fell asleep playing. I glared at the screen, trying to swipe and type without going blind. It wasn't Nathan.

A girl shouldn't just leave her soul lying around, Laney. You left yours at my door. Pier? Now? We need to talk… Bring Evan. Reese is home. Hell, text everyone.

It's almost midnight? You want us all to meet at the pier? Now?

Yes. I met you once in the middle of the night and now it's your turn. Just come.

Last time, she had met me in the middle of the night and I had disappointed her in a way that we both had to recover from. I owed her; this was my chance to reconcile us into a whole again.

"Wake up. Evan. Evan. Evan." He laughed and growled simultaneously.

"It's fine. Your parents said it's cool. We don't have to do the whole curfew freak out anymore, so you should sleep. Let's both sleep. Sleeping sounds amazing, doesn't it?" He continued to mumble something else that sounded vaguely like "sleep" while smashing his face back into my pillow. It was strange still, him taking up all the space on my bed, actually sleeping in my bed at all. Adulthood was odd.

"We have to go meet Edie. She texted me, and I need to go meet her. She wants all of us to meet up at the pier. You get it, right? That I have to go? Evan?" His fingers pinching the skin below my ribcage startled me. "Does that mean you are coming?" I asked. Two more pinches, but nothing other than his hand moved. I could go without him. I'd lived years of my life without him holding my hand. Edie knew him like she knew me and understood his sleep comas. I kissed where his hair curled up on his ear. I was happy he started growing it out ever since it turned cold. I was weirdly elated that he was taking up all my space, because in a few weeks he wouldn't be.

The house was silent without either of my parent's home. They had been taking more weekend trips, a preemptive strike on remaining together once I was gone. I dug through the basket of shoes because it was after midnight and I was picking through shoes like this was a date. The ridiculousness of my brain was reaching epic levels, and I was starving to boot.

"It's freezing outside. Stop pretending you're going to choose anything but the UGGs," Evan said from behind me. I ignored his dig that my boots were ugly. I knew they were unnaturally ugly, but it wasn't like they were Crocs. He was disheveled, his hair messy and half his face pink from being pressed into a pillow. I wanted to kiss him again, but instead I pulled on my socks and watched him rub the sleep from his eyes. It was almost like seeing him when we were kids again. He had passed out on the way home from every field trip, popping up from his seat at the end of the ride with his face full of sleep. Even when I thought boys were the bearers of the plague I found his face cute, especially his sleepy face.

"Laney, let's go. This is what you have been waiting on for months. After this, leaving will be nothing." I smiled at his words; maybe it really would be nothing. I tossed my boot to the side and picked my black Dr. Martens instead, the ribbons wrinkled from leaving them in the pile too long. The last time I had worn them had been the spring break in Venice Beach, followed by graduation.

"My phone's almost dead. I was playing Plants Vs. Zombies again and didn't plug it in. Grab your phone, Evan. Go text Reese and Nathan. I'm sure they're both still up, because Nathan can never sleep when he gets back from places and Reese doesn't exactly sleep." He shook his head in tiredness and agreement. I tightened the ribbons and responded to Edie.

Be there in 20.

It was exhilarating to text Edie back, to text her at all, and I felt high on presumed forgiveness. I had made the first move, even if it wasn't a whole move. Now she was making hers. This was worse than wanting Evan to finally see me. This was Edie and me. I needed it to be Edie and me again. I didn't want to be on the East Coast without her. She had forgiven me in the sixth grade when I had unintentionally told the entire class about her getting her period. It had been a month of radio silence, but eventually she broke down. I would break her down again.

"Ready," I said, grinning at Evan. I tossed my almost dead phone on the couch.

"Hey Laney, don't expect it to be easy. Edie needs her theatrics," Evan warned. I laughed. Texting everyone to meet her at a pier in the winter in the middle of the night was pretty much trademark for her.

"Duh. I'm going to beg her like a puppy. You know that." His laugh echoed in the living room, startling us both. I opened the door.

"Holy shit. It's freezing," Evan said. My long-sleeved thermal was rendered completely ineffectual in a single second.

"Wanna be best friends instead, Evan? I'm not going out there." A shiver traced through me, gliding on blood and ill preparation. There were definite disadvantages to being a California girl. Not functioning in weather that slid below the fifties was one. I crossed my fingers that my ass of a boyfriend wouldn't point out that this was summer weather for the East Coast. He didn't. He just started pulling the hoodie free from his shirt and passed it to me. It was still warm from his body. He had been wearing it non-stop for his two days of custody. I felt the desire to be selfless and push the hoodie back on him, but he moved past me and opened the door. To hell with selflessness.

"You need something, Evan. Want me to go get my other hoodie from the closet?" I mumbled through the fabric that was tangled between my forehead and shoulders. He tugged it down until my face was free.

"No. The only hoodie you didn't pack is the black one that says 'My Other Boyfriend Carries A Bow.' I am not wearing a hoodie that will be skintight and confesses my love for Norman Reedus. I'm secure, but I'm not a fangirl." I locked the door behind us.

"My car or yours?" he asked. He pointed to his Jeep that still had the top off, and then indicated mine.

"Mine."

"Whoa, Laney. This might be an early Christmas miracle. You driving your own Jeep and not making us walk everywhere." I glared at him, but got in regardless. The streets were empty and the fog so dense I could barely see a foot in front of me.

"This is insane. She is insane. Text Edie and tell her to meet us somewhere less insane, like Shirley's or something," I said.

"Yeah, I can't. I left my phone on the counter by the door. Let's just meet her and then toss her in the backseat. Sound reasonable?" I nodded in agreement. My driving wasn't amazing on a day when I could actually see, so in the fog it was even less so. I should have driven more, but I was never that kid that couldn't wait to have my license. Evan turned on the radio, and it was totally fate that I was driving. "Home" played and the fog fell away. It was like driving to Big Sur and both loving and hating Edie for her recklessness. I felt it, that twist in the spaces between the last time we talked and now. I missed her. I didn't even care that she wanted to relive the moment when I hurt her most on the same pier. I could hear the ocean even with the radio playing and the windows rolled up. There was a rage in the waves that couldn't be ignored. I killed the lights in the parking lot. There were only ten cars that I could see, all the late-night drinkers at Harold's. I forgot how lonely this beach town was in the winter. The storefronts were black mirrors that disappeared when we passed them. My ribs ached in the cold. A hoodie was never enough, but the cold didn't last long enough to buy an actual jacket.

"Brainy Laney, is it really you?" I ran toward the sound of Reese, her body just a blur of a leather jacket and jeans from where I stood. She was shivering, her hair wilder in the wind. I hugged her to me even though she wasn't a hugger by nature because I wanted the heat from her body to saturate me. She smelled like cigarettes and rain.

"I know. I'm going to stop, I swear. Besides, those Washington kids ain't so cool with it either." I laughed and held on to her for a few seconds longer. It was weird to not realize how much you had missed somebody until you could feel everything about them again—their skin, their smell. Happiness and misery held hands in the dark, because it would only be weeks and then we would all be lost to each other in this way again.

"I missed you too, Laney. Even these long strange hugs, and girl, I can't believe I'm admitting it, but I miss this damn town already. I have so much to tell you, things that will make all my miserable moments in high school seem like nothing. I know who I am now, Laney. I really do." she said. I laughed into the leather of her jacket, but it was just a replacement for more hugging. I wanted what wasn't real anymore. I wanted all of us to be back in the sand, taking turns at being interesting around our bonfire and empty pizza boxes in summer. I let her go.

"So, what does Queen Edie want at this hour? Hey Evan." She hadn't called Edie a queen since they had met by the swings. Edie had sat there like a dead doll waiting for someone to push her. Reese had, calling her Queen Edie and shoving her right off the swing. A friendship was born from schoolyard attitude and matched tempers.

"Who knows? Maybe she just wants us all together again," I guessed. I grabbed Evan's hand and looped my other arm into Reese's. "I miss Ry." She probably heard that all the time.

"As do I." There was an edge of sadness in Reese's reply, but excitement curbed it. "Washington is unbelievable, Laney. Everything is still green, and the rain…well, it's the rain, but it's awesome."

"You hate rain." I didn't need to remind her of how often she bemoaned any kind of weather that drove her hair to new heights.

"Yeah, but not so much now. I don't know if it's just different or what. I am totally myself at U dub I mean, in ways I didn't think I could be here, with mom and the R's. I'll tell you more about it later. Let's get this weird reunion going. Knowing Edie, she is waiting for us at the very end. It's going to rain too, but like a tsunami." She pulled our human daisy chain faster.

"Where's Nathan? Leland? Hadley?" Reese listed off our friends one by one, but didn't stop moving. The wind burned when it hit skin, the cold making my eyes water.

"Hadley went somewhere with her family to ski, Nathan should be here already if he got Evan's text, and Leland isn't coming home because his fraternity is doing some Christmas charity thing. You know, Santa and sorority sisters." I listed excuses to her.

"I haven't hardly talked to anyone. I'm so horrible, but a full class load and working at the student store is killing me. I almost lost hair while studying for finals," Reese said.

"How hard can it be drawing some naked people, Reese?" I joked. I stopped to pull the hood that had fallen down with my laughter back onto my head. Evan looked completely relaxed while I looked like I was trying to survive a blizzard.

"Shut up, Brainy. How was slinging fish and chips while I was gone?" Touché.

"Okay, fair, but you brought some of your drawings home, right?" I wriggled my eyebrows like a pervert, like Evan did when he was being gross.

"I have a variety of them." We laughed, but it was lost in the sound of the ocean. I still couldn't see Edie even though we were at the mouth of the pier. Nathan was leaning against the wood that glittered with ocean spray. He blocked out some of the stenciled words, and now all it said was "DON'T FEED." I laughed, thinking of the time that Leland and Reese had added a few words right before summer. It had said, "DON'T FEED BIRDS," and they had added some choice expletives. It was surprising how long it was left there, but then again tourists could be dense and the city itself was over it.

"So by a show of hands, who is tired as hell right now?" Nathan dropped the obvious question as he joined us, and all hands went up. "Who thinks throwing Edie off the pier is a decent price for dragging us all out here in the middle of the night and…wait…in the goddamn rain?" All hands shot up again. I felt the raindrops on my palm and tucked my hand back into the pocket. Nathan's idea to toss her over was sounding better and better while my need for forgiveness and reconciliation slid further from the front of my mind.

"Just text her, Evan. Tell her to get her ass down here," I said.

"Can't. Remember, my phone is on the counter," he reminded me. I glared at him. His face was sheepish and speckled in water. I saw a shiver trace the length of his arm and decided chastising him for leaving his phone at my house again was a waste of time.

"Well, anyone else?" I asked. Reese and Nathan shifted their stares sideways or up. "How is it possible that all of us, freaking adults out in the fog and dark, don't have phones?"

"Mine's in the truck." Nathan swept his arm in a broad gesture toward the parking by the bar.

"I didn't want my mom nagging me. 'Reese, where are you? Reese, this is my time with you! Reese, its freezing and late. Why are you out at the pier?' You know, mom crap." She grinned, her lip quirking in sync with her eyebrow.

"It's pretty comical actually. Let's drag our asses down there and then drag Edie's back to her car and get some food. We should go to Shirley's because, well, bacon and waffles, but I dunno man, it's just where we go," Evan volunteered and then moved without waiting for an answer. He pulled my hand loose from my pocket, literally dragging me down the pier. Reese and

Nathan's laughter was lost under the roar of waves smashing into old wooden pylons. I wouldn't say it out loud, but the whole pier moaned, syncopated with the waves. It was alarming. No one else seemed to mind. They were pushing each other back and forth like pinballs ricocheting through the machine at Sailor's Pizza. Between the rain and the roar, I thought for a second that the world had been narrowed down into only two sounds, crashing and pelting.

"God, Laney. You two had better skip down this whole thing holding hands after this is over. I have rarely, if ever, been this cold, or to be honest, this freaked out," Evan yelled into my ear. I smiled, my fear ebbing at the realization that I wasn't alone.

"We'll run the whole way back. She wouldn't want to make it awkward with all of us here. It's just not Edie's style, you know that. We separated and didn't want to break up the children." I would have winked, but my eyes watered and I couldn't feel my nose anymore. "We are going to die on the East Coast…" I stopped whining when I saw her. She was more of a silhouette than body, more fog than human. I dropped Evan's hand. It was weird to push down the urge to run up and shove her, to hit her for dragging us all out here.

"Brainy Laney, you came. Thank god. I almost froze to death out here. This is nothing like at school, but that ocean spray…" Edie stopped, dragging her hand down the right side of her face. I paused. This wasn't reconciliation Edie. This was broken-down-wreck Edie. This was the same girl who cried on my legs.

"Hey… Let's…" I stumbled. All the words I had in my head were in my mouth and I couldn't form clear sentences. I

391

saw flashes of her expression, her face drawn between rage and agony.

"Hey Evan. Long time no see. I sent you some texts, you know, like in October. I thought we had joint custody, Laney. Whatever. Nathan, I missed you and Reese. God, who knew we would be like this, huh? Get more than a hundred miles from our traditions and forget we even have them. I fucking missed you!" The sadness left nothing in its absence. The spaces between our bodies filled with tension and blame.

"Don't all speak at once! Laney knew…didn't you Laney? You knew that the only thing holding us all together was this!" Edie spun around in a half circle, her hand gesturing the pier, the beach at the other side, and the town beaten down by fog and rain. Tears and confusion competed on my face, but I didn't know how to fix this. I was crying in public. The last time I had was here with her.

"What is it about this pier, Laney? You're always crying at this pier because of me. You cried when you knew you were going to let me go, and you're crying now that I have no idea how to end this. How can I end years of us knowing each other like a mirror? It's us—just us and them and everything, but I don't know who I am anymore. I hate everything. I'm failing my classes. I have friends, but they don't know me, Laney. They just know I'm California and they are everywhere else. Every damn plan I ever made was for us. We were going to do it all—school, then boys, then move back here to have our brats in the sand. Didn't you get the compromise? You would wander around with me so I could come home with you. Laney, what the actual hell? You couldn't see that it was a damn compromise? You just let me go, your mind already made up, and here we are months later. You leave a necklace on my door but you don't knock, you don't say to OUR friends that maybe they should check in to see how Edie is! No, you let them console you, but I didn't let go of you. I didn't forget our plans to make my own until it was too late. God, Laney, you just let me go. You were my best friend, my everything, and I fucking hate you right now in a way that still feels like I need you to forgive me, but I didn't leave you drowning in the damn water." Edie's voice broke as I unraveled across from her. I moved toward her, convinced that if I could just hug her to me we would glue back together.

"Edie… Jar," I laughed as I choked on my tears, the badly timed joke, and the apologies that were rattling around inside my chest like fragments of something whole that was now in pieces. I was trying to… I didn't know what I was trying to do, but her face said that it was wrong. So wrong.

"Yeah, Laney, I don't have any change on me…" She stood there shaking. I moved closer, but before I could pull her to me she threw herself over the edge of the pier. I had no thoughts or consequences; I existed only as impulse and reaction. I wasn't standing on the pier across from the only heart I have ever broken anymore. I was bones, skin, clothes, and pain. I was engulfed in saltwater. I thrashed for a feeling, her hand or her leg, or anything that felt like Edie. If all your friends jumped off a bridge would you jump too?

My lungs burned as I pushed against the waves that threw me, pain biting my body with cold, with its hunger. I surfaced and screamed her name over and over. I heard nothing but the roar, and then coughing. I could hear every voice that ever mattered scattered around me before going under again. Swimming in a storm was like being swallowed and coughed up again and again until the only thing I could feel was the water around me.

"Swim, Laney! Jesus, Laney, swim the other way. I have her. GO!" It was Evan and ocean, push and pull. Our sweater was dragging me under. My muscles ached, but I waited until I was caught, the wave beating me into motion. I waited again and let it throw me closer until all I felt were my bones and the beating of my heart. The slow beat was growing louder in my ears. I was almost deafened by my own heart and the water crashing around me. Edie would jump into an ocean during a storm, because why not? There were other sounds, shouts and the wooded pylons being beat against relentlessly. I was dizzy with fear and my body tingled with cold and pain, but that last wave sent me forward. The sand was like cement, and then it wasn't like anything at all. There was nothing below me or above me for a second, or was it an hour? My mouth was salt, only salt. Was it from the water, or from my teeth pressing into sand and shells until I tasted blood? God, it was so cold.

Present:

WINTER

I was living in a bad episode of *Grey's Anatomy*. My isolation was creating hallucinations. Was it terrible that I hoped my make-believe dead friend was symptomatic of cancer? I was supposed to be reveling in life. I was living, and that was all I'd been doing. Or was I? This isn't living. I just wanted the sound of Edie's voice outside my door to seep into the wood and go still. There was no relief in the sound of her. I didn't need reminders. Her voice was all I heard every morning when I walked in from my pain and crawled into my bed, when I closed my eyes and waited for the dead. There was no comfort in the familiar after all. I had thought it was what I was missing, but now I just wanted to be thrust into a space empty of memories.

When I finally sat up, I knew. The hallucination of Edie had left fingerprints all over my things. The necklace with the gold square was hanging off the handle of the door to the deck. I saw it swinging, catching the late afternoon sun. The glint on the gold worked like a lighthouse, but I wanted to be left to crash into the rocks. I ignored it in favor of the hoodie folded at the foot of my bed and the cold glass of water. The ice had melted into rings on the wood nightstand. I drank it and took the Tylenol that had become sticky with dampness. For the first time, I thought of the pills that rattled like the apologies in my chest did the night I died and lived simultaneously. Would they clear the last of her out?

I didn't take them. I rattled the drawer to remind me that they were there. They were. I did notice with the change of the weather that the rattle had grown lighter. I knew my mother, the way I used to know myself, and there were only enough pills to help but not enough to kill. She wasn't a stupid woman, but everything I had done and all that I had lost had left her uncertain. I wouldn't take them, though. I didn't want relief as much as I didn't want to remember. I wished to be alone and empty, to be glad that the ocean and the sun no longer filled in what had gone hollow inside of me. Nothing filled in the blanks anymore, but Edie's voice kept tracing the outline of who I was in her colors, the yellows and blues of summer. My shoes rubbed mercilessly against my skin when I pulled them on, the sand dry but the canvas still holding just enough moisture to hurt. Had it really been a year? I had known last time I woke up, but now I wasn't so sure. Was that why I was pretending that I could hear her, that she is the one who left the record?

Winter was so embedded in who I was now that I should have felt surprised that she was still capable of getting to me, but I wasn't. I didn't feel anything much these days, not emotionally anyway. I felt the throb of cold in me as I stepped carefully down the deck stairs. I waited until I was almost to where the water started to crash instead of just lapping the shore. If it were to cover me, I imagined that whatever was still holding me together would be gone. I wouldn't swim this time; I would float and be dragged instead of being left behind. I always contemplated these thoughts while I walked. I thought about them even while sleeping, and they were the first thoughts when I awoke.

"You can't keep going like this, Laney. You can't. You hear me and you see me. Even if you don't want to feel it, you do," I heard. I closed my eyes to the open glass door facing the water and waited for the roar. The roar was my only source of familiarity, and her voice would be lost under it. I wanted to tell my mother that I was having hallucinations, but for what? There was nothing she would be able to do to stop it, and I wouldn't allow the doctors to help me. I pressed my lips together and sat wrapped in his hoodie, my hoodie, and waited for Edie to fade. I wanted her to let me go, because she was right when she said that I let her go first. I had, and right now I needed to do it again.

Past:

ONE YEAR AGO

WINTER

I could sense that this wasn't a hospital room. It was a truck bed and a plastic board beneath me. I was wrapped like an infant, silver blankets cocooning me. I blinked once, and the truck pulled me into nothing…

The room was brighter than the sun on still water, the smell around me was absent of salt. It was clear that I was dead. I was so relieved to be dead. There wasn't a possibility that any of us had swum out of that storm. I smiled, the lazy kind that stretches like it could be a frown. I was dead.

There was a heat that climbed through my veins. It felt like a wave building in my blood, but it wasn't. I wasn't dead. I was less than dead, but not fully alive. I was merely a body held together with IV drips and a cannula. I was definitely bruised, and I could tell that I had a broken wrist, but my heart was beating and I was alone. This was not what I thought I would wake up to. I didn't know what I'd been expecting, but it wasn't a hospital room empty of Edie and empty of Evan. Why wasn't I dead?

It only took two days after I became aware of where I was and what I had lived through to be told how lucky I was. Did Nurse Christopher understand how absolutely awful his timing was? Did he understand anything? If he knew me, he would have known that the word "lucky" didn't fit, that it would hurt like someone bending your already broken wrist. Nurse Christopher didn't apologize because I *was* lucky. I just didn't feel it.

I wasn't dead…

Present:

WINTER

"Edie, did you know when you jumped that you would die? That you would cause a chain reaction built from childhood and broken by saltwater?" I was talking through the blanket I had pulled over my face. I didn't know when I had started asking the ghost of my dead best friend questions, but I was doing it all the time now. Only in this room though; I only asked her questions here. The hallucination wasn't welcome to reside with me on the beach, to walk her feet raw like I did. That was mine and only mine. The sand and practice of soaking my hoodie in the only smell I had left of Evan was mine.

"I'm not dead. It should be really clear that I am not dead. Hallucinations don't wash your sweater and move your things around. Those are ghosts. So you have to decide: am I a hallucination or a ghost? Or are they the same thing? I don't even know anymore. I'm patient, but I feel like waiting for you to come back to reality is completely shifting my reality too. I don't even know how many of our conversations I have had alone and how many you've participated in. The only knowledge I acquired from my moment of insanity was vast and only covers loss and guilt." Her voice faded the harder I concentrated. I didn't want to be her person anymore, not even in an unstable situation where I had clearly gone crazy enough for her to exist in a hallucinatory form. She sounded just like Edie though, the way she talked and rambled. I didn't want to miss Edie. I needed to hate her. I *wanted* to hate her.

"Laney, I'm going home now. My mom gets anxious if I'm out for more than a few hours. Fallout from that one moment of selfishness stretches on and on. It only took a year to get you to acknowledge I'm alive...well, sort of acknowledge. Sadly, all we seem to have is time these days. See you tomorrow, k?" she asked. I didn't respond. I wasn't going to humor a hallucination even if it was as Edie as she ever was. I stared at the floor, the dust spinning in the fading sun. I stared at anything to avoid watching fake Edie walk out of my room. I thought I was numb, but numbness usually didn't allow for loneliness. I was saturated in it the second the door clicked shut. I was so alone that I wanted the hallucination to be real, to have Edie back even if her name was the taste of hate in my mouth. The rims of my eyes burned, but they were as dry as they always were. My solitary state wasn't enough to break down everything I had intentionally built up. I closed my eyes as the door opened and my mother moved around me as if it weren't unusual for me to sit with my knees pulled up to my chin, pretending I couldn't see her like a toddler does while pouting. Why couldn't I allow this woman that smelled like Tide laundry soap and chalk to comfort me, to let her hold me through this emptiness? There was nothing for her to fix anymore, and I didn't think I could disappoint her any more than I already had.

"I put your pills next to the cup on your dresser. You have to stop pushing yourself so hard. All this Tylenol isn't good for your stomach." I fought the urge to roll my eyes at her voice. How was she even concerned for my stomach? "Edie left in tears, so I assume today was a talking day. Maybe that girl can get in your head when the rest of us can't. She was the only one there, the only one who knows everything...I think." My mom's voice faded into sounds without definition as I concentrated her out of my head. I was imagining her saying things she wouldn't say and couldn't know. I was imagining a universe where Edie and I both survived and the families of those who didn't understood and allowed Edie to still exist in our lives. There wasn't a world like that. I don't know why I was imagining it.

Past:

ONE YEAR AGO

WINTER

"The funeral starts in an hour. You can still change your mind. The doctor said that you're still weak, but with help there isn't a reason you can't go." My mom sounded hopeful, but there were twinges of desperation in between her words. She really thought a funeral for my dead boyfriend was going to ring a response out of me. I didn't want to see what the ocean gave us back. It wasn't Evan, and there were no tears for something I couldn't understand and refused to acknowledge. I couldn't comprehend that Evan was dead, or Edie, or any of them. So instead I did what I had been doing since I woke up—I stared at the wall and waited.

"Reese's mother took the kids back to Los Angeles for the funeral, and then I believe she's going to look for a house in her sister's neighborhood. She said to give you her love, and the R's too. Ryland won't be back for eight months. The Army couldn't send him home for the funeral since Reese was just his cousin and not an immediate family member." I held still, her fingers fixing my hair as she filled my thoughts with death.

"Your father and I were thinking that you should go stay with Mara. Your aunt misses you and thinks that a change of scenery might help. I'm not an idiot in thinking it will, but being here isn't helping either. You're lost, Laney, deeply lost, and neither your father nor I can find you in there. I talk to you every day, but the only interest you have is walking along the beach until you're sick," my mom said.

Mara. The aunt I felt like I didn't have, the afterthought to wishing the family a Merry Christmas and a Happy New Year. Her relationship with me consisted of thank you cards and false promises to get together more often. They were banking on the afterthought aunt to save me. These really were desperate times.

"Do you like it?" my mom asked, her voice nervous. My eyes were still clammy from where her hands had covered them all the way from the front door to my room. I felt panic. It gripped me and cracked yet another piece off of my former wholeness. Pretty soon I wasn't going to have anything left. The walls had been stripped of all my firsts, my memories. There was no longer a Starry Night or glow-in-the-dark stars. I had lost my virginity under those stars. There wasn't a space clock throwing neon warnings on my wall that I was up too late and the next morning would be hell either. It was gone. It had been replaced. Who the hell did this to someone who had just spent two months in a room that overlooked an alley of bland rubber trash cans and wooden fences? My mother, apparently.

"What the fu..." I couldn't get the whole word out without interruption. A sharp cough came from the father I had forgotten was standing right beside me.

"Laney, jar," my mom said. The words felt like ripping fabric. The tear was never neat, and the rip often went to the side in some wonky way, ruining the cloth. With her words everything began tearing down the middle and off to the side. I was disconnected from her and from myself. I moved across the room and unhooked the hammock from the wall mounts, twisting the thick net into a ball that I placed into my father's expectant hands. His stance told me that he knew what I was doing, but his eyes still brimmed at having to acknowledge it. If everything was to go, then they had to take away all of it and live with that choice. I moved past her and lifted the arm on my record player, locking it into place and shutting the lid. That was it. All of it.

Present:

WINTER

She was real. I don't know how I knew it, but I did. She was living and breathing and aging. She was in my room more than she was out of it, except at night. Edie had been flung by the waves onto the sand, and Evan had been pulled back into the sea. I didn't know what had killed him, but it couldn't have been the water. The ocean would never treat her own like that. Reese had drowned, as had Nathan. The confusion of the storm and the fact that they were in clothes and panicking had probably killed them. I would never know, no one would ever know, but since none of them had yet to appear before me I could only assume that they were dead.

"The girl who lived." I said it simply, coldly.

"Girls. Plural," Edie responded from across the room. "And now you finally recognize it."

"Was it because I made that joke? I shouldn't have made it, but I'm awkward, man. I didn't know how to apologize any more than I had." It was there, in between the words. The grief was waiting, the tears on the horizon.

"No. It was because I didn't know how to do life alone. I was overwhelmed. I wasn't the smartest girl or the best student. My humor got lost in translation. I gained four pounds and overreacted like it was forty. I didn't have you, I didn't have anyone, and I wanted to blame everyone for it. I didn't sleep through most of finals. I stopped running and started crying all the time. I missed my mother and the mister. These are all just excuses. When you made the joke it wasn't funny to me. I had lost my sense of humor and my best friend. I just thought, 'This will show them. You want to pretend I'm not here, so I won't be. You want to make jokes like four months of total confusion didn't happen, fine.' None of it explains my actions and none of it gives weight to my choices," Edie explained.

Eighteen-year-olds should never have to use words that feel so heavy. Wait... She was nineteen now. I was nineteen. Wasn't I?

"I hate you with every single inch of my dead-ass heart, you know," I said. It was the truth.

"I know." It wasn't a whimper, but it was pained.

"I miss him, Edie. I miss him to the point of forgetting everyone else that matters. I missed you that way too."

"I know." And she did.

"Edie left crying again. That's two talking days in a row." My mom moved around my room, talking more to herself than to me. She had gotten used to me not listening to her. I could hear it in her voice. I recognized the tone from when my parents had rough patches. She cleaned and muttered when she was angry.

"She deserves to cry," I said. It felt like bleeding, my words raw and wounded. The room stilled under my voice. My mother went still, waiting...terrified. I think there may have been some gratitude as well. Even if this was all I said to her, it was still better than "What the fu…"

"She does. She has. I've never seen someone cry as much as she has this last year, or known someone to cry so little as you," my mom said. She set down the fabric hamper, every movement hesitant and small. I wanted her to crawl behind me on my bed, big spoon and little spoon together again. I didn't know how to ask anymore.

"Has she been here everyday?" I didn't want to know if the answer was yes. I didn't want anything pushing me toward forgiveness.

"No. She wasn't allowed in for a long time. There are legal and emotional repercussions to making impulsive decisions that destroy lives. I wouldn't let her in the house for months. She sat by the garage every day and waited. Your father let her in, and he was right to do it. She was so thin, her eyes just dark circles. Reese's mother would have pressed charges, but the rest of us couldn't do it. Without us, the fight went out of her. She had every right to be angry, but you can't get even, not really. You can't look at a confused teenage girl and take from her what she didn't mean to take from you. Janie left her house and her job, and Evan. She buried her son and was gone by the morning. We think she went to her father's. Her parents are all she has left. She was the first of us to forgive Edie. She held her so hard during the funeral I thought she would crush the poor girl," my mother's voice fell off. Her defense of Edie dropped between us like a slowly descending wall. I still didn't know which side I wanted to stand on. I hated Edie.

"What about the other parents? What about Big Edie?" I was hungry for answers after not asking any questions for so long. I wanted to pull them into me, stuff them into the holes that were empty.

"What about her, Laney? Her daughter almost died too. She was hypothermic and non-responsive, but when she did finally come out of it, Edith couldn't feel any joy, at least not out loud. Her daughter's rash decision took the lives of three people and turned my own child into a ghost. She was horrified and apologetic. It wasn't her fault and we all knew that. Their hearts were broken, their children dead, and it's harder than you think to either blame a confused girl or hate her. We didn't do either…most of us anyway. Kyle doesn't speak to his daughter very often anymore." I flinched, all the way into the center of me. The mister had adored Edie.

"I hate her." I said it as if I had to remind myself.

"I know," she said in a whisper.

"That's what she said too, ever the Han to my Leia. It's frustrating," I said. That was all I had. I had nothing more to give to my mother. She wasn't the mother I'd once known when I needed her. That mother had been the big spoon who never would have painted over our faux masterpiece in my time of need. My near-death had changed her.

"I screwed it up, kid," my mom said with conviction. She had read my thoughts like there was a sliver of the mother I needed left in her after all. "I almost lost you, and when I got you back I forgot everything about how you work, how you and I work together. I sent you away and then stole from you when you were gone. I didn't know what I was doing. I don't have a guidebook, remember? Even if there were, what parent would read that chapter? I should have kept your walls full of color, I shouldn't have let your childless, idiot aunt and her self-deluded 'amazing-at-parenting' advice get into my head. Since you already know what it's like to be almost dead, perhaps I should tell you what it feels like to almost have your kid die, or that if you get her back you won't recognize an entire life of memories in her face, because it's not the same face anymore. This face..." She had walked closer, but I hadn't even noticed until her fingers were lightly against my chin. It hurt to hold still. Everything from the last year was recoiling. "...was made different with your loss. Your eyes are empty. You look like you are starving all the time. For the first time in your life you need nothing and want nothing from me. It's a feeling unlike anything else when you don't know if your kid would have been better off dying than living like you've been," she said, pushing the tears off my face. I hadn't even realized I was crying. I was sobbing. It hurt, crying after a year of nothing.

"I just...all of them..." I trailed off. I couldn't process thoughts. I had never felt less like the adult I had become while I was away from everything, even my own self.

"Cry your face off, kid. You lost a lot. We lost over a year with you while you just existed." She was crying too now. She was still terrified to push too far, and I was so rusty at being human that I didn't offer to make it easier. I couldn't hug her yet, not with all my pieces still sharp and unassembled.

I cried until my father came in. We cried together as a family, and he didn't ask why. I think he knew. That's what love was with them—a snotty mess of three faces who hadn't been really seeing each other for a long time.

I pulled the hoodie over my hair, despising its length. It had grown far below my shoulders in my absence from the living world. It was strange to be going down to the sand in the morning. I had been too exhausted to pace or move after crying until my head threatened to collapse and my sinuses explode. I was still dizzy from it and had been for hours. I waited for Edie. I had left a square of gold dangling on the open glass door. It was a lighthouse after all. I didn't know if I was offering her safety or hoping to throw her to the rocks. I didn't know much, but I knew this hoodie. I knew what Evan would want. I wasn't always a giver though. It wasn't in my nature to make everyone happy just because they wished it. The year had sharpened that in me, and I was half heart and half knives.

"Your hair is long again, Laney. It makes you feel familiar and strange at the same time." I hated our twin thoughts, how without any care for our bond it still thrived, even when thrust under the water and left to die out on the sand.

"I hate you so much, Edie. I do. I really hate you," I said again. I hadn't meant to blurt it out. I had thought I would be more adult-like, more articulate even, but there it was.

"Do you think you'll always hate me?" Edie asked. She was good at getting to the point. We were the same in that way, but different in the approach. She sat beside me, dropping without grace but landing with her legs crossed. She was nervous. Her hand smoothed her hair as she bat it away from her eyes. "Can you forgive me?" she whispered. I glanced over to see her back straight and tears silent as they traced the curves of her face.

"No," I said sharply. My answer was given by the knives. I sighed at the way she was trying to match her hyperventilating to the crashing waves, like we weren't side by side and I couldn't hear it.

"Maybe," I reconsidered. That was the heart.

"I get it," Edie responded.

"That's my forgiveness," I said, gesturing at the waves and sweeping my hand across the breaking water. "It comes in so strong. I know you and I miss you, and we are Laney and Edie again…then it pulls back. I forgive you like each wave that breaks, but it's not permanent. It's a back and forth, and it doesn't settle. That's not really forgiveness, but it's all I have. Waves of forgiveness, waves of empathy, but underneath it's cold and violent and unpredictable."

"What if I was okay with that? What if I will take it, Laney? Is it that easy? Can I just have what you are offering?" she asked. I hated when she cried. It gave a nasally, whiny tremor to her words that she couldn't control. It was that same feeling of annoyance followed by guilt that I got whenever babies cried.

"You want half forgiveness?" I couldn't keep the incredulity out of my voice. There was a fragment of my old self that was begging Edie's old self to take it, to want that tiny bit of forgiveness I was offering. I missed her as much as I hated her.

"Goddammit. This is so hard. I do want it, Laney. I want any amount of forgiveness I can get. There isn't enough therapy in the world to turn me into the girl that deserves it, but I want it. I want to be us again...but different. Edie and Laney."

"Laney and Edie." I laughed at my own joke. It was the first thing I had laughed at after my life-altering changes. Edie laughed too, but it sounded foreign, and I could tell that this year hadn't been good to her either.

"I am so sorry. I am sorry for Evan and Reese, for Nathan. I am so sorry for taking away Ryland's cousin and best friend. I can't even apologize for the wrongs I have done," she said crying again and lisping the ends of her words.

"You can't. You can't apologize anymore. I'll try and you'll try, and if it doesn't work, it doesn't work. I'm awfully glad you are alive, Edie Callum, even if I wish you dead before the day is through." For what it was worth, I meant it.

"So, my hair is terrible," I stated. I stretched one of the strands away from my forehead to catch the sunlight. It was dirty.

"Want me to cut it?" Edie asked. Sarcasm and her bratty ways crept back into her voice. It was like the old Edie was back.

"Yeah, hell no." I wasn't anywhere near that level of forgiveness.

"Jar..." She stopped herself, her voice catching and filling back up with saltwater. I laughed, short and harsh. Maybe the wave was breaking on the sand. I threw a shell at her and smiled, seeing the toll that our friendship and the hardships we'd already experienced had wrought on our faces. We were nineteen now. As weird and messed up as it was, life was ahead of us now. It was finally time to start living it.

LANEY'S PLAYLIST

The Lonely - Christina Perri
Fortunate Son - Creedence Clearwater Revival
The Weight - The Band
Build Me Up Buttercup - Frank Turner
We're Going To Be Friends - White Stripes
Bonfire Heart - James Blunt
Sea of Love - Cat Power
Into The Wild - Lewis Watson
Follow Your Arrow - Kacey Musgraves
You And Me - You+Me
American Girl - Frank Turner
Me And Bobby Mcgee - Janis Joplin
Summertime Sadness - Lana Del Rey
Stolen Dance - Milky Chance
Home - Edward Sharpe And The Magnetic Zeros
Pumpin Blood - NONONO
I See The Light - Mandy Moore
Origin Of Love - Hedwig And The Angry Inch
I'll Be Seeing You - Billie Holiday
I Will Follow You Into The Dark - Death Cab For Cutie
Carry On - Fun
Riptide - Vance Joy
Youth - Daughter
Cecilia And The Satellites - Andrew McMahon in the Wilderness
The Forgotten - Green Day

Acknowledgments

My girls, you make every single thing about life more enthralling. There is no way to really acknowledge, thank, or appreciate you enough. Will starbs do?

Aubrey Williams, your patience is unmatchable, taste in books superior, and track change comments will always be my favorite. As my editor you freed so many commas back into the universe.

Shannon Morton, I could not possibly count all the Del Taco quesadillas and cherry cokes consumed in 2014. I do know that without them and our conversations I couldn't have finished this novel.

All friends and family, you made so many "She's crazy" faces at me during the process of writing this book but you still supported me. Thank you.

Birdcage Ink, Best name. Best team. Period.

Geniece Trevino, you are a kindred soul. You saw me. Thanks for doing this journey with me. You pushed me and because of you I wanted to start pushing myself again. The timing of you coming into my life was magic.

The small writing circle in December of 2019, this meeting of writers and singers started the process of bringing me back to myself during one of the darkest periods of my life. Thank you. I will never not be inspired by all of you. You gave me a community and thought my voice still full of rust from being dormant so long, was worth listening to. There is no gratitude quite like the gratitude you feel towards people who see you broken and offer you a hand up.

The central coast of California, you are my first and most lasting love. My heart is sewn to your shoreline.

More from Lori Worley
@AUTHOR_LORIWORLEY
@BIRDCAGE_INK
WWW
BIRDCAGEINK.COM

www.ingramcontent.com/pod-product-compliance
Lightning Source LLC
Chambersburg PA
CBHW030056310726
48970CB00004B/1026